STUDS
& SPURS

J.L. LANGLEY
DAKOTA FLINT
KIERNAN KELLY
ANGELA FIDDLER

mlrpress

Published by
MLR Press, LLC
3052 Gaines Waterport Rd.
Albion, NY 14411

Visit ManLoveRomance Press, LLC on the Internet:
www.mlrpress.com

Cover Art by Deana C. Jamroz
Editing by Kris Jacen
Printed in the United States of America.

ISBN# 978-1-934531-55-6

First Edition 2009

The Convenient Husband – J.L. Langley...................................... *1*

Seeing You – Dakota Flint... *77*

Judas Steer – Kiernan Kelly... *159*

Forgotten Favor – Angela Fiddler.. *233*

THE
CONVENIENT
HUSBAND

J.L. LANGLEY

"Ah ha! I should have known." AJ laughed and leaned against the rail.

Grinning at his brother, Tucker headed up onto the porch. "Should have known what?"

"Where you went. Do you have to smoke when you drink?"

Yes, and he was out of cigars, which is what he preferred with his whiskey. It was good fortune he'd stashed some cigarettes in his glove box. With any luck they weren't stale; he couldn't remember the last time he'd actually had one of them. "Self preservation, there are still guests." He'd rather face a boardroom of sharks than a horde of teenagers any day. Tucker lit the cigarette then put the lighter into his pocket. He held up his tumbler of whiskey to AJ in a silent toast, pulled the cigarette out from between his lips and took a sip. "I'm surprised you haven't hit Granddaddy's liquor cabinet as well."

"I tried but Granddad and Juan beat me to it. Dad's out of town so I figured someone in charge should be sober but, I'm hitting it after." Sitting on the rail, he studied Tucker, his head cocking to the left a little. "I'm glad you came. You need a break. You look tired."

"I'm not tired. I'm bored."

AJ snorted. "I'm surprised you didn't bring work with you."

Grinning, Tucker pulled out his phone and held it up before clipping it back to his belt. "I'm waiting for word on the Addison deal."

AJ groaned. "I should have known."

Something crashed inside and the music stopped. "Shit." AJ looked towards the door.

Tucker winced. "Want me to——?"

Waving his hand, AJ dismissed him. "I got it. Hell, it was probably Granddad or Juan, they're as rowdy as the kids. Finish your drink and cigarette, then I'll have you help me clear the rest of these kids out of here." Grabbing the doorknob, he took a deep, over exaggerated breath. "Were we this obnoxious at eighteen?"

Tucker shook his head. "I didn't become a party animal until my first year in college."

Smiling, AJ opened the door, "here goes."

Brave man. Tucker took a drag off his cigarette and walked around the side of the wraparound porch toward the back. Damn, he missed the country. The fast pace of the business world was exciting, but there was just nothing like a spring night out here far from civilization. He should really come home more often.

When he got to the back of the house, he leaned on the rail and gazed out into the back pasture. It was beautiful. There were so many stars. He'd forgotten how many. When was the last time he'd taken time to look at the stars? He'd been stuck in his high rise office working on one project or another plenty of times after the sunlight faded, but the city lights made the stars disappear. Buildings overpowered the horizon. The big city had its own appeal, but out here? Pure magic. The sky looked so big and endless.

"It's pretty, isn't it?" A soft voice asked.

Tucker started, not realizing he had company, but immediately grinned as recognition set in. He hadn't seen the pest at all tonight. Hell, he hadn't seen him in over a year. Not since the last time he came home. Taking a hit from his cigarette he turned his head toward the birthday boy and wished he hadn't.

Micah stood at the top of the back steps, a soft grin on his face. Gone were the smart little glasses he'd always worn. He'd looked adorable in them, but now, without them he was stunning. His usually messy black hair that always fell in his face was trimmed and styled neatly. Who knew he had such big eyes, those glasses had concealed a lot. The red short sleeved polo shirt pulled tightly across a slim but nicely shaped chest, and even showed off toned biceps. He was still small, but he didn't look like a kid any longer. A pair of tight jeans replaced the normal baggy ones, showing off the leg muscles he'd earned from years in the saddle.

Tucker's breath caught. Who was this gorgeous man and what happened to the scrawny kid he'd known?

Micah settled beside him, leaning his tanned forearms on the rail. He stood so close the heat of his body warmed Tucker's left arm.

"Yeah, I've missed it. Not as many stars in the city." Taking a drink of his whiskey, Tucker glanced back out at the deep, endless sky. The soft spring breeze ruffled his hair and blew smoke around him. That "someone is staring at you" feeling niggled at him, but he didn't look to confirm it. Part of him wanted Micah to be looking. If Tucker didn't know better he'd say he was lusting after the kid and... well that was just wrong. He couldn't see Juan's nephew that way, yet he was. It had him way off kilter. Or maybe it was the three whiskeys he'd had since he arrived.

"Is it all you've missed?"

Had Micah's voice always been that raspy? Apprehension trickled over Tucker, but he pushed it away. This was Micah, the kid he'd taken fishing and rode horses with, not some stranger. "Naw, it's not all I've missed. I miss my family and working on the ranch. I miss—"

Micah took the cigarette out of Tucker's fingers and took a puff off of it.

It was such an intimate gesture Tucker found himself staring. "I—I miss the quiet." He watched Micah's lips pucker as he blew out the smoke, and unbidden the image of those sweet lips kissing up his body sprang to mind. Tucker shook his head and took the cigarette back. "Since when do you smoke?"

"I don't usually." Micah shrugged. "Why don't you come home more often?"

It was the same question the rest of his family asked every time he talked to them. He hated that question. It wasn't like he didn't want to come home, but there were always deals to make and companies to sell. Mergers and acquisitions may be work, but it was also fun. He was on the top of his game and couldn't afford to be taking vacations all the time. "Work keeps me busy."

Tucker took a hit from his cigarette. It occurred to him that Micah's lips had just rested where his were. What would Micah's lips taste like? God damn where had that thought come from? "What are you doing out here? Shouldn't you be inside enjoying your birthday party?" Tucker winced at the growl in his voice.

Micah was quiet for several moments. When he spoke his voice was barely above a whisper. "I'd rather be out here with you."

Sucking in a breath of air, Tucker nearly choked but covered quickly by taking a drink. Something tickled his arm as he set his drink on the porch railing. He glanced down.

Micah's long dark fingers feathered over his arm, feeling, caressing. It was an innocent touch, but it sent the blood thrumming straight to Tucker's groin. *Fuck.* He had to get outta here. This was not good. He dropped his cigarette to the ground and crushed it out with his boot before kicking it off the porch. "Micah I—" Standing, Tucker turned and glanced right into adoring big brown eyes.

Micah bit his bottom lip and stepped closer. Once again he hesitantly traced his fingers over Tucker's forearm, moving the hair there and leaving a tickling feeling.

The innocent gesture made Tucker's cock fill fully. What was the matter with him? This was Micah. Their beloved foreman's nephew and the kid Granddad called "Tucker's Shadow." Christ, he'd known Micah since he was seven, when his parent's had been killed, and he'd come to the ranch to live with Juan.

Stepping closer, Micah raised up on tip toe, his gaze locked to Tucker's lips.

He knew what was coming, he even knew he should step away, but he couldn't. He watched, his focus on the full kissable mouth as Micah came closer and pressed his lips to Tucker's. It was like a jolt of lightning. It was such an innocent touch, it should have reminded Tucker who was kissing him, and it did, yet Tucker couldn't not respond. He wrapped his hand around the back of Micah's head and held him close. His mouth slanted over Micah's and his tongue pushed inside.

Micah jerked, gasping into Tucker's mouth. His body stiffened for several seconds as Tucker explored his mouth, then Micah relaxed and wound his arms around Tucker's waist. He squeezed Tucker tight and kissed back, his tongue sliding hesitantly along Tucker's. His breath quickened until he panted and his hands clutched at Tucker's back. He pressed forward, mashing his erection against Tucker's thigh.

Tucker's cock lurched and his own breath came faster. His free hand gripped Micah's firm little ass, urging him closer against Tucker's thigh. He pulled back, trying to catch his breath, but Micah didn't stop. He rooted his face on Tucker's neck, licking and kissing. Grunting, he thrust his hips at Tucker, grinding against him.

Fuck. This was insane. How had they gotten here this fast? He had to stop this. "Slow down baby."

But Micah didn't stop. His ragged breathing turned into moans and his hands were everywhere at once.

When Micah grabbed Tucker's cock, it was like being kicked in the stomach by a horse. Sanity returned and the voice in his head whispered "this is Micah." What the fuck was he thinking?

Tucker gripped the thick hair in his hand and tugged Micah's head back, forcing him to make eye contact. "Stop." He stared into languorous brown eyes only seconds before they went wide and Micah dropped his gaze.

Micah flung himself backward out of reach, not even looking at Tucker. "I—I—I'm sorry, I—" He shook his head then darted a glance up at Tucker. A tear streaked down his cheek then he turned and ran down the back steps toward the barn.

"Micah—" Tucker reached out before he realized it, then dropped his hand. He watched Micah disappear into the night, feeling like he'd just kicked a puppy. *Love,* his conscience whispered. He loved Micah. He always had, though he hadn't actually realized it till this moment, but the lust was new. Tucker shook his head and swallowed the last of his whiskey.

Naw, he was mistaken; he hadn't had a conscience for a long time.

CHAPTER ONE

Bong.

Blinking his eyes open, Micah stared at the dust motes floating in the stream of early morning sunlight coming in through the closed French doors. A rooster crowed and a calf called for his mama. A car door slammed and the floor above creaked. Was there anything more beautiful that this? Wait. French doors? He didn't have French doors in his room.

Bong.

Ah shit! He'd fallen asleep in the office again. All at once his body seemed to recognize what his brain had just learned, because a sharp pain shot down his spine and a dull ache settled in his lower back. "Ungh." Planting his hand on the desk, intent on peeling his face off the desk, it slipped in something. *Oh lovely. Drool.* He must have been more tired than he'd thought.

Pushing up, he yawned and stretched, wiping his hand off on his jeans. His back creaked then popped. Ouch. Sleeping in a chair sucked big fat hairy donkey balls.

Bong.

Micah groaned and looked at the monitor. Email. From Duncan Delany. Great, that was all he needed. He couldn't figure out how to pay the tab at the feed store and here was Ferguson's oldest son bugging him about the ranch again. "¡Cabrón!" The son of a bitch couldn't even have the decency to wait till his father died to try and screw the rest of the family out of their inheritance.

Pushing his glasses back up on his nose he opened the email. It was short and sweet.

Micah,

Send me the ranch's books, or I'll get my attorney involved. You aren't blood, this doesn't involve you. I want to know what I'm dealing with when my dad is gone.

Duncan

"Over my dead body, pendejo." Micah dragged the note into his personal folder and closed down the email. On the screen was the row of red numbers he'd been working on the night before. The nauseous feeling he'd had for the past two months flared to life. What was this latest threat? He wanted to know what *he* was dealing with? Did he honestly think Ferguson would leave him the ranch? Duncan lit out of Texas with his younger brother's wife and never looked back. He didn't know squat about family loyalty or running a ranch. No way in hell Ferguson would leave the ranch to him, he'd as much as told Micah so. Micah didn't know who was getting the ranch but Ferguson had hinted it'd be his younger son, Jeff, or one of his two grandsons.

Squashing down the anger, Micah looked back at the screen. No matter how many times he added the numbers they still came up negative. What were they going to do?

He leaned back in the chair he'd come to think of his since he took over management from Ferguson two months ago and mashed a fist into his stomach. Where had he put those Tums? *God, please don't let me be out.*

The office door creaked open and AJ stuck his blond head in. His gaze settled on Micah. "He's in the office!"

"Tattletale." Micah mumbled under his breath. That was all he needed, was for Jeff or Tio to lecture him about working too hard again. As if everyone wasn't working their asses off lately.

Sticking his tongue out, AJ pushed the door open fully and his shoulders sank a little. "Busted. Did you sleep in here again?"

Micah grimaced. "Coffee. I need coffee." Coffee and Tums, then he'd see what he could do with the accounts before he helped with chores.

"Bring him some coffee." AJ shouted toward the door then flopped down on of the chairs in front of the desk. "Granddad was asking for you this morning. He's not looking so good. Doc just left. Said he didn't think he'd make it through the week."

"Damn." The pain in Micah's stomach intensified. Pushing harder on his abdomen, he sat back and closed his eyes. Tears welled up behind his closed lids, but he held them back. He was a traitor. Ferguson Delany had welcomed him onto The Bar D fourteen years ago, when his parents had died, with open arms, and all Micah could feel was relief. Ferguson had treated Micah like one of his own grandsons, not his foreman's orphaned nephew. Tio Juan was a great man and had done his very best for Micah, but Micah was no fool; the Delanys had gone above and beyond what they should for an employee's kin, even if the employee was Ferguson's best friend. They'd made Micah a part of the family, even trusting him with the finances. He felt like the vilest sort of no good piece of crap for wanting Ferguson gone, but he hated to see the man, who was essentially his grandfather, suffer any longer.

"Don't start, Brat." AJ's voice cracked a little. "We've known it was coming for months now."

Once he had his emotions under control, Micah opened his eyes. "Yeah. I know, but—"

"I know…" AJ squeezed the bridge of his nose with his thumb and forefinger. He was on the verge of tears, and it tore Micah up to see it. AJ was always so strong and tough.

"Have you gotten a hold of Tucker?" Just saying the name made a whole heap of emotions run through Micah. Anger, regret, love and… anger. Tucker had abandoned them.

"I talked to his secretary. She's supposed to be getting him a message. Said he's out of town."

Nodding, Micah brought his feet up into the chair, trying to alleviate the pain in his stomach. His feet were bare. Where had his boots gone? He looked under the desk as he settled his feet onto the edge of the seat, hoping like hell he didn't look like he was doubling over in pain. He wasn't going to let Tucker Delany get to him after all these years.

"Looking for this?" AJ's hand came into view under the desk and flipped Micah the bird. *Juvenile.* "Okay seriously, what are you looking for?"

Micah grinned, the tension fading. "My boots." Micah shot him the middle finger right back, above the desk, before sitting up.

"They're on the kitchen floor."

Micah sat up, hugging his raised knee closer. "What are they doing in there?" *Merde*, his stomach was killing him.

AJ shrugged. "You're asking me?"

"Here is your coffee." Jeff walked into the office with a steaming mug and set it on the desk. He sat down in the chair next to AJ's and nudged AJ with his foot. "You tell him your granddaddy was asking for him?"

AJ nodded.

Micah pulled open the middle drawer, wondering if he'd stashed some antacids in there. "I need to finish the bills then I'll go up."

"You been down here all night again?" Jeff growled.

Micah sighed and aborted his search. "Yeah. I fell asleep."

"Kid—"

Holding up a hand Micah nodded. "I know. But until we find a way out of this hole we're in, I have to keep trying." He stared into Jeff's nearly black eyes, silently pleading with him to understand. "This is my family too, Jeff."

Jeff sighed. "Yes, it is. Did it ever occur to you that that's why I might have a problem with you working yourself into an early grave?"

Warmth spread through Micah. He knew his place here, but he liked to hear it. "All of us are working hard right now."

"How much?"

Micah thought about telling Jeff about the latest threat, but he hated to do that on top of everything else. Even the mention of his older brother or ex-wife left Jeff in a black mood for days. He didn't need to deal with that just yet, not with his father at death's door. "Can we do without the last two ranch hands? Can we handle the work between you, me, AJ and my tio?" Micah hated to pile more work on everyone, but—

"If we have to." Jeff scrubbed his hands down his face then up through the white streaked dark blond hair. "I'll let them go today. Can we give them a severance?"

No. Micah's stomach clenched, almost knocking his breath from him; he curled further into himself, making his leg press harder against his stomach. "Yeah." He'd find a way to give the men a severance pay. There was still some money left from his parent's life insurance policy. If he used it wisely, it would pay the remaining hands a nice severance and the property taxes. He'd have to find another way to pay the feed store tab and hospital bills though.

AJ sat forward, resting his forearms on his knees, a frown creasing his brow, and he stared at Micah.

Micah stared back, used to the intimidation tactic. Sometimes it sucked being treated like the younger brother, but it was also comforting with as crappy as everything else was lately. He had the urge to stick his tongue out and make faces. It was a normal impulse and if he hadn't had to yawn instead he would have smiled. "All right boys. Let's get to work. The morning's a wastin'." Jeff stood and headed out the door.

Standing, AJ dug in to his shirt pocket. He pulled something out and tossed it.

Out of reflex Micah caught it before it hit him in the face. He watched AJ disappear out the door before looking down. In his palm was a half roll of Rolaids.

After popping four of the antacids, Micah sat there for a few more minutes. He needed money. A lot of money in a big hurry.

He got up and wandered to the French doors, opened them and stepped out into the sunshine. Leaning on the back porch rail, he stared out over the green pasture with a sense of foreboding. Funny, it was early spring, the ranch was teaming with life, yet he was here waiting for his surrogate grandfather to die. It didn't seem real. He dropped his head against the post, trying not to look like he was hanging on for dear life. Losing the old man was bad enough, but Micah wasn't going to lose anyone else. Which meant he had to keep the ranch going and in Jeff's hands. Micah needed to find out what Duncan was up to. Why would he even want the ranch?

"What's on your mind, perrito?" Juan's old scarred up snakeskin boots creaked across the weathered wood porch, coming to a stop a foot from Micah's bare feet.

Micah rolled his forehead against the rough post before lifting his head. His uncle had called him that since he was a child running after the two Delany boys like an adoring "puppy." It reminded him of his carefree childhood here on The Bar D. "Just trying to figure out some stuff, Tio."

"You'll figure it out, Mijo. You always do."

That pride in his voice made Micah smile, on a day he didn't feel like smiling. "I hope you're right. Tell me about Duncan? He was gone by the time I got here." Micah didn't remember him at all, he'd left The Bar D when Micah was an infant, back when his parents were still alive. But if anyone knew about him it would be Tio. Juan had been foreman of The Bar D for the past fifty years. He'd had a hand in teaching all the Delanys, and Micah for that matter, what they knew of ranching.

"Hmm…" Juan's forehead furrowed and his eyes narrowed, then he shook his head. "Boy never did fit in. Was no surprise he run off with Vanessa. Neither of them ever cared much for the country life."

"Apparently, neither did Tucker." *Oh merde.* Why had he said that? Apparently, he had Tucker on the brain. It was kind of funny, but he hadn't thought of Tucker much the past couple months. He'd been too busy stomping fires.

"Baloney. Tucker got caught up in making money. The boy has the ranch life in his blood. He'll be back, you mark my words." Juan nodded once and spit off the porch.

Micah shrugged. "I hope you're right, Ferguson wants him home." His chest hurt and tears welled in Micah's eyes. As much as he'd adored Tucker when he was younger, Tucker was the least of Micah's problems right now.

"He does." Juan touched Micah's shoulder, gaining his attention. He stared right into Micah's eyes. "You do too."

"Me?" He shrugged again and stared out toward the pasture. The cool spring breeze brought with it the sweet fresh smell of alfalfa. It was peaceful and familiar. "I just want to make sure the ranch stays afloat and stays with those who love it."

"It will." Juan nodded and gripped the wood rail, leaning on it a little.

"I wish I had your confidence, Tio. Duncan is gonna cause problems, I just know it."

Lifting his hat, Juan scratched his head then stuffed his beat up old cowboy hat back down on his head. "How so?"

"He's been bugging me to turn over the ranch's finances to him."

"Pshaw. Ferguson handed that job over to you." Turning, Juan leaned his hip against the porch rail. "And he did so with good reason."

Micah snorted. "What reason?"

"Because he knows what kind of man you are. You'll find a way to make it all work." Juan chuckled. "Keep looking, perrito. Duncan is no threat." Pushing away from the rail, he patted Micah on the back and walked down the steps out toward the barn.

That was... odd. *Keep looking?* What did that mean? Micah frowned. What did Juan know that Micah didn't? "Tio?"

Juan waved his hand but kept walking, never even looking back.

Turning, Micah planted his butt against the porch rail and gazed back into the office. Why did old people always talk in riddles? The breeze ruffled his hair and brought a slight chill, making him shiver. He crossed his arms and stared at the computer. Was there something on there? A hidden bank account? The hair on Micah's arms stood up and apprehension and anticipation coiled inside of him. Rubbing his arms, he couldn't overcome the sense that his chill wasn't entirely from the wind.

CHAPTER TWO

"Fuck." *What is he doing here?* Tucker gritted his teeth and immediately tried to push the annoyance away. A hint of guilt niggled at him, which made him want to clench his teeth again. He was being an ass. Dennis wasn't the problem and normally he was delightful company, but Tucker had stepped off the plane from California at six this morning and been going ever since; he needed a little down time.

Dennis stood leaning against his powder blue Jetta looking elegant in his grey suit and red tie, the epitome of successful business man. He looked untouchable and... fake. It was normally one of the best things about Dennis; he pretended to be so restrained and Tucker loved to ruffle him and push that control. It was a challenge. Tucker loved challenges, but today he wasn't in the mood.

Wondering how long it'd take to get rid of him, Tucker pulled into the space next to Dennis' car. He'd had a long day and still more work to do tonight. Dennis' constant chatter would likely make Tucker's head explode. Which was another reason Dennis had to go, but maybe Tucker could talk him into a blowjob first. Dennis, who professed not to do oral sex, gave pretty decent head.

Dennis pushed away from his car and headed around it toward Tucker. He looked impatient.

Tucker checked the nav screen. It was only seven thirty-six. He never got home before seven. Dennis should know that by now. He could bitch if he wanted to, Tucker really didn't care. At least Dennis hadn't taken Tucker's favorite spot this time. He liked parking nearest to the elevators, the next space was assigned to him too, so unless someone, like Dennis, was visiting, there was no one parked beside his Jag. It was a little thing but he loved his car, he didn't want it dented all to hell. Putting his car in park, Tucker cut the engine.

Shaking his head, Dennis crossed his arms over his chest, waiting for Tucker to get out of the car.

Great. The chance of a blowjob before he got rid of Dennis wasn't looking good. Tucker gathered up his briefcase and his laptop before getting out of the car. "Hello Dennis."

"You forgot."

Yup, the blowjob was history. "Forgot what?" Tucker shut the door and locked it. He put his laptop bag over his shoulder and started toward the elevator.

"You were going to take me out tonight." Dennis maneuvered his way in front of Tucker so that he had to reach around Dennis to push the button for the elevator.

Oops. "Sorry I—"

The elevator door opened.

Digging into his laptop bag for his keys, Tucker stepped around Dennis and inside. He pushed the button to his floor just as his other hand found the keys.

"Tucker, I can't believe you forgot." Dennis followed him in before the doors closed. Huffing out a breath, he blew the elegant mahogany colored hair off his forehead and threw his hands in the air, letting them fall back to his sides with a slap. His gray eyes narrowed. "You forgot last time too. And the time before that."

Well damn. The elevator started moving and Tucker glanced up at the numbers above the door. "Sorry." That was the best he could do. Offering to go anyway was out of the question. Too bad about the blowjob though. *Floor eighteen. Almost there.*

"Sorry? That's it?"

Come on floor twenty-one. Tucker jiggled his keys. Maybe he could still talk Dennis into a hand job. It wouldn't take long, then he could get to work on the papers he brought home. He closed his eyes, trying to recall all the things he had to do before tomorrow morning. He needed to call Roger about the meeting at eight am, make sure his secretary sent the contracts to Cliff, check the stocks on Oxy Corp. again... They were so close to bankruptcy. If he could just swoop in before they filed—

The chime rang and the door opened.

Opening his eyes, Tucker headed out the door and to his apartment. "You wanna come in?" He opened his apartment door. "I'll order us some food." Maybe Mexican food from the place next door or Italian from the restaurant up the street. He was tired of Chinese. "How about pizza?"

No answer.

"Dennis?"

Still no answer.

Tucker turned.

Dennis stood in the elevator, a frown on his face and hands on his hips. The door started to close. He stuck his hand out, stopping it, and strode toward Tucker. "That's it?" He pushed into the apartment past Tucker. "You want to order pizza? And then what?"

Well shit. A hand job wasn't looking very promising either. Shutting the door, Tucker crossed and set his brief case on the coffee table and his laptop bag on the couch. He turned on the lamp beside the couch and pushed the button to open the vertical blinds. "I said I was sorry. What else do you want from me? I'm hungry and pizza sounds good. You want some?" He loosened his tie and took off his jacket.

"Un-fucking-believable!" Dennis' voice went so high it almost screeched. "So you aren't taking me out? Is that what you're saying?"

Tucker tossed his jacket over the chair closest to him and unbuttoned the cuffs on his shirt. "I've got work to—"

"You always have work to do. That is all you do. Work, work, work. You're a cold hearted bastard. You don't give a damned about anything but your fucking job and making money." He put his hands on his hips again, striking a pose that would make any drama queen envious. "You can't even take holidays off to go see your own damned family. You never go out, unless it involves business."

Someone knocked on the door, fizzling Dennis' fine pique.

Tucker pinched the bridge of his nose, relieved at the interruption, and headed toward the door. He opened the door and blinked, then dropped his hand from his nose and blinked again. He'd know those lips anywhere. He had seen that hat shadowed lower face too many times to mistake it. A smile spread across his face and excitement bubbled up inside him before he could quash it. "Micah?" He was taller than the last time Tucker had seen him, leaner. The black cowboy hat set low on his head covering his eyes and emphasizing the soft jaw, angular chin and the sensual mouth pressed into a thin line. Something was wrong. His heart sank and dread coiled in his stomach. "Come in." He grabbed Micah by the hand, noticing his duffle bag for the first time, and pulled Micah inside. Lifting the bag off Micah's shoulder, Tucker dropped it before pulling the smaller man into his arms. "What is it?" He rubbed Micah's lean back, hoping to abolish some of the tension, and felt the bumps of his spine. He was too thin. "What's wrong, baby?"

Micah's arms came around his waist loosely, almost hesitantly.

Tucker hadn't heard from or seen Micah since that night at his party, since *the* kiss. He'd been afraid to go back. He couldn't afford the temptation. The memory of that one kiss still sent Tucker's senses reeling, making him wish…

"Ahem."

Tucker jumped back, suddenly reminded of Dennis' presence. Fuck, what was he thinking? It would seem he'd been right to stay away. He hadn't seen Micah in several years and here he was pawing at him like he had every right, like Micah was his. "Micah. This is Dennis Hammond." He held his arm out indicating Dennis, without taking his gaze from Micah. "Dennis, Micah Jimenez."

With red tingeing his cheeks, Micah dipped his head toward Dennis. "Mr. Hammond." He glanced back at Tucker and pulled off his cowboy hat. He brushed a hand through his short black hair and his Adam's apple bobbed. There were bags under his eyes and he was wearing his glasses. Hadn't he switched to contacts?

The impulse to wrap his arms around Micah again was strong, making Tucker frown. What was the matter with him?

Normally he had an ironclad control on his emotions. Must be the lack of sleep.

"I'm sorry. I didn't mean to interrupt but—" Glancing at Dennis, Micah swallowed hard again. He twisted the hat brim in his hands, something Micah had always done when he was nervous. Glancing back at Tucker he asked, "Could we have a word in private?"

"I'll just be going then." Dennis stepped closer toward the door and consequently Micah. "Well good luck to you Micah Jimenez. I don't know who you are, but you've gotten more real emotion out of him in five minutes than I've seen the five years I've known him." He shook his head. "See you around Tucker."

Tucker wanted to protest, but realized with sharp clarity that he couldn't. His poker face *had* slipped and damn Dennis anyway for witnessing it. "Dennis—"

"No. I can't deal with this anymore. The sex was as phenomenal as everyone said but you take too much and give too—" he glanced back at Micah and his brow furrowed, "give too little." Shaking his head, he made eye contact with Tucker. "I can't do this." He opened the door, "If you ever want more, call me," and shut it quietly behind him.

Dragging his tie off of his neck, Tucker winced. "Guess that's a no on the hand job?" *Holy shit.* He wanted to lash out. It was a scary thought. Everything he did was with a calm calculating tenacity that served him and his interests well. He'd learned long ago not to show his hand, as it were; was that being a cold hearted bastard? And why the fuck did seeing Micah make him a fucking basket case? When he turned back Micah was still standing where he'd left him, his eyes as big as saucers, and Tucker's temper eased before it could really get going.

"Uh, I'm sorry, I did mean to interrupt. It's just—"

Tucker dropped the tie on top of his coat and went to the kitchen. "You didn't. I was trying to figure out how to get rid of him when you showed up." Grabbing the phone on his way, he punched the number two speed dial button. "Still like pepperoni and olives on your pizza?" Micah looked like he could stand to gain a few pounds.

Micah nodded, following him. "Tucker?"

Tucker grabbed two beers out of the fridge as he ordered the pizza. How long had Dennis lasted? Two months? Three? *Ouch*. Tucker didn't know. He tried to muster up regret, but there was nothing. Not a damned thing. Tossing the phone on the couch, he flopped down next to it. He set his beer on the table. "Come sit down Micah."

"Did you get AJ's call?" Micah came around the adjacent loveseat and sat, placing his hat beside him. Damn, he appeared dead on his feet. Had he driven the six hours straight from the ranch?

"I've been out of town until this morning. My secretary left me some messages but I haven't had a chance to look at them. What's wro—" Granddad had cancer. Tucker dropped his head into his hands. *Oh no*. "He's dead, isn't he?" He'd meant to go home; he'd wanted to see him one last time. Tears brimmed up in Tucker's eyes and it felt like the time he'd fallen off of his horse and flat onto his back when he was five.

"No! No, he's still hanging on. It's not going to be long though. But that's not why I came. Well, no, it sort of is, but it's not entirely why I came. I need—" He leaned his elbows on his knees and dropped is head, looking at the floor. After a few seconds he lifted his head again and ran his hands down his face. His face looked a little paler than before, or maybe the shadows under his eyes were just more pronounced in the lamp light. "I found his will the other day on the computer and your uncle has been emailing me every other day insisting I turn things over to him and—" Unshed tears shimmered in his eyes. "I can't sit by and let the ranch go under... or worse, go to your uncle."

Whoa. Wait a minute. "What do you mean go to my uncle? Granddad wouldn't—" Last time Tucker had talked to AJ— what was it a month ago?—AJ had said he was taking over as foreman and Micah was acting ranch manager. It had sounded like everything was running smoothly. Micah had always been a smart little thing and Tucker remembered thinking it was a good choice, so what had happened?

"I wouldn't have thought so either, but the way his will reads it's possible your uncle could get the ranch. I need you to find a way to break it. I don't have the money to hire a lawyer to look at it and Ferguson isn't in any shape to discuss it."

Rage built up in Tucker like he hadn't felt in a long time. "Over my dead body will that son of a bitch get his hands on The Bar D." Tucker stood, heading over to the window. "Tell me what's what with the ranch." Tucker winced at the bite in his own voice. This wasn't Micah's fault, at least he didn't think it was, but the very idea of his treacherous uncle getting his hands on the ranch did not sit well.

"We are in over our heads with your grandfather's medical bills. I've tried anything and everything I can think of and have managed most of our debt, but with the economy like it is… We need an investor." His voice cracked a little. "That's why I'm here. We—I need your help, Tucker."

Tucker stared at the reflection of Micah in the glass, watching his shoulders slump. Micah was such a proud thing, it wouldn't matter to him in the least that he was asking for help for Tucker's own family, it would still sting. Micah had always been so proud. "You have it." He said softly, hoping to encourage Micah to continue.

Micah heaved a sigh, looking slightly relieved. His eyes were on the ground, unaware Tucker was watching him. Had he thought Tucker would refuse to help?

"I felt like a first rate shit hill reading that will, but we are barely keeping our heads above water. I managed to pay off the yearly taxes, but there's nothing left. I had to do something. See if there was money somewhere else. Ferguson fades in and out. The few times I've asked about other accounts he's said there aren't any. I was hoping that maybe there was something in the will, I figured it would all be left to your dad, but…"

That's what Tucker had thought. He'd known instinctively Micah would have done everything possible to keep the ranch going. "Tell me." Forcing his focus away from Micah's reflection, Tucker stared out at the Dallas sky. It was beautiful.

The best view money could buy… and he rarely saw it. Groaning, he rested his forehead on the glass and closed his eyes. "What's in the will Micah?"

"I'd rather show you. I know it can't possibly be legal and I don't know what Ferguson was thinking, but— Do you have a computer? I brought a thumb drive with me."

No way was Tucker going to stand by and watch his uncle Duncan and his mother— "Is he still with her?"

"I don't know. His notes have been terse and demanding. Her name hasn't come up. I haven't told Jef—your dad about the emails." Micah's voice trailed off like he'd moved further away. "My tio seemed to think that Duncan wasn't a threat, but I don't know, from what the will says—" There was rustling. "It looks like he could get the ranch, unless we contest it." Micah touched Tucker's shoulder. "Here." He held out his hand over Tucker's shoulder. "I haven't said anything to AJ or your dad about the will. I didn't want to hurt them any more than they are already hurting."

Swallowing the lump in his throat, Tucker opened his eyes and lifted his head off the cool glass. He grabbed Micah's hand. He held on to it for a few seconds, extracting the thumb drive and feeling the calluses as his hand slid away.

"It's a nice view, but there are no stars." Micah yawned, standing so close Tucker could feel the heat of his body on his left side.

Tucker sighed. It didn't surprise him that Micah had noticed the lack of stars. Tucker missed them every time he looked out at the Dallas skyline.

Leaning back on the couch, Tucker read the will and took a bite of pizza. What in the hell could his granddad possibly be thinking? "This can't be real. He wants to leave the ranch to the first of us to marry?" Tucker took a swig of his beer. "It's even worded where it doesn't have to be a legal marriage in Texas or even the U.S., just a legal civil union. Technically, I could marry another man and inherit." He'd get his lawyer on this right away. "Are you sure he was of sound mind?" After a few seconds when Micah didn't say anything, Tucker glanced over at him.

With his lips tightly pressed together, Micah sat with a plate in his lap on the loveseat adjacent to the couch. A can of Dr. Pepper sat, untouched, on the coffee table in front of him. His hand rested in the middle of his chest over his breastbone and his eyes were closed. His normally tanned skin had a gray pallor to it.

Tucker's chest tightened and the protective feeling he always had over Micah reared its head. "Micah?"

Micah started, his eyes blinking open. "What?"

"Are you all right?" Tucker sat forward, putting his laptop on the table and his half eaten slice of pizza on the empty plate beside it.

He didn't look okay. Besides being tired and too thin, his big brown eyes were red. "Yes, I'm good. What did you ask?" Pressing on his chest, Micah winced and tried to pretend that he didn't.

Tucker glanced down at Micah's plate and realized he hadn't even touched his food. "You need to eat. When is the last time you had a meal? You drove straight here, didn't you? That's a six hour drive. I want you to eat, then go to sleep."

"Jeff fixed us all a big breakfast this morning. And I'm not that tired. I'll probably head back out to the ranch tonight." He set his plate on the table and rubbed absently at his chest. "After you look at that, I mean. Do you think we'll be able to contest it?"

"Yes, I think so and I'll look at the finances in a bit, but right now I want you to eat and get some rest. You look like hell." No fucking way was Tucker letting him drive back tonight. "I'll drive back with you tomorrow morning. That way I can see Granddad. I have a meeting tomorrow but I'm going to cancel it, this is more important."

Micah's eyes squeezed together and a small moan escaped. "I don't feel like eati—" His eyes flew open and he jumped to his feet. "Bathroom?"

Shit. Tucker jumped up and ran around the couch and down the hall. "Here." He pushed open the bathroom door a split second before Micah darted past him, skidded to a halt in front of the toilet and threw up, or tried too, not much came up.

"Sorry." Micah dropped down to his knees and rested his head on the rim of the toilet.

"Don't be silly. You have nothing to apologize for, but you definitely aren't going anywhere tonight." Damn. As soon as Micah dozed off, Tucker was going to call AJ and ream his ass out for letting Micah drive all the way here by himself dead on his feet. He needed to go home for a bit just to make sure the kid was taking care of himself. Tucker wet a wash cloth and took it to Micah. "Micah."

"Thanks." Micah took the rag and wiped his mouth before resting his head on the arm on the rim of the pot. "I don't know what's wrong with me. I haven't eaten anything to throw up." His other hand pressed against his chest again.

Tucker reached down to brush the dark hair off his pale forehead and saw the blood in the toilet. "Oh God." His chest squeezed tight and the hairs on the back of neck and arms stood straight up. "Come on, baby. Get up from there, you're going to the hospital."

CHAPTER THREE

Something squeezed his arm and an annoying little beep sounded. A smooth deep voice spoke softly in the distance. Micah couldn't tell what the voice was saying but it was soothing. It brought to mind a cold night with a warm fire and a fifth of whiskey. Oh nice, his lips curved automatically and he snuggled down into the warmth surrounding him. Some Glenlivet would really hit the spot. Too bad the liquor stash at The Bar D was nearly depleted. Well, no, maybe not... Lately any alcohol killed his stomach. Which really sucked, because the past month he could've used a good nip at night to lull him to sleep. Come to think of it, this was about as cozy as he'd been in a long time.

A little niggling at the back of his head said this couldn't be right. There was always something to worry over, always something to do, money to figure out... Why was he asleep? He'd gone to talk to Tucker. Micah blinked open his eyes.

The hospital. It was dim and blurry as hell without his glasses, but there was no mistaking the clinical look of the room and the scent of antiseptic. The blood pressure cuff released the death grip on his arm and another beep accosted his ears. *Merde,* he didn't have the money for this.

There was a creak, it sounded like someone fidgeting in a chair. "I love you too, Granddad." Tucker paused, and his voice hitched a little. "I'll do my best." There was another pause and a long sniff. "Yes sir, I promise. I'll make everything right."

He talked quietly, but Micah thought he heard the longing in his voice. He'd always wondered why Tucker stayed away. There was no sense in it. If he loved them, why didn't he make time to see them? To check on them? Why had he abandoned them?

"I'll see you in two days, okay? Bye Granddad."

Micah had to get out of here. Trying to shake his head into alertness, he grappled with the cuff on his arm, already edging his feet to the side of the bed and out of the covers. He didn't care what made Tucker stay away, the fact was he'd done so. All Micah needed from him now was an agreement to help. If it weren't for Jeff and AJ, Micah wouldn't even ask, but Tucker was their family and— The rip of the velcro signaled his freedom and cold air nipped at his toes. No way was he going to be able to pay for an extended stay. He'd had to have the endoscopy to make sure the bleeding wasn't dire, fine, he'd find the money somewhere, but it was an outpatient procedure, right?

A hand landed on his shoulder, pushing him back to the mattress.

Micah turned his head and met Tucker's dark eyes. Everything just stopped. Micah couldn't breath, couldn't think and certainly couldn't talk. He froze with one leg dangling off the bed and a hand on the rail to help push himself up. Here he was flat on his back—and damn his stomach ached—he was groggy and needing to get out of here, but the sight of Tucker, even fuzzy as it was, hit him just as hard as it did earlier in the evening. He'd thought his crush had run its course, thought he'd be immune to Tucker now that he'd grown up, but he wasn't. Tucker was still the most gorgeous man he'd ever laid eyes on.

"Slow down Hop-Along." Tucker released his shoulder and tucked his foot back into the covers. Twining his hand with Micah's he made Micah release the death grip on the bed rail but didn't let go of Micah's hand. "Where did you think you were going?" He smirked. One sandy brow arched in question.

"Outta here. I can't afford—"

"Don't start. I don't think the nurses would take too kindly to me bending you over my knee. The bleeding wasn't bad enough to do surgery, but you are stuck here for the next twenty-four hours at least. And I'm paying for the hospital bill." Letting go of Micah's hand, he sat in a chair next to the bed and gave Micah that stern no nonsense look that brooked no argument.

It irritated the piss outta Micah. He was not the same doting kid that hung on Tucker's every word and did whatever Tucker said. He was a grown man with responsibilities and—*Responsibilities*. Micah groaned. "Damn it. I didn't call home. And where the hell are my glasses? I can't see a damned thing."

"I've already called The Bar D." Tucker said softly. He pulled Micah's glasses out of his shirt pocket and put them on Micah's face, before leaning back in the chair and crossing his long legs out in front of him.

Now that he could see clearly, Micah studied Tucker again.

The streetlamp light coming in from the open curtain haloed him, casting a shadow on his face. Or was it a shadow? Tucker's square jaw was nearly always covered with a heavy five o'clock shadow. More than once Micah had fantasized how the prickly whiskers would feel on his skin. It had always amazed Micah that anyone with strawberry blond hair could have such a dark beard shadow.

"I talked to my granddad." Resting his head on the back of the chair, he closed his eyes.

What could Micah say to that? He'd heard. "Was he having a good day?" Micah fought the urge to reach out to Tucker by burying his hands under the blanket.

"Yeah." Tucker smiled and nodded slightly but his eyes remained closed. He looked almost fragile, making Micah want to turn away and give him a moment, but he didn't. He soaked in Tucker's presence. Funny, he seemed so vulnerable, yet his wide shoulders swallowed up the small space in the private hospital room, attesting to his power like nothing else could.

His silent strength had always made Micah feel so secure, protected. Maybe that's why he'd come to get Tucker's help. Tucker had always been able to carry the world on his shoulders so effortlessly. Micah almost resented him for it. Tucker didn't seem to be bogged down with normal wants and needs. He could go off on his own and make a fortune without missing his family, missing Micah. And wasn't that a slap to the face. Even now, he still longed for Tucker, but Tucker hadn't given two thoughts for Micah until he'd shown up on his doorstep earlier. Why couldn't Micah do the same? He was supposed to be helping and here he was mooning over a man he could never have and racking up more bills.   Micah closed his eyes and turned his head.   *A private room.*   The hospital bill was going to be outrageous.

"He told me you needed me."

"What?"   Micah snapped his eyes open and turned his head, meeting Tucker's gaze.   "You told him I was in the hospital?"

"No, AJ and Dad threatened to strangle me if I did." Tucker stood, leaning his forearms on the bed rail and looking down at Micah.   He shrugged.   "I'm not sure what he meant. Maybe he suspects something?"

Micah frowned, wishing Tucker would sit back down.   He was too big, too imposing… too desirable.   "He does know something.   He knows how bad the debt is.   I guess it's his way of reminding you where you belong and asking for help."

Tracing fingers along Micah's cheek, Tucker followed it with his gaze.   "Maybe."   He nodded.   "Probably.   But I don't understand why he didn't ask sooner?"

A tingly feeling started in Micah's stomach and spread out. His cock even stirred and the stupid beeping got faster.   Heat rushed to Micah's cheeks and he jerked his head away.   "Have you looked over the will?"

"I did.   I've got a lawyer looking at it, but that is something else I don't understand."   He sat back down in his chair and stretched out with his hands over his stomach.   "Why haven't you come to me before now?"

"Because I was handling it just—"

"Oh really?"   Tucker turned his head, one arrogant brow arched.   "You can't even take care of yourself."

"You're an asshole."   He wasn't a fucking kid anymore. Tucker had no right—   He hadn't even been around.   Micah was doing the work Tucker had been born to do—he was Jeff's oldest child—so how dare he judge.   Heat infused Micah's neck and face.   Tucker had no idea how lucky he was to still have his birthright.   Micah gritted his teeth together, the high from the anesthesia was definitely wearing off but his anger kept the pain away.

"Yes, I am. And since you already think that, maybe it's a good time to tell you what I've decided to do about the will."

A chill raced up Micah's spine and the cool, almost dead tone in which Tucker spoke. Oh yeah, the meds were definitely wearing off. "What?"

"Nothing. We're going to get married before we go back to the ranch."

CHAPTER FOUR

Micah hadn't said two words to him since yesterday. Maybe Tucker had gone too far with the marriage scheme? It didn't matter, it was a done deal—he glanced at the marriage license where it lay on the dash of the car—Micah was his for now, like it or not. At this point Tucker didn't really care what the little shit wanted. Micah had been working himself to death and this was the one sure way to make him stop, even if Tucker had to fight him tooth and nail. He couldn't live with himself if he let things go on this way. "How do you feel?"

"Fine."

Tucker repressed the urge to grind his teeth together, grab Micah and shake the shit out of him. Had he always been this disagreeable? No, Tucker knew he hadn't. Once upon a time Micah was all smiles and hung on Tucker's every word. He missed it. Okay, maybe the adoring agreement was a little much—Tucker kinda liked the new independent streak—but Tucker wanted to see that smile again. "No pain?"

"No." Micah continued to lean back in the seat with his eyes closed.

"Tell me about your ideas for the ranch."

"Doesn't matter."

Ugh! I will not slap him upside the head, I will not slap him upside the head, I will not slap him upside the head. What was it about Micah that made him so... on edge? They used to get along so well they didn't even need to talk. Tucker hadn't had that with anyone but Micah, not even AJ. "It does matter. I didn't marry you so I can just throw away money on the ranch. I want it profitable again. I want to make sure you, Dad and AJ have a home and an income. Ya'll need to be happy with it, so I need your input."

"What? What does that mean? You're just gonna get things back on track for us and split? You're abandoning us again?"

"Micah…" Tucker groaned. "I'm not abandoning ya'll. I never *abandoned* ya'll. I have a life and a career in Dallas. I can't just move back out to the ranch and pretend otherwise. I did things this way to make sure that the ranch stays with who it should. Until I can get a lawyer to look at it, this is the easiest way. It's not like I could just ask my granddad to change his will. You said yourself it's only a matter of time until—" Tucker's throat grew tight, making him have to swallow— "until we lose him. This way we have things secured. The ranch will be put in my name, I'll pay the inheritance tax on it and lend the ranch money to get it going again, but I need to know what you, my dad and AJ have in mind. What is it ya'll think will make the ranch solvent. I expect to make a profit too, but I'm not going to be here to run things, ya'll are."

Micah sighed and turned his head looking at Tucker. "Then why bother coming back? We don't need you here to spend your money. I can make the decisions and run them by Jeff and AJ. I—oh nevermind."

Ah, Tucker was starting to see the problem. Micah was used to being the go to guy. He'd gotten accustomed to running the ranch and why not? Dad and AJ hated anything to do with the business side of things, they were more than happy to stay outside with the livestock. "You think I'm just going to come in and take over?"

"Aren't you? Hell, you wouldn't even let me drive my own damned truck back. That sure seems like taking over to me."

A growl escaped before Tucker could hold it back. "We've been over that. You need the rest. I'll take you back to get your truck in a few days. Now will you quit being such a pain in the ass and tell me what ideas you have?"

Micah was quiet for several moments then he turned his head back to the front, resting it on the seat and closed his eyes. "We need to increase our herd size and AJ and I talked about adding a breeding program. So instead of just the feeding and growing outfit we can sell breeding stock. We have some excellent bulls but we'd need more."

He had given it some thought. Developing a breeding herd would take a lot of capital, but it had the potential to make more too. "What kind of herd?"

"Commercial. We wanna mess with cross-breeding."

The Bar D had always run Longhorns. "What other breeds?"

Shrugging without turning his head, Micah yawned. "Don't know yet. We've been too busy to even discuss it."

Tucker frowned. He'd noticed how tired Micah was when he'd first shown up in his apartment. But no time to discuss the ranch's future? From what Tucker could tell, Micah did nothing but worry about the ranch. Not many twenty-two year old men ended up with ulcers. The doctor had seemed to think it had a lot to do with Micah's anti-inflammatory use. Which made Tucker suspect Micah was working too hard. Sure, ranch work was hard, but— the kid needed someone to take care of him. Tucker was going to have to jump his Dad's and AJ's asses when he got home. They should be taking care of Micah better. Slowing the truck, Tucker sighed and made a left hand turn. "We'll discuss it tonight then. We're here."

Gravel crunched under the truck tires and Micah blinked his eyes open and sat up. A slow, barely perceptible grin flitted across his face.

Tucker grinned too as he drove through the open gate of rough cut lumber, with a long piece going over the top that read *The Bar D*. He swallowed hard, trying to tamp down the case of nerves that suddenly appeared. He'd ridden through this gate hundreds of times. What was so different now? Besides the fact that he could be wrong and their marriage wouldn't stand up in court?

"What if this doesn't work?"

"It will work. I talked to the lawyer. The way the will was written, the marriage doesn't have to be legal in Texas, just somewhere. It's legal in a few states and Canada, so we're good."

"I thought your lawyer didn't read it yet?" Frowning, Micah turned in his seat.

"I said she hadn't found a way to contest it yet." Tucker kept his eyes forward, hoping Micah wouldn't sense the small fib. His lawyer had said she was fairly certain it could be contested, but Tucker had decided to go this route first. They didn't want to draw any attention toward contesting the will. Duncan might contest it anyway, which is why Tucker had his lawyer looking into it, but for now they were going to try and make the marriage work for them. *Yeah right.* Who was he kidding? He wanted Micah and he took him. Seeing Micah lying in that hospital bed had really worked a number on him. For once he hadn't really thought things through. He was a selfish bastard, but he wanted more control over Micah's life. He had no clue what to do with Micah when they went back to their daily lives, but he was going to take care of Micah in the meantime. He'd let Micah go when the time came… maybe. No, he would, he had too. He knew damned well there was no such thing as a fairy tale happily ever after. If he stayed he'd be tempted to try and when it finally ended… he couldn't do that to Micah.

"Oh, I thought—¡Hijo de la chingada!"

Tucker smiled at the Spanish swear. Micah had always cussed in Spanish. As a kid, he'd gotten away with it most of the time, unless Juan was within earshot. "What are you swearing about?"

"That." Micah pointed to a gray Cadillac Escalade. The license plate read DUNCAN.

Tucker felt like someone poured ice water down his back. So help him if that son of a bitch was upsetting his dad or his grand dad…

Micah began muttering in Spanish. Tucker caught the words "cabrón" and "pendejo" and figured whatever he was saying wasn't very nice. He only regretted not knowing enough Spanish to join in.

"What in the hell is he doing here?" Tucker pulled into the drive behind his dad's beat up old Chevy and put his car in park. "Why is that fucking lowlife *here*?"

"Beats the shit out of me." Micah's voice had a growly quality to it that made Tucker look at him more closely. It was sexy and violent at the same time. Or maybe it was sexy because it was so violent sounding. At any rate it didn't sound like Micah.

"I'd like to beat the shit out of *him*. Think he brought the bitch with him?" If his egg donor was here, Tucker was going to throw her ass off the property personally.

"I don't know." Micah reached for the door handle. "I gotta go check on Dad."

Tucker caught his arm before he opened the door, wondering if he even realized he'd called Tucker's dad, "dad." "Wait killer. Your seatbelt is still on."

Micah moved to unlatch his belt, but Tucker didn't let go of his arm. As badly as Tucker would love to see Duncan get his ass kicked, he wasn't about to let Micah do it. In fact, Micah shouldn't be getting this upset. It wasn't good for him. He was supposed to be taking it easy. Tucker frowned. "Micah, calm down." Grabbing the marriage license off the dash he waved it at Micah and grinned. "Remember this? Our ace in the hole. Stop worrying. He can't get into the computer can he?"

"Only AJ and I know the password." Unhooking his seat belt, Micah shook his head and turned his body toward Tucker. He took a deep breath and visibly tried to calm himself. "No way in hell would AJ give that pendejo the password."

"Good. Relax. We'll see what he wants and send him on his way." Tucker's gaze darted past Micah for a second, spotting AJ, his Dad, and Juan coming their way. One side of his mouth hitched up. God, it was good to be home. He glanced back at Micah, noting once again the dark circles under his eyes. Tucker's chest tightened. No way was he letting Duncan stay. Micah didn't need the stress. "Come here, baby."

Micah's brow scrunched together and he glared at Tucker. "What did you call me?"

Tucker got an insane urge to kiss that glare away. He shouldn't. It would only complicate things. Fuck that, he wanted and he was going to have. Leaning forward, Tucker touched Micah under the chin and urged him closer. He slanted his mouth over Micah's in an easy caress, trying not to knock his glasses off.

A sound caught somewhere between a protest and a plea left Micah's throat before he finally kissed Tucker back. He reached for his glasses with one hand and clenched and unclenched the other in the fabric of Tucker's shirt.

Tucker wanted it to last, and the same time he knew he shouldn't, this could become addicting. He couldn't afford to get addicted to Micah's kisses. Micah may be old enough now, but their worlds moved in different directions. It was already going to tear a piece of Tucker's heart out when he had to leave The Bar D again and go back to Dallas. *Damn Micah, why did he have to be so tempting?* Tucker pulled back, hoping Micah would think the kiss was for their audience.

His family had moved toward them, and now on the porch was a man in a gray suit. *Duncan.* He looked a lot like Tucker's dad, only older. The passenger side door opened. "Well lookie here, the prodigal son has returned." Juan smiled. "Welcome back, young 'un."

"And brought a Tucker." AJ said in a surprised whisper. "Well I'll be damned. Hi there big brother."

"Juan was talking about Tucker, not Micah." Dad laughed. "Get out here boy!"

Taking off his seatbelt, Tucker opened his own door, smiling so big his face hurt. By the time he made it around the car, AJ and Juan had gathered around Micah, fussing over him. Micah brushed them off, telling them he was fine.

His dad met him in front of the car and squeezed him so tight Tucker lost his breath. He stepped back and studied his father. Dad looked older. There was more gray in his hair and more wrinkles at the corners of his eyes, but he looked... good. Like home. Tucker hugged him again. "Hi Dad."

"Glad you're home, son. You take care of our boy?" He pulled back, his eyes cutting to where AJ and Juan stood with Micah.

Micah caught his gaze. His eyes fairly sparkled with happiness for a brief moment then he looked away, saying something to AJ.

Nodding, Tucker smiled. "Yeah, he's been fighting me the whole way though."

AJ laughed. "Sounds like him." He patted Micah on the back before striding forward and grabbing Tucker in a big ole bear hug and lifting him off the ground. "Glad you're back. I should have sent the brat after you sooner."

"Besa mi culo." Micah grinned at AJ.

"All you had to do was call." Tucker laughed.

AJ flipped Micah off. "*You* kiss my ass, brat." He looked back at Tucker, the laughter and fun leaving his eyes. "You see who's here?"

Tucker looked back at the porch, his gaze meeting Duncan's. "Yeah. We need to kick his ass out?"

Duncan came down the porch steps, heading their way with his head held high. He looked so much like Tucker's dad Tucker had to remind himself what a bastard the man was. When he reached them he stepped up and held out his hand to Tucker. "So you've decided to come home. Or did the—" his gaze raked over Micah and a snarl appeared on his lips, "little faggot drag you back?"

"And by faggot I assume you are referring to my husband." He stared right at Duncan, watching the shock play over his face. "Come on. Call him a faggot again. I dare you."

CHAPTER FIVE

Micah flopped down on his bed, his legs hanging over the edge. His glasses slid up a little too far and he had to readjust them. A slow grin spread across his face followed by a giggle. Duncan was not happy. The look on his face when Tucker had announced that they were married was priceless. It made all the harassment he'd received from Duncan over the past two months worthwhile. All throughout dinner, Duncan had glared at Micah. Could Duncan resent that Micah was such a part of the family? Every time Jeff, AJ or Juan expressed joy over Micah's newly wedded state and how he was now officially part of the family, Duncan tried to divert their attention. Or was he merely a homophobic asshole? It was odd. Why did he even care? He's the one that had left and betrayed his family, Micah's placement in the family shouldn't be of any concern to him.

The door clicked shut, followed by a sigh.

Raising up onto his elbows, Micah studied Tucker.

He leaned against the closed door, his arms and feet braced out like he was expecting someone to try and get in. "Damn. He looks bad." Closing his eyes, he took a deep breath. "I should have come back sooner."

Even though Micah agreed, he hated to see Tucker in pain. He, Jeff, AJ and Juan had gotten used to how the cancer had affected Ferguson, Tucker had not. "You're back now, that is what matters. Did you have a nice visit with your grandfather?"

"Yeah. I did. He fell asleep on me though." Tucker pushed away from the door and flopped down next to Micah, making the bed bounce. "He was really happy about me marrying you."

"Yeah, I got that impression. Pretty fucking weird. I don't think he realizes it's fake..." Micah frowned. How could he not know it was fake? And why would he be so happy. "He tires easily. Rest is the best thing for him, he's not hurting when he's asleep." Micah shook his head, he didn't want to go down this road. He'd agonized and grieved too much already, it didn't help and he sure as hell didn't wanna make Tucker feel worse. He grinned, trying to lighten the mood and change the subject. "I'm still waiting for Jeff and AJ to corner me and ask why." Micah dropped to his back and rested his hands over his stomach. They'd all been genuinely happy, but they knew darn well that Micah hadn't seen Tucker in years. They knew something was up. No one wanted to alert Duncan to their business though, so they'd pretended like it was the most normal thing in the world to find out that Micah and Tucker had married. And how odd was that? They'd known Micah and Tucker were both gay, but... God, he loved his family. The weirdos.

"Yeah. I figure we'll get the third degree once Duncan leaves." He turned his head to look at Micah. The sadness in his eyes was still there, but then he grinned too. "Wonder if Duncan will pop off again and give me an excuse to whoop his ass?" Tucker's brows pulled together. "What the hell does Duncan want? Can't he tell no one wants him here? I understand Granddad is his father too, but he hasn't bothered to come visit him over the years so why now?"

Micah wanted to kiss Tucker's lips and make it all better. No, he didn't. Guh! What were they talking about? *Oh.* "Don't know. None of us has really kept our feelings for him a secret. At least he didn't bring your mother." Micah turned his head, meeting those deep brown eyes. A weird fluttery feeling started up in his belly. Swallowing the lump in his throat he licked his lips. "I think if he'd brought her, I'd have whooped his ass on sight, regardless of Ferguson's feelings. Jeff has enough to deal with right now. Duncan is either smart or lucky, I haven't decided which." He needed to get a grip. Being this close to Tucker was always harder, but after that kiss in the car... Micah couldn't stop thinking about that stupid kiss and it was really beginning to piss him off. When had he become so weak? He may be a nerd, but he'd been kissed before. *Tucker is special,* the little voice in his head said. *Callate la boca, you stupid voice.*

"You would have had to beat me to i—" Glancing down at Micah's lips, Tucker's eyebrows pulled together in a frown. His dark lashes partially concealed his nearly black eyes as he leaned forward, bringing them nearly nose to nose. Everything seemed to slow down. The tip of his tongue appeared between his lips. His breath fanned across Micah's chin.

Micah couldn't breathe. He was afraid to. If he did anything, Tucker would come to his senses and Micah didn't want to risk that. *Yes, you do, cabron! Move back, clear your throat, scratch your nose, just do something.* Because this kiss wouldn't be for show. It would be real. He wouldn't be able to explain it away.

Tucker's eyelids fluttered then flew up, making his eyes wide. He shook his head and jerked backward with a groan. "Make noise." Pushing himself up off the bed, he locked the door and checked it by turning the handle. "I'm going to take a shower."

Ah dios mio. Micah closed his eyes and took a deep breath. *It's for the best, he isn't staying, he said so himself, but damn*—"What?"

"Moan and grunt." Tucker crossed the room and pulled the curtains then went into the adjoining bathroom.

"Ungh." Micah sat up, trying to get his heart to slow down. What was Tucker doing?

"Micah…" Tucker hissed.

"Ack!" He opened his mouth to ask why, "Oh," then snapped it shut. Why not just turn on the radio? Did he really think Duncan was listening to them? He glanced at the door. There wasn't that much space under the door, probably less than an inch. It was doubtful anyone was standing outside it. Micah went to the door, laid down in front of it and looked under. His glasses shifted when the frame touched the floor but he could still see through them. It didn't look like anyone was there.

"What are you doing?" Tucker kept his voice low and leaned against the bathroom threshold, a smirk on his handsome face.

"What are *you* doing?" Groaning, Micah got to his feet.

"Looking for shaving cream. Why aren't you making noise?"

"Ungh!" Micah stomped his feet in place a few times.

Tucker rolled his eyes. "You sound like a dying cow."

"I don't think anyone is out there listening." Micah whispered back, walking closer to Tucker. "The shaving cream is in the cabinet to the left of the sink."

"Thanks." Grinning, Tucker dragged a hand over his face and through his short dark blond hair and turned back toward the bathroom. "Try to sound like you're having sex. Duncan is in the room across the hall."

"Oh." *Oh!* Micah groaned at himself. *Dork.* Shaking his head he went back to the iron framed bed. He sat on the edge, bouncing a little. The best protested nicely. This could be fun. He pulled off his shoes and tossed them away. Bouncing again, he let out a long ragged moan. Just like old times; he wondered why he let Tucker talk him into these kinds of things. *Oh yeah, 'cause you're in love with him and would do anything for him.* He was really gonna have to stop that. Micah groaned at himself, but it added to the sex noise.

"Oh lord. Don't overdo it. You just got out of the hospital, remember?" Tucker disappeared back into the bathroom.

"Oh, oh yeah. Mmm…" Crawling onto the bed, Micah hopped on his knees a little. The bed squeaked again. "Oh yeah baby!" *Take that Duncan. ¡You Pendejo!*

The water turned on in the bathroom and Micah grunted, trying to cover the sound. He climbed to his feet, wobbling a little on the soft mattress. Bending his knees he made the bed squeak again. Would the bed hold him if he actually jumped? He'd always wanted to jump on a bed. His mom would have killed him when he was little. Jostling the bed again he glanced around the room. The floor was wood. If he jumped would the bed be too loud? "Oh yes, yes, yes." He moaned again for affect. He really really wanted to jump. *¡Mijo!* His mother's voice admonished in his head. He could almost see her shaking her finger at him.

Fuck it. Micah's feet left the mattress and the headboard thunked against the wall. "Oh yeah, baby take it." His glasses slid down his nose and he had to push them back up. This was fun.

The water shut off.

"Oh yeah, take that cock."

Tucker appeared in the doorway with half his face covered in shaving cream. His mouth practically hanging open. "What. Are. You. Doing?"

Holding his glasses with one hand, Micah jumped and lifted his legs, coming down on his butt. *Clunk, clunk, screech.* The bed walked back in forth on the wood. "Oh yeah, baby!" He hopped back up, grinning from ear to ear. "You said to act like I was having sex," he whispered. Dipping his knees a few times, he made the springs bounce. Chuckling, he hopped in a circle. "You like that, baby?"

"Micah." Tucker hissed.

"What? You said—"

"I top. Stop with the 'take it,' stuff. And quit jumping on the bed, before you hurt yourself."

What? "Dios mio." Micah froze mid bounce. When he came down his teeth slammed together. Ow. "You're kidding me?"

"No, I'm not."

"You're irritated because I'm pretending to top?"

"I always top." Tucker crossed his arms and leaned against the door staring at him incredulously.

Despite Micah's resolve to get over his infatuation, that little giddy feeling started up again. He had always preferred to bottom. There was just something about having a nice hard cock up— He frowned, relieved at finding something new to be irritated at Tucker about. "Just what are you insinuating?" He hopped on the bed a couple times in a row. He was not some wuss because he liked to get fucked, damn it. And he was getting really tired of the whole, 'you are just out of the hospital,' crap.

"I'm not insinuating anything. I'm just stating a fact. I top. Always." Tucker's brow furrowed. It became apparent why opposing football players in college had feared him, why business men probably still did. But that glare didn't work on Micah.

"No one, especially my family, would ever believe otherwise."

"Well, I get to top in imaginary sex." Micah pushed the wire frames back up his nose and resisted the childish urge to stick his tongue out.

"No, you don't." Pushing away from the door, Tucker strode forward, scowling now. He looked mean.

This was the most ridiculous conversation ever. Micah should just drop it, it was beyond silly, but he didn't. "Oh yes I do." He jumped a few more times. "Oh yeah baby! Take. It. You like my big cock up yo—"

Tucker tackled him.

"Oof." He landed flat on his back in the middle of the bed with a bounce. The bed screeched across the floor and the headboard slammed into the wall. Micah looked up into wide, dark, fathomless eyes.

Tucker stayed braced above him, holding himself up with his muscular arms. His knees bracketed Micah's thighs and for several seconds, he just stared. Blinking, he shifted his gaze to Micah's lips. Half of Tucker's face still had shaving cream on it. He should have looked ridiculous, but he didn't. The chiseled jaw appeared even more masculine.

Micah licked his lips out of self consciousness. "Tucker, I, uh— Um." He cleared his throat. "Get the fuck off me."

Tucker didn't move.

It was surreal and Micah wanted nothing more than to be married in more than name. A little catch in the middle of Micah's chest made his breath hitch and his pulse race. His cock grew hard. *Oh god, please don't let Tucker feel that.*

"I get to top, Micah." Tucker's voice was barely above a whisper. He shifted, sliding his legs along the outside of Micah's. Micah should move, get out from under him.

The only sounds in the room were their breathing and their jeans brushing against each other's. Tucker's lower body pressed down on top of Micah's. A hard ridge pressed against Micah's hip, right next to his prick. He sucked in a breath.

Moaning, Tucker flicked his tongue out, moistening his lips, and his eyes closed. Tilting his head, he slanted it. His eyes fluttered open and he ground his erection against Micah.

Micah stared, barely able to breathe. He had loved this man for years. Even at the tender age of fourteen, Micah had fantasized about kissing Tucker over and over in his dreams, heck not much had changed. He still daydreamed about that, but now… he was scared. Tucker had refused him all those years ago. Not just that, he'd lit out of here so fast he left tracks. Micah swallowed, trying to get some moisture in his suddenly dry mouth. They couldn't do this. He wouldn't. Tucker was just going to leave again. Micah squeezed his eyes shut.

Tucker's finger's skimmed Micah's cheek. "You gonna—" His lips brushed Micah's.

It was nothing really, but Micah's whole body tingled, starting at his lips and traveling down his body, making him tremble. He blinked his eyes open and stared into Tucker's black eyes.

"—let me top, Micah?"

Mierda. Was he serious?

Bang bang bang. Someone pounded on the door.

Micah gasped.

Tucker jumped, rolling off of Micah and stared at the door.

"You two keep it down in there. Christ, no one wants to even know you two are having sex, much less hear it." AJ chuckled.

"Fuck off, AJ." Micah and Tucker yelled at the same time, then burst into laughter.

Micah's laugh was a little strained, but fortunately Tucker didn't seem to notice, he hopped up, held a hand down to Micah.

Taking his hand, Micah allowed Tucker to help him up. As Tucker disappeared back into the bathroom, shaking his head, Micah swallowed the lump in his throat. He knew Tucker was leaving, Micah just had to make sure his heart stayed here when Tucker did.

CHAPTER SIX

Granddad was dead and it didn't seem real. Tucker watched with a heavy heart as the lawyer left the office. Maybe he'd deluded himself into thinking that his grandfather would live forever, he didn't know but he felt guilty for not spending more time with him. He couldn't let this happen with the rest of his family. No matter what he wasn't staying away so long again. Tucker shook himself out of his daze and focused his attention on his father.

Dad looked tired. Granddad had died the night Tucker had arrived home and for the past two days they'd all been running around getting things settled for the funeral today. It was probably in poor taste to have the will read following the ceremony, but Tucker wanted his uncle gone. His presence was wearing on Dad.

"This is horse shit. You," Duncan pointed at Micah, "you little— you knew about this. You knew what was in the will."

Tucker leaned back in the chair and propped his booted feet on the desk, hoping like hell Micah didn't commence to pounding the shit outta Duncan. From the looks of Micah he was running low on patience. Tucker hadn't helped any by taking the seat behind the desk. Micah was used to being in the place of power, and why not? Dad and AJ encouraged it, but Tucker was now in control of the situation, so Micah was going to have to get used to it. "Duncan—"

AJ stood up from the chair in front of the desk, banged his fist on the top of the old oak desk and glared at Duncan. "You have no right! Just who the fuck do you think you are? You aren't even part of this family, you back stabbing bastard. And speaking of which, where's your whore?" He slammed his fist down again, making the pen holder bounce and topple, spilling pens and pencils off the front of the desk.

Tucker bit back a grin as he watched Duncan flinch at AJ's outburst. It was a spectacular show of pique, but it wasn't getting them anywhere. Whooping Duncan's ass might actually be fun but it was counterproductive. Tucker wanted the man gone and the easiest way to do that was to make it clear there was nothing else for him here now that granddad was gone.

Jumping out of his chair, Dad made a grab for the pens. "Damn it, AJ, sit your ass down and stop the hollerin'. Just because Duncan is an asshole doesn't mean you have to be."

"Fuck you, Jeff." Duncan turned his glare from Micah to Dad, but the statement had very little heat behind it. He sighed, some of the tension leaving his shoulders. He looked tired too.

Standing up from the fireplace hearth, Micah smiled and helped Dad pick up the mess AJ made.

"But Daddy—" AJ started.

"Don't but Daddy me." Dad raised from picking up a pen and pointed it at AJ, ignoring Duncan altogether. "Sit!"

AJ shut right up, dropping back into the beat up brown leather desk chair with a groan.

"Your mother left me several years ago. Found some other sap with a bigger bank account." Duncan glanced up at Jeff. "Go ahead and say I told you so and crow about how you were right."

"What good would that do?" Jeff raised a brow. "I'd say from the looks of it, you figured that out."

Ouch. Trying not to laugh at the non-confrontational jab his Dad threw at Duncan, Tucker cleared his throat to gain everyone's attention. "Duncan, my marriage is none of your business. The fact that Granddad's will left the ranch to the first to marry is irrelevant. The ranch is being put in my name, end of story. From now on if you have something to say you will say it to me, not Micah."

Micah's head popped up from behind the desk. He scowled at Tucker then went back to picking up the clutter on the floor.

Tucker smiled, noting that with the exception of his eyes being a little red from crying at the funeral, he looked much better. He had his contacts in instead of glasses, so the lack of bags under his eyes was apparent. Now if Tucker could just keep him from overworking himself again...

AJ whispered something else and Micah chuckled. The sound shot right through Tucker. He liked that sound. That was the Micah he was used to. Micah had been so playful and captivating that first night, jumping on the bed like a kid. He'd been so tempted to push things further. Tucker grinned, that was the Micah he loved, not the tired grouchy— Oh damn. A lump formed in Tucker's throat. He swallowed, trying to push the thought away, but he couldn't. He *did* love Micah. He always had. At first it was just a brotherly kind of love like he felt for AJ, but now? The realization shook him to the core. He'd wanted Micah ever since that night Micah had kissed him all those years ago. He'd tried to convince himself he'd never gotten close to anyone because of what he watched his dad go through when his mom left, but it was a lie. No one had measured up to Micah. And Micah had been too young... But he wasn't now.

"This is bullshit Tucker. We both know you have no need for this," waving his arms, Duncan motioned around the room, "place. You pretending to be a fag is a waste of your time. I'm the oldest, the ranch should go to me. When is the last time you were even here?"

"None of your fuckin' business who any of us sleep with much—" AJ mumbled.

Micah pinched AJ's thigh as he stood up and placed the last of the pens back in the penholder. "Quit antagonizing," he whispered.

Ignoring them both, Tucker dropped his feet and sat up straight. "Duncan, when was the last time you were here? Don't pretend to know anything about me. I'm only going to tell you this one more time. You had better cease with the name calling. And if anyone has a right to be upset over this it's my dad, not you. The ranch is mine now and that is that. I'll do with it as I see fit. Micah and this ranch are none of your business. I suggest you pack your bags and be out of here by tomorrow." Tucker stood. Glancing at AJ he jerked his head towards the door. He needed to think, somewhere away from Micah, and he had a feeling if he didn't get AJ away from their uncle he was going to end up replacing office furniture. "Goodbye. You are welcome to take a few mementos but you will clear them with my dad first." He walked around the desk and motioned for AJ to follow.

"Welcome back big brother." AJ slapped him on the back as they reached the back door.

Tucker tried to smile, but it fell short with all that was on his mind. "Thanks. It's good to be back." And it was. He'd missed his family something fierce. He should have been here. Sure he'd made a name for himself and a lot of money too, but family was what mattered. It was a damned shame it took his grandfather dying to drive the point home.

They headed out toward the corral, walking side by side. It was a companionable silence, one he and AJ, and Micah too for that matter, always shared. He'd missed this. The time with his brother… and Micah. Damn. What was he gonna do about Micah? He'd looked and acted so much more like himself today. Even with the weight of granddad's death and the pile of debt the ranch was under, Micah seemed much better than he had when he'd shown up on Tucker's doorstep nearly a week ago. It did Tucker's heart good. Hell it made Tucker's heart ache. He wanted Micah.

"Think he regrets it?"

"What?" Tucker glanced at his brother.

AJ stared out into the west pasture, his brow furrowed, looking a little worried. "Duncan. You think he regrets hightailing it outta here with our egg donor? Think he misses his family?"

Tucker shrugged. "Don't know. Maybe. But he burned his bridges. He was a fool. Did he really think he could make a relationship work with her? Hell, he should have known what she was like when she cast Dad and us aside so easily."

"Yeah, what kind of man falls for a woman who'd leave her children? Don't know what he has against Micah, but it's pissing me off." They arrived at the corral fence and AJ leaned his arms against the top rail and put his booted foot on the bottom. "Speaking of the brat, what's up with you and Micah?"

"I wish I knew." Tucker mimicked AJ's pose, staring out at a calf and his mother.

"He looks better. He's been running himself ragged. Don't know what we'd have done without him. I hate doing the books, Dad sucks at it and well, Micah hates it too, but he's good at it. Problem is Granddad's hospital bills nearly did us in. You know Micah used his inheritance to pay stuff off?" AJ glanced over at Tucker, making eye contact. "He doesn't know that I know."

Well, son of a bitch. "I'll make sure he gets every penny back."

"He won't take it." AJ looked back at the silver pipe fence. He started picking at the silver paint. "I would insult him by trying to pay it back." He shrugged. "You gotta pay him back without him knowing it. He's part of this family, paying him back would seem like we didn't think so." AJ flicked a piece of silver off the rail with his thumbnail. "I just hate to see him going back to worrying over the finances. Not surprised he has an ulcer. Works harder than two men. We had to let go of the hands and Micah has single handedly tried to take all five of their places, plus Granddad's." AJ was quiet for several moments, and when he spoke again it was quieter, almost a whisper. "He's happy. He don't like turning over things to you, which I guess is understandable, but he's glad you're back. We all are."

Tucker leaned forward, resting his chin on his hand that rested on the fence. He could understand why Micah didn't like turning things over to him. Micah had made a place for himself here and he saw Tucker as a threat to that. He thought Tucker was going to take over his spot. Funny, Tucker hadn't realized it before but Micah had taken over the spot he left when he moved to Dallas.

"What are you grinning at?"

"What?" Tucker turned his head, looking at his younger brother. "Just thinking that Micah took over my spot when I left."

"Nah. There's still room for you. Micah has always had his own spot."

"Yeah. I guess he has." Micah always belonged with them… with Tucker. Deep down he'd always known it, but he'd tried like hell to deny it. He couldn't have stayed. It wouldn't have been fair to Micah. He'd needed to find his own way... to grow up. Hell in the back of Tucker's mind he still felt like he wasn't giving Micah much of a choice. He wanted Micah to want him for him, not because of some childhood crush or because Tucker wanted him to, but because Micah wanted it.

"Yeah." AJ chuckled. "He has. Is it sinking in?"

"Is what sinking in?"

"The fact that Micah has always been yours."

Tucker started. "What do you mean by that?"

"I mean you can run but you can't hide. It's time to come home, big brother. Micah needs you. We all do."

"It won't work."

"Why not?" AJ scoffed. "And don't use our dad's relationship as an excuse. He didn't love her any more than she loved him. You and Micah don't have that problem."

Tucker straightened and climbed up on the top post, sitting down. Did Micah love him? "Well shit." He wanted... Could he? Was AJ was right? Did Micah love him too?

CHAPTER SEVEN

Where in the hell was AJ? Glancing at the clock again, Micah squinted, trying to read the time and decided to get up. It wasn't like he was sleeping anyway. Stupid insomnia. He glanced over at Tucker, sound asleep, and sighed. Here he was in bed with Tucker and not only was he not getting laid, he couldn't even relax enough to sleep. One would think lying in bed with the man of your dreams would be... well a dream. Not so, there was way too much to do around the ranch.

Snagging his glasses off the nightstand and putting them on, he eased out of bed, trying not to disturb Tucker. For whatever reason, Tucker had decided he was Micah's keeper and Micah really didn't want to argue right now. He checked the clock again, three twelve am. Oh yeah, Tucker would definitely tell him to get back in bed and then the fight would be on. The really warped part of Micah's brain told him to make noise and "accidentally" wake Tucker. Geez, what was wrong with him. When had bickering with Tucker become so stimulating? They never used to disagree.

After quietly gathering his clothes, he went into the bathroom. He'd told AJ to come get him at two for his watch. Maybe Miss Kitty had gone into labor. Micah and AJ always took turns when a horse was about to foal. It just made no sense for both of them to stay up and wait, especially now that they'd let go of all their ranch hands.

Taking off his sleep pants, Micah pulled on a pair of jeans, threw on a t-shirt and stuffed his socked feet into his boots. The excitement was already beginning to build. There was nothing quite like a new foal, or a calf for that matter, but they didn't have many foals around The Bar D. They only bred horses for their use. It brought to mind the first foal he'd helped deliver. He'd helped Tucker. It was the summer he'd turned thirteen. He'd come home from school and found Tucker in the barn himself. Tucker had immediately put him to work. There hadn't been much to do other than watch, but it had been exciting, not just watching the new colt be born, but spending time alone with Tucker. He and Tucker used to get along so well. Micah missed it.

Turning out the light, Micah crept out of the bathroom and out of his room. It was strange sharing his room with someone. Being quiet wasn't easy to do on the creaky old wood floor, but Micah managed it out of old habit. He knew which boards creaked the loudest because he'd snuck out plenty when he was a kid. After a stop in the kitchen to pour a cup of coffee— thank you AJ for keeping a pot on—he headed out into the cool Texas night.

He loved this time of night. It was so peaceful. The sound of the crickets was like music to his ears. Micah took a deep breath and inhaled the country air. The coffee cup kept his hands warm, but the rest of him... Brrr. It was a little chilly. Making his way to the barn, Micah alternated rubbing his arm with one hand and holding his coffee with the other. Maybe he should have brought a jacket.

Just as he reached the barn the back screen door slammed shut. He turned to find Tucker jogging toward him. His hair was mussed, making him look more like he belonged on a ranch rather than in a boardroom. He wore jeans, a t-shirt and boots, like Micah, but he looked like he'd thrown them on in a hurry, which he had. He wrapped his arms around his chest, rubbed his arms. "What are you doing?"

Micah took a sip from his cup. "I'm going to relieve AJ. What are you doing?"

Tucker stepped up to him, grabbed his cup and poured it out.

"Hey."

"Doctor said no coffee. Damn, it's fucking cold out here," he mumbled under his breath. "I came out here to find you."

Glaring at Tucker, Micah wrapped his arms across his chest to keep warm. "Well you found me. Now what?" Warmth blossomed in his chest; Tucker had been worried about him. Micah still had work to do and he wasn't letting Tucker get in the way of it, but it made him a little fluttery knowing Tucker had been concerned enough to get out bed and come looking for him. He walked further into the barn trying to conceal a grin.

"I don't know. Don't guess you'll come back to bed, will you?"

"Nope." When Micah got to the birthing stall he groaned. AJ was sound asleep, slumped against the wall, and Miss Kitty was lying on her side breathing heavily. "Dios mio. AJ wake up."

AJ jerked awake, blinking and then quickly locating Micah. He glanced over at Miss Kitty and jumped to his feet so quickly he had to grab the side of the stall. "Fuck. How long has she been like this?"

Micah grabbed AJ's shoulder, steadying him. "No clue. I just got here." The mare's eyes were a little wild and that more than anything concerned Micah. He moved further into the roomy stall and walked toward her behind. Squatting, he dragged his hand across her side, trying to soothe her. "Hello beautiful."

She huffed a piece of long black mane off her forehead and raised her head. With wide pretty brown eyes, she watched him. He glanced up at Tucker, then to AJ.

"AJ go to bed. We'll watch her." Tucker slapped AJ on the back, handed him Micah's empty mug and nudged him out of the stall. "Put this in the sink when you go in."

Micah continued to pet her as a contraction made her groan. His instincts were screaming that there was something wrong.

"What is it?"

He glanced up and noticed Tucker was staring at him. "Go get me some gloves out of the cabinet in the tack room."

Tucker nodded, already turning away. "If I remember correctly it shouldn't take too long at this point. What's wrong?"

"I don't know. Maybe nothing, but…" He shrugged.

"You obviously think something is. It's written all over your face. Should we call the vet?" He called from the tack room.

Micah shook his head, then realized Tucker couldn't see him. "No. Just hold on and let's see what we are dealing with.

Even if there is something wrong, he'll never make it here in time."

Coming back, Tucker held the one shoulder length glove open for Micah.

Micah stood and let Tucker help him. "Thank you. Just hang on to the other until I take a look at her." Scooting to the side he slipped his fingers over her rump towards her genitals. When she laid her head back down he lifted her tail out of the way and pressed into her body with his gloved hand. "It's okay mama. You're doing fine."

She made a distressed sound.

"I know beautiful, I'm getting a little too familiar here aren't I? I promise I'll get you something nice later, a little gift, huh?"

Tucker chuckled. "No wonder your love life is nonexistent."

Chuckling, Micah glanced up. "Smart ass. And who says my love life is nonexistent?" Damn, the baby wasn't in the vaginal canal. Micah felt further, finding the cervix. There was a bump. What was— A tail? *Damn it!* "The baby is breech."

"Shit." Tucker sobered. "That's not good."

"The foal's legs are back."

"Can you move them?"

Micah kept his face blank, trying not to show his concern. "I'm gonna try. You think you can help me out?"

Tucker nodded. "It's the only way I'm gonna get you back in bed." His grin was a little wicked, a little worried. He was flirting, Micah had seen it before, just not turned on him.

"What are you gonna do with me once you get me there? From what I saw, you are the one with a rocky love life." Oh shit. If he hadn't had his hand up a horse he'd have slapped it over his mouth. Why had he said that? Tucker was trying to lighten the mood, he hadn't been serious.

"My love life is not rocky. It's nonexistent, I don't have a love life I have a sex life. And I promise you I can think of a few things to do to you once I get you back in bed." Tucker squatted next to him, so close Micah could feel his heat.

A shiver went down his spine at Tucker's words, or maybe it was his nearness. It made concentrating on his task more difficult. His mind reeled with the fact that Tucker hadn't been serious about anyone. That shouldn't make Micah happy, but it did.

Tracing the foal's hip down, Micah found the right hind leg. "Suffocating me with a pillow doesn't count." Cupping the foot and fetlock in his hand, he began to maneuver it.

"I assure you I don't plan on—"

The foal jerked its foot, startling Micah and almost dislodging his hold. He must have gasped because Tucker asked, "What?"

Grinning so big his cheeks hurt, Micah held tight. It was hard not to whoop and holler like an idiot. "We got a live baby."

"Yes." Tucker bobbed his head, dislodging a piece of blond hair into his eyes. He batted at the hair. "Remember the last time we did this together? When Dotty had Waldo?"

"It was a lot more simple." Sweat beaded on Micah's forehead, dripping down into his eye. He blinked and bent his head toward the sleeve on his free arm to wipe off.

"It was." Tucker beat him to it, using his hand to wipe away the sweat then wipe it on his jeans.

Micah froze at the intimate action, staring at Tucker. This was how they used to get along, working together without words. Instinctively knowing what the other needed. A jittery feeling came over Micah that had nothing to do with his nervousness over delivering this foal.

"You still ride Waldo?"

Nodding his head yes, Micah smiled. Tucker had always been good about making Micah feel more comfortable. He was the first one of the Delanys to really make Micah feel like family all those years ago. Micah had been so awkward and shy and Tucker had always had a way of soothing him and helping him put his best foot forward. "Yeah. Waldo is out in the paddock."

The horse raised her head again, her eyes wide.

Without being told, Tucker immediately started crooning to the pregnant horse. His voice dropping to a slow sexy drawl, but his eyes stayed focused on Micah.

Miss Kitty snorted a little, but she dropped her head and listened to Tucker. Micah could listen to that voice forever. If only— *Yes!* The leg slid out of the uterus. "Tucker, in the tack room cabinet there is some brand new nylon cording, bring it to me and tie a noose at the end of it."

Tucker scrambled up and headed to the tack room again. He called over his shoulder, "What about infection? Do we have anything to serialize it in?"

"No time. We'll give her an antibiotic shot and call the vet out tomorrow."

By the time Tucker came back he was already tying a noose. He stepped up behind Micah and handed him the noose end when he was done. "Here, let me know when to pull." He sounded so sure, like he knew what he was doing, and it bolstered Micah's courage. In some form or another it seemed Tucker had always given him strength.

"'Kay." Micah pulled his arm out, grabbed the cord and went right back in after that foot. Luckily it was still there. He wasn't betting it would stay there until he got the other one though, so he looped the cord around the foal's fetlock joint. "Okay."

The rope tautened and Tucker's heat pressed against Micah's back. His hand landed on Micah's shoulder and squeezed. The little touch went straight to Micah's heart.

He went back in for the other leg, this time he tore the amniotic sack. Not much fluid leaked out, because the foal's butt was blocking it. He quickly located the other foot. A contraction clamped down around his arm making him wince. *Shit.* "I'm sorry sweetheart, we're almost there. Just a few more minutes, okay?" He moved the other leg out of the uterus. Now for the tricky part. He had to get this foal out quick.

Getting his hand around both the foal's back feet, Micah waited. "Okay Tucker, you can let go." On the next contraction Micah pulled. In a huge gush of fluid, the foal came out. Micah removed the rope from the foal and Miss Kitty raised her head, looking at her baby.

Tucker breathed a sigh of relief behind him. "Yes! We did it." He kissed Micah's cheek and stood, pulling Micah up with him. Wrapping an arm around Micah's waist he held him close, his face next to Micah. "Damn, I've missed this."

Micah chuckled, blinking back tears, and nodded his head. He was excited and relieved. His pulse should be slowing, not racing, but it wasn't. Tucker's nearness was going right to his head. He closed his eyes and took a deep breath, but he was way too aware of Tucker's body touching his. He needed to extract himself from Tucker's embrace before he did something stupid.

"Damn, isn't she the cutest thing? I forgot how exciting this was. Makes me want my own horse again." Tucker's voice was soft, full of awe, and so close it raised goosebumps on Micah's arms.

Being this close to Tucker and sharing this with him shouldn't be a big deal, but Micah was tired and his emotions needed somewhere to go now that the scare was over. He just wanted to wrap himself up in Tucker and rest. Wanted Tucker's arms around him.

A hand landed on Micah's shoulder, urging him to turn. "Micah?"

Opening his eyes, Micah spun around.

"You still have the gloves on."

Well hell, so he did. Micah peeled off one glove then the other and tossed them in the corner.

Lifting Micah's face with one finger, Tucker leaned in. His focus narrowed on Micah's lips in a dazed expression and he moved forward as if to kiss Micah.

Micah's stomach tightened into a knot and the barn was suddenly stifling.

Tucker's lips landed on his in a gentle caress. He pulled back only slightly before pressing his lips to Micah's again. Doing that once more, he traced the seam of Micah's lips with his tongue. It was tender, almost chaste.

Knowing he shouldn't, Micah rested his trembling hands on Tucker's chest and opened his mouth. The almost reverent touch was terrifying, it sent butterflies fluttering through his stomach and blood racing through his veins. Tucker was kissing him. Not because Micah had kissed him first and not because someone was watching. A moan escaped his lips and he closed his eyes, tilting his head to give Tucker better access. He didn't want to move much for fear Tucker would stop, or maybe it was fear that he wouldn't.

Cradling Micah's face in his palms, Tucker deepened the kiss. Still slow and sensual, he tangled his tongue with Micah's. It was an overly intimate kiss, one shared by lovers, and Micah's cock responded, filling.

Tucker pulled back, his lips still touching Micah's. "Mmm... even better than I remembered."

Micah blinked his eyes open.

The expression on Tucker's face was blissful, completely at ease and not a bit repentant. Why had he done that? He opened his eyes and grinned, his gaze on Micah's lips. He licked his own and leaned forward again.

Micah panicked. He couldn't take another one. He'd end up melting at Tucker's feet, begging him for anything he was willing to give. Tucker had always affected him that way, but this was worse, more intense. Probably due to the years of unrequited love. Micah winced and jerked his head away. Stepping back, he dropped his gaze, staring at his feet. He shook his head, more to himself than to Tucker. "I can't. I can't do this. I can't take you running away again." He hated appearing so vulnerable in front of Tucker, but he had to do something. His willpower wasn't strong enough to resist, but maybe he could convince Tucker to back off.

"Micah..."

Shaking his head, Micah busied himself cleaning up the stall. Putting the gloves and rope away. "I don't want to talk about it. Just leave me be."

Tucker followed him all the way out of the barn and into the house without another word. It was just as well, Micah wasn't in the mood to listen to whatever it was Tucker had to say. It wouldn't change anything. Tucker was gonna leave again. *Damn it.* He never should have gone to bring Tucker back.

As if things weren't bad enough, Micah opened the back door and locked gazes with Duncan Delany.

"Well well, if it isn't the newlywed faggots." Duncan took a drink from his coffee mug and set it on the table in front of him.

Fury washed over Micah like a tidal wave. "Fuck you, you son of a bitch. I've had enough of your mouth." He didn't even think, he just walked right over to Duncan and picked him up by the front of his shirt.

"Ah shit." The door slammed followed by boots pounding on the tile floor, then Tucker's arms wound around Micah's waist.

"Let go, you queer." Duncan batted at Micah's hands and shoved at him. Trying to get him off. It shouldn't have been hard, Micah was quite a bit smaller than Duncan, but he was beyond pissed. He'd had enough of Duncan Delany to last him a lifetime. He hauled back his fist ready to belt the cabrón a good one, and his elbow connected with skin.

"God damn it." The hold on Micah's waist vanished, followed by muffled cursing.

Micah didn't take the time to look back at Tucker, he let his fist fly, catching Duncan right square in the nose. The sickening thwack and the spray of blood were like fuel to the fire. This son of a bitch had called him names and threatened him for the last time. He shoved Duncan away from him, pleased as can be when Duncan tripped over his chair and landed on his ass with a thud that rattled the table and chairs. Reaching for Duncan again, Micah was brought up short by Tucker grabbing him and pinning his arms to his sides. "Let me go!"

Eyes wide, Duncan scrambled up, clutching his nose. Blood poured over his hand and his gaze narrowed. "You will be hearing from my lawyer. I intend to contest the will. There is no way I'm letting the ranch go to a couple of fags." He turned and walked out of the kitchen.

"Fuck you." Rage boiled in Micah and he struggled to get loose of Tucker's grasp. His glasses fell off, clattering to the ground. "Let me go Tucker." He struggled and fought, wanting to rip Duncan to pieces, but Tucker held strong. If he got out of this hold he was gonna beat Tucker's ass too. Sweat dripped down his forehead, making him blink to keep from slinging it in his eyes. His whole body was like an inferno, hot and ready to explode, but Tucker held firm, not even fazed by Micah's struggles.

"Stop it. God damn it Micah be still."

That pissed Micah off even more, but no matter how hard he tried he couldn't get loose. Gasping for air, he sagged in Tucker's arms. He was tired and he wanted to destroy something. Everything had gone to shit. Damn Duncan, damn Tucker and damn Ferguson for dying.

Tucker loosed his grip but didn't let go. He brushed Micah's sweaty hair off his forehead and pushed his head back onto Tucker's shoulder. "It's okay, baby."

Tears welled up in Micah's eyes, but he refused to let them fall. He blinked several times then closed his eyes. No, it wasn't okay. It would never be okay again.

CHAPTER EIGHT

Closing the door to Micah's bedroom, Tucker leaned against it and closed his eyes. Damn what a night. Even though he'd gotten rid of Duncan, it hadn't been an easy task. Duncan had threatened him with lawsuits and contesting the will and anything else he could think of. One thing was sure, he didn't like Micah. Tucker couldn't figure it out. Jealousy was the only thing that made sense, but why would Duncan be jealous?

Hearing water run in the bathroom, Tucker sighed and pushed off the wall. Micah was taking a shower. What was he gonna do with Micah? Tucker sat on the edge of the bed and jerked off his boots. Duncan really had it coming for the faggot remark but, damn it, now Tucker had to worry about the son of a bitch pressing charges against Micah. Tucker kicked his boot under the bed before starting on the other one. Good lord Micah was a pistol. That fiery Latino temper was something else. When had he gotten such a temper? Tucker rubbed his jaw where that bony elbow had connected and grimaced.

Kicking his other boot under the bed, Tucker ripped off his socks and threw them across the room. In the past week he realized that even though he knew Micah, Micah still had a few surprises up his sleeve. It was exciting and... frustrating. He wanted to know everything abut Micah.

The water cut off in the bathroom as Tucker stood and tugged his t-shirt over his head.

Micah opened the door and emerged from a cloud of steam. He had a dark blue towel wrapped around his hips and a scowl on his face. He looked... delicious and still mad as an old red hen. A drip of water dropped off his hair and slid down the hard planes of his stomach. Holy shit, ranch life agreed with him. He was still too skinny as far as Tucker was concerned, but he sure as hell wasn't a kid anymore.

Tucker's cock filled right up, straining against his tight boxer briefs. Shaking his head, he growled and started taking off his jeans. Stupid fucking cock, someone needed to explain to it that he was leaving, or was he? He was so damned confused he didn't know anymore.

"Did the asshole leave?"

"Yeah." Tucker kept to his task, trying to ignore the temptation Micah presented, but it wasn't easy, even with his irritation over Duncan. He and Micah had gotten along so well today. It was like old times, but not. There was a different undercurrent, a more… sexual undercurrent. But he owed it to Micah to try and back off like Micah had asked. Damn it, he didn't want to. Tucker kicked his pants aside.

"What?" Micah snapped.

What? Tucker looked up.

Micah stood with his hands on his towel-clad hips, glaring. "What are you growling about? That pendejo was asking for it."

He'd growled? Tucker shrugged, his cock twitching and his stomach tightening at the sight of Micah. God he looked edible, standing there with wet hair and nothing but a towel. "Yeah the asshole was asking for it, but now we have to worry about him charging you with assault."

Stomping past Tucker toward the dresser, Micah let the towel fall to his feet.

Tucker nearly swallowed his tongue. Look at that ass. Man oh man spending long hours in the saddle had done good things for Micah's body. His back muscles rippled as he flung the top drawer open and dug through it. Standing there, mesmerized, Tucker watched him retrieve a pair of white boxers and slam the drawer shut.

"Ow! God damn it!" Micah dropped the underwear and shook his hand out. "Son of a bitch that hurt." He brought his hand to his mouth.

Before giving it conscious thought, Tucker was across the room reaching for Micah's hand. "Let me see." He caught Micah's wrist only to have him try to pull away.

"I'm fine." He tugged his arm, but the heat had gone out of his voice.

Tugging back, Tucker inspected Micah's smashed thumb. It didn't look like anything major, just red. Probably smarted pretty good, but there didn't appear to be any permanent damage, no bones sticking out, no blood. "Stop being a pain in the ass." He raised his head and stared into big watery brown eyes. He brought Micah's lean calloused hand up to his face and kissed his thumb.

"Do you think Duncan will be able to contest the will and get the ranch? Did my punching him hurt our chances of keeping The Bar D?" He pulled his hand loose of Tucker's. "I'm sorry. I shouldn't have hit him." Turning back toward the dresser he snagged his boxers.

Everything in Tucker said it was a bad idea, but he reached for Micah, touching his shoulder lightly. Micah's obvious concern over the ranch hit Tucker in the gut. He wanted to ease Micah's worry. "Don't worry about it. I'm not gonna let him take The Bar D."

Micah turned, his face etched with worry. "Yeah?" Micah's shoulders slumped and his gaze dropped. "I shouldn't have lost my temper."

Tucker lifted his chin, intending to tell him it'd be okay, but once those big brown eyes focused on him he was lost. Catching Micah around the waist, Tucker slanted his mouth over his. He probed Micah's lips with his tongue as the heat of Micah's naked, slightly damp body pressed against his. It was absolute heaven; Micah felt so damned right in his arms, like he belonged there. Tucker had dreamed of this moment for several years.

A small whimper left Micah's lips as he opened and kissed Tucker back. His tongue tangled with Tucker's and his arms wound around Tucker's neck. He pressed against Tucker's leg then stepped back, gasping. He's gaze traveled down Tucker's body, focusing on Tucker's already hard prick.

"Oh damn." Tucker looked his fill.

Micah's stomach heaved in and out with his breath. His cock was hard and begging for attention.

Tucker's own breath caught at the sheer beauty before him. Grabbing Micah, Tucker pulled him forward by his prick, feeling the hard heat. A moan left his lips before they crashed down on Micah's bed again.

With a dazed look on his face, Micah pulled back again. "We shouldn't do this." His voice didn't sound at all convincing.

"The hell we shouldn't."

"Okay." And just like that Micah was on him, knocking Tucker back on the bed and landing on top of him. He was everywhere. His hands, his mouth. It was absolute heaven. The sounds of their breathing and wet kisses filled Tucker's head, making him ache as much as the feel of Micah against him. Why had he waited so long to do this? Never again was he going to go without this.

Wedging his hand between them, Micah shoved his hand down the front of Tucker's briefs and gripped him. He broke their kiss, gazing down at Tucker with a smirk on his lips. "I'm on top."

Tucker chuckled, feeling happy down deep in his bones. "So you are. Why don't you scoot up here." Gripping Micah's bare butt he urged him forward.

Micah groaned and scooted forward. Holding his prick with one hand, he dropped forward and rested his other hand on the bed above Tucker's head. The tip of his cock stopped only inches away from Tucker's lips. Fuck, he was something. Tucker pulled and opened his mouth, taking Micah in. His lips weren't quite wet enough to take him all the way in so he had to lick his lips.

"Ah mios dio."

Oh my god is right. Micah's smooth hard prick slid through his lips. At first he moved slowly, his prick gliding along Tucker's tongue, stopping just before the head popped from his lips. The not quite salty taste of pre cum was faint, but it was like mana from heaven. The look of pure bliss on Micah's face and the taut ab muscles had Tucker's own prick throbbing, begging for relief. He used his grip on Micah's ass to control the speed of Micah's thrusts, making him move faster.

"Oh merde, that feels good." Sitting up and still holding his prick, Micah stared at Tucker's mouth. With his other hand he traced Tucker's lips where they stretched around his cock.

Tucker moaned at the sheer excitement he read in Micah's face. Imagining the sight Micah was seeing, he reached up with his free hand, holding his fingers to Micah's lips.

Micah sucked his fingers in with relish. His eyes closed but his hips never faltered. God damn that was hot. Closing his own eyes, Tucker savored the wet heat surrounding his fingers. He couldn't wait to watch his own cock push into Micah's pretty mouth.

Crawling off of Tucker, Micah landed on the bed beside him and began messing with something on the side of the bed. His pale muscular ass wiggled.

"What are you doing?" Cupping one cheek, Tucker squeezed.

"Getting lube." Micah made a distressed groan. "Damn it, I can't find it."

Jerking his gaze away from Micah's behind, Tucker scooted up so he could see what Micah was doing.

Digging between the mattress and box springs, Micah removed a small flip top bottle. "Ah ha!" Micah sat up, his pretty prick bobbing. "Why do you still have your underwear on?"

Tucker lifted his butt and slid his underwear off, his cock slapping against his belly he pulled them off so quick. Before he even knew what hit him Micah tossed the lube at him and engulfed his dick. "Oh Jesus!" Even though he'd wanted this, he wasn't ready for it. His balls drew closer and his stomach muscles flexed. A tingle raced up his spine.

There was a muffled, "hmm," a vibration tickled his prick and Micah's hand waved toward his ass. Tucker closed his eyes, just feeling the glorious mouth on him. *Oh god, did he just—? Ah.* The tip of his cock hit soft tissue. "Oh damn, baby." He had to see this. He lifted his head and threaded his fingers through Micah's thick black hair, urging him on.

Fingers skimmed over his balls and the sexy slurping sounds started. Tucker dropped his head back down, staring at the plain white ceiling, trying not to come. His head was going to shoot right off if Micah kept that up.

Releasing Tucker's prick Micah raised his head but didn't stop caressing Tucker's balls.

When he didn't continue after a few seconds, Tucker looked down at him.

Micah blinked at him like he was trying to focus. He probably was without his glasses. "Lube."

Lube? Oh right. Tucker located the bottle and squirted some on his fingers. Closing it and tossing it aside, he trailed his fingers through Micah's crease and was rewarded with a little wiggle of Micah's hips. Oh the way Micah raised up on his knees did nice things for his cock and balls. Damn that looked obscene and… delicious. Tucker kept rubbing the puckered opening with his slick fingers but used his other hand to swat the pale ass, just to see that wiggle again. *Oh yeah there it is.* Tucker sank a finger in Micah's tight body and the moan around his cock had him gasping.

"Mmmm…" Micah's head came up and he pushed back onto Tucker's finger. Abruptly, he dislodged Tucker's finger from his ass and reached for the lube. Turning, he opened it, grabbed Tucker's already saliva slicked prick and poured lube over it.

"Micah…" Damn, Tucker sounded desperate even to his own ears.

Flicking the bottle shut with his chin, Micah tossed it toward the head of the bed, straddled Tucker's hips and lowered himself down on Tucker's cock.

Tucker couldn't do anything but watch and feel. He held his breath, savoring the feeling. He wasn't sure what was better, the tight heat of Micah's hole engulfing him or the sight of Micah's hard leaking cock. Grabbing Micah's waist, Tucker raised his head, watching as his prick disappeared. Only when Micah's ass rested on his hips did Tucker look at Micah's face. "Oh damn."

Micah's bottom lip was caught between his teeth, his head dropped forward and his eyes closed. After a few seconds, he blinked his eyes open and licked his lips. He chuckled and blinked again. "I—I can't see you."

Damn, wasn't he something? Tucker chuckled and slid his hand up Micah's tanned side, urging him forward. When Micah's face was inches from his, he rose up and kissed him on the lips. "How about now?"

Micah nodded. "Yeah." His voice was barely above a whisper. "I can feel you too." His voice quivered.

They sat there for several minutes staring at one another. Tucker knew at that very moment there was no way in hell he could leave Micah again. He'd do whatever it took to stay on The Bar D and make Micah more than a convenient husband. His eyes grew watery and he closed them. Damn, what was wrong with him? He wasn't usually this emotional.

Moving, Micah sat up, put his hands on Tucker's chest and raised up on his knees before sitting right back down.

A shiver raced up Tucker's spine and he opened his eyes. Jesus, Micah was so tight. There was no way this was going to last. Tucker felt like he should take charge but all he could do was lie there and feel as Micah began to fuck him in a slow steady pace. Gripping Micah's hips, he held on, watching the slim body ride him. The tight grip of Micah's body had Tucker gasping for breath in no time. "Come on, baby." He grabbed Micah's cock, tightening his hand and letting Micah push up into it then sink back down on his cock.

"Dios mio." Micah hurried his pace. His head dropped back and a ragged groan tore from his throat seconds before hot spunk spilled over Tucker's hand and stomach.

That was all it took. Tucker thrust up, pulled Micah down and came. His whole body shook as Micah collapsed on top of him.

Tucker wrapped his arms around the slim back and stared up at the ceiling listening to their panting breaths. Running his hand through Micah's hair, he kissed his forehead. He was hot, but he'd rather gouge his own eyes out than move the precious weight on top of him.

Feeling like his bones had melted, Tucker lay there for several minutes until Micah's breath evened out. *Asleep*. Good.

He needed it. Maybe Tucker had found a way to make the man rest. He could handle putting Micah to sleep like this every night. He'd gladly make it his mission in life, because he wasn't leaving. No way, no how. Not now. He knew without a doubt Micah loved him as much as he loved Micah. A teenage crush wouldn't have lasted this long. Leaving here to protect Micah's innocence four years ago and not coming back was the biggest mistake Tucker had made. He wouldn't make that mistake again. "You're mine Micah Jiminez, and I'm not allowing you to run away from me again."

CHAPTER NINE

Micah couldn't sleep. He'd awakened when Tucker turned over in his sleep and dislodged Micah from his chest, and now he was wide awake. His body was willing, but his brain had gone into overdrive trying to process everything that had happened in the last couple of hours. He'd made love with Tucker and made a bitter enemy out of Duncan.

He could stay in the bed, count sheep or something, but he doubted it would work. He needed to think, or maybe he didn't, he was so confused. What did their making love mean to their relationship? Micah couldn't regret it and he didn't think Tucker would either. Tucker's attempts to take care of him were starting to feel like the most natural thing in the world. It was annoying and nice at the same time. Tucker fussed and Micah pretended to get annoyed. He could get used to it. He *wanted* to get used to it. Tucker was everything he'd ever wanted and it was beginning to seem like an obtainable goal. Could he talk Tucker into staying?

Sprawled on his stomach, Tucker lay with his head facing Micah. His warm breath blew across Micah's shoulder with each not quite snore he made. He looked so non-threatening. Micah grinned, non-threatening to everything but Micah's peace of mind. It was going to kill him when Tucker left. Micah was scared shitless. So much so that the sleep he desperately needed wouldn't come. Turning his head, Micah squinted so he could see better.

For the second time, Micah eased out of bed, trying not to disturb Tucker. He grabbed a pair of sweatpants out of his dresser and a long sleeved t-shirt out of his closet and threw them on. Maybe some fresh air would help clear is mind. He headed down the stairs, through the kitchen and out onto the back porch, closing the door behind him quietly.

"What are you doing up at this time of night, perrito?"

Micah's jumped and slapped a hand to his chest. He hadn't expected anyone else to be up. "Damn Tio, you scared me."

Juan chuckled. "Sorry, Mijo." He sat on the porch rail with a cigarette in hand and a bottle of beer on the railing in front of him. "I couldn't sleep." Was that a hitch in his voice? He closed his eyes and looked away.

"Yeah, me neither. I think I fucked up."

"How's that?"

"I decked Duncan." Micah leaned against the porch post where it ran beside the steps. "He says he's gonna contest the will."

Juan snorted. "Don't worry about it. If he wants to play that game I'll have to get involved and he won't like that. Ferguson was quite clear on who he wanted The Bar D to go to. I'll make sure his wishes are upheld—" his voice definitely hitched and he cleared his throat—"until my dying breath." He took a swig of his beer, avoiding Micah's gaze.

"Tio?" Micah touched his shoulder.

When Juan turned his eyes were shiny with tears. "I'm just feeling a little… lost without— I'll get over it." He took a drag off his cigarette and let out the smoke with a shaky exhale. "Listen and listen carefully. Duncan is not Ferguson's son."

"What?" Micah's knees nearly gave out. "What do you mean?"

"Rita was pregnant with Duncan when Ferguson married her. Her daddy was a mean sum'bitch. If he'd'a found out she got pregnant by some drifter he'd'a beat that girl black and blue. Ferguson married her to protect her. She was a good woman and she made a hell of a wife. A more understanding woman I never met." He took a drink of his beer and looked back at Micah. "I don't want Jeff to know, but I'll damn sure tell everyone before I let Duncan take over. Never understood that boy. Ferguson treated him like he was his own flesh and blood but he—" Juan shook his head.

Micah let go of the post and sat on the railing before he fell over. "What about Jeff?"

"Jeff? What about him? Oh, you mean is he Ferguson's son? Yeah, Jeffery is without a doubt his daddy's boy. He may look like his mama but he acts just like his daddy." He smiled really big, then it faded. "Tell me what else is on your mind Mijo? Something else is bothering you."

Shrugging, Micah took the drink from his uncle and sipped it before handing it back.

"Don't give me that. I know you too well. What else is on your mind?" He frowned and almost as an afterthought added, "And no more beer. Ain't good for your ulcer."

Micah groaned. "You sound like Tucker."

"Tucker always was a smart one. Now give it up. What has you out here instead of in bed asleep?"

Should he tell his uncle? Sighing, Micah looked away. He didn't want to sound like some pathetic lovesick fool.

"Uh huh. I figured as much. Tucker is why you're out here."

Shock washed over Micah and he gazed up at his tio. "What makes you say that?"

"You've been in love with him since the day I brought you home." Juan took a drink of his beer.

Chuckling, Micah shook his head. "I have not."

"Well fine, since a month after I brought you here. What about Tucker has you so upset? You're married. I thought that was a good thing."

"He's gonna leave and…" He closed his eyes. Damn it hurt to even say it. "He's gonna leave and I don't want him to."

"You sure about that? About him leaving I mean. How do you know he's gonna take off again? He sure don't look like a man that has any intention of going anywhere anytime soon."

"That's his plan."

"Plans change." Taking a puff from his smoke, Juan exhaled. "Make him stay. Make him not want to leave. Life is too short to waste, perrito. Don't give up if that's what you want. Love isn't always easy, but it's worth it." His voice wavered again and he turned his head away like there was something interesting out in the pasture.

Micah looked toward the field, there was nothing. "You are too much, Tio. I thought cowboys were supposed to be antigay. Shouldn't you be damning me to hell and all that good stuff?"

He chuckled but it sounded rusty, not his usual merry self. "I'm no hypocrite, Mijo. 'Sides, I love you. I want you to be happy."

Hypocrite? Micah nearly fell off the rail. Why hadn't he seen it before? What foreman slept in the main house with a connecting bathroom to the master suite? Before he could question his uncle, the porch door opened and slammed shut.

"Am I gonna have to tie you to the bed?" Tucker's voice was laced with amusement.

Turning a startled glance to Tucker, Micah nodded. *Wait.* He shook his head.

Tucker grabbed his hand and tugged. "Night Juan."

Chuckling, Juan waved. "Night boys."

Micah followed in a daze, trying to figure out why he'd never seen it. His uncle and Ferguson had been lovers. It made perfect sense now that he thought about it. Oh damn. Tio must hurt worst than anyone. Micah couldn't imagine what he'd feel like if something happened to Tucker. Even Tucker being gone wasn't so bad, not compared to death. If Tucker died… It felt like Micah swallowed glass, his heart hurt. Pain for Tio's loss made him stop. "Tio?"

"Yeah?" Juan flicked the ashes off his cigarette.

Tucker stopped but didn't let go of Micah's hand. He squeezed it as if offering comfort. He always could since Micah's moods. "Thank you. And if you need someone to talk to…"

Juan nodded. "Go to bed Mijo. And remember what I said." He glanced at Tucker then back to Micah. "But for what it's worth, I don't think you have anything to worry about."

A smile tugged at Micah's lips and he looked up at Tucker. Tio was right. Tucker didn't look like a man hell bent on leaving. Come to think about it, Tucker would never have made love to him if he didn't love him. Maybe he could talk Tucker into staying. He was damned sure gonna try. "Night, Tio." Micah tugged Tucker along into the house feeling like a giant weight had been lifted off his shoulders. Duncan wouldn't get the ranch and Tucker was his. He just had to convince Tucker of that.

"What was that about? And why are you awake?"

Letting go of Tucker's hand, Micah stopped at the fridge and pulled out a bottle of water. He needed to work up the nerve to tell Tucker how he felt. He had a chance that his tio never did. His and Tucker's marriage might not be legal in Texas but… Didn't he owe it to Tio and Ferguson to make things work between he and Tucker? "I don't want you to leave. Stay here, let's make this work. At least commute back and forth. You married me damn it. I didn't ask you to. You insisted, so now you have to deal with it. I'm not letting you go. You have to—"

Tucker chuckled. "I'd planned on it."

What? Wow! Micah stopped with the bottle half way to his mouth. It couldn't possibly be that easy. "Are you kidding me?" He narrowed his eyes on Tucker, daring him to be joking.

"No, now will you come to bed and go to sleep before you fall over?"

Micah took a drink, then put the cap back on the bottle. Laughing and feeling like his heart was gonna burst, he shoved Tucker out of the kitchen toward the stairs. He'd let Tucker's over protectiveness go just this once. "Absolutely. But I might need some incentive to stay there."

SEEING YOU

For anyone who's lost a loved one and managed to find happiness again.

DAKOTA FLINT

"It's time for you to come home, Dylan." The strain in my sister's voice came across loud and clear over the connection, a palpable feeling despite being three thousand miles away.

"Why, Erin? What's wrong?"

"You've been gone too long. Wade… I'm worried about him." She didn't continue.

"Why's that?" I closed my eyes, trying to block out the image of the last time I'd seen Wade, standing silent by Simon's graveside, his face an indurate mask, no emotion showing through except the emptiness in his eyes.

"Every time I call to say the girls and I are going to come out for a visit, he makes some excuse. The few times I've just driven out there, he wasn't around. And the ranch… well, it looks like it's falling apart."

"What?" I couldn't keep the surprise out of my voice. The only thing Wade had loved more than that ranch was Simon.

"Yeah, I couldn't get over how many repairs need to be made and how much needs to be done, and I couldn't find Wade or Mack. You… you just need to come home now, Dylan. It's time to stop running." The last part was said hesitantly.

"I'm not running." I bit off the words that tried to force their way out after that. Did I even believe that anymore?

"The girls miss their uncle," Erin said. I didn't think the pain would be so acute, not after all this time, but thinking of eight-year-old Amelia and six-year-old Molly crying for their Uncle Simon made my stomach clench.

I gripped the phone tight, tried unsuccessfully to swallow. I said, "We all miss him, Erin."

I heard her heave a tired sigh. "No, you idiot, their Uncle *Dylan*. They miss *you*." Another sigh. "Just come home, Lynnie. We need you."

At the use of that silly childhood nickname, my throat closed up and I couldn't speak. I thought for sure I was going to lose it right there on 23rd Street, surrounded by a blur of navy blue suits swarming into the State Department buildings and an army of tourists clicking away on their cameras. Continuing my walk, I stared out at the Potomac and wondered what a dumb cowboy like me was doing busing tables in a city like this. I ignored the voice that whispered something about running. It sounded suspiciously like my brother Simon.

I stood staring at the water for a long time, watching it turn blood red as the horizon swallowed the sun. I shuddered. Erin was right.

It was time to go home.

CHAPTER ONE

Turning onto the private road that would lead me to the ranch buildings, I took a deep breath. It had been two weeks since that phone call from Erin. I didn't exactly drag my feet, but I probably could have made it back last week.

The dread ate at me on the drive back to Montana, through big cities offering nothing but traffic and problems, through the small abandoned towns that offered a skeleton of the past, through mountains and rolling hills and flat plains. Over the river and through the woods, to Wade's house I go.

My smile faded as I pulled my beat-up blue Chevy to the front of the bunkhouse. I hopped out of the truck and stood still as I tried to figure out why this place felt so… off. Not even the day after Simon's funeral had felt like this.

I walked around a pick-up truck, mouth gaping open and its intestines abandoned on a blanket on the ground, and made my way over to the corral, hooking my boot on the bottom rung of the fence. And then it hit me.

Where was all the life?

I did a three-sixty, scouring the meadow and the foothills, the ranch house, the bunkhouse, the pond, the road winding out of sight leading back to civilization, the stables and the barn, the clumps of trees lining Sweet Grass creek, the trails leading into the mountains. Nothing.

Where the hell was everyone? The hands? Mack? Wade? More puzzling, where the hell were the animals?

A breeze brushed past my neck and rustled the leaves on the aspen trees, which until that moment had stood silently at attention around the outbuildings. I stood still for a moment and listened, but I didn't hear anything other than the occasional songbird and the gurgle of creek water.

Shaking my head, I made my way over to the stables. Opening the sagging door, I walked inside and couldn't help wrinkling my nose. The stalls needed to be mucked out, despite most of them standing empty.

Walking down the aisle, I paused when I realized Simon's horse, Donner, wasn't there. I stood looking at the empty stall for a moment, but forced myself to keep looking for the other horses. I didn't see Rudy, Wade's horse, either, but my heart clenched when I spotted my Blitzen. Man, it had been hard leaving my girl behind when I left the Lazy G.

"Hey, girl. How's my pretty lady been?" I rubbed her nose, fiercely glad all of sudden that I had come home. It was too long since I had been on a horse. The unconditional love didn't hurt either.

I gave into the little boy inside of me and hugged Blitzen's neck tight until she nudged my head and I let go, laughing. "Alright. I was getting sappy, huh? Missed you though." She lipped my pocket and looked at me with what I would have assumed was a desperate eye if I didn't know any better. Had anybody been bringing my baby any treats?

"I'll see if I can scare up an apple or two later, but first I need to find out where everyone is. And where the rest of the horses are." Blitzen whickered softly, and I gave her one good rub before heading out of the barn and over to the bunkhouse. Stepping onto the sagging front step, I knocked on the door before walking in.

"Hello? Anybody here?" It was the middle of the day, so I didn't really expect anyone to answer.

"Yeah? Who's that?" The voice bellowing from the belly of the house had to be Mack, the foreman of the Lazy G since before I started working here back in high school.

"It's Dylan," I said, walking down the hallway and meeting up with Mack coming out of his bedroom wearing sweatpants and an old T-shirt, hair rumpled as if he had been asleep, his bushy gray eyebrows climbing in surprise toward what used to be his hairline.

"Dylan! I didn't know you were coming back. Wade didn't mention it. Sure am glad to see you." Mack pulled me into a bruising back-slapping hug, and I was ashamed to feel my eyes burning. I had a good excuse for it a second later, though, when Mack pulled back and smacked me on the side of my head.

"Ow, what was that for?" Guess they weren't going to slaughter the fatted calf for me.

"Boy, we're gonna talk 'bout this whole keepin' in touch thing. Twice in fourteen months don't count, and I oughta take you outside and teach you a lesson that will have you checkin' in at least monthly next time you leave."

Rubbing the side of my head, I said, "Sorry, Mack. I meant to call more, but... I just needed time."

I didn't need to say any more, we both knew why. Mack looked at me, ran his hand through what was left of his gray hair, and it struck me that Mack might have been napping. In the middle of the afternoon. That was odd. I couldn't remember Mack taking a nap in the seventeen years I'd known him.

I caught a flash of an unmade bed and bedside table sporting an array of pill bottles before Mack shut the bedroom door and turned toward the kitchen. Accepting the cold beer he offered me, I joined him at the kitchen table and tried to tell myself there was no reason to be nervous.

"So why'd you come back? You talk to Wade?"

"No, not yet. I wasn't sure exactly when I'd get in so I thought I'd... surprise him." I smiled but Mack leveled a look at me and I knew he wasn't fooled. "Actually, I talked to Erin and she thought I should come home. Now that I'm here, I can see why. Where is everyone? The horses? Wade? The hands?"

Mack fiddled with the label on the bottle, not looking at me anymore. "You talk to Wade at all since... well, since you left?"

"Not exactly." I forced myself to keep my expression blank.

Mack looked up at me and sighed, and I realized that somewhere along the way, the man who had always seemed larger than life to me had gotten old. Old and tired. How did that happen?

I was afraid I knew.

"What does not exactly mean?"

"It means... well, no."

"Shit. *Shit*. What the hell is wrong with you, Dylan?"

"I just needed time." Damn, that sounded lame. "And Wade didn't call me either." Oh, that was better. Damn.

"Christ." Mack just shook his head. "*Shit*."

"I'm sure He did. Funny, gives new meaning to the term 'holy shit.'" I knew as soon as the words left my mouth that this was not the time for jokes. Mack looked at me like he had the time he found Simon and me drunk behind a couple bales of hay in the barn when we were sixteen, and I was supposed to be mucking stalls. I tried to brazen it out, asking Mack to join us, and he stared at me with a mix of anger and disappointment. Then he hauled me up and tossed me in the freezing cold pond not five minutes later. It had been... sobering. "Sorry, Mack. Will you tell me what's going on?"

Mack sighed and said, "Wade ain't been around much since... well, I rarely see him, so he don't talk to me. I try to hunt him down to remind him to pay stuff, but he... shit, I don't know where he goes. Just out riding with Rudy I think."

"Pay stuff? Why would you need to remind him? And where are all the horses?"

"Yeah, Wade ain't been very timely with the bills lately. The feed store needs a payment before they'll fill the next order. Had to sell most of the stock."

"What? Why? What's everybody riding? How're you moving cattle? Riding fence?" Why did it feel like pulling teeth trying to get answers out of Mack?

"There ain't no 'everybody,' boy. Just two hands left 'sides myself. Can't take care of an outfit the size of the Lazy G with just three people. Had to do somethin'. And if Wade don't pay the two hands we got left this Friday, Billy and Joe aren't goin' to stick around any longer either."

"What the hell is Wade thinking?" I tried to swallow down my disbelief, but it was a funny taste.

"Don't think he is."

"He drinking?" He hadn't been, not when I'd left, but I couldn't say as I'd be surprised if he was taking some comfort from staring at the bottom of a fifth of JD every now and again.

"Not that I can tell," Mack said, sounding certain. I forced my fingers to unclench from around my sweating bottle.

"Well then what the fuck is he doing?"

"Grieving. Hiding. S'my guess anyways." Mack's faded hazel eyes looked just about as sad as I felt.

"You talk to him?" That wouldn't have been easy for Mack, forcing Wade to talk about his grief, but Mack had been there for Wade since his father died, and whatever needed doing, Mack always stepped right up to the plate.

"Won't stand still to listen to me. That is, if I can smoke him out to begin with."

"Shit." I sat back in the chair, ignoring the creaking sound, and thought about this. I should have come home months ago. "Why didn't you call me? I would have come home."

"Figured if you needed the reminder, be best if no one forced you back before you were ready to quit your wanderin'. I wasn't goin' to call you 'til things got desperate." Funny, Mack didn't look like he was kidding. I barked out a laugh anyways.

"When did this start? He seemed to be taking care of everything the first month after Simon died." Fact was, the ranch had looked like all Wade had to hold on to then, throwing himself into running it every minute of the day.

"Oh, 'bout the time you left." Mack just looked at me for a moment, and I dropped my eyes, afraid of what he might see. "You left, and what little life he seemed to have just drained right out, far as I could tell."

And just like that, I could feel the guilt pressing down on my shoulders. I mumbled some excuse to Mack and bolted outside, gulping fresh air as fast as my lungs could take it.

Instead of coming home months ago, I never should have left in the first place.

CHAPTER TWO

Walking into the ranch house, I was struck by the smell. Not the fresh apple pie smell of yesteryear, but something a little more rank. Garbage. Ugh.

Not surprising, since the kitchen sink was full of dishes and the smell got decidedly more funky as I walked closer to the spot where the garbage was kept. Realizing my mouth was hanging open, I shut it quick. Where there was garbage like that, there were sure to be flies.

The muscles in my stomach wound tight as I surveyed the mess. Wade had never been a neat freak by any means, but he'd always cleaned up after himself. Simon had been the slob. My stomach started cramping.

The door to Wade's office stood ajar, so I didn't bother knocking. Holy crap. His desk looked like a twister had blown through. The one place Wade freaked out about mess was in his office.

Starting to feel a bit like George Bailey, I called out, "Wade?" No answer.

Climbing the stairs, careful not to touch the two inches of dust on the banister, I made my way down to Wade and Si— Wade's room. I knocked softly and then louder when there was no answer. Deciding Wade wasn't in there, unless he was asleep—and hey maybe in this weird alternate Lazy G world everyone napped at 3 o'clock in the afternoon—I turned the door handle.

No Wade in sight, just a bed that looked like it hadn't been made after a wrestling match and a previously wooden floor that was now sporting a new rug I'd call "dirty laundry." Lifting my foot to step inside, I halted it mid-air as my gaze swept over the coffee colored wall and spotted a rectangle of wall that looked like someone had added a little cream to it.

I swallowed hard, and knew that if I walked into the room there would be another two naked rectangles to match the first.

Wondering where Wade had put the paintings, I listened to this weird whooshing sound for a minute before I realized it was the sound of my own breathing.

I turned around and didn't stop until I had Blitzen saddled, urging her faster and faster towards the mountains, heedless of the danger, of when I must have lost my hat, and of the wetness blurring my vision.

◊ ◊ ◊ ◊

Returning to the stables a few hours later, my steps faltered as I noticed Rudy was back in his stall. I took my time brushing Blitzen, telling myself it was because she liked it and not because I was putting off this first meeting.

Finally I took a deep breath and walked to the house in search of Wade. I found him sitting at the kitchen table, bent over what must have been a microwave dinner. He didn't look up, and I wondered how he could have missed the slamming of the screen door when I walked in.

"Hello Wade." His head shot up, and he stared at me for moment like he didn't recognize me. Then his eyes focused, and he continued to stare at me, saying nothing.

"Sorry I didn't call to tell you when I'd be showin' up, but I wasn't really sure." Still, he didn't say anything. I slid into the chair across from him. "How are you, Wade?" I clenched my hands under the table and willed him to stop looking at me like that and just say something.

It felt like an eternity while he just stared at me and breathed, and then finally he said, "Okay, I guess."

Right.

"So, uh, how come… is Mary not coming out any more to drop offer dinners and clean up?" It was obvious that the woman who used to come out to the ranch to cook and a clean a few days a week hadn't been around for a while.

"No, she said she… no, she's not. Sorry, I should probably clean up a little better."

Ya think? Jeeze. All I said though was, "Yeah."

Talk about uncomfortable. I stared at him, noting his russet hair needed some serious trimming and his cheekbones were more prominent than I remembered, although they went well with the shadows beneath his eyes and the general gauntness of his frame. He stared at me, seeing God knows what. An awkward silence like this never would have developed if Simon were—I cut off the thought.

Finally I couldn't take one more minute of this, and said, "What happened to this place, Wade? To you?" I could have kicked my own ass. What a stupid thing to say. I could tell by the look on Wade's face that he thought so, too. "Have you tried talking to someone?" Great, I was handling this beautifully.

His whole body tensed. "About what?"

I wasn't sure if I should go on. "About your… grief. About Simon. About trying to—" I stopped, because as much as I loved the sound of my own voice echoing around the now empty kitchen, I would have preferred it far more if Wade had stayed and listened instead of getting up without a word and walking off.

CHAPTER THREE

Living in different cities for over a year had made me soft.

I had blisters aplenty after a morning spent mucking out stalls, and I had all sorts of muscles screaming at me for riding for so long yesterday. Some things you just had to ease back into.

Which was why I was here in Wade's kitchen, scrubbing dishes instead of out checking grazing conditions with Billy and Joe. Wade wasn't around, and Mack had disappeared earlier, mumbling something about working on his truck. I suspected he was actually resting, since there was a minute there in the barn this morning that I swear he almost fell over for no reason. Well there was a reason alright, but I doubt if he'd tell me about it. I was going to have to force it out of him eventually, and in the meantime I ignored the tendrils of worry worming into my brain.

I was just wishing I had turned on the radio or something instead of spending so much time alone with my thoughts when the phone on the wall rang.

"'Lo?"

"Dylan?"

"Hey, Erin. How are you?"

"Good. Thanks for calling me when you got into town."

"Sorry. I just got in last night. Was about to call you actually." Small fib, but it would have occurred to me soon, I was sure. Great big brother I was.

"Yeah, right. I believe that like I believed you the time you gave me a Barbie for my birthday with a shaved head and claimed it came like that, and the only reason it wasn't in the box was because you didn't want me to have to go through all the hard work of taking it out." I could hear the smile in her voice.

"You never did believe me that it was GI Jane." I smiled to myself, but it faded at Erin's next question.

"So you've seen Wade? Talked to him?" She sounded anxious.

"Well, I've seen him. Talked to him, well that's kind of a liberal description." I rubbed my forehead. "Christ, Erin, why the hell didn't you tell me the shape this place was in? Why didn't you call me home sooner?"

"Hey, last I checked you were a grown man. Didn't think I should have to tell you that you're family *needed* you, not after Simon... not after what we've been through." She paused, and then said grudgingly, "And every time I said I was calling you to come home, Mike said I should leave you to do it in your own time."

I smiled, thinking of Erin meekly following what her big, burly husband told her to do. "And you of course listened to his advice without question."

She snorted. "What do you think? So, are you staying in the house with Wade?"

"Hell, no. Even the bunkhouse, smelling of sweat and beer, is better than this. Couldn't you have done some cleaning when you were out here?" I grinned.

Erin didn't disappoint me. "Oh, because when the little ol' female comes to visit, we should just keep her busy cookin' and cleanin', is that right? Whatever. Seriously though, the house has gotten a lot worse in the last couple months."

Well, shit, I hoped so. How long could a man live with filth like this?

"Yeah, about that. Why isn't Mary coming out here still? Wade wouldn't say."

Erin sighed and confirmed my suspicions by saying, "I don't really know. I asked her when I saw her in the grocery store the other day, and she didn't really give an answer. All she said was she felt bad, but she has a family."

"So he probably wasn't paying her either."

"What? Are you serious?"

"Yeah. Damn. I wonder if he's even looked at the books lately."

"It's really that bad? Oh God. I knew things were getting thin, but I never thought... He'll never survive it if he loses the ranch too. Never."

"He's not going to lose it. I won't let that happen." My voice came out sounding sure and strong, and I was glad.

"I'm glad you're home, Dylan. Real glad. Now come over here for dinner tonight. Mike's coming home from work early and he's anxious to hear how you got along with all the snobs on the East coast. See if you can drag Wade with you, but come without him if you can't." Her tone of voice said she had little hope I would actually be able to convince Wade to go.

"Alright. Sounds good. Tell the girls they better be prepared to help me fill my bear hug quota. I have fourteen months to make up for." More than she knew.

We said our goodbyes, and I stood there staring at the wall and thinking.

◊ ◊ ◊ ◊

Returning to the ranch later that night after dinner at Erin's, I turned off the engine of my truck and just sat there staring out into the darkness. I could hear Billy and Joe talking and laughing on the front porch of the bunkhouse, and I tried to identify the feeling that was running through me.

It felt foreign and I tried to pinpoint it as I thought back to dinner and the worry in Erin's eyes when she asked about Wade and the ranch, to the disappointed looks on the girls' faces when they realized Uncle Wade wasn't with me, to all the work I did today and the endless list for the next day, and the next, and the next.

I felt the feeling move through me, pumping my blood, quickening my breathing, tightening my hands into fists, and I recognized it from the days after Simon's death. Anger.

It had been a while since I felt anger at anyone else besides myself, and I took a moment to savor it. It actually felt good.

The next minute I was out of my truck and racing into the house, calling Wade's name. I wasn't surprised when he didn't answer, and I went tearing up the stairs, searching all the rooms until I found what I was looking for.

Fifteen minutes later I stood back and admired the way Simon's three paintings looked on the wall in Wade's bedroom. Looking at the one of Wade seated atop Rudy out near the pond, it was obvious why other people had been willing to pay Simon to teach them how to paint. What was also obvious, and what couldn't be taught, was the emotion that rolled off that painting. So much love.

I knew exactly how Simon had felt.

I was sitting at Wade's desk the next morning, digging through the mess of paperwork to try and figure out where the Lazy G stood financially, when the man himself stomped in and slammed both hands down on the desk. He towered over me, probably trying to intimidate me. It might have worked if I hadn't seen this bluff play out over the many disagreements he and Simon had over the seven years they lived together.

I decided a little preemptive strike was necessary here, and said, "Do you even know if the Lazy G is in the black these days?" Wade looked briefly taken aback, and before he could answer, I waved my hand at the mess of papers on his desk, and said, "Of course you don't."

Wade ignored that. "Were you the one who put the paintings back up?" Oh yeah, Wade was angry. Growling. Despite feeling happy at the evidence that Wade wasn't a completely empty shell, I used the residual anger I was still feeling from yesterday to hand it right back to him.

"You're damn right I did."

Admitting that seemed to take the wind out of Wade's sails. He looked away for a moment, then turned back to me and practically whispered, "Who gave you the right?"

I shot right back, "No one. But I'll be damned if I sit by and let you pretend my brother didn't exist. Who gave you *that* right?"

For a moment I thought he would haul off and hit me, actually wished that he would, but he just stood there breathing hard. He started to say something, stopped, looked at me like I was dirt beneath his boot, curled his lip, and stomped back out again.

I leaned back in Wade's chair, forced myself to relax, and couldn't help but think that had been waiting for fifteen months.

Three hours later I rubbed my eyes and tried to decide what would be better for my headache, dinner or bed. Probably dinner first.

I got up, leaving the rest of the paperwork for tomorrow. I had at least managed to establish that the Lazy G was operating in the black. Barely. And if things didn't turn around soon, the promise I made to Erin would come back to bite me on the ass. Hard.

Mack was just serving up Sloppy Joes when I got back to the bunkhouse, and I grabbed a beer and sat down. It wasn't until I had shoved the sandwich into my mouth in three bites that I looked up to find Mack, Billy, and Joe all staring at me.

Mack was the first to speak. "You talk to Wade?"

Deciding not to quibble over semantics I said, "Sure."

Mack snorted. "Well?"

"Wade agreed to see a grief counselor, helped me clean the house top to bottom, paid all the bills, and he's ready to help move cattle tomorrow." I took a swig of my beer and almost spit it out laughing when I saw the identical expressions of shock on their faces.

Seeing my laughter, Mack looked like he wanted to strangle me, Billy looked exasperated, and Joe just looked confused. "Honestly Mack, what were you looking for me to do? I landed a lot of different gigs while I was gone, but magician was never one of them."

Mack sighed. "I dunno, boy. I just thought… shit. Well have you at least looked at the books?"

"Yeah. Y'all will get paid, don't worry," I said, and the other three began to eat with enthusiasm.

I was leaning back and contemplating how much it would suck to fall asleep in the kitchen chair when I noticed Billy looking at me like he wanted to say something, but was hesitating. "You got something to say, Billy?"

Billy turned red to match his hair, the curse of having fair skin and freckles, and said, "Yeah, I uh—" he cleared his throat. "Remember when Simon first moved in with Wade? Before Wade laid down the law and told Simon he could work in any room in the house except the office?"

I had forgotten that Billy had been here at the Lazy G almost as long as I had, and I smiled as I thought back. "Shit, yeah. I don't think I ever looked at Wade swimming in the pond without busting a gut after that." We all started chuckling.

Noticing Joe looking confused, I explained, "Old Wade's not real big on words most of the time, but he sure does have a temper. He didn't want to scare his temperamental little artist off while they adjusted to living together those first few months, so when Simon irritated him he'd go jump in the pond to cool off rather than yell at Simon. Wasn't long before Wade was dunking himself two, three, four times a day." I stopped to laugh, but sobered a little as I recalled the first time I had seen Wade coming out of the pond in cut-offs plastered to his legs, water streaming down the ridges of his chest. I had gotten completely hard before it dawned on me I was looking at a *man* like that.

Seeing I wasn't going to continue the story, Mack picked it up while we followed him outside to sit on the porch, probably to give us a visual. "Well one day, we're all sittin' on this porch after dinner, having a beer, when we see Wade come slammin' outta the house and Simon's sittin' right here and says, 'I doodled on some papers on his desk. Bet ya twenty bucks he goes in fully clothed this time.' Sure enough, Wade got to the pond and kept right on walkin', boots and all, until all we could see was his gray hat floating in the water where his head had been a second before that." Mack paused as we all hooted with laughter. "We 'bout pissed ourselves laughin' and wasn't long before Wade musta decided the water wasn't gonna help that time, 'cause he was up and outta that pond before we could blink. Came up, face all red, grabbed Simon's hand and dragged him up to the house without a word. Didn't see those two for days."

Joe was laughing, but never having met Simon, he obviously needed clarification. "So Simon was doing stuff to annoy Wade on purpose?"

"No, not really. Little shit was testin' Wade," Mack said with a fond smile, and I had one of my own as I wondered if that was the first time since the accident that Mack referred to

Simon as a little shit. Hard to call the dead names, even ones you'd been calling them for years.

"Testing?" Joe looked even more confused at this.

"Oh yeah. Wanted to see how far he could push 'im, wanted to force Wade to talk stuff out if they needed to so it wouldn't build up like that. And based on the look in Simon's eyes when it was obvious Wade had been in the pond, the little shit was havin' fun, too. Kinda twisted sense of humor on him," Mack said. I snorted at the last bit. Truer words. Simon and I'd had so much fun over the years though.

We were all quiet for a moment, smiling, remembering, and it felt good. Just deep down good in my bones, thinking of Simon looking up at me with his laughing brown eyes and his brown hair, so unlike my own blond strands, always flecked with paint. Much better than the last time I had seen him, his eyes filled with pain and his hair matted with blood.

My smile faded, and I glanced over at the house when I noticed movement. I saw Wade sitting on the wooden swing in the deepening shadows of the front porch, and it felt like he was looking straight at me, but I couldn't be sure.

Mack spoke again, this time the sadness coming through in his gruff voice. "Yep, Simon sure was good for our boy over there. Just what Wade always needed."

The rain was pounding on the roof, the wind was screaming through the trees, the crack and boom of thunder keeping an even drumbeat, and I was watching it all from my bedroom window in the bunkhouse, marveling at nature's symphony and the inconsiderate rehearsal time.

Well, to be fair, it wasn't the storm that woke me up. It was the nightmare.

The nightmare was always the same. The last few minutes with Simon, looking up at me and covered in blood, saying, "Love you... brother." Then me screaming for help on the deserted highway, clutching Simon's limp body, too mindless to pull my cell phone out of my pocket and make the call.

Then there was Wade standing over us, seeming eight feet tall, fury on his face as he said, "Why Simon? Why not you?"

I shuddered, thinking back to that night in May when I lost the man that was a brother to me in every way that really counted. Most of the nightmare was so tragically real, a flashback of those heartbreaking moments, but Wade wasn't there.

No, that was just in my mind.

I hadn't dreamed about the accident in weeks, hadn't woken up sweating and crying and wondering why me in months. I had recently, in fact, started dreaming of our childhood together, of Simon and Erin and our parents, Annie and Fred. I dreamed of the day I came to live with them when I was six, bewildered by the disappearance of my mother and this concept called death, when this Simon boy sat and held my hand all night when I was too scared to sleep. I dreamed of the time a pair of nine-year-old boys thought they could hitchhike to California instead of doing their chores, but wound up waiting at Miss Flossie's house for our parents to pick us up while the town librarian fed us stale cookies and Lactaid. I dreamed of the time twelve-year-old Simon tried to convince Erin she was adopted and was really born at a house located at 666 Damnation Drive, of the moment when she looked at Simon and said, "If you're trying to make me cry, it won't work. Dylan was adopted by Mom and Dad and look how lucky we all are."

Much better dreams than nightmares of blood and death and grief.

My attention was caught by the light flashing on in the kitchen of the ranch house, and I wondered what Wade dreamed about at night. A moment later it looked like the front door had opened, and I squinted, trying to see in the darkness if Wade was outside. Then the moonlight caught him as he stood at the top of the porch steps, his face tilted up to the rain.

I watched as he made his way down the steps, over the mud and grass, to the corral fence. Puzzled, I stared. This wasn't a drizzle. It was a storm, and even if it was almost summer, a drenching would sap body heat pretty quickly. "Christ, what the hell is he doing? Doesn't he care if he gets pneumonia?"

Abruptly I realized, no, he *didn't* care. That was the point. And just like that, once again I felt the burn of anger infusing my limbs, powering through me as I dragged my Levi's and boots on, bubbling under the surface as I stomped down the hall and out the door. I didn't stop until I reached Wade, where he was leaning against the fence, and I grabbed his shoulder and whirled him around to face me.

"What the *fuck* are you doing?" I barely recognized my own voice.

He blinked water out of his eyes and stared dumbly at me before saying, "What?"

"I said, what the *fuck* are you doing out here? I know it might seem like a nice night for a walk to you, but I thought I might inform you that it's fucking pouring outside."

Wade looked away, as if he was too tired to even look me in the face, and said, "Go back to bed, Dylan." Then he turned back around to lean on the fence, dismissing me, and my anger turned to rage.

It felt like someone else moving after that. Someone else's hand grabbing Wade's shoulder to turn him around again, someone else's arm that cocked back and let fly straight into

Wade's granite jaw, someone else that watched as Wade's head snapped back from the force and he stumbled against the fence. Because surely it couldn't have been me that touched Wade in anger.

But it was definitely me that went down, without a fence to catch me, when Wade's fist connected to my own jaw. I was sure that would hurt later, but at the moment I couldn't feel anything except anger and relief that Wade was still fighting.

I scrambled back up out of the mud and then it was happening so fast, the adrenaline moving through my veins as we both grunted and swore and swung our limbs, that I wasn't sure who was landing punches where. We were like one beast, ugly and flailing. I hadn't brawled like this since Eddie Baron, one of the linebackers in high school, had called Simon a faggot when we were juniors.

The rain and mud were making things slippery, and then we were on the ground wrestling like a couple kids in the mud, both of us obviously no longer going for blood. Wade managed to roll me onto my back and straddle me, and I felt mud oozing around my head. I could barely see with the rain falling into my eyes.

It felt like the mud was seeping into my ears, which was just fucking nasty, and I stopped struggling for control and reached out, grabbed a handful of mud and aimed it for Wade's face.

It landed around his left temple and I smashed it into his hair and ear as best I could. I started laughing when Wade stopped moving and just sat back, looking down at me as if I had suddenly turned into a purple dinosaur.

I laughed and laughed until I was scared I would never stop laughing, and all the while Wade looked down at me with his mouth hanging open in shock. Which just made me bellow more as he was catching mouthfuls of rainwater like that.

Just as Wade was starting to look really concerned, the laughter just dried up and I became aware that we were out in a thunderstorm and it was pouring, and I hadn't bothered with a shirt. I wouldn't be surprised if my nipples were little blue pebbles, and I grinned at the weird thought.

That must have been the final straw, because Wade grabbed my chin and forced me to meet his gaze. "Are you fucking crazy?"

I considered this. "Probably. But if I'm crazy for lying here in the mud and laughing in the rain, aren't you crazy for watching me do it?"

Wade grinned and said, "Probably." The grin caught me off guard. It had been so long since I had seen it, making him look unexpectedly boyish despite the years carved into his face. I looked at that grin and the momentarily happy look in his eyes, and I couldn't breathe.

As if he was deflating, the look faded from his face and he said, "Why did you hit me?"

"Because I couldn't stand it one more minute. Not one more fucking second."

"Stand what?"

"Watching you give up."

"I have not." But he said it quietly, and I knew he didn't even believe himself.

"You *have*. What do you think Simon would say?" I winced as I said this, hating myself for it, and Wade looked like I had punched him again.

"I—"

"*Simon* died. Not you. I want you to stop acting like it was you that died on that highway."

"How do you know it wasn't?"

That physically hurt. "Because that's bullshit. I watched my brother die in my arms, okay? I watched and for a while I wish I had, too. You're not the only one who lost something that day, and I'm sick of watching you wish you could join him when the rest of us are doing the best we can to pick up the pieces."

Wade snarled back at me, "Why do you care now? You just left. Just packed your bags and left like I was nothing to you. Like this place was nothing to you."

That left me momentarily speechless. "I... Wade." I wasn't sure what to say. I tried again. "I just... I was trying to adjust to a world without my brother in it, and every time I looked at you

I kept waiting for you to get angry that I walked away from the crash and Simon didn't. I just couldn't stay for that." I told myself that the burning in my eyes was from the mud and rain.

Wade looked shocked. "You thought that? I... never." He scrubbed his hands over his face, not that it did any good. "Christ, I thought a million times that it shouldn't have been Simon. But I never once thought it should have been you instead."

I hoped Wade would think it was only rain leaking around my eyes. "I... thank you. Didn't want to think of you hating me."

"No." Wade was looking down at me, and I was about to ask him to get off me because I could feel my teeth getting ready to chatter, when he let out this weird choking sound. Then he said, "What do you want from me, Dylan?"

I didn't even have to think about the answer, even if this was the oddest time and place to have this out. "I want you to look around. I want you to start thinking about what you had with Simon instead of just what you lost. I want you to see that you're about to lose this place if you don't fight for it. I want you to see that old man in the bunkhouse who loves you as much as your father did, who is sick and worried about you, about keeping this ranch going. I want you to see that Erin and Mike love you and miss you, and she has two girls who cried for Uncle Wade the other night when I showed up at dinner alone. They feel like they lost all of us at one time. I want you to see that Simon would hate to see you living like this." I paused for breath, hesitating, knowing he deserved my apology. "I want you to see me, see that I'm sorry I left and I'm back to stay. I'll help you hold onto this place, I swear, but I can't do it alone and neither can Mack."

"I—" Another weird choking sound, and then Wade was sobbing, broken choking sounds. I pulled him down and held him, uncaring about the surreal quality of doing this here and now, with mud oozing into my ears. He cried as if his soul was purging itself of all the pain, and I made shushing sounds, thinking it felt different to be the strong one giving comfort this time.

When his body had stopped shaking so violently, I helped pick us both up off the ground.

I led him into the house, straight into the bathroom, and turned the water on in the shower. "Can you get undressed and get in? You need to warm up, get clean."

He nodded, looking drained and tired of talking.

"Okay, I'm going to go try and clean up." I turned and jumped a little, catching a glimpse of myself in the mirror. Man, I looked like I had the Halloween Simon and I had gone as Swamp Things, covered in mud and grass sticking to my skin and hair. Looking at Wade, I realized he looked just as bad.

Wishing I had a camera handy, I smiled until I walked back into the hallway and saw the trail of mud. Well, at least I hadn't gotten beyond cleaning the kitchen yesterday and I could take care of this tomorrow.

I mopped up the worst of the mess with towels and tossed them in the washer, shivering and starting to feel sore from the pounding of Wade's fists. A hot shower would feel great, but I decided to check on Wade before heading back to the bunkhouse.

Pushing the bathroom door open a little, I saw him still standing there at the sink, looking dazed and not a little lost. I wondered if this was the first time he had given voice to his grief. I never saw him cry after Simon died, not the night of the accident, not at the funeral, not in the month before I left. Wade was always more stoic about things than Simon and I, more prone to giving in to his temper than any other emotion, and I figured he'd let it out in his own way.

Realizing he needed someone to direct him and put him to bed, I stepped back into the bathroom, the steam swirling as if reaching out to touch me. The warmth felt good. "Wade? You should get in the shower, get clean so you can go to bed. We have work to do tomorrow and you can't lie in bed all day." No smile, no reaction to that.

I started to unbutton what looked like it might have been a green shirt, but was now splotchy brown with grass accents. Kneeling, I helped him pull off his boots, and heard the wet suction sound they made. Probably beyond redemption now.

Standing back up, I undid his belt buckle and felt his gaze on me. I ignored it and continued undressing him until he stood there naked and dirty and shivering.

I gently pushed him into the shower, watched him stand there under the spray without reaching for the soap, and made a decision I didn't want to look at too closely.

Hopping on one foot, I yanked off first one boot and then the other, and shucked off my jeans. I climbed into the tub next to Wade. Guiding Wade until he stood directly underneath the spray, I murmured, "Close your eyes."

Letting the water wash the worst of the mud and grass off of his body, I reached for the shampoo. Only an inch shorter than Wade, I didn't have to stretch like Simon would have to gently work the shampoo into Wade's hair. Thinking of Simon, my hands stuttered, but I continued when Wade made a questioning sound. By this point, my hands were practically massaging Wade's scalp, and I made myself stop and turn him to rinse the shampoo out.

His jaw was starting to discolor blue and purple, and I'd lifted my hand to trace a finger over the bruising I'd caused when he opened his eyes and looked at me. He had an odd look in his hazel eyes, and I realized that we were both standing in the shower together, naked.

I mean, I knew that we were naked, obviously, since I undressed us both, but I didn't *know* we were naked until this moment when Wade looked at me, the knowledge dawning on him as well. And since I'm a guy and I hadn't had sex in months and this was *Wade*, it was going to be painfully obvious to Wade any second that my body was beginning to *know* we were naked, too.

Feeling myself start to harden, I turned around, ashamed. Wade caught my arm. "Don't go," he said.

I looked back at him, my gaze dropping for only a second down the miles of wet flesh, but long enough to know his body already *knew* we were naked, too. "This is a bad idea."

"Yeah." He didn't bother denying it as he pulled me back in front of him.

So there we were, both naked, hard, wet, still pretty dirty— actually I was still a lot dirty—and I didn't really know what to say. This had moved past awkward and hurtled straight into weird. Wade didn't move, just stood there not speaking, not looking away from me. Finally I just grabbed the washcloth and lathered it up, motioning him to come closer.

"Did you wash behind your ears like a good boy? I seem to recall some hooligan shoving mud into one of them." The smile that followed my lame teasing was fleeting at best, and then Wade just went back to looking at me, serious, intent.

Not knowing what else to say, I started to run the washcloth over Wade's skin from the ear I had caked with mud, to his neck where I could see the pulse pounding a quick beat, to his chest where I could feel his heart thumping as quick as mine was, to his ribs where I could count each one since he'd lost so much weight.

When I reached his waistline I stopped, took a deep breath, and motioned for him to turn around. I massaged the soapy washcloth into the muscles of his back, from the top of his neck to the base of the spine. I stopped there, unsure if I should continue or not, and unwilling to break the silence that had descended. Wade turned around again. I met his eyes, seeing something there I didn't expect to see despite the hard length of his cock brushing mine.

Heat.

Then Wade took the washcloth out of my hands and repeated what I had done to him, shampooing my hair, cleaning the mud out of my ears, tracing the bruising he'd caused, lathering up the muscles of my chest and back. Only he didn't stop at my waist.

He knelt in front of me, moving the washcloth over the quivering muscles in my calves, my thighs, and he paused a moment before gently washing my prick, my balls, between my legs, and I bit back a groan.

He looked up at me, his eyes bright with so many emotions, and it was almost as if he was waiting for something, but I didn't know what. I returned his stare, and he turned me around, washing the backs of my legs, my ass, and then between my cheeks. This time I didn't bother biting back the groan that rumbled up my throat.

Still not speaking, not breaking this odd spell, we moved as if by some unspoken agreement, switching places. I knelt at Wade's feet and mirrored his previous actions, cleansing the most private parts of his body, his gaze burning into the top of my head as I hesitated a moment, looking at his prick. It was hard, I could see it throbbing, and yet there was no urgency in this moment, whatever it was. I resisted the urge to lean forward and swipe my tongue across the head of his cock, shiny and leaking pre-come, resisted the urge to finally find out after all these years of wondering what he would taste like.

Feeling the familiar guilt start to press in on me, I struggled to my feet, meeting Wade's gaze when I felt him wrap his hands around my biceps and pull me against his body, our erections trapped between us.

"This is not a good idea." I couldn't be sure who I was trying to convince, myself or Wade.

"Probably not." Wade didn't sound like he really cared.

When Wade began thrusting against me, his cock rubbing against mine, the pleasure was so intense I stopped talking. When he reached a hand down to stroke both of our cocks together, I had to fight to keep my eyes open. I wanted to see what he looked like when he came.

Wade leaned in to kiss me, and I'm not sure why, but I turned my head, his kiss landing on my cheek. I felt his lips brush my neck next, and then he was sucking on the skin there. I bit my bottom lip before foolish words poured out of my mouth.

I could feel the pleasure building, my balls beginning to tighten up, and I could tell Wade was close, too, because his hand kept losing the steady rhythm. I came before he did, my gaze locked on his, an anchor while all that feeling shot right out of me. When he came, he closed his eyes and I watched his come swirl down the drain.

Listening to the harshness of our breathing, my legs feeling like jelly, my brain like mush, I had one thought: this had been a bad idea.

"Don't go." Surprised, I glanced back up to see him looking at me again, a lock of his wet reddish brown hair curling into his half-shut left eye. I couldn't think of anything else to say except for what I had been thinking about bad ideas, and he must have read that in my face because he spoke again. "Please." His throat worked. "Stay with me tonight?"

Something in my chest cracked open at the simple request and what it must have taken for Wade to ask something like that. I nodded and we got out of the shower, toweled off, and made our way to his bedroom. He got in the king-sized bed first, and I climbed in after him, wrapping my arms around him from behind.

"Dylan—"

"Shhh. Just go to sleep." When his breathing evened out and his chest was rising in the steady pattern of sleep, I leaned my head down, kissed his shoulder, and closed my eyes.

◊ ◊ ◊ ◊

Waking up the next morning, dawn's fingers reaching through the window, it took a moment to realize where I was and who was wrapped around me. Sometime in the night, Wade and I must have traded spots because he was spooned up behind me, his morning erection prodding my ass and mine already ready to wave his hello.

I stayed there a moment, thinking, looking at the portrait of the mountains Simon had painted that I'd hung up the other day. Looking around the rest of the room, ignoring the fact that my right eye was practically swollen shut, my gaze snagged on something bright pink and gauzy hanging in the closet.

Hoping it wasn't what I thought it was, I extricated myself from Wade's hold, careful not to wake him up, and swung my legs over the side of the bed. I paused when my foot landed on something and looked down to see the corner of a notebook poking out from underneath the bed.

I reached down and picked it up, realizing it was a sketchbook, not a notebook. Opening it with a pang of guilt, I saw that it wasn't Simon's sketchbook as I expected. It was Wade's.

I flipped through the beginning pages, mostly of Simon, the ranch, the hands, a few good ones of Mack, a really appealing one of Rudy. Working mostly in charcoal, Wade never believed

Simon and me when we told him how good his sketches were, not that he had any reason to believe me. I wasn't the expert.

But Simon was. And I'd heard him telling Wade that he should do something with his work since after that very first art lesson Simon had taught in Big Timber, the art lesson I'd convinced Wade to go to—the start of it all. Wade had always replied that their relationship had enough "artist" in it without him adding to the load, and Simon had always sniffed and told Wade he better be happy for that "load."

Flipping to the back of the sketchbook, I discovered the last pages were blank, so I turned pages until I got to the last sketch Wade had done and just sat there looking.

It was a drawing of me and Simon out by the corral, Mack at the edge of the page laughing. I was glaring at Simon, and Simon was wearing my hat and holding his hand out. We had played poker that lazy Sunday afternoon, and when I ran out of money and didn't want to fold, Simon suggested he'd let me stay in if I bet my favorite hat.

He had squinted at me, his poker face firmly in place, and said, "Cash or hat." I thought I had a sure hand and was shocked when Simon snatched his winnings right off my head. The little shit taunted me, wearing that hat around the ranch where I could see him, laughing, before giving it back to me three days later. Mack was right. Twisted sense of humor.

That was a week before Simon was killed.

I put the sketchbook back in the same place I found it and checked to make sure Wade was still sleeping before getting up and walking over to the closet. Opening the door wider, I sighed. There it was, in all its hot pink glory, the long sleeve fishnet shirt—or close enough to be called a shirt in some circles I guess—that I had given Simon as a gag gift on his last birthday. It was surrounded by all the rest of Simon's clothes.

A thought occurred to me, and I walked over to the oak dresser and picked up Simon's watch sitting in the change tray. Holding the watch our dad had given Simon on his eighteenth birthday, I closed my eyes.

After a few moments resting my head on the edge of the dresser and clutching that watch, I set it back down and looked over at Wade. Still sleeping. As quietly as I could, I walked out, shutting the door softly, and went downstairs.

Looking at my stiff and muddy Levi's with distaste, I snagged a pair of Wade's from the laundry and stuffed my feet into my boots with a wince. I made sure not to slam the front door on my way back to the bunkhouse.

I slipped inside, grateful nobody else was up yet—though they be would any minute—and made my way to the shower, hoping to clear my mind. And if that didn't work, there was always mindless labor, like mucking stalls.

◊ ◊ ◊ ◊

That was actually where Wade found me almost two hours later.

Well I assumed it was Wade standing in the entrance to the stall I was working in, but I didn't turn around to visually confirm. Billy or Joe would have said something, probably called my name to get my attention. Mack was working on his truck but wouldn't have just stood there watching me work either, so that just left Wade. I was a regular Sherlock.

Not wanting to examine why, I decided to wait Wade out, keeping my back to him to see how long he would stand there without saying something. It wasn't because I didn't want to see the look on his face or anything.

"What do we do now?"

I finally turned around, looking somewhere over his left shoulder, and said, "Well, I'm going to finish these stalls. You can help if you want. Then I have some fence to fix, cattle to move, a house to scrub, a trip to town to make. And no hope of a fairy godmother to send me to the ball tonight."

"Dylan. No jokes." At the tone of his voice, I focused on his eyes, wincing when I saw that his left eye matched my right and the left side of his jaw was a deep navy blue.

"Okay. No jokes." I felt naked, more naked than I had last night washing each other. I considered his question. "I was serious though, about the work. There's a lot to do if you want to hang on to this place. Take your pick."

"No, I meant about... us." He looked like saying that was as foreign as it sounded to me.

"Wade. There is no us." I made myself hold his gaze as I said that.

"But what about last night?" Now it was Wade that wouldn't meet my eyes as he fiddled with the buttons on his blue checked shirt.

"Last night was—" I paused to gather my thoughts so I could say this right. "Was good. Nice. For you, for me. I think we both needed... something. But I don't want to be your solution to lonely nights. I'd much rather you stick with random fucks for that." I saw him stiffen, and I tried to remember that honesty was what this situation called for.

"I see." Wade was clenching his jaw even though it must have hurt like hell, and his hands had dropped to his sides and curled into fists.

"No, I don't think you do. I don't think you do at all." I hated doing this to him, but I wasn't willing to be anybody's crutch, not even Wade's. I hesitated, wishing I could leave it at that, but he needed to hear it and I needed to say it. "I'm not Simon. And I'm not a substitute for him. I need you to see that."

Wade was silent for a while, twirling his black hat between his hands. "So, what do we do now?"

I leaned on the pitchfork and forced my lips to quirk. "Well, I have to finish cleaning these stalls. And then there's some fence to fix. One step at a time, Wade. Not gonna be easy, but we'll do it."

"Well then I better go find Mack." Something about the way he said it, almost as if he was forcing a light tone, made me curious.

"Why?" I asked, suspicious and fighting down a real smile.

"To see if he'll be your fairy godmother. Gotta get you ready for the ball tonight."

I heard him chuckling on his way outside, and I laughed, feeling warm inside for the first time in a long time.

A week later I woke up feeling optimistic. The ranch wasn't so far gone that it couldn't be saved with hard work, sweat, and love.

The same could probably be said of Wade.

A week of hard work was already doing him good, giving him color, removing the dark shadows from under his eyes. A few more weeks of good eating and ranch work, and Wade would be looking much better.

Wade's body might start looking better, but his smiles still didn't quite shine through to his eyes they way they used to. The night we fought in the rain had done Wade some good, but I had a feeling he might still need to talk. Being the stubborn cuss that Wade was, I figured he also wouldn't do it voluntarily, or at least initiate it, so I saddled Rudy and Blitzen and went to go kidnap Wade for a ride.

I finally tracked him down in his office, and I stood leaning against the door jamb, one hand hooked in my front pocket, and looked at him. He was a good-looking man. Tall, strong, with lines carved into his face that said he had lived a hard life. But the lines at his eyes also suggested that Wade might be used to laughing. Or had been, anyways.

I cleared my throat and he looked up. "Hey. Didn't hear you come in."

"Well, I thought about bringing the trumpeter with me, but he was busy with his one o'clock." I walked toward the desk to see what he was working on. "How the books lookin'?"

Wade winced. "Lean. Very lean."

I nodded. I had thought as much from the work I had done in here, but I hadn't been absolutely sure. Math was never my strong point. "Fixable?"

"Yeah. Sure. Barring any major catastrophes, and as long as we all keep working hard, things should turn around. Be ready to start expanding the stock again in a few months and we might even be able to hire a couple more hands soon. We need the help."

Wade kept saying "we" and I had to admit it sounded nice.

"Speaking of help, I convinced Mack to see his doctor again. He's been suffering from dizzy spells, shortness of breath, and I'm wondering if maybe they can tweak his current medication. I'm taking him in for the appointment next week."

"I should have noticed. I'm sorry." Wade looked ashamed, and I hated the way his shoulders sat.

"None of that now. Come on. Put that on hold for a couple hours, we're goin' for a ride."

"Now? I should really finish this." But he had perked up, as if he was already mentally out on the trails.

I said, "Come on. We've been working hard. We can spare a couple hours. I've already saddled Rudy for you."

"Sure of yourself." Wade didn't sound like he minded.

"Always. Until I'm not." I winked and walked out, confident that Wade would follow.

At first we didn't talk, just content to ride side by side toward the mountain peaks looming in front of us, the immediate world blanketed in green and dotted with wildflowers, mostly yellow and red Blanket flowers. I hadn't realized how far from relaxed Wade had been until I saw him sitting atop Rudy and breathing in the fresh mountain air. No wonder he had found solace in hours spent riding beneath the endless blue sky.

I wasn't sure how to get the ball rolling, how to get Wade talking if he needed to. A few teasing lines came to mind, but I didn't think that was the best way to get Wade to open up. In the end it was Wade who opened the starting gate.

"So where'd you go?" Wade didn't look at me, instead studied the mountain peaks.

I was tempted to ask when he was talking about, but I didn't. "Made my way east. Worked odd jobs until they ran out and then I'd moved on. Stayed at motels mostly."

"Did it work?"

Again I was tempted to play dumb. The hard part about forcing someone else to talk was that you'd have to talk too, in the process. But I wanted to help Wade, so I tried not to squirm in the saddle. "Yeah, some. At first it was just nice and mindless, looking around and seeing only strangers made it so I didn't freak out when I didn't see Simon. The work was usually hard, for little pay, and I was glad. Anything that left me exhausted enough to sleep was a bonus." I didn't tell him about the nightmares. I looked over and could see him gripping tight to the reins. Yeah, he probably already knew about dreaming. "Mostly, it's just time, Wade. It mutes it. Won't ever go away, but time helps. Important to remember the good times too, and not just the end."

We came to a clearing next to the creek, rife with thimbleberry and the pungent scent of sagebrush in the air. Dismounting to water the horses, Wade and I both walked to the edge of the water, watching as our reflections rippled and swayed on the surface of the creek.

Finally Wade turned to me and said, "How do you move on and still remember? How do you keep from forgetting?" I barely caught the last part, almost lost amongst the trickles and gurgles of the water as it moved over and around rocks, fallen branches, or any other obstacles in its way.

I pulled my hat off my head and thrust a hand through my hair as I searched my mind for the right answer. "Wade, moving on with your life doesn't mean you'll automatically forget all the good times. You lived with Simon for seven years. That's seven birthdays, seven Christmases, seven years worth of nights going to bed next to him, and seven years worth of mornings waking up with him. Do you really think there is anything you can do to forget that?"

Wade seemed to think about this, his head bowed and his eyes hidden by the brim of his hat. So I continued, "The important part is to face forward. You can glance back all you want, Wade. In fact, it's important to hold on to the times that you laughed with him, that you smiled with him, that you loved him. At least it's been important for me. But you've got to face forward." I felt like a fraud preaching advice I wasn't even sure

I could take myself. But I wanted to believe. "What do you want, Wade?"

"Huh?" Wade glanced at me, looking confused.

"What do you want? You must want something out of life."

He seemed to think about that, and I kept quiet, content to wait for as long as he needed. "I… I want to smile. Want to laugh again and really mean it." He paused, turned toward me until he was looking straight into my eyes. "Not sure how, but I want to be happy again."

So simple. Two years ago this conversation would have been laughable. Now it was just life. It was so unfair. "We'll figure it out, Wade. One day at a time. Simon loved you, he would want the same thing."

Feeling drained all of a sudden, I turned and swung up onto Blitzen's back. I only knew that Wade followed when he spoke again. "So why'd you stay away?"

Surprised, I looked back at him. "I told you that the other night."

"Did you?"

"Yes." Didn't I? I went over what I remembered of the conversation we had while rolling around in the mud.

"No, I don't think you did, actually. You told me why you left. Not why you stayed gone so long."

"Oh." And this was the tough part, trying to answer truthfully without revealing how I felt about him. "Well, it's partly the same reason." I knew he deserved more than that. "But it was also… Simon wasn't here, but neither were you. Not really. I lost my brother that night. I was scared to come home and find my best friend still gone, too."

That was all true, as much as I didn't like talking about it. It was almost the whole truth even. In the way that winning a silver medal is almost like winning a gold, I guess.

The silence seemed to stretch between us, screaming, and I wondered if Wade heard the things I didn't say. I could say it, just admit out loud that in addition to all the pain and heartbreak, I left because of guilt, too. Guilt that after all the years I'd spent loving a man who wasn't mine to love, loving a man that was my *brother's*, I walked away from that crash and Simon hadn't. I wasn't sure of the logic, but I guess somewhere in there was the thought that it should have been me instead. Penance for my sin.

But I couldn't say that to Wade, and add another burden to the ones he already carried. I told Wade to look forward, to remember the love and take that with him into the future. Maybe it's time I tried that, too.

Finally Wade said, "I'm glad you're home now, though."

I nodded. "Yeah, me too."

After that, we didn't talk the whole way back to the ranch house, and I let Blitzen's plodding pace and the warmth of the late spring breeze moving against my skin lull me.

CHAPTER EIGHT

"Hey, I got that new action thug movie with Kevin Bacon. You haven't seen it have you?" I juggled the pizza, beer, and movies I'd brought back from my trek into town. Wade was bent over peering into the fridge when I walked into the kitchen. I tried not to stare.

Wade helped me set things down, saving the pizza box from a near miss. "Nope. Sounds good. Lemme warm up the pizza and put the beer in the freezer and I'll meet you in the family room if you want to shower." In that respect, living almost forty miles from town sucked. Pizza was never warm by the time you got home. I ran back to the bunkhouse to shower, oddly unwilling to use the one in Wade's house.

We eventually got settled on the couch, pizza hot and beer cold just as God intended. The movie was pretty good, although not enough to distract me from Wade, sitting only a couple feet away. I could smell him, a hint of the pine-scented soap he used in the shower and something that was pure Wade.

Over the last three months, we had settled into a pattern of sorts. Working hard sunup to sundown had paid off, the ranch gaining enough ground back to support hiring two new hands and to start expanding the stock again. It was slow going, but it was steady.

Wade worked tirelessly beside me, and he smiled, and laughed, and somewhere in the last month or so the look deep in his hazel eyes started to change. So very different from when I first got back to the Lazy G.

He still didn't go to town much, only to run errands occasionally, and never for fun. So he and I stayed here on the weekends when the hands went to tear up the town. I usually rented a movie, or we watched TV, or we went for rides. It was nice. Peaceful.

And it was always the same at the end. We'd sit here in this moment of expectation, and I would wonder how he would look at me, if it would be with warmth as he usually did, or with the heat I was starting to see in his eyes more and more. There were times that I would sit next to him, scared to move, scared not move, not wanting to screw anything up, not wanting to miss out. And there were times when I was scared that we'd be stuck like this forever, poised on the brink of action.

Blinking, the credits were rolling and I realized that I missed something Wade said. "Sorry, what?"

"I said, why don't you move into the house, Dylan?"

Whoa. And what exactly did he mean by that? "Why? I always lived in the bunkhouse, even when Simon tried to cajole me into moving in here." But it hadn't felt right, not with the way I felt about Wade, so I always said no. And maybe Simon had known why, because he stopped pushing it after the first couple times.

"Well with Simon gone... it just feels lonely here. There's plenty of space, and you spend a lot of time here in the evenings," Wade said.

I didn't know how to answer that. I was tempted. Very tempted. But that didn't mean I thought it was a good idea. I said, "I... well, that's probably not a good idea, Wade. The guys might think..." I trailed off, oddly reluctant to verbalize what Mack and the hands might think. I wasn't even sure if they knew I was gay, though they obviously never had a problem with Simon or Wade.

"Oh. Right. Yeah, they might..." Wade stopped and uttered what sounded like an uncomfortable laugh. Hesitating, he continued, "I was thinking I'd pack up Simon's clothes this week. Maybe drop 'em off in town at the Goodwill. Thinkin' about donating his art supplies to the high school." Wade paused, met my eyes.

Surprised, I waited to see how much this would hurt. Even more surprised, I realized that instead of the sharp pang I was used to, missing Simon had turned into more of a dull throb. "Sounds like a good idea."

"I think so." Wade cleared his throat. "I wondered if you'd help me." He looked away, staring at the TV, which was replaying the DVD menu loop over and over.

I thought about it, about what it would mean. Waited for the dread to rush over me at the idea of getting rid of Simon's things, more tangible proof that he was gone. But it wasn't a tidal wave, not now, more like a gentle lapping against the shore. I looked at Wade still studiously avoiding my gaze, and wondered what it felt like for him. Wondered why he asked me. I said, "Yeah, okay. I'll help."

Wade looked at me again, and I couldn't miss the relief on his face. "Thanks. I'm not sure how… easy it will be. But it's kinda nice, the idea of making somebody happy with stuff that was just sittin' around."

"Simon would have liked that idea." He really would have, his heart had been so big.

Wade nodded, and then was quiet. I debated getting up and heading back to the bunkhouse, but it was calm and restful sitting here so I decided to enjoy it before it turned into one of those awkward moments of expectation.

"Dylan, how come you've never gotten serious about anyone, never brought anyone to meet your family, never really dated the whole time I've known you?"

From calm and restful to panicking and hyperventilating in five seconds. I didn't want to answer this question, couldn't answer it. I'd been afraid for years that everyone would see, that Wade would see. I tried to stop, tried to tell myself it was wrong, he was my brother's partner. But no matter how hard I tried, I never could stop loving Wade. And the only reason he hadn't seen it, most likely, was because when Simon was alive, he was all Wade could see. As it should have been.

I tried to calm my breathing without being obvious, and I looked at Wade. Stared straight into his steady gaze and I realized he already knew why. He *knew*. I couldn't identify the emotion in his eyes, but it wasn't anger or disgust. It looked kinder than that.

Wade laid a hand on my knee, and I glanced down at it, trying to figure out what to say. "I—" That was all I could get out. I couldn't really think beyond the fact that Wade knew, and I shouldn't have felt that way, not when Simon was alive, and somehow it made it worse that I still felt that way now .

"It's alright, Dylan. He probably knew. You didn't do anything wrong." Wade's voice was gentle, as if he were talking to a spooked horse.

"I shouldn't have…" Shouldn't have loved Wade. Shouldn't have walked away from that crash when Simon didn't.

"It's alright. He loved you." At this gentle comfort from Wade of all people, something released inside of me. I could feel it, like a great big gust of air or the rush of water over the banks of the creek in spring.

I had carried this around with me for so long, and it was finally demanding to be let out.

I was the one who cried this time, Wade holding me close and telling me it would be okay.

I was tempted to avoid Wade after crying in his arms like that, but on Sunday he showed up at the bunkhouse looking pale and nervous as he asked me if I was ready to go through Simon's things. He didn't mention the conversation from Friday night, or my tears.

I didn't say it, but there are some things in life you're just never ready for.

But I followed him over to the ranch house, feeling all the dread I hadn't felt a couple nights ago when Wade first asked for my help. Why had I agreed to this? We were going to give my brother's things to strangers.

Wade didn't speak as we made our way through the house and up the stairs, and the sound of our boot heels hitting the hardwood floor was like a steady pounding drum. It echoed through me, and I forced myself to take deep breaths past the dread that was like a vise around my throat. I was scared I'd start choking any minute.

I didn't know how Wade could be so calm about this, so collected.

We stepped into his bedroom and I noticed the bed was made, the brown striped quilt smoothed neatly into place. There were a couple boxes by the open closet door, sitting at the ready, waiting for us to pack up a life. We'd put Simon's things into them and we'd haul them to town and some stranger would look at it all like it was just stuff.

Even if it was just stuff.

Still Wade didn't speak, and I looked over at him. He had his hands stuffed in the pockets of his Levi's and he stood there looking around the room like he'd never seen it before.

No, he wasn't calm and collected. He looked lost.

And then it wasn't so hard to control myself. Every breath wasn't a fight, and I didn't have to lock my knees to keep from bolting out of the room. It didn't take two guys to put some clothes into boxes. Wade had asked me because he couldn't do it alone.

"Well, I guess we'll start with the clothes. Is there anything you'd like to keep?" I asked.

"Um. Yeah. I think so." Wade sounded so uncertain and I watched as he walked over to the closet. He ran a finger along the clothes hanging there, pausing every once in a while, but he moved on until he got to his side of the closet. Then he stood there unmoving in front of the clothes for another minute before finally uttering a pained little laugh, shaking his head a bit, and turning to look at me. "No... I guess not. His hat's downstairs. I'll keep that, but... this is just stuff."

"Yeah, clothes don't maketh the man." I briefly closed my eyes, wondering why I always do that. Expecting to see a scowl on Wade's face, I opened my eyes and instead caught his small smile.

"No, they definitely don't. Especially not when Simon had such... interesting taste." Wade fingered the pink fishnet shirt I'd given Simon.

I couldn't hold back a smile at that either. "But Simon didn't pick that out. I did. As a joke."

"Yeah, but Simon liked it, I think. If he could have gotten away with it without getting his ass kicked, I think he would have worn it. It was the artist in him. Different time, different place and I think he would have shocked us all." Wade grinned.

"Yeah, Simon always was... colorful." I had a grin of my own, thinking back.

Wade snorted. "Yeah. I always told him that's why I preferred to work with charcoal. He used up all the color in our lives before I could get to it."

I chuckled, recalling a time or two when I'd heard Wade say that. Simon had always sniffed, careful not to let Wade see his smile. I opened my mouth to speak, but Wade's sigh cut me off.

"Some days I wonder if I'll ever get that color back." And just like that, the smiles were gone. He walked over to the window before continuing, "But then some days I wake up, and the world looks like it's about to burst, there's so much there."

I nodded. I knew exactly what he meant. Good moments and bad. A different reality to adjust to, and the underlying feeling that you'd never quite reach adjustment. I didn't know what to say, but then maybe Wade didn't really need me to say anything. Maybe he just needed someone to listen to him.

His back looked stiff, his muscles tense, as he stood looking out into the bright afternoon sun. Quiet for long enough to make me think he'd forgotten I was even standing there, he said, "Do you know what the worst time is?" He didn't wait for me to answer. "Sometimes I have dreams about Simon. Almost like memories. He's happy and so... alive. And then I wake up. I wake up and I remember. But it's that transition from one second to the next, one where he's still here to one where he's not. It's like losing him all over again and—" His voice broke and he went silent.

I knew exactly what he meant. I also knew..."But it's also like having him all over again. The dreams, they're the best times, too."

The muscles in Wade's back relaxed and he glanced over his shoulder at me. "I—yeah. The best times, too." He looked grateful, though I couldn't figure out why. For listening to him? I hoped he knew what it meant to me, too. I almost told him so, but my throat still felt too tight.

"Alright. Let's do this. You ready?" I didn't have any trouble getting that out.

I could see Wade take a deep breath. He said, "Yeah. I'm ready."

We worked side by side after that, folding up Simon's clothes and putting them into the boxes, clearing half the closet and emptying drawers. At one point Wade turned to me, looking straight into my eyes, and echoed what he said a few months ago, "I'm glad you're here, Dylan."

He didn't look as lost as he had when we first walked into the room. He didn't look as pale either, his tanned facing holding more of its natural color than it had all day.

For the first time in a long time, I was glad I was here, too.

◊ ◊ ◊ ◊

Barely a week later, I stepped out of the bunkhouse on my way to my truck. I was running into town to pick up pizza and a movie for Wade's and my usual Friday night festivities.

It had been a good week. After we finished packing up Simon's things, I drove with Wade into town the next day to donate it. It didn't hurt as much as I thought it would. It really was just stuff. We were keeping all the best things left of Simon.

The weather was getting cooler, the breeze carrying a distinct chill as we settled into fall. I spent the last few days helping the boys move cattle. I didn't see much of Wade, since he spent the time cleaning up his office. I felt glad about that. Even if he had been keeping up the books, the last few months his desk had been covered in papers and his filing system seemed to have taken a vacation. It was good that he was picking up old habits again.

It felt familiar, which was nice.

Wade never mentioned the conversation we had last Friday night. More to the point, he never mentioned the way I felt about him, the way I had always felt about him. He acted as if nothing was out of the ordinary, and I was grateful. If I thought about it all, my stomach would start cramping.

But it looked like things were back to normal, or as normal as they ever would be.

I was just opening the door to hop in my truck when I happened to glance over towards the pond. Just beyond it and to the left a little, a lone figure stood in the shade of the big cottonwood tree on the grassy knoll where Wade's ancestors were buried. Where Simon was buried.

I paused with one foot resting on the runner of my truck, and wondered why my stomach flipped. I knew that Wade must visit Simon's grave. Yeah, I must have known that.

So there was really no reason for me to feel like I just took a punch to the gut. Just because I was too chicken shit to face where we buried my brother didn't mean Wade was.

I had managed to avoid the spot since I came back to the Lazy G, telling myself it didn't matter. Why did I think Wade avoided it, too?

Maybe it was just a simple case of needing to see it with my own eyes.

Shaking my head, I got in my truck before Wade could turn around and head back towards the house. I didn't know what I would say to him just then.

I was still thinking about it, though, when I returned to the ranch. I thought about it during the drive into town and the drive back. Then I thought about it watching the movie. I couldn't have said what we even watched. I ignored the puzzled looks Wade kept sending my way.

I thought about it as I got ready for bed, thought about it as I lay there and prayed for a dreamless sleep.

I was still thinking about it the next morning as I walked slowly over to my brother's final resting place.

I stopped in front of Simon's grave, a quick glance showing that the headstone was less weathered than those of Wade's deceased family members. Looking up at the tree branches overhead, the leaves quietly rustling in the breeze, I tried to force my gaze back to the spot where my brother was buried, but I couldn't.

This was much harder than I thought it would be.

The tree seemed as if it were whispering to me, though the language was foreign, and I stared until I had a slight crick in my neck. Still I couldn't look down.

Wiping my forehead with the back of my hand, I concentrated on taking deep, even breaths.

"I'm sorry." My heart stuttered and I stopped breathing for a moment before I realized that I had said those words out loud. I thought that through, surprised at what I meant. A million reasons to be sorry, but only one that really mattered now.

Feeling awkward speaking out loud, but needing to get this out, I said, "I'm sorry I ran away. I was trying to outrun the pain, not your memory." I felt something shift inside of me, settling. Standing there, I looked over at the mountains in the distance, picturing Simon smiling at me. "I miss you, brother."

A bird sang softly nearby and I finally looked down at Simon's headstone. The words, "He was loved," were engraved below his name.

I cleared my throat, ignoring the burning in my eyes, and said, "Yes, Simon. You were."

CHAPTER TEN

Later that night I hesitated at the door of the bunkhouse. I had just returned from dinner at Erin's house in town. When I had asked Wade to go, he claimed he still had to finish organizing his office. Which sounded like what it was: an excuse.

A couple of Wade's lights were still on, and I made a quick decision, thinking about the disappointed look on Erin's face.

I didn't bother knocking, just walked in and headed for Wade's office. Not surprised when I didn't find him—or at how immaculate his desk looked—I headed for the family room. Wade was there, sitting in a pair of thin black sweatpants and watching what looked like, from a quick glance at the Duke, The Alamo.

"Hey," I said. Wade looked over at me, surprised.

"Hey, Dylan. How was dinner?" He straightened up from his slouch and I tried to ignore the expanse of bare, tanned skin.

"Oh, you know. The usual." I walked over and sat down at the other end of the couch. "A regular circus."

"I bet." Looking puzzled, Wade was quiet for a moment, then asked, "How's Erin?"

"Oh, you know. The usual. A talented ringleader, our Erin is."

Wade smiled briefly at that. "Yeah, she is."

When Wade didn't speak again, I said, "Why didn't you come to dinner?"

"I told you, I wanted to finish up the office. Get things done."

"Wade. Come on. I just looked in there, it doesn't get more organized than that, and I'm betting it was like that this morning when Erin called to invite us to dinner." Wade started to interrupt, but I kept talking. "Why won't you go into town for anything but errands?"

"I… I'm not ready. That sounds dumb, I know, but it's the truth." I could see the flush lining Wade's cheekbones.

"No, I don't think that's dumb. But Erin and Mike are family. They miss you."

"I, well, it feels safe here. Which sounds even dumber than saying I'm not ready, I know." Wade's voice had gone all soft and quiet, like when he was uncomfortable about something, and he was staring at his lap.

I wasn't sure what to say that wouldn't embarrass him more. I understood what he meant. The ranch was a comfort zone for him. Familiar. Someday he'd wouldn't need that—maybe that would be how I'd know he was ready to start living again—but until then, I wouldn't push it.

Much.

Trying to put him at ease, I said, "Well, I'm not sure how safe you'll feel when I tell you that I invited Erin and Mike and the girls over for dinner here next Saturday. When Erin's around, I don't think anyone is safe."

He looked up at me, but didn't smile as I expected. "Dylan—"

I cut across his words. "Ya know, when it comes right down to it, she's your sister, too. You can't keep avoiding her. And don't you miss your nieces?"

The look in Wade's eyes softened. "Yeah, I do. It just… well, yeah you're right. I do miss them, and I'm surprised Erin hasn't come barging in here demanding to know why I haven't been out to see her."

"She's shown admirable restraint." I smiled at Wade, letting my gaze drop to his chest for only a moment. One weak moment. He looked really good sitting there—and completely oblivious to my roving gaze. "Seriously though, she's been giving you the space she thinks you need, but I don't think it's been easy for her. She misses you a lot, and she worries because you rarely leave the ranch."

"I will. Just… not yet. You're right, though. I'm glad you invited them." Realizing I was staring at his mouth as he talked, wanting to move over until I was close enough to trace his lips with my tongue, I decided it was time to go.

"Good." I stood up and tossed over my shoulder on my way out of the room, "And look at it this way, Wade. The circus is coming to the ranch and we'll have front row seats."

His soft chuckle followed me into the chilly night air.

◊ ◊ ◊ ◊

I pulled the roast out of the oven just as the screen door slammed at the front of the house.

"Honey, I'm home!" Wade sounded chipper, even if his words made me roll my eyes. Okay, so a tiny part of me thought they sounded kind of nice, despite the fact that I somehow got slotted as June in this episode.

"Oh Ward, please remember to take off your boots, or I may have to skimp on your 'hunka' dessert." My '50s housewife impression left a lot to be desired, although I could try and warble with the best of them.

Wade was chuckling as he walked into the kitchen. "Aw, June, have you been slaving away at the stove all day?"

I liked that Wade got my sense of humor, and I liked even more how genuine the sparkle in his eyes was.

He seemed… happier this last week, like maybe packing up Simon's things had done him some good, deep down inside. His eyes looked warmer, if that was possible, and the jokes came more readily. Wade just seemed… easier in his skin.

I was glad.

And if I was a little frustrated that sometimes Wade would level a look at me—intense, possessive, full of heat—before turning and walking away, well I wasn't thinking about that. Much.

I just wish I knew what to expect from Wade, whether I was coming or going with him these days.

Well, I knew I wasn't coming, that was for sure. But it would be nice to know whether I was going to get the buddy-buddy-Wade or the I-want-to-fuck-you-but-I-still-need-time-Wade. Considering they both came with a dream ranch, no batteries required, and matching horsies, I should probably be happy playing with either edition.

"Yeah, Erin and Mike and the girls will be here any minute. And so will the 'special' guest." Erin had invited one of her employees, a kid named Scott who was home for the summer before he finished up his final year at MSU-Billings. She had said on the phone the other night that she felt bad for him, his parents didn't seem thrilled with his existence—according to him anyways, but that could be leftover teenage angst—and he didn't appear to have many friends. I was used to Erin bringing home strays over the years, so I told her to bring him along to dinner.

Only now it felt just a little bit more formal than it would have been with just family. Thus my meager attempts in the kitchen. I wasn't a great cook, but I was a damn sight better than Wade, so I'd been giving it my best shot for the last two hours. Not too shabby, actually, if I did say so myself. The roasted carrots and potatoes looked really good.

There was a knock on the front door, and I turned to Wade and said, "They didn't barge in, so I'm assuming that's Scott. Erin gave him directions so he didn't have to ride with the girls. You should go wash up unless you want to impress him with your eau de stables."

As I went to move past him, Wade hooked his arm around my neck and pulled my face up against his neck. "You sayin' I stink?"

Yeah he had a bit of the stables about him, but he also smelled like sweat and man. I resisted the urge to rub my nose against him as I took a deep breath to savor the scent of Wade, resisted the urge to dip my tongue in the tanned hollow of his throat. I shoved away from him before my body started to tell him how very appealing I found this headlock. "Definitely no dessert for you now." He left to go get ready.

Answering the door, I was surprised. I had been expecting some awkward, pimply-faced kid, not blond-blue-eyed-All-American-Joe-next-door. "Hi, you must be Scott. I'm Dylan." The kid met my eyes confidently, returned a strong handshake. This was the kid that nobody liked?

I didn't have time to pursue that thought because Erin and family arrived then, and there was much shrieking and giggling that took place as I squeezed the breath out of Amelia and tossed Molly into the air, straining a bit. She must have been getting too old for that, because the other option was that *I* was getting too old, and wasn't that a scary thought.

"Hey you," I said as I pulled my sister into a bear hug. I lowered my voice and said against her ear, "So why did you really invite that kid?" She didn't answer, the sneak, and I had been her brother long enough to know that something was up.

The greetings finally over, even after repeating them a second time when Wade came down the stairs fresh from his shower, I ushered everyone into the dining room to eat so the food wouldn't get cold.

We sat down, Wade at the head of the table, Scott on his right and Erin on his left, said grace, and I left everyone else to make small talk amidst the sound of clanging silverware and closed-mouthed chewing. Well, looking at Molly, maybe not closed-mouth chewing for everyone. I contemplated Scott.

"So tell me, what are you studying, Scott?" This was probably Wade's best attempt at dinner table conversation.

"I'm an English Literature major." Scott looked earnest and I didn't think I should chime in with something along the lines of, "What the hell are you gonna do with that?"

"Ah. That's interesting. Seems like Erin's coffee shop is a good place to work," Wade said. I barely refrained from rolling my eyes. Was Wade even trying? And was this how the whole evening was going to go?

I glanced around the table, taking in Mike, who was studiously applying himself to his second helping of roast, the two little girls who were conducting a whispered conversation, and finally Erin, who was looking at the exchange between Wade and Scott with interest. I looked back to see Scott blushing slightly and smiling shyly at Wade. Ding, ding, ding, we have a winner. This time I didn't bother to refrain from rolling my eyes.

"Erin, could I have your help in the kitchen?" She shook her head no, an evil grin on her face. Little sisters were still the pits no matter how old you were. "Please?"

"Dylan, you know I've never been a hit in the kitchen." Erin was truly evil. If I had said that about her, I wouldn't have turned my back on her for weeks. I opened my mouth to agree with her, damn the consequences.

And cue Mike, ever the diplomat. "But you do bake a fine chocolate cake. Doesn't she, girls?" The girls must have known which side their cookies were frosted on, because they stopped whispering long enough to agree with their father. As for Mike, he just smiled at his wife, and I cringed, thinking there was something unnatural about seeing a man look at one's baby sister like that, even if they had been married for nine years now.

But back to the matter at hand. "Oh, you know me, I'm just hopeless with desserts. I try and I try and still, it eludes me. How *do* you get your chocolate cake so chocolate? I think that's where that whole mystique problem came from. Betty's cake was just never chocolate enough." Erin rolled her eyes, but finally followed me into the kitchen, probably eager to tell me to shut up before I scared off young Scott.

I grabbed the store-bought chocolate cake out of the fridge and pulled out a plate to put it on, trying to keep my voice quiet as I said, "What are you doing?"

"I don't know what you mean. I *was* eating dinner until you rudely demanded my help." I'd seen that butter-wouldn't-melt-in-my-mouth look too many times over the years to be fooled.

"No. Scott. He doesn't look like the misfit type to me."

"He is, actually. Small town, most of his high school friends moved away. His parents are pretty hateful, though they pay his tuition." She started to say something else, but then bit her lip.

"So you thought you'd bring him out here for dinner, throw him in front of Wade, and sit back while the magic happened?" I turned around and braced my hands on the edge of the counter, consciously relaxing the muscles in my shoulders and back so Erin wouldn't know how much the idea bothered me.

"No, you dolt. Actually, I brought him out here thinking magic might happen with *you*." Her voice rose on the last bit, and I glared at her over my shoulder.

"Keep your voice down."

"Oh, like they really think I'm helping you with your cake." Her voice sounded annoyed.

"Whatever."

"Dylan." She sounded hesitant. "How long are you going to stay out here, playing house, waiting for Wade to look at you and realize he's ready to move on?"

It didn't surprise me that Erin knew how I felt about Wade. "Is that what you think I'm doing out here? Just waiting for my chance?" I'd poured blood, sweat, and even a few unmanly tears into this place over the years, and I'd worked damn hard these last few months to save that. Besides, Wade was my good friend, had been before he and Simon ever got together.

I felt her come up behind me, lay her hand between my shoulder blades, a gentle reminiscence of our mother, and say, "Not at first, no. And maybe not even completely now either. I'm not blind. I see the work this place needs. But... I'm not blind. Wade's not broken anymore, you know?" She paused, and I closed my eyes, both unwilling and desperate at the same time to hear what she had to say. "He's going to wake up someday soon and realize he deserves to be happy again, and he's going to go looking, and I'm just scared he might not go looking for you. I love you, Lynnie, and I just don't want you hurt."

I bowed my head and tried not to think about how much the idea hurt. Erin hugged my back, probably feeling bad, and I turned around to return the hug properly. For all the teasing, Erin was a gentle little thing, and she'd always hated to see anybody hurt, but most especially her brothers. "Don't worry about me, Erin. I'll be fine." I sure hoped so, anyways.

She pulled back, patted my shoulder, again so reminiscent of our mother. "We should go back in before my girls think we're eating the cake without them and come looking."

"Oh, yeah. Sure. We'll just tell them we had to make it just chocolate enough for them." I picked up the plate. "How'd you know Scott was gay, anyways? He tell you?" Kid didn't seem like the type to just go blurting that out.

Erin blushed, her pale cheeks a fiery red. "Um."

Now this looked like it might be interesting. The brother in me decided I couldn't just let it go, even if the occupants of the dining room mutinied. I set the cake down. "Spill. Make it quick though before we're discovered."

She gave a nervous laugh. "Well, the other day I saw him reading in the back room while on break."

I waited, but she looked like that was all she'd offer up. "Well, hot damn, Erin. Book the tickets for Washington. Somebody better tell those folks at the Department of Ed that it's *reading* that makes you queer." She glared at me. "So what was he reading? The Gay Kama Sutra?"

She sighed and said, "No, nothing like that. The title, *The Good Thief* didn't shriek it and the cover wasn't that obvious either, although it did have two guys on it. I probably wouldn't have given it another thought, but he blushed and stammered and raced back to the front. So I took a look."

"And?"

"And it was... well, basically a romance. But between two guys. With, ya know, sex and everything." Now she was beet red again.

"Sex and everything?" An odd thought struck me. "You read it."

"Um." She looked reluctant to answer, but then she smiled. "Okay. Yeah. I read it. When I realized what it was, I was really curious. I asked Scott if I could borrow it and when I started reading it, holy cow, I couldn't put it down. It was hot, and awesome, and I can't wait for the author's next release." With that, she grabbed the cake off the counter and walked back towards the dining room, leaving me to ponder the fact that my sister was reading gay romance.

Deciding that thought needed reexamining later, I went back to the dining room to find Wade talking about the ranch, Scott hanging on his every word, and Erin and Mike trying to settle the fight between the girls over the cake.

I sat down, figuring I might as well see how chocolate the chocolate cake was after all that. I was just digging in when Molly stopped antagonizing her sister and said, "Uncle Dylan?"

"Yeah, Molly Dolly?" How cute, she had cake on her cheek.

"You and Uncle Wade are married now, right?" She waited expectantly for an answer.

Why was it that kids always zeroed in on exactly the wrong thing to say at the worst time? The table was dead silent, and I could feel everyone looking at me, feel Wade looking at me. I didn't know how to answer, and shot a pleading look at Erin, but she was just watching me. I couldn't believe she was seriously going to make me field this one.

"No, Molly, we're not." I was saved by having to say anything else when Dwayne, one of the new ranch hands, appeared in the doorway.

"I'm real sorry to interrupt, but can I talk to you a minute, Wade?" I was curious what this might be about, but with Mack visiting his daughter in Michigan 'til Wednesday it could be any number of things.

"Sure thing, Dwayne. We were just finishing up, and then I was going to give Scott here a tour of the ranch, but I'm sure Dylan can start it off and I'll catch up. Let's go to my office."

As Wade stood up to leave, Erin said, "Well, we should be going. I have to open up the shop tomorrow morning. Don't feel like you have to go yet, though, Scott. I'm sure Dylan will be more than glad to give the tour one-on-one." She smiled at me, the glint back in her eyes.

We all said our good-byes, the girls hugging me sweetly, and Erin taking an extra long time to hug Wade and whisper something in his ear. Whatever it was made him look at me, the oddest look on his face, then swing his gaze to Scott standing near the door, waiting to start his exciting tour of ranch life.

◊ ◊ ◊ ◊

Finishing up the tour in the stables, I introduced Scott to Blitzen. He wasn't really the cowboy type, but to give him credit, he had listened and looked interested as I showed him around and he had a nice, gentle rub for Blitzen, who hung her head over the stall door.

"So what do you think? Ready to quit school and join the rodeo?" I wondered where Wade was, and why he didn't catch up with us.

Scott laughed. "Um, no, not exactly. It's really pretty out here, but the only thing I'd really want to get my hands on would be the cowboys." He blushed, as if he hadn't meant to say that. It was cute, I decided. He was cute. Cute and young, that was for sure.

"Yeah, I know what you mean."

He turned toward me, propping his arm on the stall door, mirroring my position. Barely a foot separated us. "So. You come into town much?"

I had kind of been expecting something like this. All the furtive looks at my ass out of the corner of his eye, and the subsequent blushing as we walked around. I tried to think of the best way to let him down gently. Honesty was probably the best idea. "Nope, not really. Just for errands. No time or interest for anything else." There. That was plain as day, and I could see Scott heard what I was saying by the disappointed look on his face.

"Hey, you done with the tour?" I turned to look at Wade, who was looking from me to Scott and back to me again.

"Yep. Showed Scott how glamorous ranching is, and I'm trying to talk him out of giving up school to become a ranch hand." I wasn't sure why I felt like I just got caught with my hand in the cookie jar, but I didn't like it. "Everything okay with Dwayne?"

"Yeah. Fine." Wade just continued to look at us. I could feel my muscles starting to tense.

"Um, this was really nice, but I should be going. Thanks for dinner and the tour. I had a very nice time." Scott kept shooting uncertain looks between Wade and myself, probably picking up on this weird tension.

Seeing as Wade still wasn't going to say anything, I glared at him and said to Scott, "You're welcome. It was nice having you."

We walked Scott to his car and it was only when Scott's car was a tiny red dot on the road leading away from the ranch that Wade turned to me and said something. "Nice kid, huh?" He looked at me expectantly.

"Yeah, nice kid." I wasn't sure what he wanted from me. Erin's words from earlier ran through my mind again, but I determinedly pushed them away.

"You gonna see him again?"

Huh. So that's what this was about. Had Wade wanted to see this kid again? "Probably not. You?"

Wade's eyebrows lifted. "I wasn't the one looking all cozy with him a minute ago."

I snorted my disbelief. "Cozy? Seriously?"

"Yeah, that's what it looked like to me."

"Well then, I think you might need to have your eyesight checked." Suddenly I felt weary of trying to figure everything out. I just wanted to sink into sleep for a week and forget Wade, and family dinners, and cute kids from town. "It doesn't matter. You'll see whatever you want to see, I bet."

I turned and walked off toward the bunkhouse, not bothering to say goodnight, even when I heard Wade say behind me, "Yeah, I think I'm starting to. Night."

The first sketch was left on the dresser in my bedroom a week after the dinner with Erin and the family, rolled up with a rubber band around it. Just back from checking on cattle in the south meadow, I didn't know what it was at first. I only realized it was from Wade when I uncurled it.

It was a charcoal sketch of Mack, left leg resting on the first step of the bunkhouse porch. He had a beer bottle dangling in one hand by his side, and his hat was off. Mack was laughing, looking much better than when I first returned to the ranch.

It was a good sketch, captured the feeling of camaraderie we felt sitting out on the porch in the cool summer evenings, showed that larger than life quality I'd always associated with Mack.

Feeling a bit puzzled, I wondered why Wade gave it to me, furtively left in my room like it was a secret gift. But I was glad he was sketching again.

I decided I'd go thank Wade in person, see if he'd give me a clue as to why he gave the drawing to me.

I found him eating a sandwich at the kitchen table in the main house, and I took a seat when he invited me to join him. Wade smiled at me. "You go down to the south meadow?"

"Yep, just got back. Should get ready to move cattle."

"'S what I figured." Wade nodded his head and continued to eat.

I set the sketch down on the table, and his eyes flicked down to it and then back up to meet mine. He didn't say anything.

"Thank you, Wade. It's nice. Mack probably would have liked it more than me." I let the last word lilt up as if I had asked a question.

"Welcome. Yeah, he probably would have." And that was it. He didn't add anything else, just went back to his turkey on wheat.

"Alright, then. Back to work. See you at dinner." I got up to leave, and I caught the small smile playing around Wade's mouth. It looked secretive.

Hmmm.

◊ ◊ ◊

The second sketch was left in the same place, the same way, a week later. I was curious to see what this one would be, and I felt a thrill of excitement as I unrolled it.

Surprised, I studied it. It was a drawing of Erin and Mike and the girls, sitting around the dining room table at their house, probably drawn the other night after Wade and I went for dinner. Wade had managed to capture the animation in their faces, like a snapshot in time, a sweet remembrance of a family moment.

I was still puzzled, felt as though I was missing some vital piece of information, but I pushed the thought aside. It was a nice drawing of my family.

I wondered what Wade would say, so once again I sought him out to say thank you. I found him sitting out by the pond, shirtless, sweat streaming down the curve of his spine despite the brisk air, and my step faltered.

He must have heard me, though, because he turned his head and looked at me over his shoulder.

"Hey, Wade," I said, as I joined him on the grass by the edge of the pond.

"Hey, Dylan." He tossed a pebble into the pond, disturbing the smooth surface of the green-brown water.

"I got the drawing you left today. It's… special. Thank you."

"You're welcome."

"Did you give one to Erin?"

"Nope." Another pebble was tossed. I waited.

Nothing. So that was it. I sighed, oddly reluctant to push for more.

"Mack and the hands are heading into Big Timber tonight to blow their paychecks in their usual Friday night free-for-all. I was thinking about joining them. You wanna go?" I looked at him out of the corner of my eye, absently plucking grass by his right knee. I could smell him, sweat and man and Wade with that hint of pine-scented soap, and I wondered what he'd do when we all went to town and he stayed behind.

He looked at me for a moment and then said, "Yeah. Sure."

I tried not to look as surprised by this as I felt. Wade hadn't gone out for a night of fun since I'd been back on the Lazy G. Something relaxed inside of me.

"Alright. They're leavin' in about an hour or so. Time to go find my dancin' shoes." Wade snorted at this. I got up, brushed off my jeans, and then said in falsetto, southern twang added in for good measure, "I suggest you try and find a shower. You're sweaty and that is *so* icky."

Wade laughed and said, "Sorry, darlin'. Didn't mean to offend your delicate sensibilities."

I didn't dignify that with a response, but I did put an exaggerated swing in my hips as I walked back to the bunkhouse, smiling as Wade laughed again.

I found myself whistling as I heated up the leftover chicken from last night instead of waiting for Billy to cook dinner. His hamburgers were always dry and overdone. I tried to tell myself to stop, but I whistled through my shower, too. I whistled while pulling on a clean pair of Levi's and a blue shirt Erin had bought me a couple weeks ago to match my eyes. Why I would want to color coordinate with my body parts I had no idea, but Erin had acted like that was a really good thing.

I was still whistling as I pulled on my boots, just a regular whistlin' fool.

But it felt good.

When everyone was ready to go, three piled into Wade's truck, and four into Billy's. I was squeezed between Wade and Mack on the bench seat. Wade had indeed showered, because I smelled mint and pine and clean just rolling off the body pressed tightly against my side.

We were quiet on the way to town, except for the sound of Wade humming. I fought the urge to whistle, and occasionally joined Wade's humming with my own when I couldn't help it. Hearing me join in, Wade grinned over at me, and Mack snorted and said something about young fools being "so damn weird these days."

We went into Ginny's Saloon, not a gay bar by any means, but friendly enough that Wade and I probably wouldn't get our asses kicked. Wade and I went to go grab beer from the bar while Mack and the hands grabbed a pool table.

While we waited for the beers, I said, "Shame we picked Ginny's."

Wade didn't look at me but I could see the grin fighting through. He said, "Why's that?"

"I wouldn't mind a whirl around the dance floor with you, cowboy. Don't think we'd get away with that here." I looked around at the mixture of weathered cowboys and young kids looking for trouble. Yeah, we might not get our asses kicked for admitting to being gay, but if we started twirling around together, somebody might have a problem with it.

"Yeah. I think you're right. Shame." Wade's hazel eyes looked more green than anything tonight, shining bright with... something. Something good, something I wanted to see every time Wade looked at me.

"Yep. 'S what I said." We just stood there smiling at each other like the fools Mack had called us earlier. I didn't know what this was exactly, or how things had changed from last week, I just knew it was warm and good, and it was running back and forth between us, bringing smiles and laughter and teasing. And the promises of more.

I never wanted it to end.

The moment was interrupted by the bartender coming back over with the pitchers. We paid and headed over to play some pool.

Two hours later, I was riding a nice buzz and starting to feel downright good. Excited. Which might have had something to do with staring at Wade's ass for the majority of that time while he was bent over taking his pool shots. Man had a damn fine ass, filled out his denim just right, that was for sure. I realized I was getting myself in trouble that would soon be very obvious if I kept composing odes to Wade's ass in my head, despite my slouch against the wall in the darkened corner.

Wade and Mack were playing for some serious money, competitive bastards. Billy was kicking Tom's butt over at the other pool table, Joe had left an hour ago with a blond woman who looked at least ten years older than he was, and Dwayne was currently trying his luck with a redhead at the bar. I decided to get some air.

I was leaning against the corner of the building in the shadows, inhaling the scent of early fall nights in Big Sky country, and thinking about the last few months and how glad I was that I came home when Wade joined me.

"Thought you were winnin' big in there."

"Nah. Old man cleaned me out." Wade didn't seem too bothered about it.

"Better not let him hear you call him old man. Unless you're not partial to your front teeth."

"Too late. And it's wasn't pretty." He paused. "So why'd you leave? Didn't want to stick around and see me get my ass kicked?"

"Wade, I got ideas for your ass, and they've got nothin' to do with kickin'." Shit, did I say that? I'd definitely had one too many. I leaned farther back into the shadows, not wanting Wade to be able to see my face.

"Oh really? Maybe you should tell me more about them, then." Wade didn't even look like he moved, and yet all of a sudden there he was, right in front of me, all I could see. The look in his eyes was intense, and the shadow was creeping over his face as he moved closer.

"I'm not sure..." I smelled the yeast on his breath, felt my hat tip up off my head and tumble down to the ground as his knocked into it, felt the heat of his body, felt him breathing. Then I was breathing him *in*, getting ready for the taste of Wade, finally, when the door to Ginny's slammed shut.

"Wade? You out here?" Mack. I groaned and leaned my head against the side of the building. Wade stepped back into the light.

"Yep. You ready to go?" Wade looked completely at ease, as if nothing had been about to happen here in the shadows.

I stepped into the light too, and Mack just squinted at me for a moment. Then he looked at Wade, snorted, and said, "Yeah. I'm about ready to head home. Stayin' out 'til the wee hours is for the young fools."

I studied Mack's face, tried to figure out if it was more than that. Relieved, it really did look like he was just tired.

"Alright old man, let's go home." I might have had the brass to say it, but I still put a hop in my step on my way to the truck, trying not to laugh at Mack's outraged mutterings that followed close behind.

◊ ◊ ◊ ◊

I found the third sketch the next morning, rolled up, on my unmade bed after I came back from a morning dip in the pond. Probably the last of the season, 'cause the water had been *cold*. I stood there dripping on the wooden floor, shivering, and I contemplated it. I had a feeling...

Yeah, this one was of me. It wasn't a very graceful pose. I was half bent over, hauling up a wooden slat, my hands covered in work gloves and my hat shading my face from view. I sat down on the bed and looked at that drawing, and I finally got a clue.

"I want you to see me, see that I'm sorry I left and I'm back to stay. I'll help you hold onto this place, I swear..."

I studied the sketch another minute, then I set it on the dresser until I could frame it and hang it up next to the other two on my wall.

I didn't hunt down Wade to say thank you this time. I realized he was telling me something, but I still didn't know how much he was saying.

◊ ◊ ◊ ◊

I spent a week avoiding Wade. I was unsure of what he wanted, where he was going with this, if anywhere else, so I did what I do best. I ran.

Every time I saw him coming, I went the other way, or tried to look busy, and if that didn't work, I hid. Not behavior to be proud of, really, but sometimes not knowing and hoping was better than finding out and being disappointed.

What a coward I was. I wondered if I'd find the yellow brick road somewhere on the ranch.

I didn't know if I was coming or going, and I was learning that running was still tiring even if it was partly figurative.

After an evening spent watching TV with Mack and Dwayne, ignoring Mack's mutterings—even when he called me Debbie D. for my "long face"—I said goodnight, my mind on what Wade was doing up at the house as I made my way to my bedroom.

Was he getting ready for bed? Or already in it? Was he running a hand down the smooth skin of his stomach, into the hair at his groin? Was he stroking the length of his prick, enjoying the feel of it slowly filling until he was hard and throbbing? Was he picturing someone as he pumped himself, the intense feelings curling through his body? Did he cry someone's name as his back arched and he shot his pleasure into his hand?

Realizing I was leaning against my bedroom door and rubbing myself through my jeans, I huffed a laugh and started stripping. I was naked and about to climb into bed when I noticed the drawing left next to my pillow. I wondered when he had managed to leave this one since it hadn't been here when I came back earlier and I had been in the bunkhouse since dinner.

I picked it up, unfurled it, ignoring the clenching of my stomach muscles, and gaped. The sketch was of me coming out of the pond, running a hand through my hair as I tilted my face up to the sun. I was decently covered in cut-offs, and there was nothing indecent about what I was wearing or doing. But I wouldn't show this to Mack or Erin, and definitely not to any kids.

I looked... sexual. The lines of my body, the look on my face, I don't know, but something about the way Wade had sketched me was unmistakably erotic.

Was this how Wade saw me? Was he answering my questions? Asking his own? Was he waiting for me to make my own move? I felt more confused than ever, and abruptly I was sick of the game. Tomorrow I was going to ask Wade what he wanted from me.

It was no surprise that I dreamed about his hands on me.

◊ ◊ ◊ ◊

The next morning I stumbled out of bed late after a night spent dreaming. I blinked sleep from my eyes and when my right foot slipped on something, I looked down blankly for a moment. I rubbed my eyes, not thinking it could be what I thought it was, but it was still there when I opened them again, so I leaned down and picked it up.

There was nothing subtle about this sketch. I was laying on a bed, back arched, head thrown back, eyes shut, as I pumped my cock. I looked at this drawing of me, and I blushed. This wasn't memory, it was imagination.

I stood there, my morning wood becoming actual interest as I thought of Wade spending time fantasizing about me, thinking of me spread out on his bed putting on a show just for him. I dragged on my clothes from yesterday, and was on my way out the door within a few minutes. At the last second, I turned around, rummaged through the drawer in my bedside table and stuck the lube and a condom in my back pocket.

Then I went to find Wade.

CHAPTER TWELVE

I found Wade mucking stalls, not surprised that most of the meaningful conversations in my life have taken place around horse shit.

"Where is everybody, Wade?" He obviously hadn't heard me come in because he jumped before turning to look at me.

"Mack and Dwayne ran to town. Billy, Joe, and Tom are out working cattle." Wade put down the pitchfork he'd been using and stepped out of the stall toward me.

"Good. Got something this morning." No sense beating around the bush.

"That right?" Wade's smile spread slowly across his face. He looked like he had a naughty secret.

"Oh, yeah. Think maybe you'd like it." I walked up close to Wade until our chests brushed.

"Think so?" Wade slid his right hand up my arm to my neck in one smooth caress that made me shiver.

"Oh, *yeah*. I should pass it on." Then we were kissing, tongues thrusting and hands flying as we both tried to touch as much of the other's body as possible. It was desperate and needy and a little awkward at first as we learned the way our mouths fit together.

I heard myself moan as I finally learned the taste of Wade. He tasted like coffee, a little bitter, and something else. Something that I would bet was just all Wade, rich and dark and so very good.

Good in the way that climbing Mount Everest is good, or the winning of Nobel Peace Prize good. There were no words for the feeling as he stroked my tongue with his and moved his hands down to cup my ass, bringing my hips up to rub my cock against his through denim. "So good."

"Yeah," he took the time to mutter as he sucked on my neck and we attacked buttons and belt buckles.

"This isn't going to last." I thought I should warn him of that, and then he got his hand around my cock. Yeah, no way was this going to last longer than a few more strokes.

"Last long enough to be in me?" Probably not, but for that I'd damn sure try.

"Maybe. God, that feels so good." He continued to pump my dick. "But not going to last long enough to fuck you if you keep doing that." I wrapped my hand around his cock, loving the heft in my hand as it pulsed with life.

'Shit, we don't have anything." Wade groaned and kissed me again. "We should go up to the house."

"Hell no. We got everything we need." I dug the condom and lube out of my pocket. "Turn around, hands against the wall." I wondered what he'd think of that command.

He didn't say anything, just turned around, put his hands on the wall until he was almost bent over, and looked over his shoulder at me and grinned. "You gonna show me how I like it now?"

"Sure am. Hope you want it rough and fast because anything else will have to wait 'til later." I pushed his jeans all the way down to his ankles to help him widen his stance a little. Talk about down and dirty in the stables.

"Yeah, don't hold back. Been too long." And with that we both froze as we thought about why. Then he turned his head to look at me again, serious this time, and said, "Dylan. Now."

I paused for just another moment, thinking that at some point you just had to make a conscious decision to leave the past behind, and then I finished rolling the condom down my cock.

I slid a lubed finger into Wade, listened to his breathing catch as I got him ready. When he began pushing back onto my fingers and mumbling things like "please" and "now" over and over, I lined up against his entrance and pushed in.

The feeling was so intense, the tight welcome of his body around mine, and we just stayed there a moment, my body plastered against his from where my hands covered his against the wall to the place where his body swallowed mine.

We just breathed. In. Out. In. Out. And I never knew until this moment that I'd sell my soul for the pleasure of breathing.

Then Wade groaned, and said, "Now. Please. Just move."

So I did. In. Out. In. Out. Like breathing, only this was ten times better. A million.

I set up a pounding rhythm, pumping in and out, fast, hard, and I buried my face in the back of Wade's neck, sucking on the skin there. Salt, sweat, man, Wade. I knew I'd never want another taste as long as I lived.

Adjusting the angle, I knew when I hit the right spot because Wade tipped his head back to rest against my shoulder and whimpered. Yes, whimpered. I'd never want to hear another sound during sex as long as I lived.

Wade was so sexy, and this felt so good, and I knew I was close when it occurred to me he might like a helping hand. Duh. I reached around and wrapped my hand around his cock, letting Wade fuck himself between my hand and my cock. I tightened my grip, put a little twist in, added a little rough, and then Wade was coming, his body tightening around me as he shot, and that was it. I was done. Or completely undone.

My climax left me gasping for breath and blinking my eyes to remove the spots dancing in front of me, my legs feeling like the merest wind would knock me right over. I leaned on Wade, letting him support me. "Are you okay?"

Wade snorted. "As soon as I can talk, I'll tell you. Have you seen my brain?" Those were a lot of words. I laughed and then Wade joined in, and I thought from now on I would always order hot, desperate sex in the stables with a side order of laughter for after.

When the laughter died, I turned his head and captured his mouth in a soft, wet kiss, lazily stroking his tongue with mine. We both moaned, as if adding this connection again was too much. I felt Wade stiffen.

"Did you hear that?"

"What?" The galloping of my heartbeat drowned out everything else. I listened and heard what sounded like a car door slam. "Shit."

'Yeah." And then we were scrambling to clean up as best we could and yank our clothing back on. I looked around for a place to put the condom, and finally just tied it and stuffed it in my pocket.

We looked reasonably presentable by the time we made our way out of the stables and saw Mack and Dwayne unloading feed from the truck. Mack glanced at us and gave me a knowing look that made me drop my gaze and scuff my boot in the grass.

Wade turned to me, "I need to make a couple calls, and I'd like to talk to you if you have a moment Dylan. Will you come up to the house?" By the look in his eyes, I didn't think we'd be doing any talking.

"Sure, I'll help unload and then I'll be up."

Wade nodded and walked toward the house, the slight hitch in his gait making me flush.

Dwayne paused next to me on his way to the barn, his face earnest and his eyes on Wade's retreating back. "Is Wade okay? He looked flushed and he's walking like he spent too much time in the saddle without a break."

"Yeah. He's fine." My voice sounded strangled to my own ears.

When Dwayne was out of earshot, Mack came around the truck, clapped me on my back as he hooted with laughter. "Boy, I don't even want to know what you both been up to. Just glad."

"Glad?" I wasn't sure what he meant.

"Yeah. You both been alone, and it's nice to see my boys happy together." Mack smiled, clapped me on the back one more time, and then ambled toward the bunkhouse. I helped Dwayne finish unloading, grabbed a quick shower, and then made my way to the main house, whistling.

Happy. Yeah.

An hour later I had my mouth wrapped around Wade's cock, finally learning the taste of him as I gave teasing licks from base to tip, swiping my tongue over the head, which was steadily leaking pre-come.

"Please." Wade was gripping the sheets in both hands, his head thrashing from side to side. I gave him what he wanted and sucked first on the head of his cock, and then sank my mouth down his length until I felt him nudge the back of my throat.

I threw everything I had into it after that, just getting off on the taste of Wade, on the feel of him sliding through my lips and over my tongue. I wanted him to enjoy this as much as I was. From the groaning and whimpering and the way his hands had moved from the sheets to clutching my head, I think he was.

I swallowed when he came, and that was it for me. All she wrote. I came without even touching my own cock. After I stopped trembling, I licked his dick clean, gentling my tongue strokes so it wouldn't be too much for sensitized flesh.

His voice was husky as he said, "Dylan that was… just give me a minute and I'll take care of you."

I laughed, and nuzzled the crease between hip and thigh as he ran his hand through my hair. "No need. I, uh, took care of it." He quirked a brow at me. "I took care of it by taking care of you." I blushed, not sure why I was embarrassed by that.

"Oh. Wow." He seemed to think about this for a minute, then pulled me up for a kiss. He moaned into my mouth. "Do you have any idea how hot that is? That you got off just from getting me off? And that I can taste myself in your mouth?"

I propped my elbows on his chest and rested my head on my hands as I looked down at him. I let a smile curve my mouth. "I think I have an idea. But maybe we should try it again later to make sure I *really* get it. I think I might be a slow learner."

Wade smiled. "Hmm. If we have to. But only if you cook me dinner first. I don't work for free, ya know."

I was just jonesin' on the carefree and happy look on Wade's face, but I was going to do it. Even as I told myself wait, later would be fine, I was going to get serious.

"Why the drawings?" Wade's smile faded at my words and I rushed back into speech. "Not that I didn't love them. I did. I do. I think they're great. And I think I even get what you were trying to tell me, but why didn't you say anything after that night at Ginny's? After the first drawing of me?"

"Ah, because you gave me such ample opportunity to, you mean?" He didn't sound annoyed, but I still felt bad that I had avoided him like that. He continued, "You asked for something months ago. And maybe you weren't asking for… for this, but I was just trying to let you know."

Not sure why I needed to hear him say it, I asked, "Let me know what?"

"What I see when I look at you." He rolled me over onto my back and leaned over me, rubbing a hand over the muscles in my chest and kissing me slowly. Gently. Telling me so many things I'd always wanted to hear, lip to lip. Leaning back, he said, "I see a friend, a desirable man, a lover."

I kissed him, giving him back the unspoken words.

"Can I show you what else I see?" Wade seemed slightly unsure now, not meeting my gaze anymore.

"Sure." I was curious as he rolled off of me and stood up, walking over to his dresser. He held out his hand for me and I joined him as he took a rolled sketch from his top drawer.

"Open it. See what I see." As I unrolled it, he slid his arms around my waist from behind and set his chin on my shoulder. I felt my throat constrict and reminded myself to breathe.

"You see us." Wade had drawn me on horseback. He was right next to me, and we were looking at each other and smiling.

"Yeah, I do." He tightened his arms around my waist. "Never tried to draw myself, but it was easy once I knew how I wanted to look."

"Oh yeah?" I still couldn't think of anything to say. No jokes, no flippancy, no wisecracks this time.

"Yeah. Happy was really easy to draw. Looks good on both of us." Wade kissed my neck and continued to hold me as we stared down at the drawing. More than I ever thought I'd see, right there in front of me. Right there holding me. I tipped my head back against Wade's shoulder, closed my eyes and absorbed the feel of Wade here in the silence. It felt so right.

Of course, it would have felt wrong eventually if I continued without *something* to say. That just wasn't me. "Well, let's hope you keep your good eyesight into old age then, eat your carrots and everything. Because I love your vision."

Wade snorted against the side of my neck, and then sobered. "Love. Yeah."

Love. Oh, yeah.

JUDAS STEER

KIERNAN KELLY

CHAPTER ONE

Thousands of hard hooves pounded across the prairie, churning the dusty soil into great, swirling, dun-colored clouds. Cattle, wagons, and cowboys alike were coated the same dull gold as the Earth. Nothing was spared from the bite of the prairie; not the horses, the water, or the food. Dust clogged the nose, parched the throat, and stung the eyes.

Wild-eyed steer jostled and bumped one another, their lowing drowned out only by the deafening sound of their hooves striking the ground as they raced across the open prairie. Granger got the feeling the herd was driven by fear, whipped into a panic by something more than the rolling thunder of the approaching storm. Flashes of frequent lightning gave brief, blue-white glimpses of the herd, and the cowboys who struggled to rein them in.

There wasn't anything that could stand in the face of a stampede, not God nor horse nor man. All the boys could do was to try to keep up, to get alongside the lead bulls and turn them, urge them into circling back. Milling the herd wasn't always possible, though, especially at night when the black was so thick a man might as well be wearing a kerchief over his eyes. Those times all you could do was hope the damned stupid animals didn't run off the edge of a cliff, or into a river to drown. The animals in the lead would eventually tucker themselves out, slowing and finally stopping, the rest of the herd following suit. By the time that happened, the drive might be twenty miles off course, losing a day or more.

Granger dug his heels into his horse's sides, giving a whoop. The horse reared, nearly tossing him off into the rioting cattle, then broke into a full-out gallop. Racing along the outside edge of the herd, using the flashes of lightning to guide him, his kerchief keeping the worst of the dust from choking him, Granger headed for the lead animals of the stampede. There was a big brindle bull out front. He aimed for the beast, drawing up next to him. His horse crowded the bastard, forcing him to turn.

Just as Granger hoped, the rest of the herd followed the lead bull, slowly turning in a wide arc back toward where they'd been before stampeding.

The herd finally stopped, milling around a while before dropping their heads to graze. All told, they'd only gone about a mile off course. Granger spent the next few hours rounding up strays and helping turn the herd, but as he did, he wondered what in the blue blazes had panicked them in the first place.

The stampede was only the latest knot in a long string of mishaps. The drive had been plagued by trouble since it took its first step along the trail. Cursed, some were saying, but the trail boss was quick to still those wagging tongues. It wouldn't do to have the men cowering in their bedrolls, scaring themselves silly with ghost stories.

Still and all, Granger agreed they'd suffered an odd streak of bad luck from the very beginning. Animals took sick, sudden-like. It wasn't Texas cattle fever, Granger knew that right off. These beasts dropped in their tracks as if felled by an unseen bullet. They'd lost several head already. Carcasses were left where they fell, to be picked clean by crows and wolves. Cook was too worried the meat would be tainted to butcher them. Then the rear wheel of the chuck wagon broke free from its axle. The outfit lost an entire day and a goodly amount of their supplies in the accident when the wagon tipped to a precarious angle. Pots and pans went flying, a barrel of pickles was smashed, and several bags of flour ripped open, fine powder mixing with the wind-blown dust.

Granger was only grateful they hadn't lost the coffee or the whiskey. A man could live off the land if'n he had to, catching prairie dogs or hares, and picking wild onions for seasoning, but the thought of a thousand or so miles of trail ahead without a drop of coffee or swig of whiskey to warm him at night was too awful to contemplate. If that happened, the outfit would lose men like water through a sieve, disappearing into the darkness in search of better conditions, Granger among them.

He'd gotten the job like everyone else. A bulletin was posted up in the saloon in the tiny town of Gold Creek, where he'd holed up for the winter. The sign offered two months riding the range, driving a herd to slaughter in Oregon Territory. The pay was good enough, but more than that, it offered the freedom Granger sorely missed. After spending the long winter months cramped up in a tiny boarding house room, he was more than ready to move on, to try his luck somewhere else.

A man like him tended to keep on the move, and a cattle drive was a good way to put distance between himself and wherever – or *whoever* -- he wanted to leave behind.

"Name?"

"Granger Blue."

"You got an address, Granger Blue?"

"I've been staying at Molly's Boarding House, here in town. My family's from Virginia."

"You got experience?" The foreman asked, giving Granger the once over. Granger wasn't worried – he knew he'd pass muster. He stood over six feet tall and broad through the chest. His arms were sinewy, his legs long. He looked the part of the cowboy, too, dressed in worn denims and a flannel shirt that had seen better days.

"Yes, sir. Rode with Mac Farrell's outfit three years ago, and for Wilson the year after that," Granger answered.

"And last year?"

"Been panning for gold out in California."

"That so? Any luck?" The boss asked, raising an eyebrow.

"Would I be here if'n I had luck?" Granger countered.

The boss smirked. "You own a horse? A firearm?"

Granger answered "yes" to both questions, showing the man his Colt. It was a pretty piece, bought brand-new a year ago, his one indulgence.

The boss nodded and made a mark on his list. "The Lazy J pays twenty-five dollars a month, plus fifty cents for every head you pick up and brand on the trail. Slow elk are to be rounded up and branded, not eaten."

Wasn't the best deal Granger ever got, but it was better than nothing. It didn't matter much about the slow elk, those few stray cows left behind by – or purposely culled from -- rival outfits' herds, or from ranches passed along the way. He'd still be well-fed for the two months it would take to drive the cattle west from where they'd been wintered in Nebraska Territory to the markets in Oregon. Besides, putting distance between himself and Gold Creek was his main reason for signing up anyway. The pay was only a bonus.

Something was amiss about this drive, though.

His horse chose that moment to neigh and sidestep nervously. Even Hackneyed could smell something rotten in the air, and Lord knew he wasn't the brightest critter to ever prance on four legs.

Smitty, now he'd been a great horse, smart as a whip, fast, and as pretty as a sunset. Good-natured, too, not like Hackneyed, who'd just as soon chew on Granger's fingers as his oats. Smitty had up and broke a leg in Wyoming just before the winter snows. For Granger, it was like losing a brother. He still grieved.

But a cowboy needed a horse, and grieving or not, Granger had to buy another. He'd bought Hackneyed off a farmer a few weeks before he got to Gold Creek. Cost him twenty dollars cash money, and sometimes Granger thought the price was about nineteen dollars and fifty cents too much.

Hackneyed, for all that he was a little slow and a whole lot stupid, sensed something was wrong. He was off his feed, for one thing. Nervous as a one-legged cat in a dog pen, too, sidestepping, tossing his head, and spooking at the slightest sound. Granger found himself looking forward to the time he could switch mounts, something he'd never felt with Smitty. A man needed a couple three mounts during a day's ride, lest the beast get lathered and drop, but this was the first time on a drive that Granger looked forward to trading his own horse for another.

The streak of bad luck had the feel of a human hand. Granger had ridden the trail with too many others just like the Johnson outfit not to know the difference between accidents and purposely planned trouble. He'd seen the wheel that came off the chuck wagon, had examined the axle himself. There were scrapes on the metal fittings; deep grooves that Granger was willing to bet hadn't come from the rough prairie.

He wondered if one of the drovers tampered with it, but kept his suspicions to himself, knowing that the surest way to force a drive to grind to a halt was dissension among the men, and that one poorly chosen word or accusation could lead to a well-aimed bullet. He held his tongue, but he watched everybody and everything, silently noting anything that seemed odd or out of place.

A young cowboy, one with big eyes the color of cornflowers that Granger had noticed before, was riding flank on the other side of the herd. He wondered what the boss had been thinking – or drinking – to have hired such a greenhorn for a drive. The boy's seat was piss poor; he was bouncing hard in his saddle, and Granger winced to think of what the boy's backside must look like after a solid week of that sort of punishment. It was probably redder than a whore's lip paint, and blistered to boot.

Yes, sir, there was something odd about that boy. His wide eyes looked too innocent, and he barely seemed to know which end of the horse bit and which shit. Granger doubted he was the cause of the outfit's worries – he didn't seem competent enough to pull it off – but whoever he was, he sure as hell wasn't a cowboy. The boy needed watching and figuring out, and Granger assigned himself the job.

The sun was already breaking over the horizon, and they'd have a full day's ride ahead despite the stampede. Later, when the sun was low, they'd pull up for the night again. Cook would dole out the victuals, and afterward somebody was sure to start passing the bottle around. Once the other men had a few under their belts, when they were drowsy and paying less attention, he'd try to befriend the boy, see what he could find out.

Granger filed his thoughts away for the moment, clucking softly to Hackneyed to get moving. Right now, he needed to see to the cattle, get the varmints moving in the right direction and keep 'em there.

But no matter how hard he tried, he couldn't seem to stop his mind and his eyes from drifting to the young cowboy.

◊ ◊ ◊ ◊

The prairie was lit by a dozen small, winking campfires, smoke drifting upward to blend seamlessly with the night sky. Small, quickly pitched tents dotted the land, most men sharing so as not to have to pitch their own every night. The herd settled in, soft lowing and the occasional bovine fart the only reminder that they were there, covered by the blanket of darkness, and watched over by the boys who'd drawn the short stick that day.

Cook clanged the dinner bell good and loud, and the cowboys jumped, moving faster than they had all day, jostling for position as they lined up in front of his big cast iron pot with their tin dinner plates held at the ready.

Cook was a short man, and round, the years were carved deeply into the sun-browned, leathery skin of his face. Years of practice showed in his movements as he ladled out a helping of hearty stew onto each plate. The smell drifted over, making Granger's stomach rumble, angrily reminding him it had been a good long while since lunch.

He bided his time, though, waiting until he saw the young cowboy get in the chow line, and then stepped in behind him.

"Sure smells good," he said. The boy turned, and Granger nodded and smiled at him. "Don't think we met afore the drive stepped off. My name's Granger Blue."

"How do."

Those cornflower blue eyes were guarded, wary. There were secrets there, Granger decided. What sort of secrets could a kid like this have? He didn't look older than eighteen or nineteen.

Sure, there were plenty of men who were married to plump young girls with babies on each hip by that age, but those men were farmers, or working on a ranch or at a trade to support their family, not out riding roughshod over a herd in the middle of nowhere. Cattle drives were notoriously dangerous business. In Granger's opinion, a man with a family had no business going up against unfriendly Indians, stampedes, rattlesnakes, flash floods, or any of a dozen other dangers Granger could think of off the top of his head.

Many boys, orphaned or looking for better pastures, joined up with outfits when they were barely out of short pants, but there was something about this one that seemed out of sorts, not the least of which was his riding ability.

Granger stole a look at the boy's hands. They were soft, pink from the sun. Fresh blisters dotted the pads of his fingers and his palms where calluses should be, where they *would* be by the time they reached Oregon.

Granger grunted softly to himself, satisfied that his first impression of the kid had been correct — he was no cowboy. He was no orphan, no street rat trying to survive. His clothing was new, and of good quality. The kid's boots were barely scuffed, and the heel wasn't worn down at all. *City boy, for sure*, Granger thought, *used to fancy carriages and gas streetlamps, not hard leather saddles and open campfires. What the hell is a city boy doing out here in the middle of God's hairy ass?*

The more Granger studied him, the more questions popped up, and the more he wanted answers.

"You got a name?" Granger asked the kid, as the chow line inched forward.

"Billy Bower." Again, only a two word answer. Not the friendliest cuss in the bunch, which only reinforced Granger's opinion that the kid was hiding something. Or hiding from some*body*, he amended. Wouldn't be the first time a man tried to hide from the law among the hides and hooves of a herd.

"Good to meet you, Billy Bower," Granger said. His cheek hitched in a friendly, half-smile, but Billy turned away before he could see it. *Yes sir, Billy Bower, you're hiding something alright, and I aim to find out what, if'n it's the last thing I do.*

Sinopa lay flat on his belly, sprawled across the hard gray stone of the outcrop. Four thousand head of cattle were far below him at the foot of the canyon, all prime beef, double-wintered and ready for market.

His sleek black hair was gathered into a long, braided tail, clipped with a simple leather thong and entwined with bits of bone and feathers which, along with his dark eyes and bronze skin, were clear indications of his Blackfoot heritage. He'd been with the Red Earth Gang for a year, and while he trusted none of them entirely, he stayed with them as a means to an end.

Bartholomew Johnson lay next to Sinopa, his pale blue eyes focused on the herd below. He was the leader of the Red Earth Gang, and the only man in the outfit for whom Sinopa felt any respect. Bart took what he wanted when he wanted it, and left no one alive to tell the tale. Until now, that is, and Sinopa grew weary of Bart's sudden reluctance to spill blood. Starting stampedes and sabotaging wagon wheels made Sinopa feel as if they were small children causing mischief. He took it as a personal affront to his manhood that no blood had been shed in several moons and none at all since they'd begun following the drive.

He heard Bart swear softly. His plan to stampede the herd had failed. They'd only run for a mile or so before the wranglers were able to turn them. Below on the dusty plain, cowboys were already rounding up the few strays that managed to separate from the herd. Bart was angry -- Sinopa could read his emotions on his face and in his movements as easily as if Bart had given voice to them.

The injured bull started the stampede, just as Bart hoped, and they'd watched the rampaging cattle from their perch high up on the canyon wall. The drovers managed to catch up and turn the beast, circling the herd back away from the drop-off. The stampede was over almost as soon as it began. The herd only drifted about a mile, hardly enough to inconvenience the cowboys.

Bart had been convinced the stampede was a perfect plan, and positive it would work, although Sinopa had voiced his doubts. He couldn't understand the white man's wish to destroy the valuable cattle, when it would have been much simpler to pick off the cowboys and take control of the herd themselves. Although the cattle were branded, Sinopa knew there were many traders who didn't care if the men selling the beef were the same ones who owned the brand.

His eyes narrowed, watching the brindle graze. The animal was limping, bleeding out slowly from the arrow Sinopa had sunk into his flank. He would die eventually, either from blood loss or festering of the wound, and the arrowhead stuck in his hindquarters would be discovered. If it was, there was only one man on the drive who might recognize Sinopa's workmanship. He was the one man Sinopa most wanted to kill, regardless of Bart's orders, the one who called himself Granger Blue. Sinopa hated him with a passion that burned hotter than the sun, scorching his heart until it felt withered and hard in his chest. He was the reason Sinopa rode with the Red Earth Gang.

The stampede wasn't the first attempt they'd made to disrupt the drive. Bart tried a few other things earlier on, all of which Sinopa knew were doomed to fail. He had planted a man on the inside, a weak-minded man named Cyril, who hired on with the outfit back in Gold Creek. Bart ordered him to poison a few head, and debated killing the rest of the herd the same way, but decided against it. An entire herd dying at the same time would arouse suspicion. Sinopa, for once, agreed with Bart's decision. Like the stampede, the death of the herd by poison would have been an unnecessary loss of gold for the gang, had it worked.

Cyril loosened the wheel of the chuck wagon, too, but he'd failed to cause the catastrophe Bart hoped for. It hadn't tipped completely over, and the losses from the accident were minor. Then Cyril started whispers about a curse, hoping to frighten the superstitious cowboys enough for them to leave the outfit, abandoning the cattle, but that hadn't worked either.

Sinopa knew Bart was running out of ideas and patience. Sinopa frowned. When men grew angry and let their emotions rule them, they grew careless. Perhaps it was nearing time for Sinopa to kill Granger, and go his own way. If he did, he would kill Bart and his men for good measure before he left. It was a promise he'd made to himself a year ago, and second only to his need to see Granger's blood pool in the dirt.

Sinopa backed away from the edge of the cliff, crawling on his belly until he was sure he wouldn't be seen from below, then stood up. Bart followed him, swearing, blaming everyone but himself for the failure. Everyone, that is, except Sinopa. Bart was smart enough not to incur Sinopa's wrath, not unless he wanted a tomahawk buried in his skull. He and Bart understood each other – they were not friends. Each used the other as a means to an end, and neither would hesitate to kill the other if necessary.

"Don't fucking look at me like that, Sinopa. It was a good plan, goddamn it!" Bart swore, smacking the front of his pants free from dust.

"Except that it did not work, as I said it would not."

"Maybe you just shot the wrong fucking steer!"

Sinopa's jaw clenched. "You are the one who selected the brindle. I shot him and he began the stampede. It is the fault of the cowboys that the herd did not reach the drop off. Why do you not simply kill the men?" Sinopa asked again, his impatience finally showing in his irritated, derisive tone. "Kill them, take the cattle. They will bring a high price."

"I done told you before – it's too risky. The Lazy J has too many friends in high places. Kill the men and steal the cattle and the army will be out here quicker than you can blink, searching under every fucking rock until they find us. There ain't too many places on the prairie where you can hide a few thousand head of prime beef!" Bart spat on the ground, like an exclamation point to his statement. "Why do you care so much, anyway? You've been on my ass to kill them since the drive stepped off in Gold Creek."

"My reasons are my own." Sinopa's eyes remained inscrutable, flat, black abysses that gave no inkling to his thoughts.

"Yeah? Well, I think maybe it's time to share those reasons." Anger and disappointment were making Bart careless with his tongue, a fact that did not sit well with Sinopa.

Sinopa's hand moved to the sheath at his waist, fingering the soft leather. Tucked into it was a flint blade as sharp as any of steel. Bart knew how fast Sinopa could whip it out, had seen how accurate he was with it many times. Sinopa didn't have to say a word. Just touching the blade was enough to make Bart back down from questioning him further.

He knew his stoic expression irritated Bart, saw his level of trust slip a notch, and found he didn't care. Perhaps his earlier thoughts were correct – their partnership was drawing to a close, and with it, Bart's life. Their eyes met in a silent duel, neither one willing to look away first. Bart bristled like a cougar facing down a bear; Sinopa stood as impenetrable and unmovable as a rock wall.

Bart flinched first, and that seemed to make him angrier. "Just make sure your reasons don't fuck up my plans," Bart finally growled, turning away. He nodded toward the horses, and they mounted up, picking their way down the other side of the outcrop, the horses' hooves unsettling a small slide of scree, to where the rest of the Red Earth Gang waited.

They'd earned their name in the Nebraska, Wyoming, and Utah Territories, where they left a trail of blood in the dirt from one end of the land to the other. Bank robberies, stages, and wagon trains, mostly, and a few homesteads as well, all of them resulting in a litter of corpses. Bart said it was easiest to kill everyone in sight, and then take what they wanted afterward. No witnesses meant no law on their tails. In that, Sinopa agreed with him.

The Red Earth Gang was a ragtag bunch of twenty or so men, mostly deserters from the army or men on the run from the law for one reason or another. Sinopa joined them along the shores of the Marias River, in the aftermath of an attack by soldiers on Sinopa's village.

His jaw tightened as memories of the massacre flooded back, a wave of sharp pain, heavy guilt, and suffocating hate that struck deep and fast. If only he had not left his village, enticed away by the promise of riches; if only he had not believed the lies of Granger Blue, he would have been with his people when the soldiers struck.

Sinopa was not a two-spirit. He had not lain with men before, but when Granger came into their village, handsome and strong on the back of his horse, he'd seduced Sinopa with lies and pretty words. His hands and mouth had worked magic on Sinopa's body, confusing him, blinding him with lust.

"Come with me, Sinopa," Granger said one warm summer night. They lay together under a canopy of stars, their bodies still sticky and spent from their lovemaking. "They say the ground is dusted with gold in California, and men fish nuggets the size of your fist out of the rivers and creeks. We'll be rich men, you and me."

Sinopa had believed Granger – and that was his biggest mistake. He'd left all he knew behind, traveling the long miles west with Granger. They passed through small towns where people eyed Sinopa with hate and mistrust because of his skin, across wide prairies, over mountains, all the way to the mining camps in California, where men killed one another over lumps of yellow rock.

They never found the gold Granger had promised. Most of the claims that proved rich were already taken by other white men; there was very little left to pan from the streams and rivers, and far too many men working them already. The great rush to the gold fields had already been over for years.

Sinopa accused Granger of lying, of bringing him west for no reason. Granger insisted he hadn't known, that he'd been told the gold was there for the taking. He was already making plans to travel elsewhere, perhaps to find work on a ranch or as a scout. Sinopa wanted no part of it. He wanted what Granger had promised him. Gold.

The two men fought bitterly. Sinopa wanted what little gold was to be had, wanted to take it from the miners who were luckier than they, but Granger wouldn't allow it.

"The miners are weak, Granger," Sinopa insisted. "It is always nature's way - the strong always take from the weak. We are like the wolf and the bear. We take what we need to survive."

Granger wouldn't listen. "We're not animals. We're not savages. We don't take what don't belong to us, Sinopa. Get it out of your head right now. There's the law out here in California. They'd string us up if'n they caught us."

One night soon after, a pair of miners passed through their camp with a small purse of nuggets panned from the river. They were both old and foolish, drunk from the white man's whiskey, and flaunting their find. They were careless, easy to track and kill. Sinopa made short work of them both and brought their gold to Granger, thinking it would change his mind.

"Look," Sinopa said, feeling proud as he tossed the small black bag at Granger's feet. A few golden stones rolled free. "There is no need to go elsewhere. There is gold here, we only have to take it."

Granger stared at the bag, but made no move to touch it. "Where did you get that from, Sinopa?"

"I followed the miners. They were old, foolish. They went to sleep, but will not wake up. Their gold is ours now."

Granger was outraged; he seemed horrified that Sinopa had killed the miners in their sleep. "Do you know what you've done? You murdered them in cold blood!"

"Are you so weak, Granger? Are you a warrior or a woman, cowering and whimpering?" Sinopa laughed haughtily.

They fought again, worse than ever before. This time Granger drew his gun on Sinopa, and told him to leave, to not come back.

Sinopa hardened his heart, turning his back on Granger, and traveled back to his village alone, but by the time he returned, his people were dead. Soldiers had launched an attack on his village. They'd swept in with their guns, killing nearly every man, woman, and child. Sinopa met a few survivors in Ft. Benton, who told him the soldiers had burned the dead, and then turned the few people who survived out to wander the cold plains without proper clothing or food. Most died before they reached Ft. Benton, ninety miles away.

Sinopa convinced himself the blame for the loss of his village could be laid squarely at the feet of Granger Blue. He had taken Sinopa's body, polluted him, confused him with lust and greed, and because of that, Sinopa's people were lost. He had not been there to protect them. Sinopa was a brave and strong warrior – surely he would have slaughtered the soldiers before they massacred his people.

He knelt in the middle of his burned-out village, and swore a blood-oath to the spirits of his people. He would take revenge for their deaths. The white men would weep as Sinopa carved a bloody trail through their world.

When he happened across the small camp of white men led by Bart, his first thought was to kill them. His bow was already drawn when he overheard their plan to rob the stage and murder everyone on board.

Instead of killing them, he'd joined them. With them, he was offered a small amount of protection. They knew the law, knew which areas were patrolled by soldiers and which were not. The gang wanted gold – Sinopa wanted revenge, and he took it whenever he could, killing with abandon. Most of the blood spilled in the wake of the Red Earth Gang was by his hand.

Now his path once again crossed Granger Blue's, and this time, Sinopa vowed, he *would* kill him, whether Bart wished him to or not.

CHAPTER THREE

Granger casually sauntered away from the chow line and hunkered down at the campfire closest to where Billy Bower sat alone, morosely picking at this food. Granger concentrated on eating, finished scraping the last of the stew from his plate, and spent a few minutes silently watching the crackling flames.

Granger noticed when Billy sat down he did so gingerly, like he was setting a fragile china cup onto a slab of granite. No doubt Granger was right about the boy having a blistered butt from riding all day every day for two weeks straight. It was a shame, Granger thought, Billy's rear end was small and round, the kind of ass that would fit neatly into a man's hands; the sort created for touching, for fucking, but not if it was covered in painful bruises.

Thunder had been rumbling and lightning flashing for hours again before the skies finally opened up. The rain poured down fast and furious, hitting the ground so hard it bounced back up, making the campfires sputter. Men swore, scuttling toward their tents, balancing half-eaten plates of stew or tin cups of hot coffee in their hands.

Granger had set his tent to the far side of camp. He noticed Billy hunkering near the chuck wagon, as if hoping it would shield him from the worst of the rain, and realized the boy hadn't even had the sense to pitch his tent afore dinner. Either that or he didn't have a tent to pitch in the first place, which only added to Granger's belief that he was a greenhorn.

"Billy!" Granger shouted over the roar of the downpour, "Come on with me, son. My tent's over yonder."

Billy looked up, squinting against the rain. He shook his head, and looked back down at his feet. The rain was turning the dust under them into a muddy mess.

"You can't stay out here. You'll catch the ague, or worse, and these bastards won't think twice about dumping your ass along the trail if'n you take sick. Get up now, and move! I'm getting soaked to the bone!"

Granger reached down and caught Billy's elbow, feeling nothing but cotton and bone under his fingers. *The boy is skinny as a piglet runt*, he thought. *No meat on his bones at all. He ain't eating enough. Gonna have to change that, too.* Granger pulled Billy to his feet without much trouble, and dragged him along toward Granger's tent, ignoring his protests.

Granger crawled inside the tent, dragging Billy in after him. The tent was small, barely big enough for two men, although it helped if the second was as small and stringy as Billy. Once inside, Granger started stripping out of his wet clothes, wringing them out and laying them to the side to dry. He looked over at Billy, who was shivering in his wet duds.

"Boy, you ain't got the sense God gave a turnip! Take them clothes off afore you get yourself good and sick. I got an extra blanket in here, you can borrow it for tonight. Wrap yourself up and get some sleep. We'll be up and on the trail come sunrise."

Frequent flashes of lightning lit the tent through the thin canvas walls. Billy still didn't speak, but looked gratefully at the blanket Granger handed him. Granger watched him out of the corner of his eye as he stripped down. Sharp bones looked ready to poke through his skin, making Granger again wonder how much he was eating. Not enough, judging from the way he could count every knob on Billy's spine, and every rib.

He was a pretty one for all that he was skinny. Those big, blue eyes of his drew a man right in, reminding him of sweeter things than dusty trails and mangy cattle. His hair was as pale as corn silk, darker now from the rain, falling in a dripping fringe over his eyes. The sun hadn't had a chance yet to toughen Billy's skin; it was soft-looking, lightly browned with a brighter, red patch on the back of his neck, and as smooth as a baby's bottom. Granger caught a glimpse of Billy's cock nestled against a thatch of light brown hair, his balls dusted with dark golden fuzz, and that one quick look was enough to set his own dick to waking up.

Life on the trail was dangerous and lonely, and it was often months before the drive moved close enough to a town with a cathouse. It wasn't natural for a man to go so long without tending the needs of his body, and most everyone indulged themselves now and then to relieve the ache. Most did it alone in the privacy of their tent or out in the bushes, spilling their seed onto the ground as quietly as they could. Others weren't so particular. It wasn't unusual to hears grunts and groans in the dark, or the sound of flesh slapping flesh.

Granger was a man who preferred the latter. He liked the feel of a man's body, favored it to the softer curves of a woman. Nothing swelled his cock faster than the scent of a hard-working man, the smell of sweat and leather and horse. It was one of the reasons he'd wanted out of Gold Creek – townsfolk were less forgiving of a man who fucked other men than the drovers riding the trail. He'd been less than discreet a few times, and folks in town were beginning to wonder, looking at him with hard, sideways glances. Rather than risk being branded a sodomite and swinging from the end of a rope, he'd signed on with the drive and left.

What he wanted to know was why *Billy* had signed on, why the trail boss had taken him, and whether he'd had anything to do with the bad luck that plagued the drive.

Lightning flashed again, and Granger saw that Billy had rolled over, wrapped up like a papoose in Granger's old blanket, a slim bundle of dark gray. Granger watched him until he stopped shivering and fell asleep, his breathing growing slow and steady.

Granger hadn't touched himself in over two weeks, not since the trail stepped off at Gold Creek. Now his dick roared to life, fueled by that one quick peek of Billy's privates. His hand slipped under his blanket, sliding over his hard belly, finger brushing through his pubic hair until they found his cock, already hard and leaking. In his mind's eye he saw Billy's bright blue eyes, and his prick, soft and surrounded by crisp, dark golden curls. His hand moved along his length, made slick by his own juices, and he bit back a moan. Faster, his fist squeezing good and hard, hips pumping up, his balls filled near to bursting.

He wanted to get up onto his knees, to pump his come onto that smooth, angel face, feed it into Billy's soft, cupid mouth, but he didn't dare. No doubt the kid would start screaming, raising a ruckus, something Granger didn't need to happen. Instead, he settled for rolling to his side and spilling his seed into the dirt, managing to remain silent aside from a few soft grunts.

In the darkness, his head buzzing from his orgasm, Granger never noticed Billy's wide blue eyes flash open, and remain that way long after Granger's snores had begun.

◊ ◊ ◊ ◊

"For the love of Pete, Billy, keep your goddamn heels down!" Granger shouted. He tapped Hackneyed's flanks, urging him into a trot to catch up to Billy's livelier chestnut stallion. The horse was high-strung, nearly too much for Billy to handle, especially since it was so clear Billy had little riding experience. It was yet another question Granger added to the long list he already had – what was Billy doing with such an expensive, spirited horse, when he couldn't ride worth a shit? "Lordy, you're going to be crippled by the time we reach Oregon if'n you don't learn how to ride proper!"

"I'm doing better. You said so yourself!" Billy countered. He was right – he was doing better, thanks to Granger's tutorage, but still not well enough to keep from hurting like a sumbitch come nightfall, and Granger knew it. He could tell by way Billy groaned in his sleep when he rolled over, or tried to get up in the morning. The boy was a walking black-and-blue.

They'd been sharing Granger's tent since the night of the thunderstorm. At first, Billy had staunchly protested, saying he was fine – until Granger pointed out to him that a man was more apt to get bit by a rattler sleeping out in the open than if he were inside a tent. It was a lie, of course, since the tent was only a sheet of canvas pitched over dirt and didn't do much to keep the critters out, but Billy, being the greenhorn he was, didn't know that. He eyed the shadows, as if expecting deadly serpents to be coiled there, waiting to strike, and agreed to share Granger's tent until he could purchase one of his own in the next town they came across.

Granger figured the next settlement would be Fort Bridger where the drive would turn due west, at least a month away.

That would give Granger plenty of nights to work on Billy, and get him to spill his secrets.

Lately, Granger was beginning to hope he could get Billy to spill something else, too.

Lying next to Billy night after night in his small tent was not as easy as Granger hoped it would be. He found himself more and more attracted to Billy, charmed by Billy's soft voice and subtle wit, beguiled by his boyish looks and big, blue eyes, and lusting after his lithe body. Whenever Granger took himself in hand – which was more and more often of late – it was Billy he pictured in his mind.

He stalwartly refused to make a move on Billy. He couldn't risk frightening the kid off, not now, when he'd finally begun to earn Billy's trust. He was too close to finding out Billy's secrets to risk it all because he couldn't keep his dick in his britches.

Finally, two weeks after the thunderstorm, he and Billy were sitting in front of their campfire, watching the stars wink on. Granger had pitched the tent on the other side of the chuck wagon, out of earshot from the rest of the outfit. It was a habit he'd gotten into when he realized Billy would be less likely to talk if he thought anyone else could overhear their conversation.

Granger stretched his legs out, and pulled a bottle of whiskey from his saddlebag. He'd bought it from Cook just that morning. Having had no luck in getting Billy to open up, he figured a belt or two might loosen his tongue. He took a swig then passed the bottle to Billy.

Billy took a drink and started coughing, choking until his face turned as red as the sunset. Granger rolled his eyes. *I should have known the kid would be no better at drinking than he was at riding,* he thought, taking the bottle back. "How old are you, Billy?" He asked, suddenly curious to see how close his guess was to the mark.

"Nineteen last November. How about you?"

"Me? I'm an old man," Granger laughed, taking another drink. "I'll be thirty next July."

"I got a brother your age," Billy said, reaching for the bottle. Granger gave it to him, and watching him turn red as he swallowed, although to his credit, Billy didn't choke again.

"He a drover, too?"

"Nah. Him and Pa had a falling out a few years back. He left, and we ain't heard from him since, except for once last winter when he wrote Pa for money."

"Your Pa send it to him?" Granger asked, feeling a stirring of excitement. Billy's father must have money, which only deepened the mystery of why his son was driving cattle. He got the feeling Billy's brother might have something to do with the reason Billy had joined the drovers.

"Nah. Pa said Bart was a no-account, and wasn't going to give him a nickel. Cut Bart out of his will, said he wasn't his son anymore." Billy took another swallow and hiccupped.

"You miss him? Your brother, I mean."

"Nah, not really. Sounds bad, don't it? It's the truth, though. Bart was always a mean cuss to me, my Ma, and my little sister, Emma."

Granger could see the liquor was going down Billy's pipes smoother now, and he pulled the bottle away from him. He wanted Billy drunk, but he wouldn't be able to talk if he was passed out.

"What did your Pa and brother fight about?"

"I'm not supposed to talk about Bart. Pa's embarrassed by him, I guess." Billy was swaying a bit, blinking his eyes as if he were having a hard time focusing them.

"You can tell me, Billy. I'm your friend, ain't I?"

"Yeah, I suppose so. Gosh, it's hot out here tonight," Billy said, popping the buttons on his shirt open.

Granger was distracted by the skin Billy exposed. It glowed golden in the firelight, as smooth as silk. "Er... so about your brother and your Pa...?"

"Oh yeah. See, Pa wanted Bart to hire on as a hand, work his way up to boss, but Bart thought he should be boss right off, on account of him being the ranch owner's son. They fought about it a lot, and the last one was a dilly. Calling each other names and whatnot, nearly scared my baby sister to death, and had Ma in tears. Finally Pa threw Bart out, said not to come back no more."

Granger snapped to attention. "Your Pa is a rancher?"

"Yup. Owns the Lazy J. That's why I'm here. He said he wasn't going to make the same mistake with me that he did with Bart, and wait too long to put me to work. Made me sign on as one of the men, told me to use my Ma's name, Bower, and not to tell anyone who I was," Billy said, slurring a little. He suddenly looked worried. "You ain't gonna tell nobody, are you, Granger?"

"Oh, no, Billy. I won't tell. So you're the son of the owner, huh?"

Billy nodded. "I didn't want to come. Not because I wanted to be boss, though, like Bart. I don't really want to be a rancher. Ma taught me to read and cipher numbers, and I wanted to go to this school back in St. Louis, maybe be a writer like that Mark Twain fella. You ever read his books, Granger?"

"Nah. I don't read much. I ain't too good at it, and it hurts my eyes."

"I like to read. Like to write, too, but Pa said no. He said I'm his only other son and I had to learn ranching." Billy's plump lower lip stuck out a bit, his pale eyebrows knitting.

Damn it if Billy isn't as cute as a bedbug when he pouts, Granger thought. He took another swig of whiskey and tried to concentrate on what he'd learned. *Well, that's one mystery solved. Billy is a greenhorn, and he was hired on because he's the son of the rancher.*

Granger realized he'd learned something from Billy that might be important. The drive experienced one misfortune after another, troubles that had the feel of a human hand. Desperadoes would have attacked the cowboys outright, at night when they were relaxing and there were fewer men watching the herd. Plus, bandits used bullets, not arrowheads.

He'd found only one arrowhead, in the flank of the brindle bull he'd turned during the stampede. The shaft had broken off, though. No way to tell what tribe it came from. Besides, Indians would have aimed for the men, not the cattle, and they sure as hell wouldn't have missed. If it had been a war party, there would have been a lot more arrowheads, mostly lodged in the chests and backs of the men, not the steers. If they were aiming to stampede the cattle to get the meat, they would've been whooping and hollering, chasing after the herd on horseback. The single arrow was the work of a renegade, Granger was sure of it.

But what about a man who was bent on revenge? What better way for the son of a rancher, tossed out on his ear and cut off from his father's fortune, to seek vengeance than to destroy his father's property, and to do it right under the noses of the men his father had hired to guard them? The use of an arrow on the steer might have been a decoy. Word would spread like wildfire, stories of freak accidents and stampedes, strange sicknesses, bad luck, and Indian attacks. No one would want to sign on with the rancher again. No men to drive next year's herd north to the grazing grounds of Nebraska Territory, and then west to Oregon, meant poor prices for the cattle sold in the beef-glutted south. The rancher would be ruined.

Billy held his hand out for the bottle again, but Granger placed it out of his reach. "No more. I ain't gonna spend the whole day trying to keep you in the saddle while you're hung over. You'll be puking up last week's beans and bacon. Come on, now. It's bedtime anyway. Got us an early day again tomorrow."

"Every day is an early day," Billy grumbled as he crawled into the tent. "Don't we never get a day off?"

Granger laughed as he followed Billy inside and doled out the blankets. "Next day or so we'll come to the Green River. The boss will likely want to water the cattle, and rest the horses and men for a day before following it down to Fort Bridger and turning west."

Billy yawned wide, arching his back and stretching his arms up over his head. His shirt fell wide open, exposing a sleek chest marred only by two rosy-pink nipples, and a flat stomach. "That'll be good. Be nice to rest. Maybe we could do us some swimming and fishing."

"Could be. Best get some shut-eye," Granger said, staring at Billy's skin. Lord, he wanted a taste, a lick, wanted to rub his scruffy cheek across that smooth skin. Thinking about skinny-dipping in the river with Billy had Granger hard again in the blink of an eye. "G'night, Billy."

"'Night, Granger." Billy lay down and pulled the blanket up, cutting off Granger's view.

CHAPTER FOUR

Trying not to sigh with disappointment, Granger followed suit. His balls ached, as they did most nights since he'd started sleeping with Billy. *If'n I don't stop pulling on my dick every night, my right arm is gonna be as muscled as a blacksmith's,* he thought, snorting softly. *Maybe I should jack-off left-handed once in a while, so's I don't get lopsided.*

He tried to ignore his cock, iron-hard and dripping, twitching uncomfortably against the fly of his denims. He tossed a while, turning from side to side, but couldn't get comfortable. His mind replayed the vision of the smooth skin of Billy's chest, and the hard, flat planes of his stomach. In his head, Granger pulled off Billy's shirt, lips locking on one of his pebbled nipples, hands working his pants open.

He bit back a groan and rubbed his hand over the hard outline of his cock, feeling a spot of wetness spread on the material. *Damn it! Get a hold of yourself,* he thought. *Get up and find some cowboy ready to get fucked good and proper. Stop thinking about Billy!*

Granger was about to take his own advice, when Billy suddenly rolled over flush against his back. He felt Billy's cock, hot and hard, rubbing against the crack of his ass. *The boy must be having a wet dream! Get up! Get up right now, afore you do something you'll regret!*

He couldn't make himself move. Billy's hands smoothed over his back, sliding around his waist, fingers finding gaps between the buttons of Granger's shirt, touching skin. Billy's hips ground against Granger's ass, his breath soft and sweet on the back of Granger's neck.

"Granger? I know you've been touching yourself. Most every night, I lay here listening to you. I heard other men doing it too, sometimes alone… sometimes not."

Billy's voice startled him. He was awake? Granger swallowed, suddenly feeling as dry as husk. He managed a hoarse croak. "What do you want, Billy?'

"Want… I don't rightly know what I want," Billy said, but his hips continued to press against Granger's butt, his cock nestled in the crack of Granger's ass. His breath was like butterfly wings tickling against the back of Granger's neck. "Feels good."

"You're drunk."

"I know it. Still feels good."

"Billy…"

"I know you've been with men, Granger. Seen you once, back when we first left Gold Creek. I got up to piss one night and saw you with that dark-haired cowboy, the one who works with Cook, hiding in the bushes. He had your cock in his mouth."

"What do you want, Billy?" Granger asked again, gritting his teeth against the wave of need that was rising to an unbearable level. It was all he could do not to back up against Billy's groin, to strip them both bare-assed and let Billy have a shot at the hole his cock was teasing through the denim.

"I want you to touch me. Please, Granger," Billy whispered. "I need it so bad it hurts."

Billy's soft plea cut through Granger's resolve like a sharp knife through tissue-thin vellum. He rolled over, his mouth finding Billy's in the dark. He threw one leg over both of Billy's, pinning him to the ground. Billy squirmed beneath him, hard cock pushing against Granger's meaty thigh.

Warm, soft, and incredibly hot, Billy's mouth opened for him, their tongues darting and sliding. He tasted whiskey, unsure if it was on Billy's tongue or his own, or both, not caring, only wanting more.

His hands slid across Billy's skin, feeling at last the flesh he'd hungered for, lusted after for weeks. Small and still thin, Billy had put on a few much needed pounds since falling into Granger's company. *He holds it well, it suits him*, Granger thought. His skin was so unlike Granger's, soft and pliant, not leathery and tough from exposure to sun and wind. His fingers found a nipple, the tiny, pert nub hardening under his touch. He slid his hand over it, letting the calluses on his palm massage the tender, pebbled bud.

"Granger," Billy moaned. His voice was breathless. No wonder, since Granger had barely broken their kiss long enough to allow him to breathe. His narrow hips bucked under Granger's leg, his cock seeking friction.

"This what you want, Billy? You sure? Tell me now, if'n you don't. Ain't no turning back once we get going. I ain't that strong a man, Billy," Granger said, finally forcing himself to pull back and look Billy in the eyes. He could barely see them in the dark, but what he *did* see took his breath away.

Guileless and wide, Billy's need was reflected in them, and it bored into a place inside Granger's heart that he thought he'd walled off a long time ago. He held Granger's eyes without blinking. "Yes. Yes, please. I want you, Granger. I *need*."

He needed, too. Sweet fuck, did he need! He ground his hips upward, feeling his cock brush the hard lump Billy's cock made against the course denim of his trousers. Granger refused to waste anymore time – he couldn't, not unless he wanted to spill in his pants like an untried boy. He rolled over to his back, arched up, and opened his pants, sliding them down over his hips. Freed, his cock popped up like a tall tree on a flat prairie. He felt Billy reach for him, gasping when Billy's fingers brushed his swollen prick.

"Wanna touch you, Granger."

He grabbed Billy's wrist, pushing his hand away. "No, not yet. Gonna make you come first." Granger's voice was gravelly, his need so great it was as if his throat was filled with sharp-edged pebbles. He knew that a single touch of Billy's long fingers on his prick was all it would take to send him over the edge. He rolled to his side again, quickly opening the fly of Billy's trousers, and working them down over Billy's hips.

Billy's cock was slender and pale, even in the darkness. Leaning over, Granger traced the hard edge of Billy's hipbone with his tongue, laying a wet trail across the flat plane of his stomach to its mate. Billy groaned, his fingers threading into Granger's hair. Billy's cock bumped against Granger's chin, reminding him of its presence, as if Granger might have forgotten. He felt the wetness of Billy's pre-come dapple his jaw.

No time for playing, Granger thought. *Maybe later, on another night - there would be many between here and Oregon. For now, we both need too badly.* Granger turned his attention to Billy's cock, taking him into his mouth, all the way in, to the root. He tasted soft silk and white-hot iron, heard Billy's gasp like the whisper of the wind. His fingers cupped Billy's balls, heavy, swollen, filling his palm, and tasted splashes of bitter salt against the back of this throat as Billy came, his strangled cry filtered through gritted teeth.

Granger couldn't wait another minute. He'd held back too long, fantasized about it for weeks. Awkwardly struggling to his knees, his movements hindered by his pants bunched at the knees, he loomed up over Billy's body. He wrapped his fingers around his shaft, pumping only once or twice before he shot his load.

It was only after he'd drifted back into himself, breathing hard and still enjoying the tingle that he realized Billy had lifted his head up and was busily licking Granger's cock clean. The tip of Billy's tongue flicked along his shaft, danced over the head of his dick in light feather-soft touches that were barely there, and kept at it as Granger's prick softened.

Lordy, the boy learned fast, and that was the gospel truth.

Granger slumped down on his back, quietly staring into the darkness, waiting for his heart to stop hammering. He felt Billy roll over, his cheek, stubbled with a beard too light and sparse to be seen, pressing against Granger's chest. Billy's warm breath ghosted over his skin, one arm wrapped around Granger's waist.

Most men were content to fuck and skedaddle, clearing out nearly before their peckers had finished shooting. It had been a good, long while since Granger had another warm body cuddle up to him, not since... he slammed the door shut on the memories that threatened to surface. He wouldn't allow them to ruin the moment, although why he wished to preserve the memory was something he didn't want to really think about. It wasn't the first time he'd shared his tent with another man, it certainly wouldn't be the last. He shouldn't encourage Billy into thinking there was something more between them. It wouldn't be fair.

Still and all, it wasn't every day he had the opportunity to lay with someone as pretty or as sweet as Billy. The men Granger bedded were rough, scarred by years of hard work, only looking for a quick fuck in the dark. *Yeah, that was it,* Granger thought. *Ain't nothing more than the novelty of it. No harm done, if'n it's only for a few nights. Once we hit Fort Bridger, I'll see he gets a tent of his own.*

Granger slipped an arm under Billy's shoulders, pulling him in, holding him close. In a short while, they both fell asleep.

◊ ◊ ◊ ◊

They reached the Green River two days later. The river cut a wide swath through the territories of Utah and Wyoming, its waters beckoning cattle, horses, and men alike with the promise of cooling parched throats and warm bodies. The drovers would herd the cattle south from here, following its meandering banks to Fort Bridger, but first they would rest for a full day and night, letting the cattle and horses drink their fill.

Most of the men were looking forward to reaching Fort Bridger. It wasn't much, certainly not as civilized as Kansas City or Independence, but maybe that was just as well. The drovers weren't looking for god-fearing folk and citified living. They wanted women, but not the marrying kind. They wanted the sort who wore face paint and little else, who wouldn't mind spreading their legs for a coin or two. Fort Bridger, home to several regiments of cavalry, had a good supply of such women who lived in a few sun-weathered log homes on the outskirts of the fort.

There were a few men who'd do the same. They were harder to find than the women unless a body knew where to look, as Granger did. In a small, ill-kept cabin set well back from the high walls of the Fort, there lived several men who were more than willing to drop to their knees, or shed their trousers and bend over for money. They were a motley crew, as Granger remembered, smelling of body odor and waste, covered in grime, living only for their next bottle of cheap rotgut.

The thought of touching any of them suddenly repulsed Granger, although it had never stopped him before. Three nights spent exploring Billy's firm young body had spoiled him, he reckoned.

Both nights since that first, quick time, Granger and Billy had crawled into his tent, shed their clothing like a pair of snakes slithering out of their skins, and found each other in the dark. They spent hours touching, kissing, tasting each other, trying to hold off coming for as long as they could. It was never long enough. All too soon one or the other would shoot, drawing the other's orgasm like a fish yanked out of water on a line.

Neither had breached the other's body. Their night play had been limited to mouths and hands only. Although Granger wanted Billy to fuck him, wanted it badly, lusted to feel Billy's slender cock slip into his ass, sharp hipbones banging, feel come fill him up to bursting, he held back.

Granger was used to hiding his desire. He fucked, as often as possible, but nowadays never allowed anyone to breach him. There was only one man on earth who Granger had given leave to enter his body, and that man had first stolen his heart and then trampled it into the dirt. He'd turned out to be a stranger, someone Granger hardly knew at all and found he didn't want to know, even though they'd traveled together for months.

He remembered Sinopa's hard body, the pleasure his clever fingers and tongue had given Granger. His ass clenched with the memory of the stretching, the fullness, and the burning of being taken, of the connection they'd shared. Then he remembered the reptilian coldness that pushed the warmth out of Sinopa's dark eyes when he'd dumped the small bag of gold nuggets into Granger's lap, the way he'd laughed about killing the two old miners for it.

No, he'd satisfy himself with Billy's warm, wet mouth, and his gentle hands, and Billy would have to remain content with the same. Granger might indulge himself, show Billy what it was like to be ridden hard, knees and hands digging into the dirt as a man slammed a thick, hard cock into him, but Granger would withhold that same pleasure from himself.

He would not risk losing that part of himself again.

CHAPTER FIVE

The small, nearly smokeless fire flickered, tiny embers crackling. Sinopa fed the fire spirit another thin branch, then leaned back on his hands and stared up at the night sky. A thousand stars twinkled, the hearths of his ancestors, and he pictured his slaughtered family looking down on him, wondering if they were pleased with the blood he had already spilled in their memory. *If it were me, I would not be satisfied. It will not be enough until Granger is dead, and perhaps not even then.*

He closed his eyes and thought of his people, remembered the wreckage of their village, the smell of charred flesh mixing with the heavy smell of smoke that still lingered there. He could hear their voices calling to him on the wind, crying out for vengeance. Their pain washed over him, he felt their fear, their rage, and again made them his own. His resolve renewed. He would not rest until he had avenged every drop of blood shed by his people.

The drovers had brought the herd to water not a mile away, just out of sight around the bend in the mossy bank of the river. Somewhere amid the milling cattle and horses, Granger waited. Sinopa felt every passing moment Granger lived as a personal affront, and every breath he took as a physical pain. He wanted Granger dead, wanted to bathe in his blood, and the more days that passed, the sharper the urge to kill him grew. He let it meld with the fury he'd culled from his people until he felt it surging through his blood, speeding the beat of his heart.

Scuffed boots kicked a small shower of dirt and rock into the fire, angering the fire spirit. It sputtered, hissing its displeasure. Sinopa grit his teeth at the interruption of his meditation and looked up at Bart, his lip curling in a sneer, a parody of a smile.

"Get up. I want to circle around near the boulders on the far bank of the river. We'll get a good view of the drover camp from there," Bart ordered.

Sinopa forced himself to stay his hand, even as his entire being cried out for him to kill, to take Bart's skin and wear it like a cloak. He didn't know how much longer he could force himself to remain in Bart's company without doing so. Bart issued orders to Sinopa as if he were a slave instead of a warrior; the sound of his voice grated on Sinopa like the rough bark of a tree against an open wound.

Instead, he ignored Bart for a moment, knowing his inattentiveness was irritating. He scooped dirt up with his hands and carefully smothered the tiny flames, apologizing for Bart's ignorance, and murmuring his thanks to the fire spirit. He rose slowly, insolently, to his feet, glaring at Bart. As usual, Bart looked away first, and Sinopa smirked. *Weak. They are all weak and deserve to die.*

Soon, he promised himself. *Very soon.*

The two men mounted up and urged their horses into the river, the water rising to their horses' chests as they made their way to the far side. Following the steep bank, they kept to the shadows of the trees that grew in a thick line several yards from the water, cautiously inching closer to the herd, stopping just short of the clearing where they saw the first few steer, and wisps of smoke from the drovers' campfires.

Sinopa slipped silently from his horse's back, his feet touching the sharp gravel that dusted the bank of the river. He tethered the reins to the branches of a brambly bush, and waited for Bart to dismount. Crouching in the tall grass, keeping his head low, he led Bart even closer to the camp, to the pair of large boulders sitting on the bank, partially jutting into the water. Climbing up, careful to keep the stone between him and the camp, Sinopa peered over the edge. His keen eyes picked out individual tents in the moonlight. He felt Bart climb up beside him smelling of tobacco and sweat. Hunkering down, they watched.

They could see no sign that the drovers thought they were being trailed. No extra guards were posted; only two or three men remained on horseback, keeping a desultory watch over the herd. Sinopa was sure they watched for predators, but not of the two-legged variety. Their task was to keep any of the steers from straying too far from the herd. None of the men looked especially wary; none held weapons at the ready.

The rest of the drovers lay around campfires, playing with cards or dice. One had a mouth organ, and another a squeezebox, the discordant, brittle notes drifted through the darkness. Many had bottles they tipped to their lips every so often. Sinopa could smell the strong fumes from the whiskey on the breeze that carried to them from the camp.

Sinopa counted forty men, at least a dozen less than he'd seen when they'd been back at the canyon. His smile was predatory, his teeth gleaming white in the darkness. At least twelve drovers had left the outfit, running like frightened rabbits, chased away by the streak of bad luck. Twelve men would keep their lives, a dozen too many, as far as he was concerned, but at least the one man he most wanted to kill was still with the drive.

He spotted Granger Blue after only a few minutes of searching. There was no mistaking him. Sinopa recognized his height, his broad shoulders and ambling gait. Sinopa's eyes followed him as he walked from the chuck wagon to a tent pitched at the outer limits of the camp, and squatted down near the fire. Another man, shorter, slim and fair, sat with him.

Sinopa frowned, feeling a sharp stab of jealousy pierce the hard shell of fury that surrounded his heart. Granger was not the sort of man to look for casual companionship. He had not frequently mingled with the townspeople or the miners while Sinopa had traveled with him, unless they had something he wanted. Who was the yellow-haired man? Sinopa squinted, wishing he could get closer. The man looked young, much younger than Granger. His son? No, Granger would have spoken of him if he'd sired a son.

There was something in the way Granger sat, close to the younger, almost touching, which seemed too intimate for their relationship to be merely friendly. Granger's head ducked closer to the fair-haired one, he seemed to be whispering, and the younger's shoulders bobbed as if in laughter. Sinopa remembered many times when Granger had done the same with him.

YellowHair was Granger's lover, then, the one who had replaced Sinopa in Granger's bed and heart.

He will die first, Sinopa decided, baring his teeth. *Slowly, painfully, and I will force Granger to watch as I take YellowHair's scalp. But first he will lead Granger to me, like the one the drovers call the "Judas Steer."*

The *Judas Steer*, Sinopa knew from his association with Granger and other drovers, was the one steer in a herd that the cowboys always looked for -- the docile one, the trusting one, who would walk boldly into the slaughterhouse without fear, regardless if the stench of death surrounded the place. The rest of the herd would blindly follow the Judas Steer to their ends. He would betray them. In Sinopa's mind, Granger's young lover would be such a man, trusting and docile, easily led, like Sinopa himself had been, once upon a time. Sinopa would find a way to make YellowHair betray Granger as the Judas Steer betrayed the herd.

A soft grunt brought Sinopa from his musings. "We should try to stampede the cattle again," Bart whispered. He pointed toward the left, drawing Sinopa's attention away from Granger and his yellow haired whore. "Send an arrow into that big, black bull. See him?"

"No, Bart. That would be foolish. Stampede them now and they might head this way rather than cross the river. We would be crushed beneath their hooves before we could get to safety. Even if we were not, the drovers would chase them and find us." Sinopa hissed. Either Bart was far more dim-witted than he'd realized, or far more desperate. "We must wait until the herd clears the fort. There are many ravines between Ft. Bridger and Oregon, many chances to stampede the herd, if that is what you insist we do."

Bart frowned and looked displeased, but for once listened to Sinopa's advice.

They continued to watch the camp. Laughter and song drifted across the river, along with the smell of whiskey and coffee. Suddenly, Sinopa felt Bart tense next to him.

"Over there, near the far end of camp," he said, pointing his finger toward the area. "See that tent there, on the very edge?

Those two men sitting by the fire, one is big and dark, the other smaller, and fair?"

Sinopa *had* seen them. Bart was talking about Granger and YellowHair. He nodded.

"That's my brother! Fucking snot-nosed bastard was always Pa's favorite. He gave Billy everything, never made him work for nothing. Little runt always walked around with his nose stuck in a book, like he was too good to get his hands dirty. What's he doing here?"

What indeed, Sinopa wondered. *Besides warming Granger's bed at night*, he amended. He said nothing, letting Bart work himself into a black anger.

"My Pa must be grooming Billy to take over as boss. He probably made him his heir, instead of me! It should've been mine, all of it, the Lazy J, the cattle, the money, not Billy's! He's the second son, always pretending to be better than me, hiding behind Ma's skirts when I got after him."

Sinopa's mind worked quickly. He saw his opportunity and grasped it. "Kill him. Kill him and remove the only barrier between you and your father's fortune. Once he is dead, and your father as well, there would be no one left to dispute your claim."

Bart shook his head. "There's still my baby sister, Emma."

Sinopa snorted and shrugged. "You would let a little girl stand in your way? Kill her, too. You will own everything."

He watched Bart's eyes narrow, his lip curling. "She'd be easy to get rid of, sure enough. Pa might be a little more difficult. I'll have to think on it a while. I might have to change our plans. If I'm gonna take over the Lazy J, then the price those cattle will bring at market will be mine."

"We will only kill your brother, and the man he is with," Sinopa lied. He intended to slaughter everyone he could, including Bart, when the time came.

Bart shook his head. "Not yet. Gotta make it look like an accident, just like with the wagon wheel and the stampede. Can't afford for anybody to suspect I had anything to do with it."

"Then I will kill them for you."

Bart's gaze cut toward Sinopa, and he was careful to maintain a stoic expression. He would not let Bart see the excitement that made Sinopa's heart pound, or his eagerness.

"Yeah, you can do it. Not now, though. We gotta get them alone, so's the rest of the drovers will think they abandoned the drive."

"When they reach the Fort, then. We'll ride ahead – we'll reach it much faster than the drovers – and wait for them. Most of the men will seek out the whores and the saloon. There will be very few left to guard the herd. I will slit their throats and hide their bodies, and any who might bear witness."

"What makes you think Billy won't go into town? He's young, but he's got a dick, and he must've learned what to do with it by now. He's been on the trail for over a month. Sure as shit sticks, he must be looking forward to finding himself a whore."

Sinopa grunted, shifting his gaze back to Granger and YellowHair, still sitting close together, whispering and sharing secrets. If there were two things Sinopa remembered about Granger, it was that he liked men, and he didn't like to share. He wouldn't let his lover touch anyone else. "He will be there."

"Well, we'll see. If not, we can get 'em later on, after they leave the Fort."

As Sinopa continued to watch Granger, a slow, malicious smile creased his cheeks.

◊ ◊ ◊ ◊

"I'm about as dry as an old husk of corn," Granger said, swatting the dust from his hat. "Lordy, that river sure looks tempting. What say we go take us a dip, Billy-boy?"

Billy looked up at Granger and a wide smile split his cheeks. He let out a whoop and threw down the rope he'd been coiling. With one backward look at Granger, he was off, running pell-mell toward the bank. By the time Granger caught up with him, he'd stripped down to the suit God dressed him in and was toeing the water.

He surely is a sight to behold in broad daylight, Granger thought, kicking off his boots. His eyes never left Billy's lithe body, dappled with sunshine. A quick look over his shoulder told him no one else was heading toward the river -- it was nearly chow time and the drovers were rustling up their plates and cups, too anxious to fill their bellies to take a bath. He looked to the right where the river bent. A quick swim in that direction might provide them with all the privacy they'd need.

Granger stripped off the rest of his clothing, dropping it on the bank next to Billy's, and splashed into the water. It was cold enough to make him gasp, and he ducked under, popping to the surface like a cork from a jug.

Billy was floating on his back a little further out; Granger struck out with a sure stroke. Reaching Billy, Granger wrapped an arm around him and pulled him under.

When Billy surfaced, sputtering and madder than a wet hen, Granger laughed and started swimming toward the bend in the river. "Come on, boy! Can you catch the old man?"

It was quiet and peaceful around the bend, the small beach shielded from sight of the drovers by a pair of enormous rocks that jutted out over the water. The far side of the boulders was as smooth and flat as a piece of glass, perfect for sunning and drying. Granger clambered up out of the water and climbed the rock, knowing Billy would follow.

Naked, they lay side by side, letting the hot sun dry them. Granger was all too aware of Billy's body lying next to him, smelling sweet and clean. He let his hand stray over, stroking Billy's thigh, grown strong from riding every day. Turning his head, he found Billy's lips waiting for him. They were cool from the river and as eager as his own.

Rolling to his side, Granger took his time kissing Billy, hands roaming over his thighs and flat stomach, teasing his rosy nipples, until Billy began to squirm. His cock was hard, casting a shadow over his belly, and Granger's was the same. His resolve not to let Billy breach him had withered and blown away like seeds on the wind. Their nights of passion left Granger with a deep, aching need. The more time he spent with Billy, the more he wanted him, simple as that. It was all he'd thought about for the past few days, and his need had grown stronger with each passing hour. Alone on the wide, flat rocks, the opportunity presented itself and Granger seized it "Want you Billy. Inside me. Think you want that, too?"

Billy's eyes flashed open wide, but there was interest mixed in there with the surprise. A small nod answered Granger, all he needed to see. He kissed Billy again, then rose up onto his hands and knees. He watched over his shoulder as Billy got up, too. He looked at Granger, biting his lower lip. *He's nervous*, Granger realized, and somehow the thought warmed him. "You know what to do, don't you, Billy?" He asked softly, not wanting to embarrass him, but needing too badly to hold his tongue.

Billy smirked, and Granger felt relieved. *At least he knew the basics*, Granger thought, chuckling to himself. *For a minute I thought I was going to have to draw him a map.* When Billy moved behind him and he felt the head of Billy's cock, slick with spit, press between his cheeks, he moaned softly. "Atta boy, Billy. Right there, easy now," Granger said, lowering his head to rest on his arms.

"Oh, sweet Jaysus!" Billy groaned as Granger felt him slide deep inside his body.

The stretch, the burn, the fullness, the feeling of Billy's cock buried to the hilt inside him was enough to take Granger's breath away. "Move, Billy! For the love of God, *move!*"

Billy did, probably going on no more than instinct, picking up a rhythm that was both punishing and perfect, riding Granger like a wild and powerful stallion. "Granger! Gonna… gonna…"

"Do it Billy! Come! I'm right there!" Granger cried, his hand fisting himself hard and fast. Just as he felt Billy's white-hot spunk fill him, he shot his load onto the rock, wet heat covering his fist and splashing his belly, his body wracked with spasms of ecstasy.

Billy pulled out of him and lay beside him, a silly, proud look on his face. "Done good, huh?"

Granger laughed, slipping an arm under Billy's shoulders, pulling him closer. "Yeah, you done good. Real good."

Lying on the rock, Billy's seed leaking from his body, his own drying on his stomach, the man himself cradled in his arms, Granger had a revelation. For all he'd tried to keep Billy from touching his heart, it was too late. He'd roped and hogtied it, just as sure as any cowboy roped a calf, and there was no way it would be getting loose anytime soon.

Fort Bridger had been built over thirty years prior, and hadn't changed much at all with the passing of time. Unlike Fort Laramie, a bustling and thriving center of trade, Fort Bridger remained a crude, barely civilized outpost. The walls, which surrounded the army's bunkhouses and officers' quarters, were built of rough-hewn wooden poles daubed with mud. As the years went by, several rows of cabins were built in the shadow of the Fort's walls by trappers, using the same drab, coarse materials as the fence.

Overall, the Fort was an inhospitable place, dreary, rough, and barely inhabitable, but it looked like paradise to the weary drovers after spending over a month on the trail without a home-cooked meal in their bellies, and only each other and the cattle for company. There were no saloons or restaurants as such, but there was always someone with a large kettle of hearty, fresh venison stew and thick cornbread for sale, or a few bottles of whiskey – or more likely, home-brewed moonshine – corked and ready for purchase. Someone was always ready to rattle the dice or deal the cards, and the atmosphere often got rowdy in a hurry.

Best of all -- in the opinion of most of the drovers, at least -- there were several cabins shared by women who were less than picky about whom they took to their beds, providing of course, that their suitors' pockets jingled with coin.

With faces painted as colorfully as the gaudy, tattered dresses of cheap satin they wore, the women would lounge outside the doors of their cabins, leaning against the walls, calling to any and all men who passed by. Flashing their legs and cleavage, they vied for the attention of the drovers. Finding one who was interested in what they offered, they'd take him inside the cabin. Often the cabin held only one room, necessitating several of the women to entertain their guests at the same time. Quite frequently the "entertainment" lasted only a few minutes – just as long as necessary for the woman to flip up her skirts and the man to grunt and grind and relieve himself. Coins would be exchanged as agreed upon, and the woman would return to her post immediately after, her kohl-rimmed, tired eyes scanning the crowd for her next gentleman caller.

There were many older men, mostly drunkards or gamblers needing money for their next bottle or game of cards, or trappers more at home in the wilderness than a settlement. Often wearing nothing more than long johns gone gray from overuse and infrequent washings, they would gather at a cluster of cabins near the rear of the settlement.

These were the men who offered the opportunity for the drovers to buy or barter for a few luxuries, like tobacco, soap, or dressed skins. None were of the best quality, but better than none at all, and the prices were usually reasonable. Sometimes, if a drover were of a mind, they'd offer something more personal for sale as well. A smile, a wink, a subtle touch, and they'd head off into the bushes to conclude their business.

The Johnson outfit arrived at the Fort shortly after noon three days after leaving the river. The men were in good spirits, looking forward to relaxing for two full days and nights of eating and gambling, drinking and whoring. Hooting and hollering, they drew straws to see who would be the first to leave the herd and enter the Fort. Those who drew the short sticks would be left behind to guard the herd. Come morning, a few men would come back to relieve them, although it often didn't work out the way it should. Someone was bound to get into a fight and beaten unconscious, sometimes killed. One or two would curl up in a dark corner somewhere to sleep off a drunk. Either way, it was likely that not everyone who went into town in the first wave would come back as planned. Because of that distinct possibility, no one wanted to get the short draw.

Granger would have gladly passed on drawing a straw at all. He could always ask Cook or the boss to buy him a bottle or a wad of chaw – he was content to stay behind with Billy. If he volunteered to stay with the herd, there would be more than ample opportunity to strip Billy naked. No rushing, no struggling to keep quiet – no one but the cows would be around to hear them, or care what they did. The other few men left behind would be spread out too thin to take notice.

There was another reason Granger was reluctant to take Billy into the Fort. He had no idea whether Billy would want to indulge himself with a whore, and sharing Billy with a painted woman – or anyone else -- was not something Granger was eager to do. He didn't want to admit it, but deep inside he knew he'd be busting with jealousy if Billy chose to avail himself of a woman, or worse yet, one of the men.

For his part, Billy was so excited that he'd barely stopped bouncing for three days. Every step their horses took closer to the Fort, the more wound up he became, until finally Granger suspected the grin that stretched his cheeks might just split them wide open. As much as he wanted to pass on drawing straws at all and volunteer to stay behind, Granger stepped up and took his turn. It didn't matter what length he pulled, as long as Billy pulled a short one. Granger would gladly give his away to stay behind with Billy.

Luck was against him. He pulled a long one, and so did Billy. They probably heard Billy's whoop of delight clear back to Independence. He ran toward Granger, waving his stick in the air, kicking up his heels. Granger rolled his eyes and sighed. Like it or not, they were going into town. With a little bit of luck, he might be able to convince Billy to go back to the camp early, relieve the men left behind, and still have time left for what Granger had planned for them, but he couldn't take Billy's happiness away by suggesting they stay behind.

"Lookee here, Granger! Got me a long one!" Billy cried, racing up to him. His fist clutched his straw as if it were made of pure gold, an incalculable treasure. To him, Granger supposed, it was.

"I can see it. Me, too. Guess we're going in together, huh?" Granger smiled, showing Billy his straw. He stuck it between his teeth, chewing on it. "You ready?"

"Yes, sir!" Billy grinned. He patted his pants pocket. Granger heard the telltale sound of coins jingling.

"You'd best not advertise what you got in there, Billy. I've known men to kill for less," Granger warned. "Don't show it to none of the whores, either — they'll pick your pocket cleaner and quicker than vultures pick a carcass. As a matter of fact, take most all of it and shove it into your boot. That way nobody can get to it but you."

Billy dutifully sat down and pulled off his right boot. Fishing his money out of his pocket, he dribbled all but a dollar of it into the heel, and pulled it back on. He made a face, stamping his foot down. "Feels mighty funny," he said, frowning.

"Better that than losing it to some quick-fingered whore," Granger said. He tamped down his hat, and hitched up his britches. "Well, we'd best be going afore most of the good chow gets eaten."

They melted into the crowd of men heading toward the Fort. Billy stayed close to Granger's side, his blue eyes wider than Granger had ever seen them before, flicking here and there, as if trying to take in everything at once.

"Lordy! Those women don't practically have nothing on but what God gave 'em!" Billy gasped, tipping his chin toward a cabin where three women lounged. None of them were very young, or especially pretty. Two of them had dull brown hair shot through with silver, and one was blond. The fairer one was smoking a cheroot, a ribbon of blue smoke curling around her head. All three wore dresses of jewel-colored satin cut well above the ankle, with necklines that showed dirty shoulders and grime-creased cleavage, trimmed with tattered black lace.

Granger frowned, and tugged on Billy's elbow. The last thing he wanted was for Billy to take it into his head to go visiting with any of them. Lord knows what he was apt to catch if he did — all of the women looked well-worn, and none of them looked like they'd had a bath since before Moses was a dribble down his mama's knee. "Lookee there, Billy! That fella is selling stew with fresh bread, and ain't that an apple pie? Lord, I ain't tasted apples in a good long while. Let's go get us some, afore the drovers fall on it like a pack of slat-ribbed dogs."

Billy looked torn, but eventually his stomach won out over his dick, much to Granger's relief.

They took seats on one side of a wooden table, set near a house with faded gingham curtains, a sure sign that a woman lived inside the walls. She appeared out of the back of the house, a grandmotherly woman in a starched white apron over a black, bombazine dress. The table wasn't fancy, nothing but a long wooden plank covering half a dozen sawhorses, but it was crowded, lined with hungry men. He and Billy had to squeeze in beside two other men, sitting thigh-to-thigh and elbow-to-elbow.

She took their money without a smile, slipping it into a deep pocket in her apron, then waddled off back to the house.

Their two bits bought each man a plate of stew, warm bread with fresh butter, a tall glass of rich milk, and a thick wedge of apple pie. Granger could have sat there all day, stuffing himself until he split open along the sides, but by the time he paid for and ate a second piece of pie, Billy was fidgeting, his head twisting this way and that, obviously anxious to get up and explore, but too polite to leave Granger behind.

Granger banged his chest with his fist and belched, standing up. "Okay, kid. Let's go. I want to see if anybody has any chaw for sale."

"I can use another bar of soap. Mine's worn down to a sliver I can practically see through," Billy said.

One of the men who sat next to them looked up. "Thar's a fella down that-a-way," he said, pointing one dirty finger toward the rear of the town, "who's got chaw. Don't know about soap, though."

Granger nodded his thanks and they set off in that direction. They found the man selling tobacco in a cabin nearly at the end of the dirt road that ran next to the fort's walls. He grinned at them with brown-stained teeth, and happily sold Granger two small tins of chaw. "Last two," he said, pocketing his money. "Had a few more, but yesterday them other fellas bought me out."

"What other fellas? Drovers?" Granger asked. He knew that visitors to the Fort were few and far between. Wagon trains heading west had dwindled from the vast numbers of proceeding years, when canvas-covered wagons rumbled across the plains heading for California or Oregon in long, snaking trains. To have two different groups of strangers come into town within so a short time was surprising.

"Oh no, they wasn't cowmen. They were rough boys, all of 'em, maybe twenty or so. Desperadoes are my guess. Had an Indian with 'em, too. Bastard walked into town with the rest of the gang, just like he owned the damned place," the man said. He turned his head and spat a wad of yellowed juice at ground. His dislike of the people who'd lived in the west long before his own kind set foot there was evident. Granger wasn't shocked – he'd seen it too often before when he'd traveled with Sinopa.

Granger's hand unconsciously slipped to pat his gun. "They still around here, these men?" *If there were gunslingers in the area, the boss might want to know. More guards would need to be posted with the herd*, he thought.

"Don't know. Could be, but I ain't seen any of 'em since yesterday."

"Much obliged." He tucked his tins of chaw into his pocket, and led Billy away. "I think we ought to see if we can find the boss."

"You think they might try to rustle the cattle?" Billy asked, eyes wide.

"You never know. Better to be safe than sorry," Granger replied. He didn't add that if they needed extra guards, the boss was just as likely to send the messengers back as anyone else – more so, since they'd be standing right in front of him.

"What about my soap?"

Granger paused. Another few minutes wouldn't hurt, he guessed. He nodded. "Okay, first we'll go see if anyone is selling soap. Then we'll find the boss and tell him." He looked around, saw a cabin with several promising baskets of wares set out front, and set off in that direction.

It turned out that the man who owned the cabin with the display of baskets out front was a trapper who called himself DuBois, and hailed from far across the border in Canada. He was a grizzled, stooped old man with a scar that ran from the top of his balding pate to the corner of his mouth in a jagged, bumpy white line. He held a diamondback snakeskin in his gnarled fingers, rattling the tail to attract the attention of passersby.

Granger and Billy wandered closer, nodded pleasantly, and perused DuBois' wares. He had a good selection of foodstuff and skins, making Granger wonder what Dubois had to barter for them – surely he was too old to do much trapping anymore.

One basket held a quantity of early berries – tiny wild strawberries and blueberries, and a few others. Another contained potatoes and yams, probably left over from last year's harvest. Granger smelled lye, and his nose led him to yet another basket that held small, hard, irregularly shaped wedges of soap. Piled in uneven stacks in between the baskets were the cured skins of several species of small animals – rabbits, possum, and raccoon.

"Got any sweets?" Granger asked, eyes scanning the baskets. He had a sweet tooth, and was partial to peppermint.

"No, sir, I sure don't. Had some peanut brittle t'other day, but I traded it to Ol' Moses for a few jars of his pickled beans. Had some dried mushrooms, too." He gave Granger a wink and a smile that showed pink gums and all three of his teeth. "Picked 'em myself last fall, but I sold the last to an Indian fella come through here yesterday." He pointed to a heavy buffalo hide draped over a chair on the other side of his door. It was carefully cured, with the thick head fur attached as a hood. "He gave me a fine hide for them. Got the best of the bargain as far as I'm concerned," he chuckled.

Granger smiled. From DuBois' nearly toothless grin, he figured the mushrooms he'd been selling weren't the kind a body would want to put into a stew. That would explain what DuBois used to barter with, though. Mushrooms like that, the kind that could make a man see heaven or hell, would bring a good price in skins and food.

He fingered the hide absently. It was old, balding in a few small spots. Brain-tanned, he realized, feeling the soft quality. He'd always admired the Indians' methods of tanning using brains – usually from the animal that once wore the skin -- tallow, and vegetable products to dress the hide. Running the soft fur through his fingers, he noticed a small marking stained into the skin on the underside of the hide, and felt a ghostly chill ripple up his spine. He'd seen that mark before, many times, but never thought he'd see it again. Granger picked up the skin and shook it out, pretending to admire it so that he could get a better look at the marking.

It was the same as the marks he'd seen on the skins Sinopa carried with him from his village; a small series of chevrons stacked one atop the other that distinguished Sinopa's band. Granger's fingers tightened on the hide, crushing the soft fur in his fists as a wave of unexpected emotions surged through him, anger and betrayal chief among them. For all he thought he'd known Sinopa, had trusted him, it turned out he hadn't really known the man at all. Sinopa murdered a pair of harmless old men for a bag of tiny gold nuggets. Their argument when Granger found out had been bitter and fraught with threats from both sides.

"Granger? You okay?" Billy asked, putting a hand on Granger's arm. "You look a bit peaked all of a sudden."

"Nah, I'm fine. Too many good vittles, I guess. Upsetting my delicate constitution," Granger lied, forcing his lips to curve into a smile as he replaced the hide on the chair. His mind was racing, a million questions buzzing in it like a swarm of bees. Had Sinopa been here, or did the hide belong to another of Sinopa's band? If it was his, then who were the desperadoes he'd joined up with? What might happen if their paths crossed? One thing Granger knew for certain – if outlaws were planning to rustle the herd then blood would be spilled, and if it Sinopa was indeed a member of the gang then the first blood to soak the ground would be Granger's.

"Granger?" Billy looked worried, and Granger summoned a smile for him.

"Hurry now and get your soap, Billy. We need to go find the boss."

◊ ◊ ◊ ◊

The boss refused to cut the drovers' stay in town short and call all the boys back. He insisted there was no proof that whatever gang had ridden through the town yesterday was still in the area, and if they were, that they had plans to rustle the Johnson cattle. "They're probably long gone," the boss said.

Finally, after an hour of arguing with Granger – who sunk his teeth in deep and refused to back off – the boss agreed to send a couple of men back, just to make sure everything was okay, and to help keep an extra eye out for trouble. Just as Granger had predicted, the two men closest to the boss at the time were the men he picked for the job – Granger and Billy.

That posed an immediate problem for Granger. The last thing he wanted was for Billy to be anywhere *near* the camp with the possibility that Sinopa was about. Let him spend all his money whoring – at least he'd still be breathing come morning. That might not be the case if rustlers attacked, especially if Sinopa was with them.

He didn't want Billy to overhear him, although since the boss didn't have any such qualms, he figured it was a lost cause. "He's a greenhorn," Granger whispered hoarsely, "Keep him in town. Send Brown or Abernathy back with me."

"I don't see Brown or Abernathy. I see you two,"

"I ain't afraid of them, Granger. I'm a grown man!" Billy cried, sounding younger than his years even as he argued the opposite. "I'll be fine, boss."

"Of course you'll be fine, 'cause you'll be sitting your ass right here," Granger said, without losing eye contact with the boss. "He's too green. He ain't a good shot. He ain't a good rider. He'll get hisself killed."

"Granger!" Billy yelled, giving him a good shot – the boy was stronger than Granger gave him credit for, nearly knocking him off his feet. "Mind your own goddamn business!"

"Yeah, Granger, mind your beeswax," the boss parroted with a sardonic grin. He was obviously enjoying the show Granger and Billy were putting on, but had had enough. "He goes, you go, and that's final! Now, both of you get the hell out of my sight!"

Granger opened his mouth to argue again, but a black look from the boss changed his mind. He wouldn't be of value to anyone if he was fired and tossed out on his butt. He threw Billy an exasperated look. "Fine. Come on. I'll be sure to send your Mama my sincerest condolences when some rustler plants a bullet in your thick skull."

They made their way out of town and back to where the herd grazed peacefully. Granger's eyes darted from side to side, fingers twitching over his gun every time the wind rustled the leaves of a tree, or a small animal rippled the grass. He imagined outlaws crouched just out of sight, an ambush waiting behind every bush, every boulder.

Hackneyed was just where Granger left him, grazing peacefully near Billy's spirited stallion, Thunder, just a few feet away from his tent. He watched Hackneyed carefully as he approached. For all that he was finicky, desultory, and sometime plain ornery, Hackneyed was the best barometer Granger knew of to tell of coming danger. The horse sensed thunderstorms long before a single cloud gathered at the horizon, knew the difference between plain ol' rainstorms and those that might spit out a twister. If danger was nearby, Hackneyed would know it, he reasoned, but he could detect no tenseness in his horse, no undue prancing or nervous twitches.

Seeing Hackneyed untroubled and nibbling delicately went a long way to soothing Granger's ruffled nerves. He let out a sigh and turned to Billy. "Stay here with the horses. Keep your gun ready, anything moves that don't have horns… shoot it."

"I'm not a child, Granger. Stop treating me like one!" Billy huffed. "I'm a man, goddamn it!" His cheeks were flushed with righteous indignation, his eyes sparking with anger. He looked furious, and as sexy as all hell.

"Damn straight you are," Granger growled, his voice suddenly husky. His body tightened, forcing his worry to the side. He grabbed Billy's face between his calloused palms and kissed him hard, wanting more, wanting to strip him naked, throw him down, and fuck him until he screamed and stampeded the fucking cattle. He settled for a kiss, deep and hot, a promise of things to come as soon as he made certain they weren't in any danger. "You watch this end of the herd. I'm gonna ride out to the other side, check with the drovers over there, ask if they've seen anything out of place. Let 'em know there are outlaws in the area. You see anything, you shoot first and holler second, got it?"

Billy was breathless, even more flushed, but he didn't look angry anymore. "Yeah, I got it." As Granger turned and mounted up on Hackneyed, Billy called, "Be careful."

"You bet. Ain't gonna get myself killed now. I got plans for you later on."

That put a smile on Billy's face and his own as he nudged Hackneyed's flank and started to weave his way through the herd.

Sinopa had skinned the carcass in a hurry, and it showed in the stringy tendons, clumps of fat, and bits of flesh that clung to the underside of the hide. Black flies buzzed, biting him as well as the skin he hid beneath, but he paid them no mind. The steer's skull was heavy, worn on his head like a hat. The long, curving horns would help him pass as one of the herd, at least from a distance. In a group of four thousand, he would blend in as seamlessly as a single leaf in a forest.

Instead, he concentrated on edging closer to the herd, letting the steers become used to the smell of death that clung to him. It was a necessary disguise. He would keep to the periphery of the herd, slowly working his way toward Granger's tent where YellowHair stood alone and unprotected.

When Granger kissed YellowHair, jealousy filled Sinopa's mouth with a bitter taste of nostalgia. He well-remembered Granger's velvet tongue and calloused hands, as much as he'd tried to forget how they once made him feel. It was all he could do to wait patiently for his opportunity, and not kill both men with a couple of well-aimed arrows. In fact, he debated doing just that, even though it would rob him of the satisfaction he craved in forcing Granger to watch YellowHair die.

In the end, he'd convinced himself to wait. Soon, though, in a matter of minutes, he would have YellowHair, and when Granger came for him – as Sinopa knew he would – Sinopa's revenge would at last be at hand. His village would be avenged; Granger would pay in blood for his crimes.

The stallion sensed Sinopa's presence. He danced on his toes, nickering nervously as he caught the scent of blood and man on the wind. Luckily, YellowHair was either too inexperienced or dull-witted to take notice; he glanced once at the horse and called out a rebuke, then returned to staring out in the direction Granger had ridden.

Foolish, Sinopa thought as he crept to within a few yards of him. *Bart's brother has even less sense than his elder. He lets lust blind him to danger.* Moving quickly, he threw off his disguise and dashed toward YellowHair on silent feet. A hard blow to the back of the head with the horn handle of his knife, and YellowHair slumped silently at Sinopa's feet.

Sinopa kicked the unconscious man, disgusted. "Granger wastes his affection on one so unwise," he said, bending down. He tied YellowHair's hands and feet together with a length of rope. A grim smile touched his lips when he noticed YellowHair's hat lying on the ground where it had landed when YellowHair fell. He stuck one of his arrows through it, embedding the sharp flint arrowhead through the wide brim and into the ground.

He was tempted to take YellowHair's horse – the stallion was in his prime and worth a good price – but the beast was already unsettled by the smell of death that clung to Sinopa. He might be difficult to handle, and Sinopa couldn't risk a bucking, agitated horse attracting attention of the drovers on the far side of the herd. He left the stallion where it was and, moving quickly, still smiling a death's head grin, dragged YellowHair toward the shelter of the trees.

◊ ◊ ◊ ◊

Granger checked with every cowboy who'd been left to guard the herd, and nobody'd seen a single, fucking thing out of the ordinary. No outlaws, no Indians, nothing but horns, hides, hooves, and cow pies. Granger turned Hackneyed around, heading back toward his tent. His instincts must be off, or maybe he was just getting old. He'd let himself jump to conclusions, and now he'd look a fool to the boss and Billy. What was he thinking? Getting himself all worked up over a marking on a hide; could be the hide was traded to another Indian, or stolen. It definitely wasn't proof that Sinopa was in the area.

Granger chided himself as he threaded his way between the steer. If he had a lick of sense, he'd make this drive his last. Find himself a cabin somewhere up in the mountains, and spend the rest of his days fishing, maybe do a little trapping.

Get set up on a nice little homestead, nothing fancy, just a cabin in the middle of a whole lot of nowhere, someplace where the ghosts of his past couldn't find him. Maybe he could even convince Billy to come with him.

Granger smiled, feeling his body harden as he thought of cold, snowy nights holed up in a cabin like that with only Billy's lean, young body to keep him warm. Now, that was a life a man could get used to in a hurry. His balls swelled, cock filling, pressing against the fly of his denims, and he urged Hackneyed forward, suddenly anxious to get back to his tent and Billy.

Funny how a stringy little beanpole like Billy could set fire to Granger's skin, but he couldn't deny that Billy's body got him hot and bothered every damned time he thought about it. There was more to it than that, when he considered it. He liked the way Billy's eyes shone with admiration whenever Granger told him stories of Granger's younger days, how he was always eager to touch Granger, or have Granger touch him. The way Billy leaned in when Granger kissed him, and the noises he made when he came.

His dick twitched eagerly when he remembered how sexy Billy looked when he'd been riled up. He grinned, Billy would be lucky if Granger waited until they ducked inside the tent before he stripped him naked.

As he cut around the outside edge of the herd, he could see his tent. Granger frowned, eyes darting from left to right. Thunder was still there, although from a distance the horse looked agitated. The tent looked fine, but there was no sign of Billy anywhere. A sudden, icy-cold finger tickled Granger's spine, and he urged Hackneyed into a trot.

He froze when he spotted a crumpled cowhide, recently skinned with the skull still attached, and nearby, Billy's hat lying in the dirt with an arrow stuck through it. Granger's heart did an odd flip-flop in his chest, and his stomach dropped, leaving him feeling nauseated.

Sliding out of the saddle, he stared down at Billy's hat, feeling the blood drain from his head to his feet. The arrow was frighteningly familiar. He'd handled others just like it, admiring the smooth, chokecherry shaft fletched with three crow feathers, and carefully knapped, razor-sharp head.

Sinopa had always taken great pride in his workmanship.

Granger yanked the arrow out of the ground, and pulled it free from the brim of Billy's hat. A quick inspection of the earth and hat thankfully revealed no blood; Sinopa had taken Billy but not killed him. A whirlwind of questions whipped through his mind. Was it happenstance that crossed his path with Sinopa's again, or had Sinopa been tracking him all along? If so, why had Sinopa waited until now to make his move? Surely there were many times Granger had been wide open for attack. It would have been easy to pick Granger off during the drive. Why now, and why take Billy?

The answer came to him easily.

Sinopa had spied on him and Billy; he knew Billy and Granger were lovers. He wanted revenge, and took Billy as bait. Sinopa knew Granger would try to get Billy back, and was using him to lead Granger to exactly where Sinopa wanted him.

It would be stupid to follow. Sinopa was a deadly hunter; Granger had seen him in action too many times not to know that he could make himself virtually invisible, blending seamlessly in with the brush, until it was too late. By the time Sinopa revealed himself, Granger would be dead. Billy was probably already gone, and if he weren't, he soon would be.

Billy, too young, too green, who'd never hurt anyone, who only wanted to please his father, the trail boss… even Granger. Billy, who tried so hard to be a cowboy, who'd touched Granger's body and his heart, and who'd never done anything wrong. He was being used as a pawn, caught up in a deadly game between Sinopa and Granger that should have ended years ago at the moment Sinopa laid the small bag of gold at Granger's feet, and Granger had seen the black hole where Sinopa's heart and conscience should be.

Granger knew he'd acted like a coward, although he'd never let himself admit it before. Instead of killing Sinopa, instead of ending it there and then, he'd chased Sinopa away, then packed his things and fled.

Now his past had caught up with him, and poor Billy was going to be the one to pay the price for Granger's cowardice.

It was his fault, Granger's, all of it.

Impotent rage fired his blood, and he snapped the arrow in two, tossing both pieces as far from him as he could. He threw his head back and roared his fury, both Hackneyed and Thunder shying at the sound.

His mind was a black cloud of anger as he stalked to where Hackneyed stood, the poor creature's flanks twitching nervously, and tore through his saddlebag. He popped open the chamber of his Colt, making sure it was fully loaded, then shoved a fistful of bullets into his shirt pocket, the casings jingling. He strapped a sheath to his right thigh, tying the ends of the rawhide tight, and slipped his Bowie into it. Another knife was stuck behind his belt at the small of his back, and yet another slid into the side of his right boot along his lower calf.

He knew he was walking right into Sinopa's trap, but he was going to be prepared when he got there. If he was to die, so be it, but he knew one thing – he was going to do his damnedest to take Sinopa with him.

Granger forced himself to stand still for a moment and take a deep breath, to calm down. He was going to need his wits about him if he was going up against Sinopa. Sinopa held all the cards – he knew who Billy was, what Billy meant to Granger, and that Granger would come looking for him, ready to kill to get him back. Sinopa would be ready for him when Granger caught up. He couldn't afford to go barreling after them half-cocked.

Bending down near the spot where he'd found Billy's hat, Granger carefully examined the earth. He spotted a footprint, soft and rounded, pressed into the dark dirt. There was no boot heel, or toe marks. It hadn't been made by either a cowboy boot or a bare foot, but might have been left by the soft buckskin moccasins favored by the Blackfeet. The grass was bent; a large area flattened entirely, the earth disturbed. Something – or someone – had been dragged across it

A grim smile creased Granger's cheek as he followed the trail, heading off toward the dark, closely wooded forest at the edge of the clearing. He followed a trail of snapped twigs, softly rounded footprints, and broken stalks of grass deep into the tree line. It veered east, continuing on for a spell until it cut north, going ever deeper into the forest. The trail was easy to follow, Sinopa had made damn sure Granger could track them.

Sunlight dappled the ground, filtered through the thick canopy of interlocking branches overhead. Birds twittered in the distance, but fell silent as Granger drew near. He listened carefully for anything that sounded out of place, but heard nothing out of the ordinary. He knew that even though he was being led – herded, like a fucking steer – to where Sinopa wanted him, Sinopa wouldn't be stupid enough to give away his position. He kept his right hand held ready over the butt of his Colt, his skin itching with nerves. Every step he took intensified the feeling that he was being led into a trap. His instincts were howling, he was close, and getting closer by the minute. Alert for the tiniest sound, a scent, anything that might give away the position of his former lover, he pressed on.

CHAPTER NINE

It would not be long now, Sinopa mused. He crouched behind a thicket, screened from view by the brush. In the center of a small clearing before him, YellowHair lay still upon the ground, bound hand and foot. He wasn't dead; Sinopa was saving killing him for when Granger arrived, although he had been sorely tempted many times during his trek through the forest to slit YellowHair's throat and leave a trail of blood for Granger to follow. YellowHair's chest continued to rise and fall, but he had not gained consciousness since Sinopa had hit him over the head.

Not that it mattered if he ever did. It was not YellowHair's eyes Sinopa wished to see when he killed him – it was Granger's. Sinopa wanted to see them widen, see the pain YellowHair's death would paint in Granger's expressive eyes. Would he weep for his lover? Or was YellowHair like Sinopa himself, easily cast aside?

He hoped for the former. He wanted Granger to suffer before he died.

His thoughts turned momentarily to the Red Earth Gang. Bart would be looking for him. He was supposed to return with news of the drovers' positions, how many men had stayed behind, and where they were in relation to the herd. He had promised Bart he would not kill Bart's younger brother or Granger beforehand, but when the opportunity to take YellowHair presented itself, Sinopa had seized it.

He shrugged and shifted his weight minutely to ease the cramping in his thigh from remaining crouched for so long. Let Bart fume, once Granger was dead, Sinopa would kill Bart and his men as well.

YellowHair moaned softly, and his head rolled from one side to the other. Sinopa tensed, waiting to hear a shout or cry of protest, but none came. YellowHair's eyes never fluttered open, and his voice never rose above a pained whisper.

Sinopa's brow knit. He would rather YellowHair be awake and screaming. He found himself hoping Granger was not as adept at tracking as he remembered him to be; the longer he took to find them, the more time YellowHair would have to recover.

Granger would be armed, of course, but it wouldn't matter. Sinopa was close enough to YellowHair to reach his side in an instant. The moment he heard Granger approach, he would move from the brush, and use YellowHair as a human shield. Granger wouldn't dare fire.

Once Sinopa had slit YellowHair's throat, Granger would be too blinded by grief to see Sinopa's knife, still red with YellowHair's blood, fly through the air until it was embedded in his chest.

The thought brought a smile to Sinopa's lips, and he settled down again to listen and wait.

◊ ◊ ◊ ◊

Granger forced himself to slow, although every fiber in his being urged him to rush ahead, crashing through the brush until he reached Billy's side. Through a small gap in a thick screen of leaves, he could see Billy curled on his side in the dirt, hands and feet bound. Bits of leaves and bark dusted his blond hair, his face and hands were scratched and dirty.

But he was breathing, and that was all Granger needed to know. He felt an easing of some of the tension that had knotted his back. He wasn't too late. Sinopa hadn't yet killed Billy, and instantly Granger knew why. Sinopa wanted to murder him in front of Granger, make Granger witness the terror in Billy's eyes as he died.

Not in my lifetime, he thought. *Sinopa, you're a dead man, even if you don't know it yet.*

He pulled his Colt from his holster and almost smiled as he wove his way silently through the brush, taking care not to make the slightest noise, knowing Sinopa would be nearby, listening for his approach. It was Sinopa himself who'd taught Granger to move like a ghost through the forest, never suspecting that a time would come when Granger would use that skill against him.

Slowly, Granger began to circle around the clearing. Sinopa was here, he was sure of it, hiding in the bushes, waiting for Granger to show himself. He knew Granger would be armed, knew how good he was with a gun. No doubt Sinopa planned to use Billy to shield himself. The only hope Granger had was to reach Sinopa before he knew Granger was there.

He took one step, then another, placing his feet with care so as not to disturb a single leaf or branch. More than once he forced himself to pause, to listen, his ears straining to catch the slightest sound on the breeze. A movement nearly caused him to fire a shot from the Colt, but it was only a rabbit. It scurried across Granger's path and down a hole, out of sight. *Damn it!* Granger swore, taking a deep, calming breath. *Can't be shooting at shadows, not now.*

He crept around the trunk of a giant oak, and stopped, his heart pounding in his chest. Through the tangled bramble of a blackberry bush, he caught the sight of a dark head and a long braid knotted with feathers and bits of bone. Sinopa was crouched not twenty feet away, staring intently at the spot where Granger knew Billy lay. He raised his Colt, sighting carefully, his thumb slowly cocking the hammer. It clicked, and he fired.

The sound of the hammer clicking was like thunder in the silence of the forest, and Granger realized it was all the warning Sinopa needed. Sinopa didn't hesitate, he threw himself forward through the brush, scrambling to reach Billy, and Granger swore as the bullet whizzed by so close to the side of Sinopa's head that he surely felt the breeze it made. Granger fired again, but it did nothing but kick up a puff of dirt and leaves near Sinopa's right foot as he broke into the clearing and raced to his captive. His knife was already in his hand as he yanked Billy up and held his body against his, facing the direction where Granger hid.

"Granger! Show yourself!" Sinopa cried, putting the blade to the soft skin under Billy's chin.

"Don't have to happen this way, Sinopa! You kill Billy, I kill you. Let him go, and you live. It's that simple." Granger struggled to keep his voice from betraying the wild beating of his heart. One slip, one false move, and the knife Sinopa held to

Billy's throat would slice through it. He prayed Billy didn't regain consciousness. If he did and began to struggle, he'd die.

"No. You will be the one to die here today, Granger," Sinopa replied, his lips curling in a sneer. He dropped his arm from around Billy's waist, grabbing a fistful of blond hair. He snapped Billy's head back, exposing his throat and the knife pressed against it. "You and him."

Granger held his tongue, and began to edge slowly to his left. If he could get far enough to the side, he might be able to get off a clean shot without hitting Billy.

"Show yourself!" Sinopa yelled again. He moved the blade slightly; it broke the delicate skin of Billy's throat, drawing a thin trickle of blood.

The sight of red against the pallor of Billy's throat refueled Granger's rage. His breath caught, and his fingers reflexively tightened on the Colt. "Stop it! I swear to God if you hurt him—"

"What do I care what you swear to your god? Because of you, my people are dead! Because of your lies, your treachery! I swore to them I would take revenge for them!"

"What are you talking about?" Granger asked, moving again to his left. "I did nothing to your people!" *Keep him talking, keep him distracted,* he thought. The sight of Billy's blood had shaken him. It was only a scratch, but the next cut would be much deeper, he was sure of it.

"I trusted you, followed you! I was not there to fight because of you!" Sinopa roared.

"As I recall, you wanted to come with me," Granger retorted, and took another step.

"Liar! You confused me, seduced me!"

Billy chose that moment to begin to stir, moaning softly. Granger froze and held his breath, if Billy woke up with a start, he'd slice his own throat on Sinopa's blade. He had no choice, not if he wanted Billy to live.

"I'm coming out, Sinopa!" He called, tossing his Colt out of the bushes. It landed in the dirt outside of Sinopa's grasp.

"And your knife!" Sinopa yelled, and Granger cursed him silently for knowing he'd have one. It followed the gun. Granger stepped out from behind the screen of brush, holding his hands in the air.

"Okay. Here I am. Let him go, Sinopa." His blood froze at the grin that bared Sinopa's teeth. It was more a grimace than smile, malicious and insane.

"G-Granger?" Billy's eyes blinked rapidly as if he couldn't quite focus. "W-hat...?"

"Shh, Billy. Don't move," Granger said, willing him to listen and understand. "Sinopa, let him go."

"Why? He is your man now. You took my family from me, and I will take your man from you!"

"No!" Granger yelled. He judged the distance between himself and Sinopa. There was no way he could reach Sinopa before the deadly blade bit deeply into Billy's neck.

Suddenly, there was a loud noise coming from the direction of the herd. Granger heard bodies moving quickly through the forest, and the voices of men shouting to one another.

"Here! There's footprints here!"

"This way!"

Sinopa's head whipped from side to side, first looking toward Granger, then toward the sounds of the strangers' voices. From the look on his face, Granger understood that while the voices were unfamiliar to him, they weren't to Sinopa. He knew who was coming.

A man with dark blond hair burst through the brush on the opposite side of the clearing. He looked vaguely familiar to Granger, although Granger couldn't recall meeting him before. Then Granger realized he looked a lot like Billy, although older.

"What are you doing, Sinopa?" The man spat out, advancing on Sinopa. His gun was drawn, and aimed at Sinopa's head.

Sinopa moved, dragging Billy around to shield him from the gun. It was the moment Granger had been waiting for. He dove for his gun, took aim and fired.

The shot brought the attention and the guns of the blond man and his companions to bear on Granger, but he didn't care. All that mattered was that his aim hadn't been off. The bullet hit Sinopa in the meaty part of his arm, and he dropped the knife he'd held to Billy's throat. Uncaring of the guns trained on him, Granger dashed across the clearing and pulled Billy free from Sinopa's grasp.

"Granger? What's going on? What happened?" Billy asked, leaning heavily against Granger. He touched his head and winced. "Who's the Indian?" Looking around he gasped. "Bart? Is that you?"

"You know this man, Billy?" Granger asked, nodding toward the blond.

"Yes, he's my brother, the one I told you about."

"Yeah, we're brothers," the blond said, his lip curling into an ugly sneer. "But I'm about to be an only child. Sinopa jumped the gun, so to speak. The stupid bastard wasn't supposed to kill Billy until after we got a report on who was guarding the herd." The gun in his hand swung to point directly at Billy's chest. "Guess it can't wait now. Gonna have to kill both you and him."

Granger turned, putting himself between Bart's gun and Billy. "You want the herd? Take it! Be my guest!"

Bart laughed. "Sorry, that's not good enough. Gotta get rid of Billy, since our father went and made him his heir. When I get back to the Lazy J, I'm gonna kill the old bastard, too. The whole operation will be mine, then... well, after I get rid of our Ma and little sister."

"No!" Billy screamed, trying to twist toward Bart. "Not Ma and Emma!"

"Oh, shut up, you little mealy-mouthed baby! I listened to you whine for almost eighteen years and I'm sick of it! I'm gonna kill this sodomite you've been sleeping with, and then kill you!" Bart barked.

Granger heard the click of a hammer, and closed his eyes, thinking for sure the next thing he heard would be the bullet shattering his skull. He heard the shot, but felt no pain. Instead he heard a howl of agony coming from in front of him.

Opening his eyes, he saw Bart fall, Sinopa's knife embedded in his chest. Granger turned again, pushed Billy roughly to the ground and quickly took aim.

Gunfire erupted from the weapons of the men who'd come with Bart. Sinopa did a crazy dance as the bullets tore into him, blood soaking his buckskins. He died on his feet, gone before he hit the ground.

Granger and the men of the Red Earth Gang stood staring at one another for a few long, tense moments. Between them, Bart's breath bubbled, and finally stopped.

"We're no threat to you," Granger said softly. He made eye contact with each of the men, then slowly lowered his gun. "We have nothing you want. You want the herd? Take it. Just leave us in peace."

One of the men looked down at Bart, then turned his head and spat on the ground. "Never did like the asshole anyway," he said. His small eyes flicked toward Granger. "But we didn't come all this way, and through a heap of trouble for nothing. Don't want the herd, not enough of us to drive 'er, and we're too close to the Fort to chance it. What else you got that'll convince us to let you live?"

Granger nodded, then slipped his hand inside his shirt, slowly, and pulled out a small black bag he'd kept in the waistband of his pants. He weighed it a few times in the palm of his hand, then looked at Billy and smiled. "This was never mine in the first place. Couldn't bring myself to spend it; couldn't bring myself to throw it away, neither. I'm glad to be rid of it," he said, tossing the bag at the feet of the man who'd spoken. "Take it. There's more than enough in there to pay for your troubles, I reckon."

The man cocked an eyebrow and scooped the bag up from the ground. He fussed at the rawhide that held it closed, and opened it, spilling some of its contents into his hand. The gold caught the last few rays of sunshine filtering through the leaves, glittering in his palm. His cheek twitched in a half-smile, and he nodded. He motioned to the other men. "Let's clear out afore the law comes sniffing around."

Granger breathed a sigh of relief when they turned and melted into the forest, leaving Billy and him alone in the clearing with the bodies of Bart and Sinopa. He turned to Billy, who was shaking and pale. "You okay, kid?" he asked, gently probing Billy's head. The wound had stopped bleeding, but he knew Billy would have a headache for at least a couple of days afterward.

"He was my brother, Granger. I knew he hated Pa, and he was always as mean as a badger, but I didn't realize he hated me, too."

"He was twisted up inside with greed, Billy. I knew someone just like him," Granger said, glancing at Sinopa's body.

"That was a lot of gold you just gave away," Billy said softly.

"Yeah, well, I ain't the greedy sort. As long as I have what I need, I figure I'm doing okay." Granger smiled softly at Billy, running a thumb along the curve of his jaw.

"Yeah? You got what you need now, Granger?" Billy asked, leaning in to him.

"That depends. You gonna stay with me after we see the herd to Oregon?"

Billy smiled up at him. "I never did want to be a rancher."

"Well, then I guess I have everything I need then," Granger said softly. He drew Billy close and kissed him, then held him just because he wanted to, and he could. When he finally let go and began to lead Billy out of the clearing, he felt lighter, as if he left a heavy burden behind him.

They returned to the clearing the next day and laid both Sinopa and Bart to rest under the sheltering arms of the trees. Neither felt inclined to say a prayer, instead they spent a few moments in silence, both thinking about the men they were burying and the way their paths had crossed.

Then they turned their backs and left the glade, knowing they'd never return.

The next two months were hard, but not because of the work. Billy continued to improve as a drover, under Granger's tutorage, quickly growing competent as a rider and a cowboy. What was difficult was keeping their growing feelings for one another secret. They had to constantly be on guard to keep their distance when in sight of the other men.

What a man did after dark to relieve the loneliness of the trail was one thing, flaunting it in broad daylight was another. At night, Granger was glad to tuck himself and Billy away in his tent, but during the day, he kept Billy at an arm's length, and with each passing hour, it grew more and more difficult to live the lie.

Finally, though, they brought the herd in. Granger and Billy watched from horseback as one of the drovers shooed the Judas Steer into the pens that surrounded the slaughterhouse, the rest of the herd following meekly behind.

From there Billy and Granger rode south to California, along the sheer cliffs that dropped away to the rolling waves of the Pacific. Neither had any specific place in mind to settle down, but when they happened across a small valley not far from the Baja border, they both knew they'd found it.

They were living in Granger's old, worn tent, slowly hauling wood from the forests that edged the valley, eventually to be hewn into logs for a cabin. The sun was a burning hot, yellow ball in the sky, and both men were soaked with sweat when they decided to take a break. Billy washed up in a hurry then stretched himself out under the shade of a nearby tree, arms tucked up under his head, hat pulled down low over his face.

Bending over the creek, Granger scooped the clear cold water into his hands and splashed his face. Suddenly, something glittering at the bottom of the shallow creek caught his eye. Reaching in, he scooped up a handful of silt, letting the gently babbling water sift through it, washing away the dirt. In his palm lay three small golden nuggets.

He laughed, thinking Fate had a funny sense of humor, tossed them back in, dusted off his hands, finished washing his face, and went to join Billy under the tree.

FORGOTTEN FAVOR

ANGELA FIDDLER

PART ONE

When Mark closed his eyes, he felt the fall. It hadn't been Butter's fault. Mark should have seen the change in the ground, but the early morning gallop had felt so good. They had been on the road for almost a month, placing well in the money in several of the small town rodeos. After all that time living in the front sleeping quarters of his horse trailer and riding about in finite spaces, he was home on the ranch where the earth seemed to stretch on forever and there didn't seem to be an end to the sky. He'd felt free.

He remembered looking down. Just as he was about to pull back on the reins, he felt Butter trip. For a second, he thought that she would recover. Then she stumbled again, and for another heartbeat they both were weightless. He grabbed the reins, his feet kicking free of the stirrups as though on autopilot, and he knew, even as he saw the ground hurtling up towards him, that this was going to hurt. And his next thought was a prayer that Butter would not be.

He hit the ground hard. That was a given. He remembered the sickening crunch from the shoulder but he had no memory at all of Butter coming down on his leg. He supposed that was a blessing, though in his dreams he still imagined the snap.

And also in his dreams, he saw the hooves. Black as night, as death, as sin. The ground was soft, the rational part of his mind knew that, but when the hooves struck it, sparks flew. He also heard Butter's frantic breathing just a few yards away. His own pathetic attempts at drawing air into lungs too stunned to remember their most basic function was just as hard. There was more than just the two of them in his dream. No matter how hard he had tried to look up, to ask the riders on the horses for help, or for somebody to check on Butter and find out why she wasn't attempting to get up on her own, he couldn't breathe.

Through the pain, and stress, and anxiety, he was terrified.

Mark woke up in the hospital. Not for the first time, but for what seemed like the hundredth. He was alone in the semiprivate room, and the television overhead was muted. His leg ached dully, almost resentfully, and he knew from how high the sun was in the sky that it would be another hour before the nurse came with more painkillers.

To distract himself, he stared at the walls that no amount of bleach would ever get truly white again. The washed out green curtains matched the green summer weight blankets on each of the three beds. The get well cards on the table beside him—the last of the accompanying flowers had been thrown out a couple days ago—were buried beneath insurance forms, half finished crossword puzzles and magazines that predicted the outcome for the last set of Olympics.

The worst of the damage was not on the femur, which by itself would have kept him in traction. When Butter had fallen, she had rolled over him. It could have been worse; other than his spleen, there had been no other internal damage. One of the ranch hands had seen him fall and called an ambulance. If Mark concentrated hard enough he could feel the metal plates holding his pelvis and thigh together under his skin. The fiberglass cast kept him from touching the surgery scars, and they woke him at all hours of the night with unholy itching.

Though if he had died, if he was being perfectly honest, hell would not be too different than a semiprivate room that lingered with the smell of dead flowers.

A shadow crossed the door. Mark looked up. As much as he hated being poked and prodded, at least the nurses on their frequent rounds were some break from the monotony of his life. His father had visited, twice, his stepmother more often, but she'd just been there the day before helping him move from the hospital room to the rehab center for the extended care he couldn't get at the ranch. He still had a stack of books she'd brought him as well. Some of the ranch hands and a few of his roping buddies had stopped by in the beginning, but they tapered off by the time the flowers they'd brought had wilted. He didn't blame them.

And his father... he didn't want to think about his father, Edward McCoy. He would use the ranch as an excuse not to come more often, and on the surface Mark accepted the excuse for what it was. Though Edward did own one of the largest cattle ranches in southern Alberta, he also had more managers than some fast food chains and accountants up the wazoo. The fact was they did far better as employer and employee than they ever had as father and son. Up close and personal...well, that wasn't so good. He had moved out of the big house to the apartment over the new stables when he was eighteen, the disgraced heir apparent. A good year was measured by how many conversations they didn't have. Things had gotten slightly better once Edward had remarried, but Sunday dinners were still frosty.

The door opened. The man who walked in was familiar, achingly so, but it took Mark an extra second to recognize him. He sat up as much as the traction would allow and swallowed. "Jake Alastair," he said, and was glad his voice didn't break. When he thought about the strained relationship he had with his father, he had to think about Jake.

Jake hadn't changed all that much over the past five years, since the hayloft. He was taller, more tanned, and broader across the chest. He was dressed in Sunday go-to-meeting jeans, and a white western shirt that had obviously never fallen off a horse, but the hat he held nervously looked as though it had survived a stampede of wildebeests once or twice. His blond hair had been recently combed and his blue eyes, always a bit too wide and a bit too deep, were exactly the same. Mark swallowed again.

"Mark," Jake said. And despite his boyish looks, his voice was low and comforting. Mark couldn't help but think of the loft again, the smell of the hay, the dust dancing in the sunbeams, and the way Jake's lips had felt on his throat. Not that anything more had happened. It was bad luck his father had come home so early. Mark had been eighteen, just finished school and hadn't found Butter yet, and if he hadn't had his father's support, he would have had nothing at all. It was a lame excuse to cave in to his father's threats, but he had. After an awkward year of avoiding Jake for fear of his father finding out they'd had contact, Jake had dropped out of the rodeo circuit entirely.

Jake looked him over, and his mouth twitched when he saw the lump in the bed the cast made. Mark shrugged, though it hurt his shoulder to do so, and motioned to the chair on the other side of the bed. "You can sit if you want," he said, knowing the words were awkward. There had been long, hot nights in his life where he would imagine what he would say if he ever saw Jake again, but sitting arrangements had never been one of the topics of conversation.

Jake nodded, but didn't come any closer. "You know my dad got sick," he said. His mouth opened and closed a couple times. The awkwardness between them was wrong.

"No," Mark said. "I didn't. I thought you fell off the planet. Is that why you stopped riding?"

A flash of pain crossed Jake's face, and he bit his lip. "Mostly," Jake allowed. "My dad needed help at his ranch. It was a rescue center. Is a rescue center, I mean."

"Okay." Mark realized his mouth was dry and reached for one of the plastic cups, the same washed out green as the rest of the room. The water inside tasted plastic as well, but he gulped down half of it. His leg throbbed as though punishing him for not making the pain the center of his attention for the past couple minutes, and he rubbed the cast with the palm of his hand until he could manage the pain again.

When he looked up, Jake's face was pale despite the tan. He swallowed with a mouth so dry Mark could hear the clicking sound his throat made, and he offered what remained in his cup to Jake. "The pitcher has ice in it, or it did an hour ago."

Jake took it gratefully, filled and emptied the cup up twice before putting it down. The room was air-conditioned, but he was sweating. Mark frowned. "Are you okay?"

Jake waved his hand and shook his head. "No. I hate hospitals. I never liked them, but after dad got sick, well..."

Mark didn't ask him to finish. "You didn't have to come."

"Yes, I did. I told you, I run a rescue center now." Jake hesitated. "So when I saw her in the kill pens, I had to save her. I didn't think you would... I knew you wouldn't..."

Mark felt sick, like he'd just had an overdose of morphine, and the room started to spin. He gripped the blankets and where he touched it he left damp handprints. "Who's she?" he asked, forming the words carefully. But he knew the answer. He just needed to hear Jake say it.

"Butter," Jake said. "She'd been sold on with her papers but I knew it was her the moment I saw her. She was hurt, her knee was pretty banged up, but she's okay."

Mark shook his head. "No. That's not possible. My dad told me she was fine. She was back at the ranch. He wouldn't -- " But he would. Mark felt cold inside. He looked up. Jake continued.

"I have her. The vet says it was just a bone bruise. The x-ray didn't show anything broken or chipped. We've been keeping her pretty immobile and she's recovering."

"Thank you," Mark said. He knew he sounded distant. "I can't... thank you."

"You don't have to," Jake said. He approached the bed like a marionette controlled by a rank beginner. The hand holding his hat tightened, crumbling the straw brim, but he made it without falling over. He took Mark's hand, the one attached to his bad shoulder, but Jake's touch was so gentle that Mark didn't fear the potential pain. "I missed you."

Mark cleared his throat. "I missed you, too." It was an understatement that burned his throat with all the words he wanted to say. "After..." Mark waved his hand over the cast helplessly. Jake nodded, telling him he understood, and Mark relaxed.

"Of course you can come," Jake said.

The door opened again and a nurse came in with two pills in the tiny paper cup. Her scrubs, with the bright balloons and teddy bears, were the only real colorful thing in the room. She smiled at Mark, a genuine show of affection, and tipped the paper cup so that the pills rolled into his palm. "Your friend can stay, but these will make you really drowsy."

Jake stepped back from the bed. "I really have to go, ma'am."

Mark wanted to say something, to be perfectly honest he wanted to ask Jake to stay, but Jake looked so uncomfortable Mark couldn't do it. "Thank you," he said. "For everything."

"Weren't nothing," Jake said, sounding double his age, and made his escape. Mark would have given anything to join him. Instead, he took his pills.

◊ ◊ ◊ ◊

There was a strange disconnect between what was happening in the cities and what was happening in the dusty rodeo grounds and racetracks that made up so many hot summer weekends. Despite the victories in court and the acceptance Mark saw on the television, "gay" was still a synonym for all things inconvenient, and "faggot" was the ultimate putdown above all other putdowns. Mark learned quickly to keep his head down, to fake interest in the buckle bunnies that hovered around even the smallest rodeos, and to never show emotion over words that were used for posturing. It was hard.

But then Jake was there, they were both in the roping events, and the thing about rodeos was that there was always a hell of a lot of hurry up and wait. They had to wait for their event, wait for their turn, wait in the box, wait for the string to snap, and then wait for the gratifying way the rope floated down around the calf's neck. Jake made the waiting better.

There is no world smaller than that of the infield of the chuck wagon racetrack, where cowboys set up camp between the days of the show. For long hours there was nothing to do but shoot the breeze--though in any other world it was straight gossiping. There was so much Mark wanted to talk to Jake about, or just touch skin on skin in a way that wasn't covered with denim, leather, or dirt. But that just wasn't possible. And from the cryptic looks Jake gave him, Mark only hoped it was reciprocal.

Mark honestly could not remember the excuse Jake had made to drive up that fall day six years ago. It could have been a saddle, either to sell or buy, or a forgotten something left over the last weekend. That part of the day was a complete blank.

It had been a hot day and even with the sun parallel to the earth, the ground itself radiated heat. Rodeo season meant two and a half if not three days away from the ranch, which meant all the work from eighteen-hour days seven days a week had to be compressed into five, sometimes less. And the sun going down on Edward McCoy's ranch was never an excuse to pack it in if one was related to the man.

Mark was working on a tractor. It was less than three years old, the green paint still shiny, and yet the engine had stripped something and huge bellows of black smoke kicked out whenever it started. It was only two months past the warranty, as was always the case. He and Devon, the boss hand, were up to their elbows in grease and little specks of metal that were never a good sign in any type of gear work when Jake's red truck came barreling down the road.

Devon saw Jake through the windshield, looked at Mark's face, and understood. Jake came out of the truck holding a bridle--that had been the ruse. They had talked about it in one of the few seconds they'd had alone. Mark remembered now. Jake looked almost sheepish, dressed in clean jeans and a clean white shirt. Mark glanced back to Devon, his tongue tied like a teenager trying to come up with some excuse that would give him and Jake more privacy, but Devon just nodded and squeezed Mark's shoulder.

The smell of the anti-grease soap had been particularly offensive in the work sink of the barn. The hair on the back of his neck prickled with awareness of Jake standing right behind him. They were alone, and would be for a while. Only one horse was missing from the stables. His brother, Peter, had taken his gelding out to try to find what had happened to a lost steer in the northern field. Mark's dad was gone for the day, as were all the paid day employees, so Mark took the extra second to take off his shirt and wash away some of the day's grime that had worked up his sleeves and down the waistband of his jeans.

He remembered turning to Jake, half naked, yet feeling completely exposed, and if it were possible to feel a gaze on his skin, he felt Jake studying him. It didn't feel wrong. Still, they were right out in the open. Anyone glancing through the huge open doors would see them beside the sink. Jake knew it too.

He glanced up to the hayloft, a Motel 6 for any ranch hand, and waited for Mark to nod before heading up the old ladder.

It was early fall, and the second cutting of hay was still on the field. The small square bales made comfortable surroundings. Both their shirts made the lowest pile an okay bed and it was Mark's turn to be able to look at Jake. He traced Jake's clavicle with clean, if slightly raw fingers and was amazed at the sinewy strength Jake had over his shoulders and down his arms. Mark would've kept going, to feel his way down Jake's chest, over his belly, and further down to places his sudden shyness wouldn't allow him to think the names of, but his overactive imagination had great plans for, when Jake kissed him.

It was soft, in a way that Mark did not think possible. Devon probably knew what was what the moment he saw that Jake had shaved at five o'clock at night. His cheeks were smooth. Mark pulled away, knowing that his own cheeks weren't, but Jake didn't let him go free. Nor did Mark truly want to be free.

Jake parted his lips, an open invitation, and slid his hands around Mark's hips to pull him closer. This was the part with the buckle bunnies that had always disgusted Mark. It was like his mouth was a box of cereal and whoever had their tongue in his mouth was looking for the special prize. He had to have been pretty drunk in order to have gotten that far, and more times than not he'd pushed the poor girl off of him and stumble away to sleep off his too high blood alcohol level.

This wasn't that. It almost seemed two completely different acts. Mark awkwardly parted his own lips, hesitantly following Jake's lead in his hand placement in relation to buttocks, and felt a jolt shoot through him the first time their groins were aligned. This was very, very good and he had been stupid to wait this long.

The next bit should have been automatic. The jeans were to come off, they were to lie down over their shirts naked and... be together, however that was supposed to align itself. He'd been somewhat fuzzy on the mechanics at the time, and in this dream state Mark only had a tenuous grasp on the line between present-day knowledge and memory. It would be so easy to insert the memory of an orgasm on that day... the sweet hay, the smell of dust that perpetually tickled the back of his throat, the sun soaked smell of the old wood, the calming, reassuring smell of the horses beneath them. Floating in his hospital bed, it seemed the easiest thing in the world for Mark to be able to rewrite what had happened that evening.

But he couldn't. He had unbuttoned Jake's jeans, but hadn't yet managed the zipper when he heard the clatter of hooves below them and outside. It wasn't possible. There were no pavement or cobblestones for that particular sound of shod horses clattering against a hard surface, but he heard it nonetheless. He wondered, there in the hospital room, what would've happened if he'd kept to the task at hand, but instead he'd gone to the single, grimy window that let in the filtered orange light of the sunset, and looked down to the yard.

It was a posse. They were dressed all in black, on big, black horses, and their faces were covered in black bandannas that hid all but the too large black irises in their white eyes.

Jake wasn't looking at him. He was adjusting the shirts, a dozen feet away, and didn't stop making the nest that they had created more comfortable. He couldn't have seen the riders. He didn't see the way the riders had looked up almost the instant Mark had come to the window, and he didn't see the way the leader dipped the rim of his hat at him all cordial like.

Mark had taken a breath to call Jake over, but the words died in his throat when his eyes locked on the leader. If he could have, he would have curled up under the window, hugged his knees to his chest and hid his face until whatever terrible thing that was below them rode on without ever acknowledging them again. But he couldn't. He couldn't look away, and even under the bandanna, Mark knew the rider was smiling. And if he raised his hand and beckoned Mark down, Mark knew he would go. He didn't have to look away from the leader's face to know there would be at least one horse without a rider, waiting for him.

But the man didn't beckon. Probably because the motion from the front gate distracted him. It was only when the man looked away from Mark's eyes that Mark was able to follow his gaze and see another riderless horse trotting down the lane with the saddle it still wore, stirrups swinging back and forth. It was Camper, his brother Peter's big sorrel gelding. And it was alone.

The leader looked back up to him, again touching his hat, and if ever Mark had been told, "another time then," it would never be as clear. And Mark would have screamed, but all that was left from that initial breath he had taken before seeing the black riders was a tiny little squeak. And even that was too loud. The leader smiled again, the action visible only in his eyes, and he motioned his riders to follow.

More clattering of hooves. Sparks shot up where the black horses struck the ground and it wasn't until the last rider had passed through the gate welcoming visitors to Bar Nunn that Mark was able to pull himself away.

Jake looked up, and Mark realized how few seconds had passed between him going to the window to him stumbling away from it. "What's wrong?" Jake had asked. Mark remembered the words five years later because it seemed so ridiculous that the only concern Jake had at that moment was that Mark had developed cold feet. But there were no words to describe what he'd seen and he knew he couldn't even attempt it. So he didn't. He went down the ladder, still half naked, and Jake followed, calling his name.

Mark supposed, distantly, that if Jake had taken the time to put his shirt back on, it might have changed at least some of the events that evening. But he hadn't. It was easy enough on a hot summer's evening for one young man to be shirtless. But when his father had driven up and found Mark trying to catch a still spooked Camper half-naked, with another half-naked young man behind him with his jeans unbuttoned, well, there was no explaining that. Especially when Mark was, in his father's words if not his own, the younger, more delicate son, the conclusion his father leapt to was not altogether off base.

And when the younger, more delicate son was found half-naked with another man on the same night that his older, more rugged son was found dead in a ditch a quarter mile from the gate, well, those sorts of nights are never really forgiven, forget forgotten.

Mark opened his eyes back in the hospital room. The euphoric part of the drugs had worn off, leaving him in a pain-free, if restless state. Now that Mark was awake, the black riders became a distant memory, like something he'd been told rather than something that had terrified him.

He'd been young enough that his father's good will had meant everything to him. And if swearing he would never look at another man again, or have anything at all to do with Jake Alastair, meant that the two of them could sit down at dinner across from each other and discuss nothing more personal than whether to allow a field to lie fallow the next year, then at the time Mark considered it to be a fair deal.

Things got easier two years after Peter died. Edward remarried, to a blond haired will-o-wisp of an ex-barrel racer. Her name was Mitsy, and within a couple months she brought civility, and not just forced politeness to the table. She didn't involve herself much between Mark and his father, but she was always willing to brew a cup of strong coffee in the big house's kitchen. They didn't say much, they didn't have to, but it was good just to sit at the table until the frustration of dealing with the block-headedness of his father passed. Mitsy was there for him, but she also loved his father for reasons Mark never really understood.

The cast had come off before Mark's father visited him again. The skin under the fiberglass had gone fish belly white, and when he stood there wasn't a single part of him that trusted the leg to hold his weight. An old wheelchair and a pair of crutches stood by the bedside, but when his physiotherapists weren't watching he used the cane the most, despite their dire warnings of its inefficiency.

Even though it clearly made him nervous, and the rescue center was at its busiest in the middle of summer vacation, Jake had visited him twice. Not for very long, but Mark didn't mind. He enjoyed Jake sitting with him -- even when he was too doped up or in pain to be much of a conversationalist, it felt good to have him there.

They spoke of inconsequential things, but that was okay. Their empty conversations had nothing to do with the thick silence Mark had always associated with dinnertime. Finally, Mark approached the topic of getting out of the hospital with all the caution of approaching a wild bull in the chutes.

It had been in the late spring, and he was able to sit in the chair facing the window. The sun was bright, and the world outside was full of so much early color that when he had to look back into the room and see the washed out greens and dirty whites again, it made his head hurt. Bar Nunn bred its cattle for an early spring delivery to maximize growth, which meant by mid-May even the most stubborn of young heifers had finally given birth. The crops were already planted. The spring showers -- if they were very, very lucky -- turned the riverbed and most of the back forty into green blankets of new growth that never lasted but spurred what seemed to be new growth everywhere.

If he were on the ranch, he would have more chores than hours to do them in. His father had never really replaced Peter, which somehow gave Mark four times as much stuff to do, but it kept him busy and too exhausted to think that life could be anything else but work. He hadn't had this much time to think in his entire life and he was almost sick from the monotony and exhaustion healing seemed to take.

So when the door opened, and Jake walked in, Mark embarrassed himself by how eager he was to get the hell out of the hospital room and into some place that didn't smell like antiseptic and recycled air. Dressing was something he could not quite manage without help, but once he made it down the stairs and out the door, and into the park, there was a strong enough wind to make the bathrobe he wore over his pajamas -- which he was going to burn later -- acceptable.

Jake looked good. It was only late spring, but he was already starting to tan. The constant exposure to the elements had left him with lines around his eyes that showed just how much of his day he spent smiling. It was a ridiculous thing for Mark to notice, but he did.

He must have been comfortable enough with Mark because he was no longer wearing his dress blues. The old pair of jeans he wore hugged him in places no brand new pair ever would, though the new shirt had obviously just come out of plastic.

He had a distracted look in his eyes that kept him from being all the way with Mark, and when Mark asked about it all he said was there was a special place in hell for developers and their like.

Jake then told him, in a deliberate act of changing the subject -- a faux pas Mark allowed him -- of the first spring auction he had gone to. It was an easy time for him, spring was full of hope and more people came down to the local auctions to buy riding animals than at any other time. They quickly priced out most of the meat merchants who could not go above a dollar a pound and still make money. It was the fall that was hard, Jake said in his quiet way that broke Mark's heart. The cost of hay inevitably rose over the winter, and too many perfectly healthy young horses were sold to the auctions. Almost no one else bought for the same reason they were selling and the meat buyers made a killing. Literally.

Mark swallowed. It took him three attempts to broach the topic, and when he did the words piled out unceremoniously like rodeo clowns out of a barrel.

"I'm not going to be here forever," he said.

"I should certainly hope not. It's rather an unbearable thought." Jake leaned against the handles of the chair, and his hat shaded them both from the sun. Despite the wind, it was getting too hot. Mark felt naked without his own hat, despite the almost four months he had been without it. But if there was one person he felt comfortable being naked around, it was Jake.

From across the street, the school bell rang like it did every school day. A moment or so later the first of the kids riding bikes came pouring out of the park. Mark wanted to go inside, not wanting to be seen as yet another freak being aired out like his mother's hall runners, which she beat off the back porch every Sunday like clockwork when she was alive. He was about to open his mouth and asked Jake if they could move when Jake reached down and touched the line of his spine.

Mark jolted, but then got control and leaned back into the touch. "You're not going to be here forever," Jake repeated.

Mark hesitated, but then realized Jake was trying to encourage him to continue.

"I don't want to go back." Mark would have given anything to have been able to watch Jake's face for any kind of reaction before continuing on, but that would've required a significant amount of flexibility he no longer had. Jake stroked his neck again, this time using both his forefinger and his thumb, and Mark knew it was going to be all right. "I want to stay with you."

The touch on the back of his neck hesitated, but didn't stop. Mark felt his heart beat on the roof of his mouth but he didn't say anything else. He had said quite enough, thank you very much.

"Okay," Jake said.

Contracts were sealed with less. Mark relaxed into the wheelchair, and Jake didn't stop petting the back of his neck. Suddenly, Mark could not think of a better way to spend the afternoon.

Now it was high season. The park outside the window of the hospital had a string of bicycles moseyed up to a bike rack as though it were a hitching post, but it was so hot the kids they belonged to sat listlessly on unmoving swings or in what shade the slides provided.

Mark was listless, too. The scars from the operation itched in a way no mosquito bite ever could. He was to be released the next day, under dire threats from the physio department not to do anything stupid. What they considered to be stupid took up most of a binder currently sitting on the end of his bed. Mark already hated its rusty red cover. Arrangements had been made for his truck to be waiting outside, and he had even gone out illicitly during the day to check if the familiar blue Ford waited for him. Seeing it in the long-term parking lot, he was much more pleased than the situation warranted. It took a second to gather up his courage, but when he looked in the cab behind the seats, the suitcases were there just as Devon had promised they would be.

So when the door opened, Mark honestly expected it to be Jake, despite the fact Jake had told him there was no way he could get away from a fund-raising event. From the tone of his voice over the phone Mark knew exactly how Jake felt about fund-raising events, but to use Jake's words they needed every freaking dime.

It wasn't Jake.

His father walked into the room, his cowboy boots making a click that echoed down the halls. For the past four months, Mark had been accustomed to the silence that came from the hospital where even the muffled coughs of other patients seemed loud. Just standing there, Mark's father filled the room with noise and Mark knew he no longer wanted any part of it.

"Why did you sell Butter?" Mark said instead of a greeting. It was rude -- he had meant it to be rude -- but his father did not react to the challenge. He did not even look surprised that Mark knew he had passed Butter on.

"I don't keep dangerous horses in my stable. You know that."

Mark definitely knew. He hadn't sold Peter's horse, Camper. Despite Mark's protest, he had taken the handsome gelding out to the back forty and shot it as crow bait. It was yet another thing Mark could not forgive.

After that, to Mark at least, they did not have much more to talk about. They had long since given up their relationship as father and son and it was a lot easier to tender his resignation to his boss rather than his father.

Again, there was no recognition or surprise. His father nodded, once, and Mark was glad he'd asked Devon to pack up his things. At least there wasn't a question of back payment owed. Without a goodbye, not that Mark expected one, Edward McCoy spun on the back of his heels and walked out of the room.

That was that. The sense of discomfort left and it seemed the easiest thing in the world to wait until morning.

PART TWO

The GPS told Mark in a clipped voice to turn down a rural road that seemed to lead into a farmer's field. Mark almost didn't do it. The gravel road he was already on wasn't much better, yet still he passed the fresh cut wood bones of houses. The lots were barely staked out, yet the stone wall that surrounded the gated community was completed. The gate that was to separate the owners of the huge monstrosities from the rest of the rabble was elegant in its warning to stay away.

For the hundredth time, Mark checked the crumpled piece of paper where he'd written the address down. His left leg cramped up, shooting pain up his spine, half real, half imagined. He slowed down enough to take the turn one handed and rubbed the scar tissue along his hip. It was far too early to link the pain to a change in the weather, but the heavy black storm clouds chasing him didn't make it any easier. The real source of the pain was probably the hour it took to get out of the city and the other hour and a half on bouncy, dirt roads after months of hospital and rehab living.

The sky to the west was certainly growing dark, and prairie summer storms were the worst. There was nothing to stop the clouds from gathering for miles and miles. He licked his lips, knowing the hard packed dirt road here would look like a mud bog after the deluge, but he was committed, and he wasn't planning on leaving anytime soon. He shifted up to third, but didn't dare take it up any faster for fear the truck might rattle to pieces.

The air stilled. With his window open, the cicadas in the ditch were deafening. Mark took off his hat long enough to scrape his hair off his forehead. Another turn, and out of nowhere -- or as much out of nowhere as could be in a landscape with almost a zero gradient -- the ranch was ahead. It was obviously built in the only dip for miles to cut back some of the wind. The two red barns, painted the same ubiquitous red of all red barns everywhere, grew in the distance. The house beside them had yellow siding on it. The rest of the outbuildings were in various stages of care, but there was none of the elephant graveyard of equipment that most of the farms and ranches Mark had passed had in their front yards.

The horses in the first field had the glossy sheen of all well taken care of beasts. The two sorrels were neck to neck, scratching each other's shoulders, and their penny-colored tails switched lazily in the still air. They both turned at the sound of his truck. One started trotting, the other ran to catch up, and that became a gallop to the narrow human gate that separated their field from the barn. When they reached it, both of them turned on a dime and set off in the opposite direction, their tails streaming out behind them.

Mark parked next to the two trucks in the gravel patch in front of the barn. An eight-horse trailer rested off to the side with its hitch on the ubiquitous stump that all ranchers used for that purpose. Nothing new here, but everything was in good repair. Mark shut off the engine, hearing it ping in protest, and he took a moment before opening the door. His leg twinged again, but he ignored it. Sometimes it felt as though he could feel every screw that had gone into both metal plates.

He got out, and to his credit didn't limp. Jake came out of the barn and leaned against the sign that announced this to be the Sweetgrass Rescue Center.

Jake was different here. He stood taller, his shoulders were wider. The desire Mark felt for him, and it felt good to put a word onto the emotion he'd felt the first moment he saw Jake, all but exploded from the box and had the calf on its side and double hitched in under seven seconds. It wasn't admiration or respect for his skills, which was the justification he'd been hiding his need behind for so long. It was desire, and he wanted Jake. And he was going to have him.

There wasn't anything inherently sexy about the jeans and shirt that were more washed out and dusty than any particular color, and the boots looked as though they were at least, in part, duct tape. A wife or a mother would have thrown them out years ago, but Mark understood.

A boy had come out of the shadows with Jake, no higher than Jake's shoulders. Jake handed him two halters and leads and pointed to the two horses still trotting after other each along the fence line. "Billy, go get the girls," he said.

The boy nodded, glancing to Mark curiously, but trotted down the path and hopefully out of earshot.

Jake straightened, uncovering the sign that said Mark was arriving between visiting hours. Mark supposed that was when the real work was done. The back door to the small house had 'office' printed in the same neat handwriting. The ranch had been Jake's father's labor of love, Mark knew, and the reason why Jake had stopped competing in rodeos on his father's death to take it over. But studying Jake, perfectly at ease in the middle of his land, Mark saw that Jake didn't miss competing.

Jake didn't say anything as Mark approached, but the way he looked down to Mark's left leg showed concern he would never talk about.

"Jake," Mark said. His voice didn't crack even though it was the first word he'd said since he'd left the rehab. There was so much he wanted to say, the gratitude, the need to push Jake back into one of the empty stalls and do all the things he'd meant to on that hot day so long ago, or even simpler, to kiss Jake where he stood and be kissed back and to have everything, finally, fit into its place. He almost forgot about Butter in that second, but all things considered, he could forgive himself that.

"Mark." It was just one word, and his inscrutable face hadn't changed, but Mark knew Jake heard him. And it was okay.

Billy returned with the two horses, but hesitated at the unspoken conversation hanging between them. Jake's eyes remained locked on Mark's for another second, then he stepped out of the way. "Put Queen and Tick away, Billy. Do you need a ride back to town?"

"No, sir," Billy said, but stared at Mark as though trying to categorize him. When he came up blank, he decided to ignore him entirely. "My dad's coming to pick me up."

"If it starts to rain before he gets here, you can wait in the office."

"Yes, sir," Billy said, and clucked to the two horses he led. They entered the building without complaint, and Billy had no problems putting them both away.

Jake hadn't turned around. Mark got the impression he wasn't watching the boy, but looking through the other open door to the field beyond. There was a distant smaller stable, surrounded by a seven foot pipe fence that still looked new. Mark was going to clear his throat, to catch Jake's attention again, but instead he said Jake's name.

Jake turned back. "Yes?"

"May I see her?"

Jake nodded. Billy passed them on the way back to the office, again shooting a worried look at Jake, but Jake shook his head and headed for the office. The storm was almost on them, but before Billy reached the red painted door of the office a blue minivan pulled up and Billy hopped into the passenger seat. The driver made a four-point turn and was gone before Mark spoke. "Where is she?" All the horses visible in the big barn were various shades of sorrel and bay. There wasn't one single cream Palomino.

"She's not here--these are the horses up for adoption," Jake said. He motioned with his head to the smaller red barn that was visible from the road. "Come on."

The other barn was a hundred yards or so away. Mark tried again to prepare himself -- he'd been told she was injured, he reminded himself. But his throat was tight and his leg throbbed as Jake threw open the second barn's door. As though reading his mind, Jake exhaled, sharply. "Most of the swelling's gone. But you know how knee injuries are. My vet's been looking after her, and she's pretty confident she'll make a full recovery."

Mark nodded. This barn only had ten or so stalls, five on each side, and a much smaller tack shop. Only half of the stalls had horses in them.

Butter whickered when she recognized Mark, a deep-throated mare's call that was half welcoming, half demanding, and Mark barely heard Jake say, "And she says Butter's pregnant."

"You got my mare pregnant?" Mark asked, turning to him.

"Well, not personally." Jake's didn't crack a smile, but Mark could see in his eyes that he was fighting it.

The rain, this close to the open doors, swept in, cooling Mark's skin where it touched. After the long hours in the truck, it felt good. The familiar smell of horse, wet grass, and old barn was heady. Mark opened his mouth, wanting to speak, but he had nothing to say. Nothing at all.

The rain also made Jake's skin slick. Mark touched the side of his face, and his fingers slipped down to the corner of Jake's mouth. Jake looked at him, and Mark just couldn't bear a single question as to whether he really wanted to do this, or if he was okay with it. So when Jake opened his mouth and drew in a breath, Mark kissed him hard, pushing him back so that his shoulders hit the door frame. There was a wall of rain inches away from them, and the smell of the ozone the rain brought was everywhere. But it couldn't hide the smell of Jake's wet skin. He smelled of the sunshine in the rain, of the horses he loved, and though he didn't match exactly the way he had in the hayloft, Mark didn't care.

Shirts with snaps were the best invention Mark had ever heard of. He yanked open Jake's shirt just so that he could feel more skin, and Jake didn't protest. Mark kissed his way down Jake's throat, sucking the last bit of salt off his skin that hadn't been washed away, and he nuzzled his way across the line where suntan met the white skin of Jake's chest.

Jake put his hands on Mark's shoulders to steady himself. Mark found Jake's nipples in the fine dust of blond chest hair and when he gave them each an experimental lick, Jake groaned again. He was exceptionally sensitive and quite responsive.

Mark looked up. Jake's mouth was open and his eyes were closed. He had turned his face to the rain. "I would definitely ride you with a snaffle bit," Mark said, and watched Jake lick the droplets of water off his lips.

"We can discuss choice of tack later, I'm sure," Jake said. "But for right now…"

Mark cupped the bulge in Jake's jeans. He let his fingers slide along the hot length he found. "Task at hand. Got it."

"Good." Jake arched his back and stretched, clasping his hands over his head. It revealed a whole new set of muscles between his pectorals and the waistband of his jeans, and if Mark had the patience, he would have been pleased to investigate each and every individual muscle with his tongue and fingertips.

Instead, he kissed his way down the well-defined line of Jake's abdomen. The jeans stopped him for at least thirty seconds as he fought with the wet denim to slide it down Jake's thighs. Roping cows was easier, but he finally succeeded. The boots had to come off first. Jake was naked but for the modest pair of white boxer briefs growing increasingly wetter and, as a consequence, translucent.

Jake looked down at Mark on his knees. Mark felt the gaze and tore himself away from Jake's cock pressed against the white material, and looked up to meet his eyes. He didn't open his mouth to speak. Nor did he need to tell Mark he didn't have to do anything he didn't want to, and Mark didn't have to tell him that his hesitance was not reluctance.

He shifted forward so that he could easily kiss the crown of Jake's cock through the cloth. He rubbed his cheek up and down the length, and took the time to suck on Jake's balls. Again the rain had robbed him of most of the taste of skin, but there was enough to be a promise for things to come.

He peeled the thin wet cloth from Jake's skin. It had revealed a lot, and Mark felt a shiver of pleasure down his spine and straight to his groin at the naked sight. He had to be at least seven inches, cut, and when Mark reached up, hesitantly, to wrap his finger and thumb around it, his fingers could barely touch.

"Getting cold," was all Jake said.

Mark didn't want that. He shifted forward again, lifted himself off his ankles despite the protests from his new hip -- he was so going to feel this tomorrow -- and took Jake into his mouth. The slippery feel of pre-come on his lips was interesting. So was the reaction he got when he slid his tongue all the way around the crown and then flicked the small hole with the tip of his tongue.

Jake dug his fingers into Mark's hair, but didn't try to force his cock any further down Mark's throat. Mark didn't think he could handle that strictly from the gag reflex point of view, and Jake apparently agreed. Jake did, as a compromise, wrap his free hand around the base of his cock and began sliding it up and down to keep pace with the bobbing motion Mark gave him.

It couldn't have been ideal, with the rain and the saliva Mark smelled on Jake's palm being the only lubrication, but it was enough. Jake tensed, his entire body rock still, and when he groaned one last time it was pure desperation. Mark cupped Jake's ass with both hands, and felt him start to shoot in his mouth. Both of Jake's hands were now on Mark's head, but he still didn't try to force Mark any further down.

Salty, thick and warm semen filled his mouth. Mark took over, releasing Jake's ass reluctantly and sliding his fist up and down Jake's cock and let the last little bit inside him. He swallowed, but didn't let the cock out of his mouth until Jake pulled away and helped him to his feet.

Jake tried to kiss him, and for the first time Mark hesitated out of reluctance, but Jake caught his chin easily. "It's okay. You don't have to run inside and brush your teeth quite yet."

"My toothbrush is in the truck," Mark said, knowing he sounded stupid.

"See, impossible. Now shut up and let me kiss you."

There was no arguing his logic. Mark shut up and let Jake kiss him.

It became impossible to ignore how cold the wind was, and small rivers of rainwater began to cut paths through the cement they stood on. Jake made a face, pulled up his soaking wet clothes until he could once again move in them, and together they closed the two doors, instantly turning the day into twilight.

"Okay, come with me." Jake let him pass the stall with Butter. The one right next to her was empty but for half a dozen square bales and it only took a second to make a half decent bed out of them. Mark was grateful to be able to sit down, then lay down at Jake's insistence. He closed his eyes, and liked the haphazard way Jake touched him as he slowly unbuttoned his shirt one by one.

When he finished, Jake stood up but only long enough to pull Mark's boots off. Mark bit his lips, not wanting to say anything but knowing there was such a difference between removing enough clothing to get the job done and being completely naked. Jake was obviously not going to be satisfied until Mark was stripped, but he couldn't have been more delicate when it came to working the jeans. They were baggy after all the months of hospital food, but he was still gentle. He pushed them down Mark's hips, down his thighs and then off completely. A second later Jake's clothes joined them.

Mark was more touchy about the puffy pink scars from the surgery than he was about being completely naked. He almost covered them, but Jake saw and caught his wrist before he could. He kissed the palm of Mark's hand before putting it by his side. Jake bent down, but didn't kissed his cock like Mark had been expecting. Instead he touched the first long scar that went up and over his hip bone.

"Don't ever be ashamed," Jake said. He looked up, and Mark couldn't look away from his blue eyes. "Never again. Promise me."

"I promise," Mark said. He would've said anything, spread out naked as he was for Jake that instant, but he was surprised to feel that he had meant it. Jake finished kissing his way down the longer, uglier scar and then straddled Mark's thigh so that their groins were aligned.

"You've done this before," Mark said.

Jake shifted, took Mark's cock in his right hand and his own in his left, and smiled. "A couple times."

"Do you want to tell me what happens next?" Mark asked.

"Oh, I would so much rather show you."

The grip on his cock was loose, much looser than Mark liked when he was alone. But when he was alone, he didn't have Jake over him, moving his hips and keeping perfect rhythm so that Mark was fucking Jake's hand. He looked up, eyes wide, and Jake smiled at him, picking up the pace. He'd been practically hard since leaving the hospital, definitely hard since pulling up into Jake's yard and achingly hard on his knees in front of Jake taking what he could into his mouth. It didn't take much of Jake's wild ride to pull the orgasm from him, and when he came, his insides felt raw from the over stimulation and intense need. Jake didn't slow down as he was coming, but let him ride out each of the aftershocks that shook him. His come shot up over his belly and almost to his pectorals. Jake licked him clean an inch at a time and then curled up next to him in the warmth and safety of the barn while the worst of the storm passed over them.

There were worse ways to spend an afternoon.

The sound of the rain slacking off on the roof of the barn woke Mark from his light nap. His body told him more than the watch on his wrist that it was time for another pill, but he ignored the pain as he sat up. Jake was already awake, if he had been napping at all. He was still naked, leaning back against the stall wall. Mark couldn't help dropping his gaze downward to Jake's cock.

It was nestled in blond pubic hair, and it was beautiful even flaccid. He forced himself to look back up to Jake's face, and then couldn't help but smile just because Jake was smiling. "Good afternoon. Sleep well?"

Mark sat up, and stretched. After so many nights in the hospital and in the rehab center, if he spent the rest of his life sleeping on hay bales he would've been happy. There was something else in the question, something deeper. If he was going to freak out afterwards -- though why he would freak out when he had just found that thing he was missing -- it would have been the time to say something. Instead, Mark reached his foot out and stroked Jake's leg. "Yes."

Jake relaxed. "Good. If you put some clothes on, I'll show you around the center. Not that there's much left to show you."

Mark nodded. Together they got up and dressed.

The rain had let up and the sun burst through the dark clouds brilliantly, bathing the world in light that seemed to magnify the colors remaining in the hot autumn day. The barns seemed more red, the hay waiting to be cut more golden and the blue sky poking through ahead of the sun even more sapphire. The world smelled of wet, but also of promise. Jake glanced up at the sky as though to decide if the dark clouds had truly finished, and then nodded.

"Right, then. I'll show you around."

Mark nodded. Jake showed him the different pastures; he had a quarter section, and while most of it was used to grow enough hay so they didn't have to buy any on good years, he also had fifty head of Black Angus cows. The small barn away from everything was the quarantine area.

Lastly, Jake showed him the office, a small add-on to the house. The room was big enough for a desk, a couple filing cabinets and spare helmets that probably belonged in a tack-shop.

"That's the grand tour?" Mark asked.

"It is. I would show you the house, but I want to check on the herd before we lose any more light."

Mark was going to nod, but stopped. A huge truck, black at one time but now as muddy as the road, roared into the compound. It slid as the driver slammed on the brakes, and came dangerously close to hitting Mark's truck. Jake's jaw clenched, once, the only sign of displeasure from him, and then his face returned to the bland politeness he'd kept around the nurses.

The man getting out of the oversized vehicle just this side of a monster truck struggled to get his belly out from behind the wheel. His face was red, despite the cool breeze the rain had created, and he took the time to hitch up his pants before slamming the door closed.

"Alistair," the man called, with the raspy voice of a chain smoker. Mark came down the step of the office. Jake followed him. Even though his face was nothing if not polite, there was a tight line around his mouth.

"Mr. Rendell," Jake said.

"Did you get my paperwork?" He glanced to Mark, standing just off to the side, and then he looked back to Jake. He nodded to himself, and while the self-satisfied smirk only lasted a tenth of a second, Mark knew Jake had seen it as well from the way he tensed.

"Who's your friend?" Rendell asked.

"My friend," Jake said.

"If he's here to give you a better deal..." He didn't finish. But something hung in the air. Just because Mark couldn't see it or understand it didn't mean it wasn't there.

Jake crossed his arms over his chest. "I got the papers. But as I told you the half dozen times before, I am not interested in selling. I need the land to grow my hay." Another minivan pulled in beside the monster truck, and a mother with three girls piled out. Jake nodded to them, motioning to the first stable, and turned back to Rendell. "Is there anything else, Mr. Rendell?"

"That section has the best view of the river. I need it. And I'm going to have it."

"Good evening, Mr. Rendell."

Rendell crossed his arms, a mirror of Jake's body stance, but if he assumed Jake was going to partake in the stare-down, he was wrong. Jake simply stepped past him and followed the girls into the barn. The girls led out three of the smaller horses. "Are you coming?" Jake called, speaking to Mark alone. Mark shrugged his shoulders at Rendell, and followed Jake into the second barn.

"Damn fool," Jake said, under his breath so the girls couldn't hear him. "I told him that stretch is a flood plain, but he won't hear me. He says his developers gave him to go ahead, but it's flooded once every ten years or so since my dad bought the land."

Mark nodded. He didn't like the look Rendell had given Jake at all. "Has he threatened you?" He followed Jake back to the private barn, where he was more than a little pleased to see Hank, Jake's champion roper. When Jake had stopped competing he could have sold the big gunmetal gray gelding for twenty grand, easy. Hank took up the slack faster than even Butter could.

"Of course I kept him," Jake said, ignoring the asked question and answering the unasked one. "It was the least I could do to give you an unfair advantage as to not having to compete with the greatest cow pony in Alberta, if not western Canada."

The cow pony stood at least sixteen hands at the shoulder. "The very least, eh?"

Jake nodded and gave him a big boned dun Appaloosa mare named Chancey. They saddled up and then joined the girls in the yard. He mounted on the wrong side, using his right leg to pull himself up. Getting his leg up and over the saddle probably wasn't in the rusty red binder, but it had been too long since Mark had sat in a saddle.

"Is that okay?" Jake asked, and put a hand on Mark's upper thigh. It was tight, and muscles he'd had his entire life felt atrophied, but it was okay. And the hand on his leg was even better. He nodded.

"Good." Jake slapped Chancey on the ass as he walked behind her. Chancey swished her bob of a tail good-naturedly.

The girls waved to their mother, who was in the office at work with the door open and the fan on. "She does the books," Jake explained. "And the girls volunteer with the horses. They seem to think I'm doing them a favor by letting them muck out stalls."

"Do you have help year-round?"

"Mostly. The money isn't tight, most months it's nonexistent. If we didn't raise the cattle, some months there'd be no money to pay even utilities."

Mark got down at the first gate and opened it then closed it behind them. The girls took off on ahead, their blond ponytails streaming out behind them, but Mark kept behind with Jake.

"You didn't answer the question. Has he been threatening you?" It wasn't his place to pry, Mark knew it, and Jake knew it. It fell under the sacred realm of "personal business," and if Jake didn't answer this time, Mark knew he could never ask again.

"Not exactly threaten," Jake said quietly. "A gate gets opened. Was it left open or did it get opened? A dead animal falls into the drinking water. An accident? Little things. Things that happen all the time. It's just a hay field, but the way the price of hay skyrockets so quickly in a bad year, if I can't feed the herd I'd have to cull it and how ironic would that be?"

Then he hesitated. "And there was a dead calf," he said. "With the herd. It could have been wild dogs, or an accident and they just found the corpse, but I swore around the edges of the throat where the most damage was, it looked cut, like with a knife. He probably just came by to see if it spooked us."

"Did you call the cops?"

"They came out. Even if its throat had been cut, there was no way to prove Rendell had done it. He's been nothing but just another polite good ole boy. And his offer for undeveloped farm land that floods is really quite generous, but not enough to keep me in hay for the rest of our lives here. We owe the bank so much for back taxes on the land, and it would be so easy to agree to it. It just seems I'm going to lose this place either way."

Ahead of them, the girls slowed, spun around and came barreling back. The horses that they rode were sleek, healthy and happy. That they had been sold for their meat price was an abomination. Mark looked to Jake. This hadn't been his life. It hadn't been his fight. But he knew, the same way he knew just how fiercely he loved Jake, he loved this world, too.

And when Jake looked back at him, he smiled. And he knew. He raised an eyebrow, already lifting his reins to give Hank his head, but Mark's hip was hurting. He reined Chancey in. "You go. I should head back."

"Are you sure?"

Mark nodded. One of the girls shrieked ahead of them, a joyous sound, and Jake really did have to check on the herd. He reached over, touched Mark's cheek. The evening had chilled thanks to the sudden rainstorm, and the touch was hot enough to burn. The thought of even more skin being pressed up against him turned the slight heat to his skin into a full flush, and Jake smiled as though he could read his mind.

"Tonight," he promised. He turned Hank away, not even having to kick his flank, but just leaned forward in the saddle. They took off, kicking up wet clods with the just turned smell of grass and dirt as Hank dug in for those first couple bounds. Despite the ache in his hip, Mark was home.

Chancey fought with him, just for a second, wanting to take off after her buddy, but when Mark turned her away, back to the barn, she sighed and ambled back. Mark took the time to rub his hip, taking deep breaths to help manage the pain, and by the time they got back to the gate the pain had settled to a constant ache.

He carefully slung his right leg over to the left side, over the pommel of his saddle, and slid down Chancey's side slowly so that his right leg took all his weight when he landed. He undid the gate, led Chancey through and closed it again. He was a hundred yards from the barn, and chose to walk it rather than mount up again.

Behind his truck, though Mitsy's little Fiat could have hidden behind a Shetland pony, was the familiar green two-seater. Mitsy herself was in the office, chatting with the office lady, but the moment she saw him leading Chancey into the yard, she was down the stairs in a flash.

She wore jeans that shouldn't have been flattering on her, considering she was ten years older than Mark, but she pulled them off. The men's work shirt she wore was loose enough, and her blond hair, all natural if the almost ghostlike eyebrows and eyelashes were any indication, was tied back in a ponytail. She was an aging beauty queen and she knew it, but she kept her makeup to an absolute minimum, and time was, and would probably always be, kind to her.

"Marcus James McCoy. You did not just ride that horse," she said, crossing her arms over her chest. "Tell me you were not that stupid."

"Would you believe me if I said no?" Mark asked, keeping his face innocent.

"For the sake of our relationship, I suppose I'm going to have to. Just this once, you understand."

"Just this once," Mark promised, but had obviously crossed his fingers. She eyed him critically, then nodded to herself. "You look better. How's Butter?"

"Jake says she'll make a full recovery."

"Good," Mitsy said, and took Chancey away from him. Mark lamented the fact that his cane was still in his truck; he really could have used it right about then, but Chancey didn't seem to mind him following and throwing his arm over the saddle for support as Mitsy walked her back to the second barn. Mark leaned against the doorframe, trying not to flush at the thought of Jake leaning against the exact same spot, but Mitsy didn't look up from stripping Chancey down and brushing her out. After Chancey was put away, they both moved to Butter's stall. "She's looking good," Mitsy allowed. Mark said nothing.

Mitsy, of course, noticed. She held up her hand. "You can blame your father for selling her on," she said. "Lord knows I tore a strip off him for you, but he didn't do it to punish you. You should know that."

Mark shrugged. He didn't believe her, but felt it impolite to argue the point. She turned to him angrily. And when Mitsy got angry, it was best that everything light enough to throw was firmly tied down. "You don't think he turned pale as a ghost when he saw Butter come back alone? Who do you think found you out there first? It wasn't Devon. You were passed out and bleeding from your damn fool head, and your father held your hand until the ambulance arrived. He even rode back with you. You don't remember that part, I'm sure, but he was there."

Mark stared at her. He shook his head, not remembering much at all after the crash and being too afraid to look up and see the black riders. But he did remember, if he stretched out the memory as far as he could, the feeling of his hand being held was there. "That was Dad?"

"And he was pretty sure he'd just lost his second son. He needs you, Mark."

The ride back had obviously taken far less time than the ride there, because just as Mitsy finished, Jake appeared at the door, leading a sweating Hank behind him. The sweat turned Hank's gray sides black, but there was still plenty of pep in his walk. Mitsy glanced at him, then looked back to Mark. "Your father still loves you. And he'll accept you, after a fashion."

"I'm not asking him to accept me after a fashion or not," Mark said. Jake had frozen where he stood, shifting his weight from foot to foot in embarrassment, but obviously pretending he couldn't hear them. Mark didn't care if he did. "This is what

I am," he said, quietly. "And if it took the fall to get me here, I'm glad I did. If Dad needs me to go home, tell him I already am."

Mitsy tsked, then dusted some imaginary dust off Mark's shirt--or more like smacked it off, but in a kind, loving way. "You two boys are going to give me wrinkles. I should be getting back, daylight's wasting, and I need to shower before work. Emergency phones don't answer themselves."

Mark knew she didn't need to work at the dispatch for the local RCMP detachment. He suspected she did it just to get out of the house. She picked up the graveyard shift, every other day, and was damn good at being that calming voice on the other end of the line. Mitsy smiled at him, brilliantly. "According to the sign on the wall, visiting hours are almost over. I'm sure your man over there will help you move the rest of the books I brought you."

He looked over to his man over there, and couldn't stop the smile. "I reckon he will." Mark kissed her cheek. "Thank you for coming."

"You don't be a stranger," Mitsy told him. She walked past Jake, eyeing him up and down appreciatively, and touched his arm as he bowed his head to her.

"Ma'am," he said.

"Indeed I am," Mitsy said, and jumped into her little car. The girls finished their own chores, their voices carrying on the new wind, and all piled back into their mom's car. She drove off as well, albeit at a much slower pace, and Jake and Mark were alone again.

"Well?" Jake asked.

"Well what?" Mark hurt. He had the fine grit under his clothes that happened when rain-wet denim dried without being washed, and after days and months of a busy day involving two trips to the communal television room just to get out of his eight-by-ten cell of a room, he was exhausted.

Jake took his hand. "Dinner's cooking on the crock pot on the counter. Another hour or so won't hurt it one bit."

"Well," said Mark. Together, they wedged off their boots on the corner of the step on the porch and went inside the small yellow house.

The house was small, and the main hall — what there was of it — opened into the kitchen. The living room was off to the left through an open arch and the two doors to the right, both of them closed, were probably the bathroom and bedroom.

Beneath the aromas of dinner, the house smelled like home. It couldn't have been just the smell of the slow cooked beef and onions simmering in the small crock pot beside the sink. His mother had been a fine cook, despite her wealthy upbringing, but Mitsy sure wasn't.

The living room was an untouched museum display. Mark could almost see the card missing off to the side. In neatly typed letters it would say "living room, late 1950s setting." A plastic dust cover swathed the huge flowered chesterfield and dark wood was used in everything from the coffee and end tables to the crystal display cases. Jake obviously kept the room dusted, and the pale pink carpet was in pristine condition.

The kitchen looked much warmer. The stove was a huge gas beast and the green enamel finish came from another era. The fridge matched. The kettle rested on the back burner of the stove, because that was where all farm kitchens had kettles. Unlike Bar Nunn's decorative pot that got moved every decade or so, this one looked as though it got some regular usage.

Mark glanced to the second door, the one that probably led into the bedroom, and glanced at Jake. "Shower, first," Jake announced and took Mark's shoulders. He propelled Mark into the bathroom, which turned out to be the first door after all. The green sink and tub were both scrupulously clean but had long since lost their shine.

"Strip," Jake ordered.

"You're putting on airs now?" Mark asked, but couldn't keep the smile, despite how much he wanted to pretend a scowl. "Big words for a man who has a doily collection."

"Those were just the everyday doilies. Wait until you see the company coming chest."

There was a chest Mark wanted to see, but it didn't involve any frills or lace. He put his hands over Jake's heart and the even beats calmed him.

Jake put his hand over Mark's. "I said strip," he said. His low voice was barely more than a growl. Mark looked up and saw the slow curl of the smile that touched Jake's lips. He undid his shirt buttons, one by one, and remembered how it felt to have Jake do it for him.

"Is this the way it's going to be?" Mark's own voice felt thick. His shirtsleeves caught over his wrist and he had to pull them off one at a time.

"Unless you have any objections," Jake said. As he spoke, he stepped forward and pinned Mark against the sink. He moved his hands up Mark's thigh. He waited, and Mark held his breath before Jake finally cupped the palm of his hand against Mark's already mostly hard cock. Mark had to fight with himself not to grind against it. "Are there, Mark? Any objections I mean?"

And Jake looked at him, his blue eyes intense. There was a time Mark could have stared in them for hours, but right that second there was a burning heat between them, and Mark had to do something before the moment passed. He was going to get fucked. This man was going to put him on his knees and stick his dick into Mark's ass. Mark found in the second he had to think about it that he had no issue with that whatsoever.

"No objections here," Mark said. His now fully hard cock ached for more than just a touch. But Jake stepped back and Mark felt cold with the absence.

"Good. Then can you finish stripping for me?"

Mark found that he could. His jeans came off, his socks, his shorts, and his wristwatch. He was completely naked. Jake looked down to Mark's bad leg. Mark wished he could stop the tremble, but Jake saw it. "It hurts?"

"Yes," Mark said. He couldn't lie. Jake nodded.

"Do you think you can step up into the tub?"

"Yes," Mark said, and there was a bite in his voice he hadn't intended. "I'm not a complete invalid."

"Begging pardon," Jake said. "But you are, in fact, in pain. Do you need help?"

"Yes," Mark said reluctantly.

Jake kissed him softly, and pressed their foreheads together. "That wasn't so hard, was it?"

"Asking for help, or your dick against my leg?" Mark asked, as innocent as he could.

Jake laughed. He pulled away but held Mark up against the sink with a look. He stripped down himself. There was so much naked flesh for Mark to touch. Instead, they got into the shower. Mark used Jake's shoulders for support and even with that, his bad leg twinged again as he stepped in.

For how old the rest of the house was, the water pressure and showerhead were both wonderfully modern.

Mark braced himself against the tiles, letting Jake slide slippery hands up and down his body in places no one else had ever touched him. He flinched when the soapy finger slipped between his ass cheeks, but Jake was there, whispering things to make him relax and assure him that everything was going to be just fine. As soon as the tension left Mark's shoulders, Jake tried again. This time, Mark let him. It stung at first, though that could have just been the soap. Jake took the showerhead off the hook, snaking the metal hose past Mark's shoulder, and held the warm stream of water over the small of his back. All the while, he kept pushing his finger further into Mark.

It didn't feel good, not at first and especially not when Jake slipped a second finger inside him. But Jake added something from a bottle, conditioner, probably, and that took away most of the burn. It left Mark feeling uncomfortably full for another second, but then the pressure that was building suddenly became pleasurable. He groaned, and leaned back into Jake's body.

Jake had to lean forward to kiss the back of his shoulder. "There you are," he said.

Mark closed his eyes. There he was, indeed.

They moved to Jake's double bed. The blue sheets were clean, and the pillows were surprisingly soft. Mark's leg hurt too much to kneel down on it, and the edge of the bed was not high enough. They settled for Mark on his side, with the pillow supporting him. Mark didn't watch the preparations. There was something else in a bottle, the tinfoil crackle of a condom wrapper, and Jake's fingers went back inside him working through the first amount of discomfort with something cold that seemed to melt. He waited for Mark to start pushing back to get the fingers deeper inside him before he even lay down.

"Ready?" Jake asked, and held onto his hip. Mark hugged the pillows under him and nodded.

Jake was much bigger than his two fingers, but there was so much lube inside of Mark and on Jake's cock that Mark felt too slippery to clamp his muscles down and stop Jake, not that he wanted to. Jake pressed against him, his chest to Mark's back, and kissed the nape of Mark's neck.

"Still good?" Jake asked.

"Yup," Mark said, and then groaned again as Jake pushed the rest of the way inside. He moved his hand to Mark's cock. The lube had warmed to his body temperature, so when Jake closed his fingers around Mark with just the right amount of tightness, Mark gasped. Jake jerked Mark's cock a couple of times, deep and hard enough that it worked from the base of his cock to the very sensitive crown. It took Mark's attention away from the pressure in his ass, and the next time Mark thought back to it, the discomfort had passed. "You're a tricky bastard," Mark said.

"Yes." Jake licked his way down Mark's neck. "You should see me get a colt into a trailer for the first time."

"I hope you don't use this exact technique." Mark got the lobe of his ear bitten, but he supposed he deserved it.

Jake began to fuck him, slowly at first. It took Mark a little longer to get to like the in and out feeling. Jake's hand kept pace so there was always sensation. Jake shifted, and moved into long, slow strokes. It just about drove Mark to push away, the sensation was so much it was almost easier to pull back than take it all, but Jake didn't let him go.

Jake laughed, again, and Mark wanted it harder, thrusting into Jake's hands over and over as sparks he didn't even know he had the plugs for began to fly. He tried lifting himself off the bed to get his dick deeper into Jake's hand. His whole body flushed as the orgasm pushed him with hot dizzy strength.

Jake growled, pinning him down and four hard, quick strokes later, his whole body tensed and he was coming, too.

The bed shifted, Jake had collapsed behind him, and against his shoulder blade he felt how fast Jake's heartbeat was. It matched his almost perfectly. Mark grabbed Jake's hand, pulling it over his side, and curled up to it. Jake didn't pull away. Mark just meant to close his eyes just until Jake turned over to the other side, but when he opened his eyes again, it was dark out and the smell of food made his stomach clench hungrily.

The tray Jake carried was made of the same old wood as most of the living room, and if it were any less quality it would have bowed under the weight of all the food it carried. The stew filled two cereal bowls, the egg noodles were on the side and smelled of butter and chives. There were green beans, still steaming, and a huge salad made of iceberg lettuce. Two long-necked beers, a jug of water, and one small pill bottle completed the meal.

Mark grabbed one of the small white pills and swallowed it dry. "If I thought I loved you before, I'm certain of it now." He looked up, swallowed again, and felt the burning trail the pill had left. "Or are we not at that stage yet?"

Jake adjusted the pillows behind Mark's head and sat down cross-legged on the other side of the tray. The pill in him reacted quickly in his empty stomach. "I've pretty much loved you since I saw you at the rodeo," Jake said. He touched Mark's thigh, now under a blanket, and Mark wondered when or how that had happened. The world was in a gentle fuzz, and it just seemed right as he reached over and touched Jake's cheek.

"That's so sweet," Mark said.

Jake kissed his hand. "That's nice, but I know it's just the prescription talking."

"I wish you'd fucked me in the hayloft," Mark said. Jake gave him a bowl of the food, and put the beer he'd brought for him out of reach on the floor.

"Me too," Jake said.

Mark pointed his spoon at Jake. "Just think how many spectacular orgasms I've missed. I bet you can do things with your tongue I've never even heard about."

Jake picked up the pill bottle as well, read it, and put it out of reach, too. "I can teach you tongue tricks," he said, soothingly.

"I learn best by being shown," Mark said. The drug made it hard to form the words properly, so he tried extra hard. He pointed the spoon again, but then distracted himself with the swooping motion it made at the end of his finger. "Bet you never signed up to be a nursemaid." He was fairly certain he'd gotten all those words right. At least Jake's face looked pained.

"I signed up for you. On lay-away, but you were worth the wait. Go to sleep."

That suddenly sounded like an excellent idea. Mark closed his eyes and felt the tray beside him being lifted. He didn't hear Jake leave the room.

Mark dreamed. The drug-induced sleep was a tenuous one at best, and he felt himself pushed up against the line between waking and sleeping a dozen times. Yet still he slept and dreamed.

He walked down the path from the house to the barn. He'd walk that path a million times, knew every bump, every rock. His head was down, and he was tired. It had been a long day, not that the fact narrowed down the time frame much. He could still smell the hot plastic fake leather of school bus seats in the summertime, so he must have been elementary school aged at least, and the horse he was going to collect was really just a pony named Smokey, now over fifteen years dead. They had never really gotten along; he'd been Peter's pony for years and had grown stubborn and mulish in a way that only old cantankerous ponies could become.

Time in the dream passed, or maybe he just came back to being aware of the fact that he had been dreaming. He was on Smokey, on the dirt road between fields. And he remembered what day this was. If he could, he would have shaken himself awake, but he was deep asleep now, and the gossamer strings that had seemed so thin and so close to waking were gone. He was stuck in the dream, riding shotgun in a younger version of himself.

The sun beat down and the crickets sang in the safety of the long grass. His very important task was to check the depth of the watershed in the cow pasture and record it in the book he swore no one else had opened but him. But at least he got to ride Smokey and all his other tasks were far less pleasant.

Except today. A grader had passed in the night and the road that was usually packed dirt, perfect for horses, now had more small stones that took forever to be covered and made safe again for shod hooves. So for today, Mark had pushed Smokey into the soft cut grass shoulders of the road. It wasn't as good as the dirt, there would be no galloping at least, but it was okay.

Until Smokey kicked the ground wasp nest. Mark felt Smokey flinch, shaking his whole body the way horses did, then he started to cow hop, bucking with his back legs in quick succession. Mark stayed on for the fifth or sixth hop, but after that he lost count and his stirrups at the same time. Luckily they were still on the soft grass, and falling from Smokey meant that there wasn't much distance between him and the ground. He landed on his ass and his dignity and bounced up quickly.

The adult Mark who was watching this in the young Mark's head closed his eyes. He didn't want to see this next bit, but he had no ability to block out the memory. Smoky had taken five or six steps forward and had gotten distracted by the bright yellow flowers that grew next to almost every road Mark knew. Mark called to Smokey, and made it almost close enough to step on the fallen reins and get back on before anyone knew he had fallen, when Smokey crowded him, swinging his ass end towards him in a deliberate threat.

And Mark knew he should have been more careful. But instead he slapped Smokey's dusty brown coat with his hand, making a cracking sound that echoed over the prairie.

Then Smokey kicked him. Mark saw it, saw the hoof with the perfect V-shaped frog heading toward him, he felt the wind on his face, but even as he tried to turn and get away it was too late. A new cracking sound echoed over the prairie, but it was his skull that made the sound.

In the dream he woke again, still on the side of the road. The sun was still hot, Mark felt it on his cheek, but when he opened his eyes the world was black and white.

The adult Mark knew that any child growing up on a farm or ranch had more than half a dozen *almost died* stories. It was a true triumph of human spirit that any boy or girl survived their childhood growing up where so many things could -- and did -- go horribly wrong.

The dirt road was no longer graded. It was no longer what could be exactly called dirt, either. It was a wagon trail. Two of them really; he was on an old crossroad. Neither one of them looked well traveled. He touched his temple, and felt the blood. It was a good thing Smokey's hooves had been far too hard to shoe.

A man ran past him, holding his side. And if the blood Mark had on his fingers was black in the manner of old movies, the man's side was red. Blood red. Ruby blood red that ran down his side and coated the hand that held him together. It wasn't the wound that scared him -- Mark had seen blood before -- it was the look in the man's eye. Even wounded and obviously running for his life, he still looked at Mark possessively, like there were things, bad things, the man wanted to do to him and only the time constriction kept him from doing them. The man took his good hand, or the clean one at least, and pressed it against his lips. It wasn't done as a co-conspirator like Peter had done so many times before when he was up to the fun kind of no good, but as a dire warning.

Mark shrank back. The man took off, slower this time and not east or west, but through the field of long grass southwesterly. The grass around him shimmered once and stilled.

The silence didn't last. Hoof beats like an oncoming storm shook the earth and seconds later the black riders were all around him. The leader, the same man who had nodded to him when they waited (would wait?) to collect Peter, looked down at him. He didn't ask the question, but his eyes were cold and expectant. Mark pointed into the long grass. This close he felt the horses' breath on his bare arms and it was hot enough to burn. His teenage self had seen compassion in the man's eyes, and the nod to him then was not a threat, but a promise: Mark knew Peter would be quick, and he wouldn't suffer.

None of those promises were here now. The man nodded a second time, or first if Mark was to count it chronologically, and the black horses with their black riders rode into the tall grass. And even on the soft grass, the hooves cracked like thunder.

Mark woke to the same sound. He remembered now, waking up with a splitting headache and a goose egg. Smokey had been waiting a half-dozen steps past where he'd been the first time. Getting up made Mark sick enough to throw up, and thinking back he'd probably had a severe concussion, but he got back up on Smokey and continued on, forgetting there ever had been black riders.

Mark was wide awake, as he often was once the euphoric part of the painkiller had passed. Jake was asleep beside him, naked and on his back, his mouth open, and if it wasn't for that sound, Mark would've gotten up for a completely different reason. He got dressed -- Jake had left out a clean pair of jeans he must've gotten from Mark's suitcase -- and he pulled them on commando style.

The porch had a bunch of stuff for the kids lying about. An old saddle, the chewed up leather latigo only good for securing it to an old hay bale, an old harness bridle for a draft horse the length of Mark's arm, the bit itself a good nine inches across, and an old lasso still coiled correctly. He looked up. "You've got to be kidding me," he said.

No one answered him, thankfully. He took down the rope. What he had taken as thunder was actually the crack-boing sound that was unique to old gas cans. The darkness hid him. He didn't need the thin crescent of the moon. The man who worked by the private barn did so with a bouncing ball of flashlight light that gave off more than enough light to see.

The smell of gas filled the air, and Mark knew there was no more time to waste. The lasso in his hands, even after the months of absence, belonged there. Before the arsonist could strike his first match, Mark had him roped around the waist and was yelling for Jake to call the cops.

The arsonist took a run at him, bound as he was, even as the bedroom light snapped on. Mark saw it coming and stepped aside -- his night vision hadn't been ruined by the flashlight. He tripped the man, and let him drop hard without his arms to break his fall, and used the end of the rope to tie off his ankles. It wouldn't have broken any world record, but it was still neat work.

Jake was outside a few seconds later and they secured the man to the hitching post together. They took the time to evacuate the stalls before the police arrived.

Pictures were taken, evidence bagged, and the arsonist, who hadn't said a single word, was carted away. Emergency crews were called to deal with the gasoline clean up, and Mark went to the station with the constables to make the formal statement. Jake went in the house just before they left and brought back a shirt for Mark. The RCMP constables all looked away in the second it took him to dress. He didn't think that Mitsy would have been the one to take Jake's call until he saw her worried face through the window of the dispatch room. Another woman took her headset, squeezing her shoulder at the pass off, and she stood up and went outside.

Mark sat down in the gray interview room and wrote down his statement on the yellow legal pad. He signed it, watched it being witnessed, and answered what few questions the constable had. Mark didn't know what had woken him, he'd just woken up. The horses were fine, there was no property damage other than the gasoline spill that had to be treated like hazardous waste, and the horses, including poor Butter, would be just fine out in the pasture for the night. He didn't say anything about Rendell, other than to confirm the fact that he'd been out to the center the day before, and after that there were no more questions to answer. His leg hurt, in a dull kind of way, but he promised himself he would never take another one of those little white pills.

The constable, Jackson was his name, a bald headed black man who smiled and nodded encouragingly without giving Mark the feeling he was being coached into what to say, gave Mark a refill of his coffee. Mitsy came in and sat down on the table, and Mark was suddenly very tired. She rubbed his shoulder, leaning forward to do so. Jackson came back in with his coat on.

"If you don't mind, Mr. McCoy, I would like to drive you back to your house," he said, his hat in his hands.

Jake would come and get him, if Mark was to ask, but Mark wouldn't wake him. "I would appreciate that," he said and stood.

"I'll tell your father," Mitsy said.

"You don't have to do that," Mark said, and meant it. His first night of being a full-on fag, and someone tried to burn down his barn. His father would just love that.

As though reading his mind, Mitsy slapped his shoulder. Not hard, of course, but enough. He supposed she didn't have to read his mind, he was tired enough that his face probably gave away what he was thinking.

"Your father loves you," she said. "And I'm sorry it's so tough for him to accept this, but he will because he loves you. You moron."

Mark stared at her, wondering whose kitchen table she had sat at during all those awkward meals. But then it did seem his father followed his roping, and was more supportive when he was not in the money than when he was. He nodded.

"What was that?" Mitsy demanded.

"You can tell my father." Mark didn't even mumble.

She grinned at him, and Mark saw why she had won so many pageants in her career. It was all in her smile. "That wasn't so hard, was it?"

"Mitsy, don't push it."

She fussed with his hair, though she had to stand on her tiptoes to do it. "Silly boy. If you don't push a McCoy, you don't get nothin' done."

He supposed she would know. He wondered if his father knew what exactly he had married. Johnson opened the door and led the way back to the patrol car. Even in the front seat, Mark felt weird, like he'd done something wrong. It was a quiet drive, and they didn't pass another car the entire way. After all that darkness, it was strange to see the house fully lit. The cleanup crew had left, and it was only Jake sitting on the porch with a cup of coffee, waiting for them.

Mark got out of the car first, but hung back not really knowing why. Constable Johnson came around the car as well and walked up to the porch. He stuck out his hand, and Jake stood up to shake it. "Thank you for bringing him back," Jake said.

"It was nothing. We appreciate his willingness to come in and make a statement. If you don't mind, I'd like to arrange a time when we can come out here and discuss this unpleasantness with you. We do have a few questions as to who would want to burn down the barn."

Constable Johnson looked as though he wanted to say more, but then glanced at Mark. Mark was a potential witness, after all. Mark shrugged, letting Jake know he was willing to go inside if they needed privacy, but Jake shook his head.

"I'm here all day tomorrow. If I'm not at the house, I'll be in one of the barns. You're welcome to come find me."

"I do appreciate that. Again, thanks so much for your trouble."

"I could say the same to you," Jake said. They shook hands again, and Mark went up the stairs to the porch as Jackson returned to his car. They both watched and waited for the unmarked police car to turn around and drive and head out, the two angry red eyes growing distant, until they were completely alone but for the crickets.

"The horses okay?" Mark asked.

"Don't change the subject," Jake said.

"I hadn't been aware we were talking."

Jake looked angry, or at lease terrified masquerading as angry. "He could have had a gun," Jake said. "He could have shot you dead."

"Yeah, and he could have had a Zippo. With wood that dry, it would've gone up in seconds."

"I don't want to... I can't... I'm not going to lose you again. Not to your own stupidity, not again."

"You would've done the same thing." Mark looked at him. "Gun or not, you would've done the exact same thing."

Jake looked at him, willing to argue, and shut his mouth. Just for a heartbeat. "No. I would have done it a second and a half faster."

"Oh, you think so, old-timer?" Mark said. He pulled off his boots, using the corner of the step as a wedge.

"I know so," Jake said. Mark made a rude noise, and Jake shut him up with a kiss. "Get inside, you idiot."

For a day that Mark had been called a moron and an idiot, almost had his mare burned to death, and spent several hours in a police station, it was still one of the best days of his life. In the bathroom, he found a large jar of no-name aspirin and downed three of them. Jake was waiting for him in the bedroom, and it seemed the most natural thing in his life to strip off and join Jake in bed. He ran his hand down Jake's chest, played with a few of the curly hairs on Jake's lower belly and fell asleep, his hand on Jake's cock.

The sad part about living and working with animals was that no dispensation was ever granted on the basis of what time one has gone to bed the night before. Jake's alarm went off what seemed like twenty minutes after they had gone to bed, and both of them, lifelong ranch workers, got up without hitting snooze. They got to grumble, that was okay, and so was bumping into each other in the kitchen when they made coffee and toast and searched around for a frying pan. Mark kissed the back of Jake's neck, because he could, and when Jake reached around him to grab milk from the fridge, he cupped Mark's ass on the way by.

By the time they finished, the first of the volunteers had arrived for the morning hours, and Mark took care of the private barn while Jake oversaw the controlled chaos of five overeager teenagers. Oddly enough, Mark had finished first, so he went into the office. The filing cabinet was unlocked, the account receiving book out in the open, and it didn't take long to see how much in the hole the rescue center really was.

Jake brought him a coffee halfway through, and leaned against the doorway. "I can't charge an adoption fee that even comes close to how much it costs the vet and the amount of food the horses consume. The fundraisers help, but it's constantly begging with my hand out and I have to keep five or six thousand dollars in ready cash to keep some of the finest horses I've ever seen being turned into dog meat. We do what we can, but it's month-to-month, and I just can't see a way out of it."

Mark nodded. "I see that." He looked up. "You can go back to the show. Hank's still young enough, and the purses are getting bigger and bigger. One good season and you can bankroll this place."

"It's something to look into. But this isn't the kind of place you can bugger off and leave three or four days of the week. It's a twenty-four/seven, three hundred sixty-five days of the year kind of gig."

Mark stood up. "You're not alone anymore."

"I know." Jake took another sip of coffee. "Just don't think I'm not going to work you to the bone."

Mark looked at the shabby numbers in the books, and then out to the small window to the barns and the fields beyond. It would be work, ridiculous amounts, but he was okay with that. "Deal."

"You drive a hard bargain."

Mark was going to take the coffee cup from Jake's hand, and take his first payment, formulating in his head some crack involving the words pound and flesh for what was owed, when he heard a truck pull up. Jake had already turned, and frowned to see Rendell's black truck stop in the middle of the yard. Mark got a bad feeling, and out of the clear blue morning he heard the distant thunder of hooves. He was already picking up the phone when Jake told him to call 911. He nodded, and punched in the numbers.

The kids were all in the field. He could hear them whooping and hollering from a long way away, so Mark wasn't afraid for them. Jake walking up all alone to the huge black beast made every inch of his spine crawl. The woman on the other end of the phone asked him what the nature of his emergency was, and Mark almost told her that the black riders were coming.

Instead he shook his head. "There isn't one, not yet but I think there's going to be."

The almost bored tone in the woman's voice ended. "Could you be more specific?"

Mark watched from the doorway. Rendell was wearing a thick leather jacket despite the warm morning, and he and Jake were still exchanging stony-faced pleasantries. "I think the man who tried to burn down our barn -- " *Our barn*, Mark thought. *Already it's our barn.* "--is on the property. And I think he's going to try something."

"My name is Sherry, whom I speaking with?"

"Mark." He gave the address, and didn't try to explain how he belonged here.

"Has he said or done anything threatening?" She asked. He could hear her typing in the background. He only hoped she was sending somebody.

Mark glanced out again. Rendell was trying to force a stack of papers into Jake's hands, who was refusing to take it. "Yes," Mark said. It was only a small white lie.

"I'm sending somebody right now, Mark," Sherry said. "I want you to stay on the line with me."

Mark agreed, but if he saw the riders, all bets were off. A second truck rolled into the yard. The Bar Nunn crest had been repainted since Mark had seen it last. He looked over, back to Jake and Rendell. They were shouting at each other. Or Rendell was shouting, Jake had opened up the black truck's door and was trying to get him back inside. Mark's father was out of the truck now, looking slightly smaller than Mark remembered now that he wasn't so afraid of his opinion. Mitsy was at his side, grim-faced and immovable, regardless of her height.

Sherry had asked him a question, but it was all just white noise. The black riders stood patiently by the hitching post, just as tall and dark as he remembered, and the second to last horse was riderless. Through the doorway, the leader found him and nodded his head a third and final time.

Rendell had pushed Jake back, and Jake had lost his balance. He was falling down on his ass just as Rendell was taking an old Colt revolver out of his pocket. He either hadn't seen Mark's father approach, or he didn't care, but Mark knew with one hundred percent certainty that Rendell's warning shot, to show Jake that he was serious, was going to ricochet and go straight through his father's heart.

Jake let the telephone receiver slip from his hands. It clattered to the floor and he took a giant leap out of the small office, and nothing he saw moved. It was like a painting. A horrible, true to life rendition of his father's death. Mitsy had seen the gun, and was trying to pull Edward down, but it was going to be too little, too late. None of them were fast enough to avoid this.

"Stop," Mark shouted. He looked at the leader, saw the black eyes and wasn't afraid. "Stop this right now. You owe me. You know you do. Stop this, let him live, let Jake and Mitsy live, and we're even."

The leader stared at him, but that smile was back behind the bandanna. His horse struck the ground, sending sparks out where the gasoline had been, but even if it had still been there, Mark doubted it would have ignited.

"Please," Mark said.

What seemed like an eternity passed. The leader kept his level gaze on Mark, and if it hadn't been for the hours and hours of staring games he and Peter had played as children on long snowy days, Mark would've looked away. But he didn't, long after his eyes stung in his mouth went dry. He kept the leader's gaze, and didn't let him look away. This wasn't right. It wasn't fair. And Mark wasn't going to allow it.

Finally, the leader lifted his hand off the pommel of the saddle. He twisted his wrist and one by one the riders slipped away until it was just Mark and the leader. This time there was no doffing of the hat, no nod, no smile. One instant he was there, the next he wasn't. Mark dropped to his knees, his eyes stinging although they were plenty wet enough, and the crack coming from the gun wasn't a bullet, it was a misfire. Mitsy finished knocking Edward out of the way, Jake regained his footing and knocked the gun out from Rendell's hand, and Constable Johnson pulled up in his unmarked in time to see it all. Or most of it at least.

But when Edward looked across the yard to Mark for the first time, it was as though he knew what had been avoided. And if it were possible, how it had happened. Edward touched the rim of the big white cowboy hat he always wore, and bowed his head. Mark bowed his head back.

The squad car that the 911 operator had called for arrived about ten minutes later, once Constable Johnson had Rendell in cuffs. He said tersely that he couldn't talk about an ongoing investigation in front of witnesses, meaning Mark, but Mark read between the lines and figured that the arsonist had already rolled on the man who hired him. Mark stayed outside as Jake and Constable Johnson went into the house for Jake's statement, and that left Mark alone with Edward and Mitsy. He looked at them both. With his dad and Mitsy, he corrected himself. The words instantly felt better.

"So this is you now?" Edward said. He looked around the yard and the barns. He'd said nothing about Jake, but Mark had watched him study Jake carefully as he led the way into the house.

"This is me."

A muscle in Edward's cheek twitched. But he nodded. "And your leg?"

"Getting better. Not there yet."

"And this place."

"Needs a lot of work. And time. And money."

"Mitsy said." Mark had definitely not discussed finances with his stepmother. And he doubted Jake had either. But he supposed looking around the center showed there was no hiding how much of the work was done with a spit and a promise. Mitsy looked ready with a well-timed slap, should the situation have called for it, but Edward willingly reached into the inside of his jacket. "Your mother was quite wealthy," Edward said stiffly. "She would have hated to see you struggle." Mitsy smacked him for his efforts. He cleared his throat and tried again. "I would hate to see you struggle," he tried again, and Mitsy beamed at him.

Mark didn't know what to say. Edward handed him a check for a hundred thousand dollars, and then quickly crossed his arms over his chest. "We only wanted what was best."

"Thank you," Mark said. It was woefully inadequate, but Edward nodded. The matter was now officially closed. Mark folded check and put it in his pocket. "If you want, for dinner sometime? It would..." He didn't finish, but Mitsy responded as though she'd been handed an engraved invitation.

"Why, Mark, we would be delighted. How does next Thursday sound?"

Mark looked quickly at his father, willing to keep the invitation as an indefinite sort, if that was what he wanted, but his father shook his head. "Next Thursday it is," Mark said, and that matter was settled as well.

Mark showed his father the operation, as much as there was of it, and by the time he finished the grand tour, Jake had finished with his questions. Jake came back outside, walked Constable Johnson back to his car, and then went and stood awkwardly behind Mark. Edward, this time without any prodding -- or physical violence -- from Mitsy took the first step and offered his hand. Jake shook it somewhat hesitantly.

"Mr. Jake Alastair. I saw you in Calgary. 6.95 seconds, with a double tie to boot. That was a beautiful thing."

"It was another lifetime ago," Jake said. "But thank you."

Edward looked around. "And you do good work here. Are you a registered tax-deductible charity?"

"I am. Do you want to see the paperwork?"

"I do," Edward said and together they walked back to the office. Mark hoped one of them noticed the phone was off the hook.

"I had to almost drag your father kicking and screaming into the truck this morning," Mitsy said, and put her hands on her hips. "He kept going on and on about this bad feeling he was having. That misfire..." She didn't finish, and Mark didn't want her to. "Things will get better."

Mark listened for the sound of thunder, but heard nothing but the morning birds. "Yes. I think they will."

Jake and Edward came out of the office together. Jake was only slightly taller, his father was only slightly thicker around the waist. They shook hands again, and Mark and his father shook hands, and when that felt woefully inadequate, Edward hugged him, stiffly, but it was the first hug Mark had gotten in years. "Thank you again," Edward said. He looked Mark in the eye, and though Mark wanted to ask if his father saw the riders too, it seemed like a far too personal question to ask at the moment. Edward and Mitsy got in the truck and drove away.

"Your dad took almost all the information I had about the place. It would've been nice if he had left a check," Jake groused.

Mark reached into his pocket. "Say, like this one?"

Jake unfolded it, looked at all the zeros, and went very white. "You're kidding me."

"Nope. Not kidding."

The kids were coming back, it was time for lunch and Mark was both surprised that it was only noon and very glad they were going to be very alone very soon.

"You... I..."

Mark figured Jake was going to be speechless for a while so he made sure the adoptive horses were put away and all the kids had rides back to town, marveling at how easily this responsibility thing came to him. When he took Jake's arm and led them back to the house, Jake went willingly if still a little stunned.

Mark locked the door. He wished he could have dropped to his knees, but overcoming death in a staring contest didn't exactly heal all wounds, and he was still stiff from the ride the day before. So instead, they went into the bedroom. They took off their clothes, one article at a time, until they were both naked, and standing braced against the dresser didn't hurt Mark as much as he thought it might. Jake kissed his way down the line of Mark's spine, starting from his hair line, and took extra special care working the small of his back. Each kiss was a heartbeat of wet tongue and soft lips, and each kiss dragged slowly from one spot to the next.

Mark could smell Jake behind him but every time he tried to turn around Jake must have seen his weight shift, because he got a stinging slap on his ass that should have annoyed him to hell and back, but instead was strangely erotic. More than erotic. His cock had gotten hard by the third slap, and he found himself shifting over from foot to foot just to feel it again. Jake laughed, biting down on his ass, and reached around to take his cock in his hand. "Now you're doing it on purpose."

"Is there a problem with that?" Mark asked, jerking forward, but Jake just pulled him back.

"No. I just want you to know I know."

"So now I know you know?" Mark asked, leaning to the left, and got a hard smack on his right cheek. The good sort of pain went right to his cock, and Mark groaned.

Jake laughed again. He kissed Mark's tailbone, then moved to his bad hip and kissed every quarter inch of skin. By the time he finished, Mark couldn't stop gasping. If Jake had plans to go down his bad leg, Mark didn't think he could bear it.

But Jake stood up, and Mark almost sighed in relief. His shoulders slumped and he leaned further over the dresser. He heard the now familiar tube open up, the condom wrapper, and tried to adjust his legs even further apart so that his bad one was just this side of not hurting. Two fingers at once, more painful than one, but after the slaps that heated up his skin, Mark didn't mind it much at all. He was going to embarrass himself by coming just from the way Jake moved his fingers inside him; he knew exactly where Mark's prostate was and he pushed it, sliding his fingers over it time and time again.

Mark arched up to his toes. "Keep doing that and I'll come," Mark warned, not able to stop the sparks inside him. He tightened his muscles, hoping by sheer will alone he could stop the amazing heat from building up much too deep inside his cock, but it only made the screaming need to just come already worse.

"So come," Jake said.

Mark felt him shrug against him. He relaxed, as much as he could when his whole body was in lock down. He came hard against the wood of the dresser, and slumped forward. "That wasn't fair," he said, when he could.

Jake kissed him. He gathered up Mark's come with his fingers and licked it off. "Pull yourself up," Jake said. The dresser was a good two and a half feet deep and the only thing on it was a glass display case for all Jake's old championship buckles, which was easily pushed aside. The only problem he had with turning himself around was that his legs had gone boneless on him. But he managed it, and on the second attempt was able to lean with his back against the wall.

"Like this?" Mark asked.

"Perfect." Jake got up beside him, his knees on either side of Mark's hips, and sat up off his heels so that his cock was now at the perfect height.

"Is there a manual for this kind of thing?" Mark asked. "I mean, how do you just know your parts will line up with mine?"

"I have a good eye," Jake said. "And you have a great mouth. Will you open it for me?"

Mark did. Jake leaned forward so that he was all Mark could see, and his sun-baked skin was all he could smell. Jake was already starting to smell different, and Mark realized with a start it was because of him and the way they mixed.

Jake took hold of his head, carefully. Mark wrapped his hand around Jake's dick, leaving as much exposed as he felt comfortable swallowing. Jake pushed inside his mouth carefully, just until Mark felt his own fingers against his lip. Jake began thrusting, but regardless of how hard his cock was, or the sounds that came out of the back of his throat, he never pushed past Mark's fingers. Mark pulled his mouth free, gasping for air, but used both hands on Jake's cock to make up for it. Jake gasped, his fingers tightening in Mark's hair as Mark rubbed his cheeks against the crown before popping just the head in his mouth. Jake went rigid, letting Mark choose the pace, and with both hands in constant motion, his saliva producing all the lubrication needed, Jake only had to hold onto his head and keep his shudders under control.

"God, Mark," Jake whispered, and cupped the back of Mark's head as he came. This time Mark swallowed it all and kissed the head of Jake's cock before Jake collapsed beside him. Mark was semi-hard again, but that could wait. He put his head on Jake's shoulder, and Jake swung his arm over his. Naked, sitting on a dresser, Mark had never been more comfortable.

"I want a bigger bed," Mark said.

"I think that can be arranged."

Mark looked around. "And closet space."

"Sure."

"And room in your buckle display case for mine."

Jake stiffened.

Mark laughed, though it was soundless and really nothing more than his shoulders moving up and down. "Just kidding."

About the Authors

JL LANGLEY is a full-time writer, with over ten novels to her credit. Among her hobbies she includes reading, practicing her marksmanship (she happens to be a great shot), gardening, working out (although she despises cardio), searching for the perfect chocolate dessert (so far as she can tell ALL chocolate is perfect, but it requires more research) and arguing with her husband over who the air compressor and nail gun really belongs to (they belong to JL, although she might be willing to trade him for his new chainsaw). You can find JL on the internet at: http://www.jllangley.com or her yahoo group http://groups.yahoo.com/group/the_yellow_rose/

DAKOTA FLINT lives in upstate New York and currently spends her days dreaming up lots of interesting situations for two men to meet and fall in love. While she hasn't yet managed to attain the fame and fortune she's sure will come her way through these tales, Dakota has managed to convince the employees of her local Starbucks not to give away her usual table. Any story she publishes can be dedicated--in part--to the iced white mocha. To find out what's going on with Dakota and her writing, check out her website. http://dakotaflint.com/

KIERNAN KELLY lives in the wilds of the alligator-infested U.S. Southeast, slathered in SPF 45, drinking colorful tropical, hi-octane concoctions served by thong-clad cabana boys. All right, the truth is that she spends her time locked in the dark recesses of her office, writing gay erotica while chained to a temperamental Macintosh, drinking coffee, and dreaming of thong-clad cabana boys. Sigh. You can find Kiernan on the internet at: http://www.KiernanKelly.com or http://kiernankelly.livejournal.com

ANGELA FIDDLER lives with her wife in Alberta, Canada. She got her first pony the same Christmas she got a six-foot high inflatable Godzilla and the complete Narnia series. It was the Best. Christmas. Ever. Her vampire "Masters of the Lines" series is available through Loose Id and has several books through MLR Press. Horse rescue centers, like the one depicted in *Forgotten Favor*, try to save even a small portion of the thousands of completely healthy and sound animals who would otherwise be sold for their meat. Angela can be found on the internet at: http://www.angelafiddler.com

MLR Press Authors

Featuring a roll call of some of the best writers of gay erotica and mysteries today!

Maura Anderson
Victor J. Banis
Jeanne Barrack
Laura Baumbach
Alex Beecroft
Sarah Black
Ally Blue
J.P. Bowie
P.A. Brown
James Buchanan
Jordan Castillo Price
Kirby Crow
Dick D.
Jason Edding
Angela Fiddler
Dakota Flint
Kimberly Gardner
Storm Grant
Amber Green
LB Gregg
Drewey Wayne Gunn

Samantha Kane
Kiernan Kelly
JL Langley
Josh Lanyon
Clare London
William Maltese
Gary Martine
ZA Maxfield
Jet Mykles
L. Picaro
Neil Plakcy
Luisa Prieto
Rick R. Reed
AM Riley
George Seaton
Jardonn Smith
Caro Soles
Richard Stevenson
Claire Thompson
Kit Zheng

Check out titles, both available and forthcoming, at
www.mlrpress.com

THE TREVOR PROJECT

The Trevor Project operates the only nationwide, around-the-clock crisis and suicide prevention helpline for lesbian, gay, bisexual, transgender and questioning youth. Every day, The Trevor Project saves lives though its free and confidential helpline, its website and its educational services. If you or a friend are feeling lost or alone call The Trevor Helpline. If you or a friend are feeling lost, alone, confused or in crisis, please call The Trevor Helpline. You'll be able to speak confidentially with a trained counselor 24/7.

The Trevor Helpline: 866-488-7386

On the Web: http://www.thetrevorproject.org/

THE GAY MEN'S DOMESTIC VIOLENCE PROJECT

Founded in 1994, The Gay Men's Domestic Violence Project is a grassroots, non-profit organization founded by a gay male survivor of domestic violence and developed through the strength, contributions and participation of the community. The Gay Men's Domestic Violence Project supports victims and survivors through education, advocacy and direct services. Understanding that the serious public health issue of domestic violence is not gender specific, we serve men in relationships with men, regardless of how they identify, and stand ready to assist them in navigating through abusive relationships.

GMDVP Helpline: 800.832.1901

On the Web: http://gmdvp.org/

THE GAY & LESBIAN ALLIANCE AGAINST DEFAMATION/GLAAD EN ESPAÑOL

The Gay & Lesbian Alliance Against Defamation (GLAAD) is dedicated to promoting and ensuring fair, accurate and inclusive representation of people and events in the media as a means of eliminating homophobia and discrimination based on gender identity and sexual orientation.

On the Web: http://www.glaad.org/

GLAAD en español:

          http://www.glaad.org/espanol/bienvenido.php

Printed in the United Kingdom by
Lightning Source UK Ltd., Milton Keynes
140739UK00001B/20/P